The Beautiful
and the Grotesque

ALSO BY RYUNOSUKE AKUTAGAWA

Rashōmon and Other Stories

The Beautiful and the Grotesque

Ryunosuke Akutagawa

Translated by Takashi Kojima
and John McVittie

Edited by John McVittie and Arthur Pell

Illustrations by Yuko Shimizu

LIVERIGHT

NEW YORK • LONDON

Copyright © 1964 by Liveright Publishing Corporation

Previous edition published under the title *Exotic Japanese Stories:
The Beautiful and the Grotesque*

Manufacturing by Courier Westford
Production manager: Devon Zahn

Library of Congress Cataloging-in-Publication Data

Akutagawa, Ryunosuke, 1892–1927
[Short stories. Selections English.]
The beautiful and the grotesque / Ryunosuke Akutagawa ; translated
by Takashi Kojima and John McVittie ; edited by John McVittie
and Arthur Pell ; illustrations by Yuko Shimizu.
p. cm.
Previous edition published under the title Exotic Japanese Stories:
the beautiful and the grotesque.
Includes bibliographical references.
ISBN 978-0-87140-192-2 (pbk.)
1. Japanese fiction–Translations into English. 2. Short stories,
Japanese–Translations into English. 3. Japan–Social life and
customs–Fiction. I. Kojima, Takashi. II. McVittie, John. III. Pell,
Arthur R. IV. Title.
PL801.K8E96 2010
895.6'342–dc22

2010004278

Liveright Publishing Corporation
500 Fifth Avenue, New York, N.Y. 10110
www.wwnorton.com

W. W. Norton & Company Ltd.
Castle House, 75/76 Wells Street, London W1T 3QT

1 2 3 4 5 6 7 8 9 0

Acknowledgments

WISH TO CONVEY my thanks to those who have been intimately associated with me in the publication of this book.

Above all, through the insistence of the translators, this book has been dedicated to its most worthy parent, Arthur Pell, Editor of the Liveright Publishing Corporation. Without his faith, inspiration, guidance and untiring assistance over a number of years this work would never have been possible.

To my colleagues, Prof. Takashi Kojima and Masakazu Kuwata, I must bow many times with thanks for their splendid cooperation.

Too great to be repaid within one lifetime is the debt which I owe to my wife, Rosaleen—my painstaking critic—my right hand!

JOHN McVITTIE

Contents

The Beautiful
and the Grotesque

A Sprig of Wild Orange

Introduction

My dear Rosaleen–

As FIRST READER of the translations–and first severe critic, representing the many who in the course of time will read this book–you deserve a more intimate interpretation of the numerous intriguing facets comprised in these pages.

Even as in Akutagawa's imagination, the spirit of Wei Shêng was reborn, so have I often felt during these modern times, notwithstanding so much encouragement from my critics, that I cannot write anything of any worth, but am always waiting for a love that never comes.

That love which never comes is resignation, that complete understanding of life to which in the Far East we often hear applied the word "enlightenment." In *my* life, *time,* like the river, is swelling with the tide; the world's many people with their robes fluttering in the wind, and the carriages with wheels rumbling pass me by, tempting me to join the throng, and my years like the day are deepening as I wait so patiently for my Lady Enlightenment to come. But there is some comfort for me now that I have learned from the experience of Wei Shêng and feel that it is not for my love to come to me, but for me to go forth to seek her out wherever I might find her.

In his literary journey, Akutagawa rambled leisurely, rode furiously, sought fervently this Lady through to the extremities of Japan. From the Heian era to modern times he sought, and at length made his decision to await her coming his way. He was Wei Shêng who waited on the river bank as the night closed in about him. By degrees the dusk deepened; in his moments of expectation the sound of the wind, the sound of reeds, the sound of water—even the cry of the heron—were captivating sounds; he paced the river bank, conscious that the waters were rising with the tide. As Wei Shêng calmly accepted his destiny when the Lady did not come, Akutagawa would accept his, too.

Surely it is a romantic notion for me to assume that, since I was born at almost the very moment when Akutagawa died, that I, too, have inherited the spirit of Wei Shêng; and, indeed, I have sought through many countries of the world for the Lady Enlightenment, especially through the many enchanting byways of Japan; and many times have I paced the river bank awaiting the Lady, but always have I set out once more to seek her out, and never have I felt her presence so close as I have throughout the hours when I was absorbed in the translation of these stories; yet she has always been elusive.

In these stories I feel that I shall find her, as already I am inspired by the conviction that Akutagawa has bequeathed to me the task of searching for her in the haunts where it is evident he felt she might be found; he has repeatedly given the clue to the state of mind in which the captivating task should be undertaken; the clue is *belief.*

Nothing in Japan may be done directly; to the Japanese, life is not direct but is as circuitous as it possibly can be, so he does not bother to learn the elements of logic in an attempt to establish a standard way of thinking. We, too, can begin our pilgrimage through these stories indirectly with an act of *belief* which Akutagawa anticipated might startle the reader–the belief that badgers can change their form. Why should it be so difficult to convince modern man that badgers can change their form? He can believe that an inverted basket or a lamp shade becomes a hat when used by a woman *as a hat,* but he cannot believe that the man next door could be a badger which has changed its form; he will even use a table knife for a screw driver, but will scorn the idea that the barman at his club could be a badger. I remember a weird rumor that circulated among my fellow philosophy students at the university to the effect that a certain awkward student called Myrtle had a tail. I really cannot say whether or not Myrtle had a tail as I was not responsible for the rumor, but I do know that there were many plots against Myrtle to ascertain if the rumor were true–so there were certainly some who *believed.*

On a loftier plane we can say that *belief* in His Majesty, Emperor Hirohito, as linear descendant of the Emperors of Japan for the past two thousand five hundred years or so has saved the Japanese nation from elevating Lenin to Imperial status.

So naïve, so formal a study as "The Badger" presents one of the most satisfying–though sometimes one of the most cruel– aspects of the Japanese mind. The Japanese has still not lost the capacity to *believe.* In summer, ghosts are a popular conversation topic, and on television programs and in the cinema these ghosts– lurid figures with matted hair, ragged clothes, gnarled limbs, and one–only one–remaining eye, bloodshot and terrifying to look on–make frequent appearances. To us, summer is an odd season for ghosts, for in the West, ghosts have always been associated rather with long dreary winter's nights when the windows rattle and the stairways creak; but the Japanese say that their "summer ghosts" send a chill down their spines, an acceptable phenomenon on hot summer nights. If you are able to live long enough in Japan, you will be fascinated by the Japanese will to believe, and you will yourself gradually begin to believe. In Tokyo I made the acquaintance of an unusually timid student; she was timid probably because she had some congenital malformation of the skin on her hands–and such children in country villages (and perhaps even in the cities) are believed to be the offspring of foxes; such is a manifestation of *belief* at its cruelest–it is only a variation of the worldwide tendency to believe in the guilt of a man once he is under the suspicion of having committed a crime. There is something enlightened about the Japanese contention that we cannot discern much distinction between what *is so* and what is *believed to be so.*

With respect to badgers, it is not so much, submits Akutagawa, that the badger came to bewitch people, as that it was *believed to bewitch.* Yet, between bewitchment and belief in bewitchment there would not be much distinction.

The author's assurance that this is not only confined to badgers is more provoking to thought; he asks–is it not that any *existence* is but what we *believe it to be?*

Only a few moments before I took up my pen, my younger son, gazing up at a pine swaying over the rooftops, asked me: "Pappa–why are there trees?" So I replied with a counter-question: "Why are *you?*"–and he was spontaneous in countering: "I don't know, Pappa–why are *you?*" I made no reply because he would not have understood if I had said: "Because I *believe* I am so."

How pathetic a character I would be if my parents had insisted as I grew up that I was *not* so–that I did not really exist!–How wretched I would be if I could not believe that Lady Enlightenment really exists! Want of belief, therefore, is surely destructive to the human mind and morale. The readiness of Japanese belief has assisted the Japanese, in their misery of defeat after World War II, to recreate Japan as a prosperous nation. And for over a century and a half belief has preserved the inviolability of the United States Constitution, and there are ample psychiatrists and child welfare officers to testify that all men are not equal; but, whether men are equal or they are not, it is imperative for the preservation of democratic principles that they be believed to be equal.

As a man is capable of belief, so is he capable of being an *individual*. In Japan as in the West the several media that have been termed "mass communication" have been vying for control of men's minds; but some who wish to remain *individuals* seek relief from this tyranny. Those "some"–who form the advance guard of the many–becoming weary of the constrictions of mass thinking, will be most readily drawn into the spirit of these stories. But first I must hold up a finger and say, with the companionable smile that the Japanese themselves so blithely bestow: *"You must believe in badgers!"*

In such sympathetic company as those of you who are still with my introduction, I would go along to renew acquaintance-ship with one who has chosen to sever relationship with our society so completely that we must pity him. He has gone so far in his belief in and reliance on *Kappa* beings that he has lost faith in humanity. He is Patient No. 23. As, until recently, I lived in Tokyo, adjacent to Japan's largest mental institution, I would like to believe that we could find him there; and the author's description of the mental asylum in "The Kappa" seems, as far as it goes, to match the hospital I have often seen in passing. Also, it is interesting to believe that on many a night the *Kappa* would surely have passed along the waterway behind my house in their journeys to and from the hospital. A psychiatrist from the same hospital was a frequent visitor to my home, but I hesitated to ask him if he had ever seen a *Kappa*, for I know that–as he is a psychiatrist–he would never care to admit that he had seen a *Kappa*.

To the Western reader it surely suffices to say: "If you believe in the Japanese you will have no difficulty in believing in the *Kappa*." Western businessmen, at least, will contend that the Japanese are surely as elusive as the *Kappa;* and Patient No. 23 insists that "both sides of the (main) street (of the *Kappa* city) are not in the least different from the Ginza," the business thoroughfare of Tokyo.

As for the attributes of the *Kappa*–the lady who had the utmost talent for deceiving her husband reminds us not only of some Japanese ladies we know; and the fact that the *Kappa* can change the color of their skin in sympathy with their surroundings does remind us in an abstract way of some people we have known in many parts of the world. It is amusing that the *Kappa* do not wear clothes, but it is more amusing that we humans *do* wear clothes; and it is odd to think how the Japanese are abandoning their comfortable kimono for our archaic suits, and their wooden *geta* for our crippling shoes. It is so easy to believe in the *Kappa*–surely easier than it would be for the *Kappa*, if they had not actually seen for themselves, to believe in us humans.

The *Kappa*, it seems, do believe in humans, and even go so far as to say that humans are happier beings than *Kappa* because they have not reached as high a state of evolution as have the *Kappa*. They say also that this unhappy disposition could spring from the fact that *thought* of any consequence reached its zenith three thousand years ago, and that since such time we have but added a new flame to old kindling wood.

In the religious thought of the *Kappa,* there is something reminiscent of Shintô, the Japanese Way of the Gods, which pays reverence to a multitude of deceased dignitaries and inanimate objects to which Shintô shrines are dedicated; but it would be out of context here to discuss the nature of Shintô. One does suspect, however, that the *Kappa* temple which floats "like a weird mirage in a desert of sky" would be as commercially interested in visitors as the innumerable temples and shrines of Japan.

As we pass from chapter to chapter of "The Kappa," the constant satirical references to Western religions and philosophies indicate the nature of the prevailing interest of Japanese thinkers of the 1920's. There are references to Darwin, Dostoyevsky, Napoleon, and others whom the *Kappa* evidently venerate; but rarely is there any reference to Japanese heroes or to Japanese men-of-letters. Akutagawa did not survive to see the latter twenties or the thirties when he might have deplored even more than Western intellectualism, the new bushido movement that forced on Japanese society the most aggressive qualities of Japanese tradition.

Be that as it may, "The Kappa" should be read in the same spirit as that in which it is related by Patient No. 23 who will tell the story to anybody who happens to come his way. When the time comes for us to move on to the next story, we are conscious that we have, like the student in the story, looked through our legs at the world upside down and found that, after all, it is the same place.

This is a splendid thought to bear in mind for a fuller appreciation of the other stories, all of which are more consciously

Japanese. If you have felt some sympathy with the *Kappa*, there is every chance that you will feel drawn even more closely to the Japanese characters of the stories, bearing in mind that howsoever odd the Japanese might seem to be, and howsoever upside down, the world we view is, nevertheless, the same place.

It is not the world itself that differs so much as one's sense of values. The course of a few days' experience in Japan provides much bewildering evidence of the divergence between Japanese and Western values. A brief study of advertisements in modern Japanese magazines indicates more prudence on the Japanese side, partly because Japanese evaluation of the things of everyday life is more conservative than is our own.

Akutagawa was aware of some superiority in the Japanese sense of values when he wrote "The Dolls."

The dolls of this story were not the "ordinary" dolls little girls carry about in all countries of the world. They were dolls for display on or about March 3rd, during the festival that has been popular in Japan for over three centuries.

Sometimes this quaint festival is referred to as *Jômi no Sekku*, the Girls' Festival. On March 3rd, tasty food and *shiro-zaké* (a sweet saké) is prepared for the dolls, but the little girls themselves visit the houses of their friends and enjoy an adequate share of the delicacies on that day. It is a day when little girls—with their magnificent dolls displayed in the alcove reserved for the display of family treasures—can feel important; and even in the most "modern" households of Japan the place of the daughters is overshadowed by the far loftier importance of the sons.

Soon after Japan was reopened to intercourse with the West (1868), and the Meiji Emperor began his historic encouragement of Western ways and thought, many of the finest families of Japan, impoverished directly and indirectly by the collapse of the feudal system, began to dispose of their Japanese treasures; this to some extent was in their attempt to survive financially, and to some extent because traditional things were inconsistent with their new way of life and inhibited their enlightenment. It can well be imagined that one of the family heirlooms disposed of might have been the set of *Hina-matsuri* dolls.

"The Dolls" embodies an expression of the author's failure to find satisfaction in his own studies of Western ideals. In all of his works there is no more boorish a creature than the young man who in "The Dolls" compares the brightness of the new kerosene lamp to the brightness of the "new learning."

When mother is ill, O-Tsuru is as dutiful a child as any Japanese daughter should be. Only when mother is feeling more comfortable does she give some voice to her own suppressed desires. She wants to see her dolls once more before they are sold. Her entreaty is in vain; but she does have her reward in a singular way; she learns that in her uncompromising father there is still a yearning for the elegance of old Japan–a yearning that he must suppress in "modern times" for the material welfare of his family. O-Tsuru's revelation can never be proven, but she has gained a lifetime of spiritual comfort from her *belief* that it is so.

For the Western reader, "The Dolls" is a humbling story; it makes us feel awkward and unrefined. We feel that the Japanese could never learn anything of enlightenment from us who are such unenlightened people.

We have been prepared to give to Japan but not to receive. Okakura Kazuo, in "The Book of Tea," points out that the Christian missionary, too, has gone to Japan to give, but not to receive. It is not enough to read these stories in a spirit of curiosity and tolerance; if you are not prepared "to receive" you should lay aside this book.

In this volume there is a Japanese who feels impelled to help the Westerner towards some interpretation of Japanese culture. Most educated Japanese prefer to be silent on matters pertaining to their own culture, either because they are afraid of the ridicule of people who cannot fully appreciate them, or because their attempts to reconcile the somewhat incompatible elements of Japanese and Western culture usually lead to confusion.

The Professor in "The Handkerchief" has long dreamed of being "a bridge between East and West." Presumably he found some outlet for his ambition by marrying an American woman who had a passion for Japanese culture. "It was safe to surmise that the fancy lantern, suspended from the ceiling of the veranda, did not represent the Professor's taste, but was rather an expression of his wife's enjoyment of the things of Japan."

Professor Haségawa in "The Handkerchief" is really a portrait of Dr. Nitobé Inazo who sprang from a samurai family which so well understood the principles of bushido that his work entitled "Bushido" is considered a standard text and has been published in several languages.

It was his belief that if this bushido could be revived in the existing current of Japanese thought, it would be advantageous in facilitating mutual understanding between the European-American peoples and the Japanese people. Or, it would be a means of advancing international peace.–He himself had long dreamed of becoming such a bridge spanning East and West. The principles of bushido–loyalty, sincerity, courage–could be emphasized because of their universal acknowledgement as virtues.

But it was Professor Nitobé's awareness of how bushido could become a mere *mannerism*, empty of understanding, that is the burden of "The Handkerchief." . . . And in contemporary Japan there is the sad fact that the Japanese are fast losing their faith in their own traditions.

Propriety is a mild term for some of the great acts of sacrifice perpetuated under the name of "obligation" that are to be found recorded in Japanese history. Sometimes the fulfillment of obligation can be ironic, and even sometimes terrible, as it is in "Gratitude."

After twenty years' separation, destiny has once more brought together a notorious thief and a renowned merchant. The extreme predicament in which the merchant, Yasoêmon, is placed, demands quite naturally of Jinnai, the robber, an acknowledgement that he must satisfy his debt of gratitude.

Quietly the steaming kettle set the atmosphere of impending tragedy. Jinnai, who evidently understood the significance of "tea," would have felt this mood–a difficult mood for the reader to sense if the reader be uninitiated into the philosophy of tea. Okakura in "The Book of Tea" contends that the average Westerner, in his sleek complacency, will see in the tea ceremony but another instance of the thousand and one oddities which constitute the quaintness and childishness of the East. It will surely be a serious affair when many of Japan's heroes are understood to have partaken of tea with their intimate friends before they have committed *seppuku* (better known in the West under the more vulgar term *hara-kiri*).

As the story progresses, we wonder how the author can resolve the dilemma between the conscience of Yasoêmon, a Christian, accepting money that would surely be stolen, and the Japanese demand for the fulfillment of obligation. Akutagawa's genius is equal to the task, and his story, "Gratitude," consequently becomes one of the really great short stories of the world.

Jinnai, one of Japan's most notorious villains, becomes a noble being as he hurries with all possible dispatch along the snow-covered road, his wicker umbrella-hat glimmering in the moonlight. As to who is the hero of the tale–that is for the reader to decide; perhaps it is the man who has been shamed into remembering his own debt–his filial duty–who finds such contentment as occurs only once in a lifetime. Could this contentment be the resignation that comes from enlightenment?

The theme of "obligation" recurs in the tale of "The Dog, Shiro"–a story that moves briskly and lightly.

Any being–dog or human–might well be ashamed when he reflects on his failure to assist a friend in a moment of crisis. Nor is there anything particularly Japanese about that sentiment. Homeless and desperate, unworthy Shiro subsequently tempts fate in his daring exploits.

From my own experience I can remember a moment of selfishness, the memory of which still brings pressure to bear on my conscience. I was returning home one night in winter at about nine o'clock, traveling on the Tokyo suburban section of the Chûô Line. Gasping for breath on the tightly packed train, I was relieved when it pulled into Shinjuku Station where I had to change trains. A little old man had been pushed before the mob as it burst from the doors of the train; and by the time I myself had stepped down onto the platform he was leaning against a wooden pillar, hemorrhaging and barely able to stand. The crowd scrambled past as though it saw nothing of the old fellow who was one of the many victims of the overcrowded Tokyo suburban trains. As the Keiô Line train bore me closer home, I wondered how the Japanese, usually kind and courteous, could show such unconcern for the distress of a fellow human being. But suddenly a jolt of the train reminded me of my own place in the events of the previous half hour, and I was ashamed that it had not occurred to *me* to offer the old man my own assistance. But to be sure of one's obligation is one thing, and to act upon it is another.

Being myself of an unfilial nature since my childhood, I do not remember much of my father's advice, but I do remember his words which were prompted by a visit from Dr. Kagawa Toyohiko in the 1930's: "The great men and women of history have not been those who sought to glorify and advance themselves, but those whose aim and ideal in life has been to do as much for others as they possibly can."

"The Dog, Shiro" is the simplest of illustrations of the influence of this power of compassion. . . . He will be the most perverse of individuals if this naïve story does not prompt him to feel at its conclusion that Shiro has attained the state of resignation that comes only from enlightenment.

"The Kappa" and "The Dog, Shiro" are unique in Japanese contemporary literature because they are two of the few Japanese stories that have been written in the lighter vein. Both stories, however, are serious in their assessment of the place of the individual in society.

Yet, neither enlightenment nor resignation can ever come to a person in his capacity as citizen of a state. It can come to him only in his capacity as an individual. So, although he must serve his state, he must never lose his individuality.

Confucius, whose life was devoted to expounding his views on the place of the individual in society, has been a source of much inspiration to China and Japan for two and a half thousand years. If Confucius had been born in the China of today he would by now be in prison. In the "Great Learning," a Confucian classic, we read: "The men of old who wished to spread complete virtue throughout the world ordered well their own society. Wishing to order well their society they organized the affairs of their families; wishing to organize the affairs of their families, they cultivated their own persons; wishing to cultivate their own persons, they rectified their hearts. . . ."

In the background of Akutagawa's stories there is evidence of this process of rectification. If we were able to ask Akutagawa himself why he wrote a certain story, he would probably say that he had no end in mind, but that his stories were his own personal interpretation of life as he understood it to be. In writing "The Robbers" he had no idea in mind of pointing a moral, but if we were to nominate a story which illustrates how individuals "rectified their hearts" (though the rectification was far too mediæval for current approval) we would suggest "The Robbers."

"The Robbers" is set in an age when might was law; provided a man were strong enough there was little inhibition–killing, praying, mating, eating–every desire was satisfied provided the man was strong enough. But, if in those remote times one were not strong enough–then there would be little chance of survival to inflict one's weaknesses on the succeeding generations, or to be a burden on one's fellow men. Such was the natural order of things; and what is natural is sometimes cruel; but it was rather a physical cruelty, and far more tolerable than the degree of mental cruelty which arises from our present-day unnatural and so-called humanistic society. . . . Power in our own age is ever shifting from one group to another, but such power can never be advantageously suppressed, for the weakening of one clique spontaneously strengthens another. In the history of the human race, power has always been an idol. "Power is the grim idol that the world adores" (Hazlitt). The preoccupation of man, whether primitive or civilized, has been at all times a struggle for "the idol."

In present times we have learned to be subtle enough to conceal "the idol" lest others discover our treasure and covetously deprive us of it. In the era in which "The Robbers" of Akutagawa's story were active in the capital of Japan, there was no subtlety attached to the possession of power, and there was constant battle for it between rival clans and between honest warriors and rascals–the distinction between an honest man and a rascal not always being clear.

Always fascinating is Akutagawa's presentation of the mood of that early period. It is true that even today the archaic atmosphere of "The Robbers" of a thousand years ago, still lingers in Kyôto provided the reader is prepared to go there in the heat of summer. If he catches the prevailing plague in the course of reading this story, his relaxation will have been genuine and his attempt to appreciate the art of Akutagawa psychologically, a success.

"The breathless sky, hung with humid summer heat, spread over the houses; it was a certain noon in July. At the crossroads where the man had paused there was a willow–the leaves on its sparse branches so long and slender that one might think it suffered from the prevailing plague at the time; it cast its meager shadow over the ground; and at this place there was no wind to stir the leaves withering in the sun. . . . Everywhere fiery dust bathed the crossroads, and but for the foul-smelling putrid water oozing from the wound of a snake, there was not one drop of moisture. . . . The green flies swarmed over the dead snake–emitted a slight whirr of wings as they swarmed and settled again."

We meet with the old woman of Inokuma—as gnarled and desperate a character as anywhere in literature or history. The Japanese have not forgotten the ruggedness and ugliness of the commoners of the feudal ages. It is not so long since the grandfathers and grandmothers of many old Japanese would have smelt strongly of hay, and had deep crevices in hands and faces, and broken and missing teeth. In those times the classes of society must have seemed like different races of mankind; in those times men and women became aged early in life and if they were fortunate (or unfortunate?) enough to live beyond fifty years of age they were surely pitiful figures by the time they reached their three-score-years-and-ten.

But coarse as she might have been, any young wench would nevertheless have been sufficiently desirable to the hardy men of the times. It is around such a raw theme that "The Robbers" revolves, the passion of one generation devolving on the next. The things about us change sometimes beyond recognition to those who see them after a long absence; but the nature of lust does not change.

We trudge through the old Capital, and at every step the city's desolation more and more reveals itself to us. "Between the houses, the sagebrush fields smelled strongly; in places there were old walls standing in a line, with scarcely any of the pine and willow of old times remaining. Everything we see prompts us to associate this ruined city with the faint odor of the dead. . . ." There are few people abroad in the heat of noon. ". . . Restless swallows flashing their white bellies, from time to time, skimmed the sand of the street; over the shingled and cypress-bark roofs the crowding dry clouds of fused gold, silver, copper, and iron showed no sign of movement. The houses built on either side

were so hushed and still behind the wooden shutters and bulrush blinds that it might have been doubted that throughout the
whole city any were still alive." . . . The metal trimmings of an
ox-cart "glittered dazzlingly in the sun and flashed before the
eyes." ". . . The water of the river which was narrow, almost dry,
like a white-hot sword reflecting its water in the sun between
clusters of houses and leafy willows, made a faint gurgling sound.
. . . There lay naked under a wide fence the decomposed bodies
of two children, dumped one athwart the other. Perhaps because
they had been beaten upon by the fierce sun, some parts of the
discolored skin protruded glutinous flesh, and on them both,
blue flies–countless–had settled. . . ."

At length, under the heat of day, in moments of treacherous
intrigue, the plans have been made for the robbers' assault on the
mansion of Judge Tô. Action that has been painfully slow under
the summer sun, promises to be swift as the night darkens. There
are a few moments of suspense while the robbers gather at the
appointed place. "In the heavy darkness, as far as the eye could
reach, the Capital was silent, asleep; the surface of the Kamo
River faintly reflected the stars and shone dimly white. . . . Around
Rashômon at the end of Suzaku Main Street, there was the sound
of bow strings; at that unexpected time, just like the sound of
bats' wings, they answered each others' calls; one person–three
persons–five persons–eight; figures of men appearing, gradually,
suspiciously, appearing from somewhere, gathered together."

The scenes of the bloody skirmish that follow, belong to a
long past age; but the human principles involved are ageless.
There is a moment of treachery when a youth and a girl, planning
a murder, "feel the awful will to agree." Fortunately for man's feeling of security, there is not so much homicide in modern times

as there was in feudal ages, but there is something less despicable in the murder of a man than in the present-day compromise—the murder of his reputation. There is a moment when we peer on a dead face and feel ashamed that, in the normal order, a human face in death should appear holier than a living face.

"The Robbers" has a satisfying denouement in that two characters in whom our interest is aroused, though utterly confused by the intrigue around them, were able, either from conscience or instinct, to "rectify their hearts." Here we have a pleasant contrast to much of Japanese fiction and drama which assumes that man is not good by nature, and that where the forces for good and evil are matched together the latter more often prevails.

In some respects, what is good and what is evil differ in definition from nation to nation and from man to man; but certain principles of good have established themselves over thousands of years through the trial and error of thousands of millions of human beings who have tested all possible actions and reactions of which mankind is capable in all possible situations.

It is inspiring to read a story in which men have "rectified their minds."

"The Garden," also, is a story in which a man was inspired to rectify his mind, and is a stimulating "manual" for those who have some urge to do the same. Since I read "The Garden"—first in Japanese—I have longed for a wilderness to convert into a garden. The Buddhists say: "An old pine tree preaches wisdom," but it is not the wisdom itself of old gardens that is the essence of this story, but rather the creation of the garden—not the discipline involved in creating, but the *fait accompli*.

It is a story, writes Akutagawa, "about the garden of Nakamura's old-style house that had been an official post-station inn;"

but we prefer to write that it is a story of a man who, like a judô wrestler, yields to circumstance for the purpose of fighting it. There was no especial reason why Second Son defied the ravages of his mortal illness, the burning heat of the sun, and the choking stuffiness of the grasses, to re-establish the garden. He had no absorbing interest in gardens, nor was he consciously looking for enlightenment; but just as we have a *feeling* that these stories might conceal the Lady Enlightenment, he addressed his whole strength to the creation of the garden, aware that the completion of his task might bring him some satisfaction.

But, before any spiritual revelation can come, we must master the physical laws of life. A wilderness must be disciplined before it becomes a garden; in disciplining the garden, Second Son was disciplining the wilderness of his own soul, as it is the same principle that is involved. At least one knows where to begin with a garden; one can see, touch, hear, and smell a garden. In disciplining the Japanese garden, consideration must be given to the natural tendency of every tree, shrub, and plant; rocks, pathways, ponds, mounds, bridges, and summer houses have their "natural" place in a garden.

If we ask a priest of the Zen sect what is the first move to make towards enlightenment, he would be expounding a principle of his faith if he were to say: "Walk on!"

Once spurred towards the rectification of his mind, Second Son rose from his bed and "walked on." He expended all the energy which was required for his task—no more, no less. There was no time nor inclination on the part of Second Son for idle sentimentality about the beauties of nature; sometimes he committed the sin of reflecting on his work—but when, in a state of physical exhaustion he was forced to rest, "looking back" on his work was generally rather in the mood of deciding whether what he had thus far accomplished might be right or wrong.

Eldest Son had hearkened to the advice of devotees of the new learning, and in response to the utilitarian teachings of the venerable Fukuzawa Yukichi, had planted fruit trees in the garden. Like the impact of much of this Western learning, the fruit trees in Nakamura's chaotic garden, only emphasized the ridiculous.

When Second Son commenced his work in the garden, "nankin weeds had begun to float on the pond. In the thickets there seemed to be a mingling of withered trees"–"the waterfall had ceased its splashing."

"But, with hands blistered, with nails torn, he swung his mattock every day; somehow he felt compelled to carry on. Then when autumn came. . . ."

My purpose is not to relate whether Second Son achieved his aim, but to assist in drawing some attention to the inspiration that may be found concealed in the story of "The Garden."

Already I have referred to the changing face of the material world. In this, Akutagawa is more pertinent than I could be. He simply writes: "The steam train pulls into the station every day, then leaves again." Some people thrive on that kind of routine–perhaps such people are "enlightened" enough not to want anything beyond routine. But this could be so only if they had accepted routine after a long lifetime's experience of the *laws of change*. Discipline that does not come as the aftermath of chaos is moronic; such discipline is good only for the blind donkey which grinds the mill.

On my study table there is a very small Buddha with an amiable smile. He says: "The beauty of the garden is not in the discipline of it, but what grows by virtue of it."

When you have read "The Garden," you might not understand the exertion of Second Son, but transparent enough will be "what grew by virtue of it."

The Lady Rokunomiya was not as fortunate as Second Son who chanced to be graced with implicit faith in life, provided he could succeed in what he was impelled to do.

I do feel some sympathy with the father of the Lady Rokunomiya who had sprung from royal lineage but was "formal in manner" and "unadapted to the spirit of the times in which he lived." Assuredly the father's incompatibility to the current of the times had some adverse influence on the soul of the Lady Rokunomiya.–I pray that our own daughter, Louise Teruko, does not suffer on account of my own uncompromising nature and lack of acquiescence to "the spirit of the times."

"The Lady's demeanor was at all times modest, in conformity with the training she had received from her parents. It was a life in which there was no awareness of sadness, nor yet of happiness; and, although the Lady was secluded from the world, she did not feel any marked discontent. Her parents' well-being was all that really mattered to the Lady."

Such implicit devotion as the Lady had acquired as a virtue befitting her rank, was–besides elegance and some accomplishment on the *koto* (harp) and verse making–the only understanding of life which she was privileged to have. When her parents died and she was left alone in the world, she was far too bewildered to be overcome with grief.

The Lady was inconsolable. When a solution was suggested to overcome both her impecunity and her loneliness, "all the while she hid her face in her sleeve." She became convinced, however, that "there was no way in which to defeat the course of events." She believed it her lot to drift with life, withersoever the course of events happened to bear her.

Six difficult years went by. When a further solution was suggested by her only servant and friend, "both her body and mind had become too weary." She said: "I just want to wither quietly with age. . . ."

From that time onwards "the Lady's wretchedness was far beyond my power to describe."

Yet we can hardly be sympathetic with one who would not attempt to bestir in herself any spirit to resist the flow of events. Such abandonment must never be confused with resignation. One prayer–but one act of faith in the merciful Buddha–might well have altered the course of her destiny. In the 10th century a famous Court poet, Ki-no-Tsurayuki wrote: ". . . Step by step from the first movement of the foot, distant journeys are achieved in the course of time, as grain by grain high mountains are piled up from the mere dust at their base until their peaks are lost in the drifting clouds of heaven." Thus could the life of the Lady Rokunomiya have become rich and abundant.

As the Lady lay gravely ill, a Buddhist monk assured her: "We have no power over transmigration. Without effort on your own part we cannot invoke the name of Amida Buddha (the Merciful Buddha)."

Perhaps for the first time in her life the Lady murmured the name of Buddha. There was indeed some response to her faint-hearted prayer.

"Beseech Buddha with all your heart," implored the monk almost in rebuke. "Why is it you do not call on him with all your heart?"

But the Lady had no spirit to pray. She uttered some words in imitation of a prayer, but she saw nothing.

"I see nothing. . . . only the wind in the darkness–only the cold wind comes blowing."

About the precincts of that place the smell of pines was wafted on the night air. Whether the Lady were to have survived or not, the smell of pines would still have been wafted on the night air, just as the mercy of Buddha is ever-present. Only faith in the mercy of Buddha could have saved the Lady of Rokunomiya from a premature death; and the mercy of Buddha is no less than life itself.

Faith in *life* is not an abstract idea to the Buddhist. Faith in life is faith that as long as one foot precedes the other, the journey will be accomplished. So the priest advises us to "walk on!" We should proceed with our lives as we find them–seeing with the eyes, smelling with the nose, hearing with the ears, and touching with the fingers. When we derive satisfaction from seeing, hearing, smelling, and touching–from sleeping and waking–from the everyday experience of life, then we are able to enjoy the resignation that comes from enlightenment.

As for being aware of attainment to a state of resignation, I am told that there comes a time when the enlightened mind ceases to see, to smell, to hear, and to touch, but rather *is seen, is smelt, is heard,* and *is felt.* It is satisfying to have some feeling that in the translation of these stories, I was not translating the stories, but *being translated* by them. The reader might even begin to feel that he is not reading the stories, but *is being* read by them; such, it is written, is the nature of resignation.

We find in "Heresy," a Lady who, like the Lady Rokunomiya, was left alone in the world on the death of her parents. Different in disposition from the Lady Rokunomiya, the Lady Naka-mikado had the spirit to challenge her destiny.

"Heresy" is a sequel to "Hell Screen" inasmuch as it is a story about the young Lord of Horikawa. It is a valuable work as a study of character; we do not begrudge the many pages in which Akutagawa compares the young daimyô with his terrible father to whose extreme conduct we have been introduced in "Hell Screen."

"Previously I have told of the origin of the 'Hell Screen,' the astounding incident which occurred during the lifetime of the Lord of Horikawa; and now I want to tell you of the one strange event in the life of the young Lord, his son. . . ."

"Between the Lord and the young Lord, though they were father and son, from appearance to disposition there would scarcely have been anything not contrary. . . ."

The author compares the Lord's grandiose and valiant actions which "never ceased to intimidate people," with the elegance of the young Lord. He compares the preference of the Lord for the martial arts with his son's enjoyment of poetry, song, and music. We can never interpret Akutagawa's portrayal of the young Lord as being that of an effeminate young man, when we read of his courage in the face of mortal danger as he faces Heidaiyu and his band of assassins. The young Lord lived in an age when music and poetry were designed to reflect all aspects of life.

The Emperors themselves, wrote Ki-no-Tsurayuki, "on blossomy spring mornings and moonlit autumn nights, called together their courtiers, and bade them compose verse on various subjects. Some would celebrate their wanderings in different places after the blossomy sprays of spring, others their unguided rambles in the darkness of night to gaze upon the orb of the rising moon of autumn." These poems would be examined by the Emperors who could determine the degree of proficiency of the poets.

The young Lord, then, being strong in his complacency, "father and son watched each other as would two falcons hovering in the sky, each wary of the other at every instant."

In our eyes the young Lord appears as the personification of Japanese chivalry—a portrait still admired by those Japanese who have not divorced themselves from their Japanese heritage in order to ally themselves with Western "enlightenment." It is this Japanese chivalry which fortifies the young Lord in his challenging the aggressive Christian against whom the laconic Buddhists have proven no match. Akutagawa has no enmity towards the Christian, nor towards the Buddhist, but he seems to sense that neither of those two religions—in the form in which they appear in Japan—are *as religions* any match for the inspiration which Japanese chivalry has *derived* from the principles of Zen. He seems convinced that religion as religion is unrealistic—either as a result of superstition or as a yearning for the ceremonial, that the mystic develops from religion, and not religion from the mystic, as it should do; and mysticism is mystic because it is religious, not religious because it is mystic, as it should be. He interprets the mystic not as religious manifestations that are beyond human comprehension, but the relationship between mind and matter which, though experienced in everyday life, we find beyond human comprehension because our finite minds cannot comprehend the infinite, just as our languages—symbolic as their phraseology might be—cannot adequately discuss the nature of the eternal or the infinite. Purely religious discussions are a game, as, for instance, the debate as to whether God can tell a lie; if He cannot, He is not omnipotent; if He can He is not all-perfect.

Bushido is not lost in abstractions. It relates man to life as it *is*–not life as man considers it should be, nor to life that might be after his decease, nor to life in places other than this earth to which man so far has been confined. Because it is the study and perfection of what is found to be the best in life *as it is,* or as it is genuinely *believed to be,* the only prerequisite for one's understanding it is that he should be content to acknowledge life *as it is* or *as it is believed to be.*

"From the day, therefore, that the young Lord succeeded to the headship of his House, never had there been an atmosphere of such serenity throughout the mansion; it was the serenity of a spring breeze."

Later in life the young Lord described his youth "as days of dreams." They were days when love was love, and youth was youth, and youth and love were synonymous. In his desire for the renowned beauty, the Lady-Naka mikado, the young Lord dispatched to her a letter of admiration, attached to a sprig of wild orange, and was rewarded by an invitation to attend upon the Lady.

"Thereafter, the young Lord was almost a nightly visitor at the Mansion of Nishi-no-Tôin." The scene depicting the attendance of the young Lord upon the Lady is one of the most picturesque and elegant in Japanese literature. ". . . The starlit water of the pond glistened through the bamboo blinds, and a faint perfume from the scattered remains of wisteria pervaded the cool atmosphere."

"In this world, all love," she asked as though in soliloquy, "is it always as transient, I wonder?"

The young Lord explained that we tend to forget Buddha's laws on change "as we bask for a while in the wondrous pleasures of the lotus world; and we can best achieve forgetfulness in moments of love." (He stole a glance at the Lady)–"So, the bounty of love could be said to be infinite. . . ."

Throughout the room the scent of wisteria grew stronger.

As the conversation drifted, a suggestion was put forth that an interest in the new Mary Religion which was then being preached about the Capital might be a novel expedient to assist in forgetting the inevitability of change.

I have known many contemporary evangelists who have fervently preached through the countryside, but it would be surely difficult in our times to find one as wild and fanatical as the Mary Priest who was believed by some to be a *tengu* demon. He gave eyes to the blind, legs to the lame, and tongues to the dumb; he pronounced fearful punishments on those who denounced him; he turned well water to foul smelling blood; he made antagonistic vestal virgins unsightly lepers. Rapidly his converts, fascinated by his dynamic preaching of the wrath of God and hell-fire, became more and more numerous. He spoke as though he were personally acquainted with the millions of the heavenly host–and with facility he summoned them to protect him, with their war-chariots, fiery horses, and halberds–lurid dragon-like apparitions.

What appeals to us is not the burden of the Mary Priest's preaching, but the authoritative manner with which he preaches it. Fascinated by this dominating character, I can the more appreciate the assertion of one of the most renowned atheist philosophers of the British Commonwealth, Professor John Anderson of Sydney, who died only recently; he asserted that he could tolerate religion best in its most uncompromising moments.

The uncompromising nature of the Mary Priest is similar to that of a communist "Sunday agitator" on his soapbox in a Sydney park. "When communism comes," he shouted, "you people will all be able to live in magnificent houses." A voice from the crowd interjected: "I'm not interested in houses." "...When communism comes you will all have your own cars to drive." "–I don't like driving!" At length the agitator in the heat of annoyance proclaimed: "Listen, you fool, when communism comes, you will have to do precisely what you are told!!!"

The scene on the river bank where in the light of the refuse fires, the pariahs wildly abused the two retainers of the House of Horikawa, when "men and women swarmed about us peering with hate-filled faces; ... from before and behind, left and right, those leprous faces–shutting out the stars, the moon, the night– and the straining scrawny necks, seemed to belong to another world," is indeed extraordinary. We have before us the ugliness of deformed humanity in an age when deformity was not concealed; where such wretchedness was ever-present, the doctrine of uninhibited love of one's fellow man would hardly have been popular.

Relief from the ugliness and hysteria of "Heresy" comes for a moment when Akutagawa reverts to the Buddhist theme. We hear a voice reading the doctrine, there is the tinkling of bells, and we smell the fragrance of incense as it rises unceasingly and recedes into the clear autumn sky.

The last militant adherent of the gracious dignity of bushido was Saigô Takamori, unyielding leader of the Satsuma rebels, who lends his name to one of the stories in this volume. Saigô is referred to in Oliver Statler's "Japanese Inn" as "a stocky, hearty man, a warm friendly man with a great booming laugh," and by Akutagawa as "a corpulent, mountain-like man with a white beard"–a man with "a lofty countenance."

The personality of Saigô is not, however, as important to the story as the "historical fact" that Saigô died at the Battle of Shiroyama after his defeat by General Yamagata's National Army.

In the story, "Saigô Takamori," Akutagawa suggests that historians should acknowledge that most historical material could be said to be hearsay and not necessarily factual; much of history, he points out, is not so–but only *believed to be so.*

Akutagawa has also given us an authentic and intimate picture of a Japanese student. . . . The foreign tourist in Japan will be astounded to see such a vast throng of young men in formal, brass-buttoned black uniforms and will be even more astonished to learn that the young men are not army cadets or young police trainees but are university and high school students. And the picture of the student drawn by Akutagawa fifty years ago is authentic even for the student of today.

One must not be misled by the numerous collective political demonstrations–rightist and leftist–staged by the students of the major Japanese cities. Students individually show no deep grasp of politics, and no evident tendency towards social aggression.

During our years of residence in Tokyo we have found the student reserved in manner and polite to seniors, with extreme respect for the *sensei* (teacher), and ready to listen to any constructive theory that one senior to him might care to expound. Even after an acquaintanceship of some years it is difficult to bring the student to the point where he will express an opinion contrary to that of one senior to him–especially if the opposing opinion is held by his teacher; but when he is ultimately encouraged to speak freely his contradiction is usually plausible and worthy of consideration.

The student, Honma, had taken advantage of the spring vacation to explore some of the historic sites of Kyôto. On his way back to Tokyo, by accident he met an elderly man who was familiar with his own line of research.

We should take special note of the elderly man's appearance since Akutagawa's description is typical of the many scholarly old gentlemen one can see seated opposite one on the suburban trains even today. ". . . On the bridge of his prim pointed nose he wore metal-rimmed spectacles. The impression he created was altogether a graphic one. He wore a black lounge suit, and at a glance it would seem that his clothing was by no means stylish."

This old professor was able to illustrate from experience how erroneous historical accounts can often be accepted as being authoritative and true. He convinced Honma that one must be careful to *select* from conflicting ideas on what is *believed to be so,* for there are few events—even those in our own experience—of which we can be certain. Presuming that our historians have the best of intentions, all we can be sure of when we read from history is that what we read is *believed to be so.*

When others do not rely upon us for accuracy in our recollections or selection of evidence, one may for the sake of entertainment be more fanciful in what one cares to believe. In such mood has Akutagawa written "The Greeting," which is the story of a young man, Yasukichi, who became infatuated with a girl who happened to pass his way from time to time. He could not remember her appearance in any precise way, but he did remember that "she had beautiful eyebrows," and he liked to believe that she was desirable.

There are occasions when Yasukichi is reminded of "a certain young lady," although he is too preoccupied with tomorrow to think of yesterday, but—

This young lady who would sometimes pass him by on a rail-road platform was no "paragon of beauty." It did seem to Yasu-kichi, however, that the acknowledgement of a flawless beauty hurts the dignity of our contemporaries, since most novels written either in the East or in the West write of their heroines, "She was not beautiful, but . . ." This might well raise a smile, since it does seem apparent that in neglecting their personal appearance women often use the excuse that "the soul" transcends "the flesh."

With respect to the "certain young lady," we are told that "Yasukichi, at sight of her, did not remember his heart having throbbed–it was the same feeling as when he saw the familiar face of the Commandant of the Naval Base, or the cat from the newsstand.... So, when he did not see the girl, he felt somewhat disappointed, even if it were not a keen sense of loss.... Actually he felt much the same disappointment when the newsstand cat had been missing for a few days."

There is something comical about this attitude, and one does feel that it is consequently no compliment to the young lady with the beautiful eyebrows. But much that enlivens us to an awareness of truth may be said to be comical.

A time did come when Yasukichi discovered his interest in the girl to be stronger than he had imagined it to be, and he began to wonder if he were not *in love*.

Yasukichi's chances of even establishing acquaintanceship with the girl were remote. Japanese society still demands that one should not be misled into marrying in response to one's infatuation. Through the intervention of a "go-between" one wanting to marry is introduced to a prospective partner chosen after careful consideration of suitable social background and education. In current times the final decision is left to the discretion of the young couple.

Japanese society still insists that only people of experience are qualified to advise the inexperienced how to go about choosing a partner in marriage. Never would it approve of Yasukichi in this instance cultivating more than a passing acquaintanceship. It would only be a rare chance if the girl's social status were on a level with Yasukichi's; it might be on a higher or a lower level; in either situation there would be a danger of incompatibility. Much more facile is it to approach a variety of prospective marriage partners through the services of a discriminating intermediary, examining carefully the ages, academic careers, pastimes, dispositions, health, and status of the parties—so that two persons of similar background might be wedded, and two families of mutual status might, for their mutual benefit, be allied.

Many side issues arise from "The Greeting," of which the most interesting to the Westerner is the manner in which the Japanese boy meets Japanese girl. Irrespective of what magazines publish to suggest that the Japanese are becoming "modern," the truth is that Japanese boy does not meet Japanese girl unless there is ample reason for it. Rarely does one see boys and girls together in public places in Japan; there is no freedom of social exchange. Sometimes boys and girls who work together go in *groups* on week-ends to pleasure resorts—but it is universally true that the most intriguing people are those whose acquaintanceship is not easily made.

We suggest that this is also true of literature and that the reader has an interest in Japanese literature because it is at most times difficult to become acquainted with—it being by nature somewhat elusive.

One of the most elusive stories in Japanese literature is "Withered Fields," which is rather in the mood of a confession than a story.

Those who already, through their readings in Japanese poetry, are familiar with the works of Bashô may come to mourn his passing in "Withered Fields." "His years but fifty-one, quietly he would soon withdraw his living breath, 'even as the warmth of buried coals declines.' "

Bashô's disciples have come even from remote places to pay their last respects to their Master. There is a sympathy apparent between all those present, as all had learned to rely upon the Master.

Among the adherents of Buddha, death marks the transmigration of the soul into either a higher or a lower stratum of existence, ultimately the soul's shuffling off the edge of life into nirvâna, eternal bliss. Those who have some feeling of obligation towards the deceased are fastidious about the last rites which must be carried out with appropriate dignity and sincerity.

The atmosphere of which we are conscious in "Withered Fields" reminds me of the solemn atmosphere of tea ceremony. There is the same restraint of movement, and the silent acknowledgement of the spiritual presence of the living Buddha. If we are aware of conscience, it will be most transparent in those spiritual moments. If you have never instinctively been conscious of a spiritual presence at any time, be it a baptismal, nuptial, communion or funeral ceremony, or when left alone with the stars at night, or in the sunshine on the summit of a mountain clad in snow, or been privileged to witness and be moved by an act of benevolence—if you have never instinctively felt that presence, neither Akutagawa nor I myself could explain the elusive "some-

thing" of this story, for you have been born without the capacity
to experience spiritual existence; and if you have been born blind,
of course, none can ever adequately explain what beauty the eye
can see.

On the other hand, those who are conscious of that spiritual
existence, even if only momentarily, will be moved to examine
their thoughts in a desire to "rectify their minds. . . ." Do we
believe ourselves to be what others *believe* us to be?–If there be
some discrepancy in this it may not matter–and we do have a
tendency to emphasize the importance of what we believe about
ourselves and what is believed about ourselves; but if the discrepancy be "wide" (and what is "wide" is again a matter to decide
upon honestly) we can suspect that either our minds or others'
minds need to be rectified, and we can be sure that it is our own
mind that is in need of therapy if we find a natural tendency to
meddle with the minds of others.

At least there is an air of honesty about the last rites of Bashô
inasmuch as there are no words spoken in glorification of the
deceased. Christian clergy, among others, have all had some
training in comparative religion, but for those of them who have
forgotten what they learned about Buddhism in the throes of
their studies for seminary or theological college examinations,
we recall that the appreciation of Bodhidharma who introduced
Zen in 527 A.D. depends not on his speech or actions, but on
his mind as we are given to know it. . . . The solemn moments of
death should be free from the prattling of the living as the dying
man himself cannot receive comfort from obituaries; the dying
man is what he *is,* and when dead he was what he *was;* people
who go to mourn, mourn in contemplation of what they understood the man to have been; if they need reassurance that the
man is worth mourning for, they should not attend. It is inspiring

to attend the last rites of Bashô, when no word of praise for the Master is spoken. But, in modern times the Japanese are even more inclined towards garrulous mourning than are Westerners; Fukuzawa Yukichi, who had an all-consuming interest in things Western, was unkind enough to introduce the "speech" into Japanese society in the Meiji era. I have in recent years attended gatherings where no less than fifty speeches have been inflicted on those assembled, and this was thought by some to be an afternoon's entertainment.

Akutagawa, to the last degree, analyzes the introspection of the disciples attending the last rites of Bashô. They are all accomplished writers of *haiku* (seventeen-syllable verse), and therefore accustomed to introspection and critical observation of life. The degree of honesty inspired in each of the disciples by the spiritual atmosphere in the room where Bashô lay dying provides some further indication as to how one should go about rectifying the mind in preparation for enlightenment.

For those interested in Japanese literature, one man-of-letters touching on the affairs of another might have some spiritual interest. In "Withered Fields" we are drawn to feel respect for the Master, Bashô.

A similar sentiment is apparent in Akutagawa's treatment of Bakin, with whose name the Westerner is likely to be even more familiar. Personally, I like the mood of "Absorbed in Letters." The story is concerned with Bakin's self-conscious nature and has an optimistic movement. Throughout the translation of "Absorbed in Letters" I often felt that I shared much with Bakin–spiritually if not materially.

As I write, the fluorescent lamp on the table of my garden retreat is humming–as such lamps often do–reminding me of Bakin. As he sat within his quiet room he could hear the oil gurgling in the lamp, and from outside came the chirping of the crickets as they spoke vainly of the long night's loneliness. And, but for the noise of the lamp, the interior of the room is quiet like the forest.

Akutagawa was ever-conscious of the apparent whims of destiny and the weaknesses of human nature—an attribute of the most mature writers of all nations but unique in a young man, and entertaining in Akutagawa because at times it prompts his pen to satire, though never to cynicism.

In his "Absorbed in Letters," Akutagawa quotes Shikitei Samba's words: "Deities, Buddha, love, heartlessness—all are visitors at the public bath." Indeed, there are, also, all of them present in the stories of Akutagawa.

"Absorbed in Letters" is especially interesting for those who wish for a more intimate knowledge of Akutagawa himself. It was suggested that Bakin had no knowledge of current affairs, that he was an incorrigible fellow who could not make any money from pursuits of any worth, that when he was writing he would be oblivious to all other things.

For all Akutagawa's self-detachment, his works were created in "the mental state of being absorbed in letters," so we must assume that his self-detachment is an actual one and not a literary device. Therein lies the difference between Akutagawa and other writers, East and West, who are acclaimed as being "objective." In his writing he is oblivious to any misgivings about adverse criticism, though he did entertain such misgivings in his non-creative hours.

When Akutagawa wrote that Bakin had towards his readers always felt goodwill, he was surely enlarging on his own attitude. With Bakin such goodwill did not influence his evaluation of the people who read his works; hence at the one time he was able to feel both contempt and goodwill.

Perhaps, like Bakin, Akutagawa had not the courage to be too introspective. He hid from the public his own uncertain attitudes. There is some indication that, as with Bakin, there had always existed in him the insoluble problem of reconciliation of *himself as a moralist* and *himself as an artist.* He deplored the affectation of writers who sought to satisfy the public artistically and morally.

We must not, he contends, assume that the writing of mere fiction is easy to achieve. Right mind and right setting are as important to fiction writing as are knowledge and experience. Akutagawa's brush has all these advantages behind the mind that propels it, and like Bakin's brush, it sometimes zealously slips down the pages, writing of itself, as though it writes in veneration of some god.

In the story "Absorbed in Letters" there is a recurrence of the theme, the acquisition of "right mind." To Bakin, neither conceit about his ability to write *haiku* if he chose, nor his preoccupation with his readers' criticism could induce a state of mind satisfactory for his writing. The hot water of the public bath was evidently relaxing, and assisted in diverting his mind sufficiently to bestir his imagination, but it is only a temporary indulgence, and his attention is soon arrested by the "bathhouse critic" who addresses an acquaintance close by him in the foggy atmosphere.

". . . It can be said of all Bakin's works that in writing them Bakin uses only the tip of his brush. His works have no substance. When his works do have anything to convey, it is just as if he were a (history) master of a temple school. . . ."

Reflecting on such criticism, Bakin decided that an author

who drew only from the prevailing taste of the time would fall into the peril of failing to express his own sentiments in his works, and would write only in response to the taste of his readers.

Izumiya Ichibê, the publisher, endeavors to persuade Bakin to write "in response to the tastes of his readers," but Bakin is as contemptuous of the idea as he is of Izumiya himself. I can understand how contemptuous of his "blankfaced guest" a forthright man such as Bakin could have been. I know a Japanese who is like him in every way—except that Izumiya smokes a pipe, and my own acquaintance does not; he is polite and solicitous to the point where one feels the satire of it; and one does not like being a party to a satirical sketch; he is easily awed by somewhat trifling circumstances; he has a soft and effeminate voice, and, above all, the outcome of his professed intentions is always entirely opposite to what his intentions were professed to be; curiously enough, he has a strong will which he exercises at the most unreasonable times; his most disturbing trait is that, like Izumiya to Bakin, he often turns on me a "placating face."

If Izumiya is so much like my own acquaintance, I suggest that he would know well that Bakin would soon become irritated with his thinly concealed criticism, and that it will come as no surprise to him when Bakin calls his maidservant and asks if Izumiya's shoes (left at the door of the Japanese house) have been turned, as is the custom, towards the street, ready for his departure.

Then Bakin, "the possessor of a liberal area of warm sunshine," turns to the garden to assuage his wrath. "When ten minutes later Sugi, the maidservant, came to inform him that his midday meal was prepared, he was leaning vacantly against a veranda post, still altogether enwrapped in dream."

"Until a short while ago, it had been my aim to write a great work which had no rival in this land. But there again, in that, too, perhaps there existed the kind of vainglory common to all men. . . ." His strong *ego* had filled him with passion too ardent to allow him the refuge of *enlightenment* and *resignation*.

But Bakin was to gain spiritual satisfaction from the unexpected and simplest of sources, as such satisfaction may often be gained.

In the evening when he settles down in his study to write, "a power that would shatter the stars, was flowing swiftly through his mind, infusing him moment by moment with strength, urging him onwards. In his eyes there was neither advantage nor disadvantage, neither love nor hate. The flowing torrent in his mind had washed away the dregs of life, and life glowed resplendent like a new ore."

We leave Bakin completely "absorbed in letters," seated with legs cushioned beneath him, upon the *tatami* (matting) of his room, one arm on the low-set desk, writing. Outside his study the crickets are chirping to acclaim the autumn.

Akutagawa assumed that, allowing for the influence of heredity, destiny could be said to be a compromise between faith, environment, and chance–to which three entities, through decades of painful and pleasurable experience, we learn to be resigned, and through resignation to be comforted. *Chance* is the romantic, the unexpected element in life. *Environment* is just where one happens to be. *Faith* is, as is written in the Epistle of St. Paul to the Hebrews, "the evidence of things unseen," or, we might say for consistency of style, "the evidence of what is believed to be so;" and all life can be said to be no more than what is believed to be so.

We cannot always be sure whether another man is *resigned* or whether he is not. If he be a soldier he might be resigned, but if he be agitating for an aggressive war, then he is not resigned. If he be a social agitator demanding more and more material benefits from life, he is not resigned, for he is under the misapprehension that impetuosity is strength and that material advantages strengthen rather than weaken a man. Unlike Yasukichi of "The Greeting," a man who is resigned does not live for yesterday and tomorrow, but for today—conscious that life and death, yesterday and tomorrow are swift, but that the present instant is eternity. The man who is resigned will enjoy the tranquillity of the crescent moon either above the pine forest or above the restaurant roof, or through the bathroom window; beauty has no special place to be seen or not to be seen.

May we pray that these stories respond to the search for inspiration and of themselves suggest the ways in which, if need be, the reader may "rectify his mind." To be enlightened the human mind should be disciplined as a garden is pruned, swept and watered. And is enlightenment to be found in the process of such discipline? Buddha was careful to rebuke those who were too devoted to their own style of discipline. "The beauty," he said, "is *not* in the *discipline* of the garden." . . .

. . . Then, Rosaleen, let me hope that this "letter in A Sprig of Wild Orange" will be a sufficiently entertaining introduction to this book. I have the more confidence in your judgment in that I have witnessed your serenity when you serve tea; your serenity, as you might imagine, inspires me more than the taste of the tea. Sometimes my own words have the bitter flavor of that tea,

so I suppose when you read this introductory epistle–which is
not really for you alone–in the same spirit as that in which you
serve tea . . . , well, in any case, you do appreciate, I know, that
the beauty–the inspiration–of the garden is not in the discipline
of the garden, but in what grows in the garden by virtue of it.

JOHN McVITTIE
University of Tokyo

The Robbers

Introductory Note:
The title "Chûtô" is liberally translated as "The Robbers."
"Chûtô" is a Buddhist term and means either "robbery" or "a
robber." It is referred to among the five Buddhist precepts.

Like "Rashômon" this story is a story of Kyôto in the period
of its decline as the capital city of Japan. It was not unusual
that Kyôto was so devastated, when one considers the feudal
conflicts that raged in the Middle Ages. To some extent, Akuta-
gawa draws his ideas for this story from the "Konjaku Monoga-
tari" an old classic, TALES PAST AND PRESENT.

One of the greatest of contemporary orientalists, Prof. A. L.
Sadler of the United Kingdom, in his book, A SHORT HIS-
TORY OF JAPAN (Angus & Robertson, Ltd., Sydney and
London, 1946) briefly describes Kyôto as it was in the Heian
period; ". . . it was laid out in a chessboard pattern, and was
about three and a half miles north to south and about three east
and west. Straight down the middle ran the Shujaku High-
way, 280 feet wide, leading from the South Gate of the city to
the front gate of the palace quarter which lay at the northern
extremity. Parallel to this ceremonial highway were three others
on each side of it–one 100 feet wide and two, 120 feet. Between
these again were others of 80 and 40 feet. At right angles to

these were the avenues numbered one to nine, 80 or 120 feet wide, with the exception of the Second Avenue (Nijo) running across in front of the palace quarter which was 170 feet. Across it and facing the palace were the Imperial Pleasure Park and the university, while to the south between Sixth and Seventh Avenues were the two market quarters, each intersected by the two canalized rivers that flowed through the city. The capital was laid out in square units of 50 by 100 feet, each called a "chô." Four of these formed a row (hô) and four rows made a block (bô). The city was eight of these blocks wide, and the space between the cross avenues was one block. Similarly, the length from south to north was nine and a half of them. A smaller residence might occupy one unit, but that of a great court noble might spread over four or six."

At the close of the Heian period there were plagues of small-pox and other unidentified diseases rampant throughout the city. Dead were often found even in the streets.

"The Robbers" was completed on April 20th, Taishô 6 (1917).

I

"GRANDMA!–Grandma Inokuma!"

At the crossroads of Suzaku Road and Aya Street he called out to the old woman to stop; the ugly one-eyed samurai, wearing a *momi-é* hat and dark blue hunting garb, raised his *hiraboné* fan.

The breathless sky, hung with humid summer heat, spread over the houses; it was a certain noon in July. At the crossroads where the man had paused there was a willow–the leaves on its sparse branches so long and slender that one might think it suffered from the plague prevailing at that time; it cast its meager shadow over the ground; and at this place there was no wind to stir the leaves withering in the sun. And, on the highway scorched by the sunlight, where presumably because of the intense heat there had for some time been no passer-by, there wound in long sweeps the trail of an ox carriage that had passed some time before; a small snake had been run over by the wheels of the carriage; at first the tail with its raw wound had wriggled, but at length the snake had turned over on its belly and had moved its scales no more. Everywhere fiery dust bathed the crossroads, and but for the foul-smelling putrid water oozing from the wound of the snake, there was not one drop of moisture.

"Obaba!"

"Eh?"

The old woman looked back with a start. At a glance she would seem to be about sixty years of age. Tarnished hair hung down over her soiled hemp gown and cypress skin; trailing heel-less straw sandals, she leaned on a stick shaped like the leg of a frog; her bulging eyes and the size of her mouth made her face more reminiscent of a toad's than of a woman's.

In a voice parched by the sun she exclaimed:

"Ah, Tarô!"

The old woman, dragging her stick, moved back two or three paces before speaking, and she licked her upper lip.

"Have you anything for me?"

"No, nothing special."

The one-eyed man, forcing his pock-marked face into a smile, spoke with resolution.

"I'm wondering where Shakin is these days."

"If you have any business it's always with my daughter. . . . A kite has been known to hatch out a hawk, hasn't it, Tarô?"

"I wouldn't exactly call it *business;* but I haven't yet heard the latest about tonight's plan."

"Why would you think there'd be any change in the plans? The meeting place is Rashômon, the time—nine-thirty. Everything's just as previously decided."

In saying this the old woman craftily looked about to left and right; perhaps she would be assured that there were no passersby; she licked her thick lips.

"My daughter says she's looked over almost the whole interior of the house. None of the samurai, she says, are worth a thought. Tonight she will give you the details."

Hearing this, the man called Tarô, behind the yellow paper fan with which he shaded the sunlight, scornfully contorted his mouth.

"Then Shakin has become intimate with the samurai there?"

"Perhaps she went there as a peddler or some such character."

"Whatever she did to get inside, is her own affair, but she can't be trusted, can she?"

"Always suspicious, aren't you?—There's a limit to jealousy."

The old woman, laughing sardonically, poked with her stick the dead body of the snake on the roadside. At times the green flies swarmed up, then settled as before.

"Listen, if you're not careful, Jirô will take Shakin from you. That's all right. It wouldn't matter much if that would be the end of it; even my husband, for that matter, changes the color of his eyes. You do, too—only more so."

"I know that."

The man, frowning in vexation, spat onto the root of the willow.

"I don't understand you at all. You're indifferent now, but when you found out about the relationship between my daughter and her stepfather you were like a madman, weren't you? As for my husband, he'd better exert a little more care, too, or you'll both come to blows."

"That's already a year ago."

"Doesn't matter how many years ago! What's done once can be done thrice, can't it?–If *only* three times, then that's all right. As for me–I don't know how many times I've done the same foolish things."

As she had spoken the old woman had bared her speckled teeth and laughed. "That's hardly a joking matter; but what's more important is tonight's company, Judge Tô. So, everything's already arranged?"

With a somewhat irritated expression on his sunburned face, Tarô changed the subject.

It seemed the path of the sun had encountered the peak of the clouds and suddenly the neighborhood darkened. Meanwhile, the oil from the entrails of the dead snake seemed to glitter more than before.

"Even though it *is* Judge Tô's, I'm an old hand at tackling four or five of the younger samurai there."

"Hm, you've a fine spirit, Grandma–how many of us will there be then?"

"Twenty-three as usual, besides my daughter and myself. . . . As Akogi's pregnant we'll have her wait at Suzakumon."

"She certainly is pregnant–it must be her last month."

Tarô again scornfully contorted his mouth, and almost at that moment the sky cleared, and the sunlight once more became bright enough to smart the eyes.

For a time the old bent woman of Inokuma laughed like an Azuma crow.

"The fool! Nobody knows who made her that way. Akogi's keen on Jirô, but it certainly wouldn't have been Jirô."

"Apart from us finding out the father–everything'll be a bother to her while she's pregnant."

"There're many ways she could be helpful, but she's not co-operative–that's the trouble. So it's left to me to be the contact for the group. After I leave you, I have to visit three houses–there's Jûro of Makino-shima, Heiroku of Sekiyama, and Tajômaru of Takechi. . . . Ah, well–I've been here selling oil to you, and it's already two o'clock; you'll be tired after so much chatter."

As she said this she began to move her frog's leg stick.

"And Shakin?"

There was a tremor on Tarô's lips; it was an imperceptible tremor perhaps, as the woman did not seem to notice it.

"Probably she's at my house at Inokuma having an afternoon sleep.–She hadn't been home till yesterday."

The one-eyed man looked directly at the old woman, then afterwards in a subdued voice he said:

"Then, anyhow, let's meet again after sunset."

"Yes, until then you'd better take a quiet nap, too."

The old woman of Inokuma, thus replying in her talkative way, dragging her stick, walked off; eastwards along Aya street the monkeylike hempen shape, raising dust with the backs of its straw sandals, walked on, heedless of the severity of the sun. The samurai who had farewelled her, with sweat spreading over his forehead among the creases, once more spat on the root of the willow and then slowly turned on his heels.

The two having parted, the green flies swarmed over the dead body of the snake—emitted the usual slight whirr of wings as they swarmed in the sunlight and settled again.

2

THE OLD WOMAN of Inokuma, the roots of her yellowed hair wet with sweat, went off tapping her stick, heedless of the summer dust that clung about her legs.

Though often she had passed that way, when she now compared her own younger self of years ago in these surroundings, everywhere she showed change beyond belief. She reflected how at one time she had been a kitchen maid in an aristocratic house, and had been wooed by a man of higher station and had at length borne Shakin; compared with that time, except in its name, the Capital bore few vestiges of the old times.

In those times there had been roads by which oxcarts had come and gone, where now only the thistles bloomed desolately in the sunny spots between the half-fallen fences, and now there were fig trees with their unripe fruit, and flocks of crows, unheeded by anyone, gathered at the waterless ponds even by day. And she—her hair had bleached and her skin had wizened, and her body had bent from the hips—she herself had become aged. Even as the Capital was not the old Capital, she, too, was not herself of old times.

Not only had her appearance changed, but also her heart. When she had first found out the nature of the relationship between her daughter and her present husband, she could well remember how she had wept in her fury. Even in considering the matter now, she could not think of it as a natural thing. Yet, even to steal and to kill had become as household tasks; perhaps it was that her heart had grown wild like the highways and byways overgrown with weeds, and no longer did such things distress her. So, everything was changed, and yet in another sense all was the same as it had always been; what her daughter was doing now, and what she herself had done in old times were unexpectedly similar. And, too, what Tarô and Jirô were doing, and what her husband had done in his time, would not be so much different. In this way the people of all times would do over again the same things. So, if she thought of it in that way, here still was the old Capital, and even she herself was her old self.

In the heart of Obaba of Inokuma, such thoughts came vaguely fleeting. Perhaps she was moved by this sad lonely feeling. Her round eyes had become soft, the toad-like flesh of her face had in time become loose; but suddenly the old woman contorted her wrinkled face into a spirited grin, and began to enliven her face and the frog's leg stick she carried. But there was nothing unusual in that.

About four or five *ken* in front of her the road and the miscanthus, a wispy autumn grass, were divided by a crumbling roofed-mudwall–here presumably had been somebody's spacious garden–and beyond the wall were several silk-trees which had passed their prime, and over the moss colored sunbaked tiles hung faded red flowers. There against the sky, with its four corner posts of withered bamboo and walls hung with old straw matting, was a hut–lonely and strange. In appearance the place seemed to be the abode of a beggar.

What especially drew the attention of the old woman was a young samurai of about seventeen or eighteen years of age; he stood with arms folded, wearing a sword in a black scabbard over hunting garments the color of withered leaves. For some reason he was gazing intently into the hut. Beneath his naïve brow, his drawn cheeks had not yet lost their boyish appearance. At a glance the old woman knew well who it was.

"Jirô—what are you doing here?" she asked.

Obaba of Inokuma walked over to him; she propped her frog's leg stick and lifted her chin. Taken aback, the man turned, and looking down at her withered hair, her toad-like face, and the tongue licking her thick lips, he bared his white teeth in a smile, and without a word pointed to the inside of the hut.

Inside the hut on a torn *tatami* mat spread over the bare ground, a slightly built woman of about forty years of age, with a stone for a pillow, lay on her side and only a linen cloth about her waist covered her nakedness. Looking at her breasts and abdomen, so swollen and yellowish did they seem that only if poked with a finger they would ooze water and bloody pus. Especially where the sunlight pierced through the torn matting walls onto the flesh, there could be seen darkish spots like rotten apricots at the armpits and at the base of the neck, whence a strong smell seemed to be emitted.

By the pillow there was an earthenware cup with a broken rim, seemingly discarded; and if they were to judge from the grains adhering to the bottom of it, it might have been used for rice gruel. Somebody, perhaps in mischief, had arranged in the bowl five or six muddy stones; and in their midst were the withered flowers and leaves of a sprig of silk tree, perhaps in imitation of the *kokoroba* with its colored celebration streamers hanging from the *takatsuki*.

Looking on this, the stout-hearted old woman of Inokuma frowned her characteristic frown and stepped back a pace; and at that moment there crossed her mind the memory of the dead snake she had seen a little while before.

"What is it?–Hasn't she got the plague?"

"That's right. Her people somewhere in the neighborhood probably decided it was all over with her and dumped her here. There's nothing anybody can do for her in that condition."

Jirô again showed his white teeth in a smile.

"Why are you looking at her?"

"When I came by just now, two or three stray dogs had found she was good feed; they were trying to eat her, so I shooed them off with stones.–If I hadn't come along her arms by now would likely have been torn away and eaten."

The old woman, resting her chin on her frog's leg stick, took a keen look at the body–at what shortly before the dogs would have eaten, and noticed how the upper arms obliquely protruded through the torn *tatami* of the wall into the sand of the track outside, and there was moisture on the earth-colored skin where three or four sharp purple teeth marks had been impressed. The woman's eyes were firmly closed, and it was not evident as to whether or not she was breathing. For a second time the old woman felt severe repulsion as though she had been struck in the face.

"Is she alive or dead?"

"I don't know."

"She's at peace, this person. If she's dead and the dogs eat her, it's all right, isn't it?"

The old woman, as she spoke, raised her frog's leg stick, and keeping her distance, turned to strike at the woman's head. The head fell from the pillow stone, and trailing the hair on the sand, fell smoothly onto the *tatami* matting, but even then the woman, her eyes closed, moved no muscle on her face.

"It's no use doing that. Just a moment ago when the dogs were gnawing at her she didn't make the least movement."

"Then, she's dead, eh?"

Jirô smiled, for the third time showing his white teeth.

"Even if she's dead it's still cruel for the dogs to eat her."

"Why's it cruel? If she's dead she won't feel any pain if the dogs bite her."

Then the old woman stretched out her stick and rolled her eyes as she continued leisurely:

"If she's not dead, but close to it, it's far better for her to be bitten in the windpipe once and for all by the dogs."

Obaba of Inokuma licked her upper lip.

Jirô said: "But I can't stand by while a person's eaten by dogs."

"Just the same," said Obaba impudently, "don't we look on without caring while human kills human?"

"That's true."

Jirô, scratching his sidelocks, showed his teeth a little once more as he stared calmly at the old woman.

"Where are you going, Grandma?"

"To Jûro of Makinoshima—then to Tajômaru of Takechi.—Oh, yes, and I wanted to ask you if you had any message for Hiroku of Sekiyama."

When she had said this, Obaba of Inokuma, holding onto her stick, had already walked on for two or three paces.

"Ah, I can go there myself if you like."

Jirô caught up with the old woman at the back of the plague-stricken hut, and ambled along the road under the burning sun.

"Seeing that person has made me feel quite ill."

63

The old woman gave an exaggerated frown.

"–Well, Hiroku's house–you know it, don't you? Go straight along the road, turn to the left at the Ryuhonji Gate, and go on till you come to Judge Tô's mansion. It's one *chô* further on from there. You'd better make a preliminary inspection for tonight and have a look about the mansion on the way."

"Yes–I'd already intended to take a look at it. That's why I'm here."

"Oh, did you?–That's sensible. If they see your brother their suspicions might be aroused, so we can't ask *him* to take a look around. If *you* go it will be all right."

"I don't know that I like the way you refer to my brother."

"I speak better of him than anyone. What my husband says about him couldn't be repeated."

"That's because there's trouble between them."

"Even so, he doesn't speak ill of you, does he?"

"Perhaps he thinks I'm still a child."

They strolled along the narrow road, chatting in this way. At their every step the Capital's desolation more and more revealed itself before them; between the houses the sagebrush fields smelled strongly; in places there were old walls standing in line with scarcely any of the pine and willow of old times remaining. Everything they saw would prompt one to associate this wide ruined city with the faint odor of the dead.

On their way they passed a crippled beggar–just this one person, holding his high clogs in his hands. . . .

"–Then Jirô, be careful!"

Obaba of Inokuma happened to recall the face of Tarô, and with an involuntary bitter and fleeting smile she said:

"Your brother is quite obsessed with my daughter."

These words seemed to have greater effect on Jirô than she

might have expected. A frown suddenly appeared between his shapely eyebrows, and he cast down his eyes in displeasure.

"Even *I* have to be careful."

"Then do take care!"

The old woman was surprised at this drastic change in the man's feelings; she muttered, licking her lips as she would often do:

"Yes, you should take care."

"But my brother's dreams are my brother's dreams; I can't do anything about them, can I?"

"If you think that way, we might as well say that *both the contents and the lid are lost.*"

"As a matter of fact, I saw Shakin yesterday. And come to think of it she said she'd be at the front of the Temple at three o'clock this afternoon and that she'd meet you there. She told me she'd managed to avoid your brother for a fortnight. If Tarô knew that much even, there'd be trouble between you."

Jirô nodded many times in irritation as if to interrupt the old woman's incessant chatter; but Obaba was not easily discouraged.

"I was with Tarô at the cross-streets over there for a while. I gave him some good advice. If there were trouble between you and Tarô who are of our band, you would be sure to come to blows and my daughter would be the first to suffer. I'm worried about it. It would be just like my daughter; and Tarô is obstinate. I'd like to ask you a favor. . . . Even if a dead person is bitten by dogs, you are too kindhearted to look on. . . ."

Even while she spoke the old woman tried forcibly to subdue the anxiety that was aroused in her, and she deliberately laughed hoarsely. Jirô, with brooding face, walked on deep in thought—his eyes downcast.

"I hope there'll be nothing serious."

Obaba of Inokuma, quickening her frog's leg stick, prayed from her heart in that way.

ALMOST AT THAT very time three or four of the towns-children, with the dead body of the snake suspended over the end of a stick, happened to pass the outside of the hut where the woman lay; one mischievous boy among them, leaning over from as far away as he could, threw the snake onto the woman's face; the blue belly, oily, fell and clung on the woman's cheek, and then the tail, wet with foul water, slid down below her chin; at that moment the children, shouting all together, scattered in fear.

Until then the woman had seemed to be dead, but at that same moment suddenly she opened yellow eyes beneath heavy lids, and dimly those eyes—like the whites of rotten eggs—she cast up at the sky; she moved her fingers a little in the sand, and something like her voice—or only her breath—was emitted from between the dry and broken lips.

3

HAVING LEFT Obaba of Inokuma—at times fanning himself, and without choosing the shade—Tarô ambled northwards along Suzaku Road.

Throughout the middle hours of the day there were scarcely any people passing in the street; but there was a lone samurai mounted on a *hiramon* saddle on a chestnut horse, followed by a man carrying his armor in its casket; he was sheltered from the sun by an *ayaigasa*. At length, when they had passed by, restless swallows, flashing their white bellies from time to time, skimmed the sand of the street, over the shingled and cypress-bark roofs; the crowding dry clouds of fused gold, silver, copper, and iron, showed no sign of movement. The houses built on either side were so hushed and still behind the wooden shutters and bulrush blinds, that it might have been doubted that throughout the whole city any were still alive.

As Obaba of Inokuma has said, the fear of Shakin's being taken by Jirô has been gradually presenting itself before me. That woman having recently given herself to her stepfather, would it be at all strange that she forsake me who is pockmarked, one-eyed and ugly, for my brother who is sunburnt but well featured? Since he was a child, Jirô has regarded me as his idol; I believe that Jirô will not yield to the temptation, but will at least have that much discretion. Yet, considering what has recently transpired, it would be ill-judged for me to place too much confidence in my brother. No, as for overestimating my younger brother—it would be a mistake to underestimate Shakin's flattering technique. It is not only Jirô; the number of men ruined by that woman's one glance is more numerous than the swallows flying about in the scorching sky. For instance even I, after I first met that woman, have been gradually degrading myself. . . .

At the cross streets of Shijô-bômon, a woman's oxcart, ornamented with red thread, quietly passed Tarô's way; the passengers could not be seen, but with its row of silk blinds—arranged from light red to dark crimson from top to bottom—it was fascinating enough to arrest attention in the desolate streets. The boy who was pulling the cart and the servant at the rear suspiciously cast their eyes towards Tarô, but the oxen only lowered their horns, waved pompously their black lacquer-like backs, and ponderously trod on, not turning their heads. But, for Tarô, though he was submerged in rambling thoughts, the metal trimmings of the cart glittered dazzlingly in the sun and flashed before his eyes.

He stopped for a while to let the cart pass by, then casting his one eye towards the ground, quietly walked on.

In looking back to the time when I was a low grade official at the Migi Jail, I feel as if it were long ago. If I consider myself at that time I did not forget to respect the Three Treasures; nor did I neglect to follow the Imperial laws.–Now I thieve; I sometimes commit arson; and not only two or three times have I murdered. Ah, myself of old times–with my companions among the low ranking officials–I gambled at *shichihan* as such people do; I revelled in it and found entertainment in such gambling.–That Self of old times–looking at this Self as I see myself now, I did not know how happy I was then.

In my thoughts those experiences seem only of the day before, when I pause to think of them in this way; but in fact already a year has passed. That woman at the time was charged with stealing from a *kebiishi* officer of the law and had been imprisoned in the Migi Jail. It happened that through the lattice bars we talked together, and our conversation waxed more intimate, and one day we began to reveal to one another the story of our lives.

At length I pretended not to observe the members of the robber band who entered the prison with the old woman of Inokuma to assist the girl to escape. Many times from that night on I went in and out of the house of Obaba of Inokuma; Shakin, gauging the time I would likely appear, from between the slits in the shutters would peep at dusk into the street, and seeing me there would, in a voice like a rat's, ask me to go in. Within the house, except for the humble maid, Akogi, there would be no other person. Soon Shakin would firmly close the shutters and light the tripod oil-lamp, and on some *tatami* mats, a four-cornered tray and a rice-stand cluttering the place, we would enjoy a meager drinking party–just the two of us. At length, having laughed, cried, quarreled and been reconciled again, as it were, we would do what any lovers do, and would lie awake through the night.

Having gone there at sunset, I would return home at dawn. For a month it was like that. Meanwhile I came to understand that Shakin was the child of a former marriage of Obaba of Inokuma and had become the chieftain of twenty odd robbers who from time to time disturbed the heart of the city; she lived, too, as a harlot–such matters I came to know of. But, contrary to expectation, her deportment served only to enshroud her with a mysterious halo, as told in old stories, and the matter aroused not the least feeling of vulgarity. Of course, the woman sometimes asked me to join her members, but I would never agree; so she would say I was a coward, and would make a fool of me. I was often angry at that. . . .

There was a voice urging on a horse–"Hai!–Hai!" Tarô hurriedly gave way. A lowly person wearing a cotton kimono was leading a horse which bore four rice bags–two on either side of it; the man turned at the crossroads of the Sanjô-bômon, and not pausing to wipe off the sweat from his face, he proceeded under the burning sky towards the south of the main street. In the shadow of the horse, which branded the earth blackly, a swallow with nimble shining wings flew crosswise up into the sky; then, as if it were a small stone, it dropped down right in front of Tarô's nose and entered beneath wooden eaves. Tarô walked on, apparently in reverie, waving and flapping his fan back and forth.

While such months and days went by interminably, I realized, and by chance, the relationship between the woman and her stepfather. I had already known that I was not the only man who had made Shakin do his bidding; even Shakin herself had proudly told me many times the names of the Court nobles and priests with whom she had had relationships. I had felt that this woman's flesh was known to many men, but that the woman's heart was occupied only by me. True—woman's chastity was not of the body; believing this, I suppressed my jealousy. Of course, in spite of myself, I had learned something from this woman's standard of morality. In any case, as my thoughts ran in such a way, my pained heart was somewhat at ease.

Yet, the relationship between Shakin and her stepfather was different. When I realized it, I felt unspeakable displeasure. If parent and child did such a thing, killing would not be good enough. Her mother, the old woman of Inokuma, observing it and saying nothing, is more cold-blooded than a beast. With this in mind, every time I see the face of the drunken old man I do not know how many times I put my hand to my sword. But Shakin at such times is especially severe in making a fool of her stepfather. Her transparent technique strangely blunts my heart. When she says, "It can't be helped that my father is detestable," I can hate the stepfather, but by no means can I hate Shakin. Between me and the stepfather to this day, beyond staring at each other, nothing has happened. If the

old man showed the least bravery–yes, if I were in the least
brave–one of us long ago would have died. . . .

Tarô having some time earlier turned at Nijô, raised his head
when he saw that he had come to a small bridge spanning the
Mimito River. The water of the river, which was narrow, almost
dry, like a white-hot sword reflecting its waters in the sun, made
a faint gurgling sound between the clusters of houses and leafy
willows. On the lower reaches of the river, two or three black
points, like cormorants, disturbed the flow of light; perhaps they
were towns-children bathing in the water.

In Tarô's mind, in a moment of reminiscence, he recalled his
boyhood of long ago when, with his younger brother, beneath
the Gojô bridge he would fish for dace; his nostalgic recollections passed through his mind like a breeze through the scorching sky. But he and his younger brother were no longer as they
had been in those far-off days.

While crossing the bridge a severe expression flashed over
Tarô's thin pock-marked face.

Then, suddenly one day the news came that my brother, who
had been a low grade official in a provincial office of Chikugo,
having been suspected of theft, was thrust into the Hidari Jail.
I, who was a low-ranking officer of the peace, knew more than
any the pain of the interior of a prison, and it was as if it were
I myself who had been sent to prison. Discussing the matter
with me, Shakin found no difficulty in saying: "Wouldn't it be
a good idea to break open the bars?"–and Obaba of Inokuma,
who happened to be present at the time, eagerly urged me to
do so. Making a decision at last, I called together with Shakin

five or six robbers, and that same night without any difficulty,
I rescued my brother. The wound which I then suffered is
even now scarred on my breast; but more unforgettable than
that, I then, for the first time, cut down and killed an officer
of the peace; the man's sharp shriek and the smell of blood
I cannot sever from my memory. Even now in the sultry air
this thing pervades my heart.

From the next day onwards, my younger brother and I
stayed out of sight at the house of Shakin of Inokuma. Since
I had committed a crime, my living honestly or my leading
a precarious life would be the same thing in the eyes of the
officers of the law. If I were to die, at least I would live on as
long as I could. With this in mind, at last I became obedient
to Shakin; together with my brother I entered the fraternity
of thieves. From that time I burned, I murdered. There are no
evil deeds that I have not done, though, at first, of course, I
acted unwillingly; but after I had committed such acts there
was no longer any inhibition. I began to believe the doing of
evil is natural for human beings. . . .

Unconsciously Tarô turned at the corner. At the crossroads there
was the mound of a grave, piled about with stones, and on the
mound, side by side, were two stone tablets upon which the noon
sun beat down. At the foot of the stones a number of lizards had
made their bodies the color of black soot, weirdly lying flat. Perhaps frightened by Tarô's footsteps, as soon as his shadow had
fallen on them, they scattered squirming in every direction; but
Tarô showed no sign of having noticed them.

The more crimes I committed, one after another, the more
I became attracted to Shakin. My killing and stealing—all

was because of that woman. Even the breaking of the prison bars, besides my trying to help Jirô, was because I feared that Shakin would deride me if I did not take steps to help my brother. Thinking in this vein, I did not want to lose her whatsoever the exchange.

Now I must face the fact that Shakin is being stolen from me by my brother; she is being stolen by Jirô whom I helped at the risk of my life. It is not clear to me whether she *will be* seized or *has been* seized from me. I, who did not doubt Shakin's heart, allowed her relationship with other men for the sake of the carrying out of our evil deeds; I even have permitted her relationship with her stepfather; closing my eyes I could allow her that much, believing that she had been seduced unwittingly under the spell of the old man's parental authority. But with Jirô her relationship is different. My younger brother and I seem different in character, but we are not really so. As for facial features—the smallpox of seven or eight years ago marked me heavily and my younger brother lightly—his features being as they were when he was born, Jirô has become handsome, while I, having lost an eye on account of the smallpox, have become unnatural and deformed. If I, so ugly and one-eyed, have until now captivated Shakin's heart— even though this might be self-conceit—I am sure it must have been by the power of my soul. And even my younger brother, born of the same parents, has the same spirit as I. . . . But my brother, compared with me, is handsome in everybody's eyes; it is reasonable that Shakin is attracted by such a man as Jirô. Besides, in comparing him with me, I doubt he could resist her allurement. Yes, I am always ashamed of my ugly face; almost always in love affairs I am modest. Even such as I have loved Shakin to distraction; and Jirô, who is handsome, could not but fall foul of her flattery. When I think of it, it is reasonable that they should come together. But because it is not unreasonable—just for that alone do I suffer. My younger brother will take Shakin from me; he will take all of Shakin from me; at some time he will surely do so. Ah—but my loss is not only Shakin alone; I shall lose my brother, too. And instead, I shall have an enemy called Jirô; and I give no mercy to mine enemies. Nor would my enemy give me any mercy. That being so, I know well the place we will go from here. Would I kill my younger brother, or would I be killed . . . ?

The smell of death, striking his nose, frightened Tarô; the death in his heart had no odor. Looking around in the vicinity of Inokuma Bystreet, he found that there lay naked under the wide fence the decomposed bodies of two children, dumped one athwart the other. Perhaps because they had been beaten upon by the fierce sun, some parts of the discolored skin protruded glutinous flesh, and on them both blue flies—countless—had settled. Nor was that all, for under one of the children who lay face downwards, the swift ants had already attached themselves.

Tarô felt that before his eyes there was revealed to him his own future. Then, unconsciously, he bit hard on his lower lip.

Especially these days Shakin avoids me. Occasionally when we do happen to meet, at no such time does she seem pleased. At times when we come face to face she even abuses me; and at those times I am angered; I have beaten her; I have kicked her; but while beating her and while kicking her I always feel as though I am punishing myself. That is not unreasonable. My whole twenty years of life dwell in Shakin's eyes. Therefore, to lose Shakin, and to lose myself, until now would it have been the same. . . ? Losing my brother–with that loss I completely lose myself. Perhaps the time will come when I will lose all. . . .

He was still pondering over this when he came to the door of Obaba of Inokuma; the doorway was hung with a white cloth; to this place he had borne with him the smell of the dead bodies. Beside the door a loquat tree with hanging green leaves cast some of its shade coolly on the window. Passing under that tree, how many times he had entered the door he did not know, but from this time . . . ?

Tarô, suddenly feeling tired, with sentimental air and the moisture of tears, quietly crossed the threshold.

It happened at that moment.–From inside the house the sudden sharp shriek of a woman, mixed with the voice of the old man of Inokuma, pierced his ears. If it were Shakin he could not leave without doing something. . . .

Raising the cloth over the doorway, he hurriedly stepped forward into the dimly lit house.

4

JIRÔ, heavy of heart, departing from the old woman of Inokuma– as if he counted them one by one–mounted the steps at the gate of the Ryûhonji, and went up to the round pillars, peeling their lacquerware surface in various places, to drop to his haunches as though he were tired.

Inhibited by the jutting tiled roof, even the summer sun, hot as it was, did not penetrate there. Looking behind in the dim light he could see a pair of *Deva kings* standing on a blue lotus, with raised wooden pestles in their left hands, swallows' excretion clinging about their breast; unobtrusively they protected the noonday precincts. Jirô, having at first come to this place indifferently, began to feel meditation in his heart.

The sunlight, whitening the roadway before his eyes, shone on the wings of swallows flitting about like pieces of black satin.

Holding over himself a broad sun-umbrella, a man in white hunting dress and carrying a book with a green bamboo binder, passed slowly in the heat where on the far side of the mud-wall there was not even a dog to cast its shadow.

Jirô pulled out the fan which was thrust into his waistband, and opening with his fingers each blade of black persimmon, closed them again one by one, all the while recalling the matters pertaining to his elder brother and himself.–

Why should I be so distressed? My only brother looks on me as an enemy. Whenever we meet and I speak to him, he answers evasively and suppresses the conversation. It is certainly not unreasonable considering the present situation concerning myself and Shakin. Especially after meeting him I feel sad, and often yearn for my brother's friendship, and secretly I weep for a long time. Once I really thought of going off to the east country, without saying anything, and leaving my elder brother, and Shakin, too. If I did, my elder brother would not hate me, and I myself would not forget Shakin. With this in mind each time I went to my brother's place, thinking this would be a secret farewell, he all the time dealt with me coldly; and when I would meet Shakin–then would I forget the decision I had made. But at such times, how I would believe myself to be at fault!

But my elder brother does not know of my distress; he

thinks of me as an enemy in love. If my brother abuse me that is all right; if he would spit in my face, it would be all right; and if in these circumstances he were to kill me, that, too, would be all right. But I want him to understand how I hate my own misbehavior, how I do sympathize with him—that is all. It would be enough if he were to understand my feelings, and if, as well, I were to die any death, even at my brother's hands. Yes, rather than be distressed at this time, how happy I would be just to die!

I myself love Shakin; at the same time I hate her. It angers me only to think of that woman's fickle character. Besides, she's a ceaseless liar; furthermore, even when my elder brother and I myself would seem to hesitate, she will commit a cruel murder indifferently. Sometimes I stare at her wanton sleeping figure, and puzzle as to why I might have been attracted to such a woman, especially when I find she has given herself to men she barely knows; I feel even as though I might kill her with my own hands. So much do I hate Shakin. Yet, looking into her eyes, I feel still more her fascination. There is no other like her possessing such an ugly soul and beautiful flesh.

My brother seems not to know of my hate. My brother, by nature, does not seem like me to hate her bestial mind. For instance, when observing the relationship between her and other men, my brother's outlook is entirely different from mine. My brother keeps his silence when seeing her with anybody else. He seems to permit her such whims as though they were passing fancies; but I myself cannot do so. To me the fact of Shakin soiling her body is the same thing as Shakin soiling her mind; and, of course, I cannot permit her to turn her mind towards other men; it is still more painful that she has given her naked body to other men. Because of that I am jealous also of my brother; in my feeling of sorrow for him there is jealousy. In this way of thinking would there be much difference in outlook if I compare my elder brother's outlook and my own? And this very difference would worsen our relationship. . . .

Looking out dreamily onto the road, Jirô turned over in his mind these problems. Suddenly a blusterous laugh, shaking the dizzy sunlight, came from somewhere along the road. Then, a woman's shrill laugh and a man's lisping, heedless of being overheard, went on exchanging indecent jokes. Jirô, thrusting back his fan into his waistband, stood up.

The man, wearing a birch and cherry-patterned ceremonial Court robe and a soft twilled *é-boshi,* who pompously bore an embossed sword–a man of but thirty years of age–seemed to be drunk. The woman, who wore a kimono of a mauve design on a white background and a veiled *ichimégasa,* judging from voice and appearance, would have been recognized by all to be Shakin.

As Jirô went down the steps, biting his lip, he turned aside his eyes. The two did not seem to see him.

"Well–is everything clear?"

"Clear enough. Since it's myself you've told about it, you can feel as safe as if you were on a great ship."

"But I'm risking my life; it's natural for me to remind you of that."

The man, opening his red-bearded mouth so wide that his throat could be seen, laughed and stroked Shakin's cheeks a little with his finger.

"It's my life, too."

"You're smart, aren't you?"

The two having passed in front of the Temple gate, went down to the crossroads where Jirô a little while before had parted from Obaba of Inokuma, and stood there for some time, unashamed of being seen in their flirting. Soon, the man walked away, turning back many times, and continuously bantered something; then he turned the corner and went off towards the east. The woman, too, turned about, and still giggling, went back to where Jirô waited below the stone steps; there Jirô, moved by an emotion both pleasant and sorrowful, blushing like a child, welcomed Shakin's big black eyes staring at him from beneath her veil.

"Did you see that fellow just now?" asked Shakin, laughing, and opening her veil to reveal her perspiring face.

"Of course—why wouldn't I see?"

"That fellow. . . . Anyway, let's sit here."

Shoulder to shoulder the two sat down at the foot of the stone steps of the stairway. Fortunately, there outside the gate was the shade of a red pine with a gnarled though slender trunk.

"That fellow is a samurai at Judge Tô's mansion."

Shakin said this, half squatting on the steps, as she took off her *ichimégasa*. She was a woman of twenty-five or twenty-six years of age, of medium stature, and she moved her limbs as lithely as would a cat. Her face was a mixture of an awful wildness and extraordinary beauty. Narrow forehead and tender cheeks, fresh teeth and sensual lips, sharp eyes and arrogant eyebrows— all these cannot be expected in one person, but strangely she had them all. There was not the slightest flaw; most wonderful was the hair falling over her shoulders; as the sunlight shone bright blue on black, we might say that her hair was no different from the feathers of a bird. He felt the never-changing fascination of this woman to be rather distasteful.

"So, he is one of your lovers?"

Shakin, narrowing her eyes and laughing, innocently shook her head.

"Nobody as stupid as he!–Doesn't he obey like a dog whatsoever I say? Because of him I've found out everything."

"What about?"

"What do you mean, 'What about?'–The set-up at Judge Tô's. The fellow chatters excessively. Just a little beforehand he told me everything, even to a horse that had been bought lately.–So I thought we'd get Tarô to steal that horse. The fellow said it was a three-year-old from Michinoku. Altogether it's not a bad proposition."

"My brother'll obey in everything you say."

"I don't like your jealousy–especially your being jealous of Tarô. Though I did think something of him at first–now I don't care."

"Someday the same sort of thing will happen to *me*."

"I don't know about that," she said.

Shakin again laughed in a high-pitched voice, and said:

"Are you angry?–Should I say it will never happen to *you*? Inside you are a female demon."

Jirô, frowning, picked up the stone beside his feet and tossed it a little away from him.

"Perhaps I am a demon. Misfortune is inflicted on you by such a demon.–Seriously though, do you still doubt?–If you do, I don't care."

While saying these words Shakin stared up at the roadway for a short while; then suddenly she turned her eyes on Jirô, her cold smile fleeting across her lips.

"If you doubt so much, shall I tell you something good?"

"Something good?"

"Hm."

The woman brought her face close to Jirô's. From the smell of her light cosmetic mixed with perspiration, pungent to his nose, Jirô felt an impact so strong that his body tingled; he turned his face away.

"I've told that fellow everything."

"What!?"

"I told him about everybody going to Judge Tô's mansion tonight."

Jirô did not believe his ears. Even the stifling stimulation of his organic function ceased for a moment. In doubt, vacantly he turned towards the woman's face.

"No need to be surprised. It's nothing important."

Shakin, lowering her voice somewhat, took on a scornful tone.

"What I told him was this: 'The room I sleep in is right near the cypress hedge facing the highway. Last night outside the hedge I heard some men–perhaps they were robbers–about five or six of them, talking about breaking into your place; and, moreover, they were to do this tonight.' I said: 'I'm telling *you* because I know you well; if you don't have ample protection, it'll be dangerous,' I said. . . . So, perhaps they've already arranged for tonight. The fellow has now gone off to collect some friends. I'm sure they will muster together about twenty or thirty samurai."

"Why did you give us away?"

Jirô, appearing ill at ease, perplexedly watched her eyes.

"I didn't give *you* away."

Shakin's laugh seemed unpleasant. Touching with her left hand Jirô's right, she said:

"I did it for *you*."

"For *me*?"

In uttering these words Jirô felt somewhat apprehensive. Surely not!–

"Don't you follow yet? If we speak to Tarô and ask him to steal the horse–howsoever he tries he can't succeed alone; if others were to go his help you know what would happen.–If we ask Tarô to do it, you and I will be all right, won't we?"

Jirô felt as though water had been poured over his body.

"You mean we should kill my elder brother?"

Shakin, toying with her fan, nodded naïvely.

"Would it really be so bad to kill him?"

"Not only bad–it's treachery to lead my brother into a trap."

"Then, you can't kill him?"

Jirô felt Shakin's eyes keen like a wild cat's peering at him, and in those eyes there was a fearful strength, and gradually his own will power seemed to be crippled.

"But it's despicable."

"It can't be helped if it is despicable, can it?"

Discarding her fan, Shakin took Jirô's right hand in hers. Jirô said:

"Even if it were all right to kill my elder brother, that's no reason for exposing all the fraternity to danger."

Even as he spoke in this way Jirô was aware of his mistake. Confound it! He thought–Of course this crafty woman would not overlook this opening.

"If we kill only *one* man, then it's all right?–Why?"

Jirô, pulling his hand from hers, stood up; with the color of his face changing he walked to and fro in front of Shakin.

"If it's all right to kill Tarô, it will be all right to kill any of our companions."

Shakin, looking up from below Jirô's face, had spoken briefly.

Jirô said: "What will you do about your mother?"

"If she should die—I'll think about it then."

Pausing to look into Shakin's face, Jirô saw her eyes burning with contempt and passion, glowing like a charcoal fire.

"For you, I can kill anybody."

In these words there was something to pierce a man like a scorpion. Jirô felt again a kind of shudder.

"But my brother?"

"Am I not throwing away even my parent?"

Speaking in this way, Shakin lowered her eyes, and suddenly relaxed the strained expression on her face; onto the burning sand she dropped tears reflecting the sunshine.

"I've told the fellow already—I can't take it back again.—If it comes out, I—I will be killed by our fraternity, possibly even by Tarô."

At her hesitant words a desperate bravery came springing up spontaneously in Jirô's heart. Pale and dumbfounded, Jirô fell to his knees on the ground and took firmly in his own chilled hands the hands of Shakin.

The two of them, alone together, their hands clasped, felt the awful will to agree.

5

TARÔ raised the white cloth, and as he stepped into the house, he was astonished.

On looking about him he saw in the narrow room that a screen door, which opened into the kitchen, had fallen onto the folding screen of split pine; at the same time an earthenware mosquito incense stand which had broken in two was rolling and scattering its ashes; what was left of the green pine fronds was still burning. A lowly servant of about sixteen or seventeen, fat, of poor complexion, her dishevelled hair strewn with ashes, was in the arms of an old baldheaded man–fat from over-imbibing; the mean cloth covering the front of her body was askew, as she kicked her legs and screamed. With his left hand holding fast the girl's hair, the old man held up high in his right hand a broken lipped *heishi*, and he was forcibly pouring its sooty liquid between her lips. The grayish liquid hardly entered her mouth, but flowed down at random, over the girl's face, over her eyes, over her nose. The more the old man tried to force open the girl's mouth, the more vexed he became. The girl would not drink one drop of it, and though her hair was held so tightly, she so vehemently shook her head that her hair, it would seem, might even be torn out. Hands and hands, legs and legs tangling together and untangling. . . . Tarô, coming from the brightness of outside and suddenly confronted with the darkened room, could not distinguish one body from the other. But he knew at a glance who they were.

Impatient, Tarô slipped off his *zôri* and jumped into the disarrayed room. In an instant, he had caught hold of the old man's right hand and without difficulty wrenched from him the *heishi*. The old man roared angrily:

"What are you doing?"

Tarô's sharp words were very quickly snapped by the old man's reply:

"What are *you* doing?"

"Just what I *am* doing!"

Tarô threw down the *heishi* and released the old man's grip on the girl's hair. Then he raised his foot and kicked the old man onto the screen. Akogi must have been surprised at the unexpected help. Confused she crawled away one or two *ken*, then looked up to see the old man fallen on his back. She turned towards Tarô, her hands clasped as though she prayed to Buddha; trembling, she lowered her head. At that moment, unconcerned at her disheveled appearance, she turned aside and, worming through the white hanging cloth, ran barefoot off the veranda. A second time Tarô kicked the old man of Inokuma who had started off in furious pursuit, and as he fell into the ashes, gasping, the girl ran off under the loquat tree on the southern side of the house.

"Help! Murder!"

The old man screamed out. His former spirit lost after his fall across the screen, he tried to escape towards the kitchen. Tarô, quickly stretching his long monkeylike arms, clutched at the light-yellow hunting dress, and pulled the old man down.

"Murder! Murder! Help! Murder!"

"Stupid! Who's going to kill you?"

Tarô laughed loudly and derisively, as he pushed the old man under his knees. All the while the wish to kill him was so strongly aroused in Tarô that it was hard not to put it into effect. To kill would not, of course, be difficult. With only one stroke–if he were to strike only once at the nape of the neck in the loose skin, it would be all finished.

In the point of the sword's responding to the *tatami* he imagined he felt that agony of the body approaching death, and when he pulled back, there was the smell of welling blood; such imagining made Tarô's hand of itself extend towards the arrowroot vine-binding on the hilt of the sword.

"It's a lie. It's a lie. You're always thinking of killing me.– Help me someone! Murder! Murder!"

Fighting desperately the old man of Inokuma screamed out, and tried to spring up onto his feet, as he looked through into Tarô's heart.

"Why were you treating Akogi like that? Tell me the reason. If you don't tell. . . ."

"I'll tell! I'll tell!—I'll tell you. Even after I've told you—I know your way—you'll probably kill me."

"You shouldn't speak in that way—are you going to tell me or aren't you?"

"I'll tell you! I'll tell you! I'll tell you!—But first let me free. I can't open my mouth because I'm choking."

Tarô seemed not to hear the words and repeated irritatedly in a threatening voice:

"Are you going to tell me?—or aren't you?"

"I'll tell you," said the old man of Inokuma in a strained voice all the while struggling to obstruct Tarô.

"I'll tell you. It was only that I was trying to make her take some medicine. But that idiot Akogi wouldn't drink it at all.— So I had to deal with her violently. That's all I was doing. Well—not only that.—It was my wife who made up the medicine. I don't know anything about it."

"Medicine?—It's abortive medicine, isn't it? Even if she *is* idiotic, to lay hands on the girl when she doesn't want it is immoral."

"Just as I thought. You told me to tell you, so I told you, but you still want to kill me. You're a murderer! You're a wicked fellow."

"Who said I'd kill you?"

"If you're not going to kill me why are you holding your hand on the hilt of your sword?" shouted the old man, turning his sweating bald head, his glance cast upwards, his mouth frothing at the corners. Tarô was startled.

. . . If I am to kill him the time is now—the idea flashed into his mind. Without any further thought, grasping the hilt, Tarô rested the weight of his sword on his knees, and stared at the nape of the old man's neck. Under the back of the head, partly covered with a few remaining grey hairs, two sinews unobtrusively smoothed out the wrinkles of red goose-flesh. When Tarô examined that nape he felt an odd pity.

"Murderer! Murderer! Liar! Murderer! Murderer!"

The shouts of the old man of Inokuma increased till he sprang up from under Tarô's knees. As soon as he was on his feet, he protected himself behind the fallen screen door, casting his eyes hither and thither as if to run away if the least chance presented itself. When Tarô then looked into the old man's crafty face, with its distorted eyes and its nose red and swollen, he regretted not having killed him. But, gradually relaxing his hold on the sword hilt, his lips broke into a bitter smile as if to pity himself, and reluctantly he sat down on the old *tatami* nearby.

"Now I have no sword in my hand to kill you."

"If you kill me, it would be patricide."

The old man of Inokuma who by this time was feeling secure in Tarô's presence, edged from behind the screen door and emerged by degrees. Restlessly he settled his body crosswise on the *tatami* on which Tarô sat.

"If I were to kill you, why would it be patricide?" asked Tarô, casting his eyes towards the window, as though he spat out the words. Through the window, which framed a square of the sky, gleamed the loquat tree, its leaves, bathed in the sunlight, bunching at the top their various greens—light and dark.

"It would be patricide. I'll tell you the reason. Shakin is my stepchild by marriage. So aren't you also my child if you have relations with her?"

"What are *you* if you have relations with her?–a beast, aren't you?"

The old man, giving some attention to the sleeve of his hunting dress, torn a little beforehand in the fight, spoke in a whining voice:

"Even a beast would not kill its parent."

Drawing thin his lips, Tarô derided him:

"Glib with your tongue as usual."

"What do you mean?"

The old man of Inokuma swiftly and sharply stared at Tarô's face, and soon again began to sneer.

"So, I ask you–do you not believe I'm your father? Can you not believe I am your father?"

"No need to ask."

"You can't believe it?"

"No, I can't."

"You're conceited. . . . Listen–Shakin is the child of my wife's former marriage. She is not *my* child. If I must think of Shakin as my child because I married her mother, so you must think I'm your father because you married Shakin. But you don't think of me as your father. Not only do you not think so, but according to the circumstances you'd strike me, wouldn't you? For what reason did you tell me I should think of Shakin only as my child? Why is it bad for me to have relations with Shakin? If I am a beast because I have relations with Shakin, are you not a beast because you want to kill your parent?"

His eyes flashing, the old man with triumphant air pointed his wrinkled forefinger at Tarô and continued to chatter.

"Now? Am I reasonable? Am I *not* reasonable? Shouldn't even *you* be able to understand such things? My wife and I have been old sweethearts since I was a petty official of the Sahyôèfu (palace guards). I don't know what she really thought of me, but at least I was in love with her."

Tarô had never thought to hear from the mouth of this drunken, cunning, mean old man such talk of bygone days. No–rather had he thought it doubtful whether the old man had any ordinary feelings. The old man of Inokuma who had loved the old woman of Inokuma, and had been loved in return–in thinking of it Tarô felt the quiver of a smile come fleeting.

"Meanwhile I noticed that my wife had an admirer."

"And so, did she come to dislike you?"

"A lover can't prove that he's disliked.... If this talk is bothering you, I'll stop."

The air of the old man of Inokuma was serious as he paused, but soon again, sliding on his knees he crossed over to Tarô; chewing his saliva, he went on:

"–My wife meanwhile became pregnant with the lover's child. This was nothing. What I found surprising was that soon after she gave birth to the child I was not able to discover where my wife had gone. On inquiring I was told either that she'd died of the plague or that she'd gone down to Tsukushi. According to what I heard later–well–she stayed for a while with some acquaintance at Nara-zaka. Suddenly from that time I lost interest in life. I drank and gambled. At last, at others' invitations I let myself fall easily into thieving. If I stole patterned cloth, then it was patterned cloth; if I stole brocade, then it was brocade; all reminded me of my wife. Ten years went by after my wife had gone–fifteen–before I met her again."

By this time the old man who sat with Tarô on the same *tatami*, having spoken thus far, and perhaps because he was gradually becoming overwrought, for a short time let the tears fall down his cheeks, and though he moved his mouth he said nothing. Raising his one eye, Tarô looked on the old man's sobbing, and it seemed as if the old man had become a different person.

"When we met again, my wife wasn't the woman of previous years. I, too, was not myself of that former time. But when I saw her child, Shakin—who was with her, this Shakin was so much like my wife of former times that it was as if my young wife had returned. Then I thought—if I were to part from my wife I would have to part from Shakin also. In order not to part from Shakin, I would have to stay with my wife. All right—then, I would remarry the old woman. Having decided to do this, I set up this poor household here in Inokuma."

The old man of Inokuma brought his weeping face close to Tarô, as he concluded his story in a crying voice; the unpleasant smell of saké, that until then Tarô had not noticed, pervaded the air around them. Taken aback, Tarô hid his nose behind his fan.

"—Then, this wife from those old times, the woman whom I've loved to the point of risking my life, is now the Shakin of the present. You called me a beast when you had the chance. Do you hate this old man so much? If you hate, it's all right to kill—it's all right to kill me now. If you were to kill me, I'd be satisfied. But don't you understand that to kill a parent would be the action of a beast?—Beast kills beast—that'd be amusing."

As the old man's tears dried he resumed his former sullenness and abusiveness, and he waved his wrinkled forefinger.

"Beast kills beast. Then kill me! You're a coward!"—he laughed:— "Since it was you who got angry a little while ago when I wanted to give Akogi medicine, then it must have been you who made Akogi pregnant. If you're not a beast, who *is* a beast?"

Feeling himself to be in peril for having spoken thus, the old man quickly jumped back behind the fallen screen door, and showed an inclination to run away, all the while twisting hate-

fully the features on his purplish face. Tarô could not be so abusive; holding himself in check he rose to his feet and grasped the
hilt of his sword. Then with swiftly moving lips, he spat over the
old man's face, and said:

"That's just like the beast you are."

"Stop calling me a beast. Shakin's not only yours; isn't she
Jirô's woman too? So, because you steal your younger brother's
woman you must be a beast."

Tarô, for the second time, regretted his not having killed the
old man. At the same time, he feared to arouse in himself the
desire to kill. His one eye flashing like fire, but saying nothing,
he kicked at the *tatami* on which he had been sitting, and made
as if to leave. But the old man of Inokuma, waving his forefinger,
bathed him in abuse from behind.

"Did you think the story was true? It's all lies!–about the old
woman having been my sweetheart–and it's a lie what I told you
about Shakin being like my wife used to be. Understand? All are
lies. Even if you want to blame me, you can't. I'm a liar. I'm a
beast. I'm the vile wretch you failed to kill."

Letting fly such invectives, the old man gradually became
incoherent, but gathering still more all his hate into his pellucid
eyes, he stamped his feet, and continued to shout words with
no meaning. Assailed by a feeling of hate difficult to bear, Tarô
blocked his ears, as he hurriedly left the household of Inokuma.
As the sun was somewhat declining, the swallows could be seen
as usual gliding airily about in the sunshine outside.

"Where should I go?"

Outside, Tarô unconsciously inclined his head when he happened to remember the reason why a little while before he had
come to Inokuma; he had wanted to see Shakin, but he had no
idea where he should go looking for her.

"–Well–I'll go to the Rashô Gate and wait until sunset."

In this decision, it is true, his wish to meet Shakin was somewhat lurking. He recalled how lately Shakin had liked to wear men's clothes at night when she went to steal, and that all the clothes and weapons had been put into leather boxes concealed in the roof of Rashômon. Having made his decision, he walked with long strides along the bystreet towards the south. Then turning west at Sanjô, he went down to Shijô on the far bank of the Mimito River.

It was when he came out onto the main street at Shijô that it happened. There Tarô saw two–a man and a woman–talking as they passed under the wall of the Rippon Temple; they were walking south along the main street at a distance of one *chô*.

The hunting dress, the color of withered leaves, the mauve kimono, their double shadow leaving behind bright laughter, passed from bystreet to bystreet. Among the flight of giddy swallows the man's black sword scabbard glittered in the sunlight; at that moment they disappeared.

His brow unconsciously clouding, Tarô halted his footsteps on the pavement and muttered painfully:

"After all–everybody is a beast."

6

THE SUMMER NIGHT darkened. Just as quickly came the half hour after ten. Not yet had the moon risen. In the heavy darkness, as far as the eye could reach, the Capital was silent, asleep; the surface of the Kamo River faintly reflected the stars and shone dimly white. Gradually the intersections of the main street and bystreet had become indistinguishable; the Imperial Palace, the miscanthus field, the town houses, together under the quiet sky, color and shape vaguely extended without limit over the broad surface. Furthermore, the Left Capital was indistinguishable from the Right Capital; and everywhere it had become exceedingly quiet; hardly, beyond the noise of the cuckoos flying up and down, was there any sound. If there were even but one friendly flickering of fire, and if there could be heard any faint voice, then it might be in the precincts of the Dai-ji, where incense would be rising before the image of Kujaku Myô-ô—the peacock Buddha painted with gold and mottled with verdigris—worshippers there were guided by the ever-burning lights; or under the bridges of Shijô and Gôjô, there would be groups of mendicant priests passing the short night in the shadow of fires from burning rubbish. Or, again, night after night, it is said, the old foxes of Suzakumon which threaten people from the roof tops and the grasses, light spirit fires; there were points of fire like that. As well, to the north, up to the south boundary of the Toba Highway where the smell of mosquito repellent was buried deep under the night's color, as if unaware of the breeze, the leaves of mugwort moved on the river bank; and the night quietly unfolded.

At that time, north of the Imperial Palace, in the Rashômon vicinity at the end of the Suzaku main street, could be heard the sound of bow strings. Unexpected at that time and like the sound of bats' wings, they answered one another's calls; one person—three persons—five persons—eight; figures of men appearing, gradually, suspiciously, appearing from somewhere, gathered together.

If we were to gaze through the dim starlight, some might be seen bearing swords, some arrows, some axes, some halberds—everybody armed with weapons, and aptly wearing leggings and straw boots, crowding, forming lines in front of the gate. Right at the head was Tarô. Following next was the old man, who, it would seem, had forgotten the quarrelling of just a short time before as in the darkness he pompously flashed the point of his halberd. Immediately behind Jirô was the old woman of Inokuma, somewhat aside from Akogi. Shakin stood in the midst, a little apart, wearing black hunting dress and a sword—a quiver slung from her shoulder, she used her bow as a support. Looking around them all, she charmed them with her commands.

"Listen . . . tonight our task is more formidable than at any other time. Bear this in mind—everybody. At first fifteen or sixteen men, with Tarô, will enter from behind; the others will enter from the front. The most precious booty is the horse from Michinoku in the stable at the rear. That I charge to Tarô.—All right?"

Tarô, who had been scanning the stars, nodded when he heard this and drew in his lips.

"I warn you," went on Shakin, "not to take any women or children as hostages. It would be too troublesome later. Then, if we're all here, let's make a start."

Having thus spoken her commands, Shakin raised her bow in summons. Looking back at Akogi who was standing biting her fingers dejectedly, she added gently:

"Well, wait here. Everybody'll be back in two to four hours."

Akogi, child-like, looking vacantly into Shakin's face, quietly assented.

"Then let's go. Make no slips, Tajômaru."

The old man of Inokuma, clamping his halberd under his arm, looked at his companion nearby. This man wore a purpledyed hunting dress, and from his direction came the metallic sound of sword meeting scabbard, and a voice murmuring only "Hm. . . ." Beside him a young bearded man who shouldered an axe spoke up:

"*You* there—don't be afraid of shadows."

At this, twenty-three robber confederates with Shakin in their midst, all laughing to themselves, pushed out into the Suzaku main street; like crowding rain clouds the air of the band was tenacious. Like muddy water overflowing a ditch, drawing into the hollows, wheresoever they had gone, they disappeared in a moment, absorbed in darkness.

After they had left, the solitary moon came out against the dim sky and the high canopies of the Rashô Gate, facing the main street. Here and there, came and went the cuckoo's voice. Even Akogi, who had been standing on the fifth of the seven long stone steps, could no longer be seen—but soon in the turret of the Gate, a dim lamp was lighted, and one window was slid open; from that window a woman's small face could be seen looking at the far-off rising moon. Akogi, looking down on the Capital which gradually lightened before her eyes, felt all the while the movement of the fœtus; she smiled, seeming to feel a lonely pleasure in this.

7

STILL ENGAGED in battle with two samurai and three dogs, and brandishing his blood-stained sword, Jirô retreated down a bystreet towards the south for two or three *chô,* not able to give a thought to whether or not Shakin was safe. The samurai were relying on their over-all strength to take him off-guard, to cut him down. The dogs, too, their bristling backs rearing, jumped up at Jirô from both front and back. Under the moonlight the street had become bright enough for Jirô and the samurai to avoid each other's striking swords in the face of death.

To Jirô there was no alternative but to kill or to be killed by his opponents. In his mind it was natural for such a resolution gradually to increase his strength; parrying the swords of his opponents, forcing the swords aside, and at the same moment thrusting aside the dogs which were snapping at his legs–these actions he did almost at the same time. At the moment of thrusting his sword to force the opposing weapons aside, he was obliged to defend himself against the fangs of the dogs which came from behind. As might be expected, he seemed at some time to have been wounded, as in the moonlight a red-black line could be seen mixed with the perspiration which trickled down his sidelock. But Jirô, in his desperation, did not feel the pain. The prominent eyebrows on his pallid forehead were drawn into a frown. Like any person who has lived by the sword, he crossed swords in all directions, unmindful of the loss of his *é-bôshi* hat and the fact that his hunting dress was ripped.

It would be difficult to know how long this went on. But at length one of the samurai, while brandishing his sword, suddenly overbalanced, and gave out a wild scream; Jirô's sword had swiftly cut his abdomen near his waist; the sound of cutting bone resounded dully, and the glinting light of the sword sweeping sideways, broke the gloom. Jirô's sword, prancing into the air, had in the instant swept aside the other samurai's sword, and his opponent was severely cut in the elbow and ran off instantly in the direction from which he had come, while Jirô, in pursuit, tried to cut him down; almost at the same time, one of the hunting dogs, bounding like a ball, bit Jirô's hand. Jirô jumped back a step, swinging his blood-stained sword over his head; he felt discouraged, as though all his muscles had slackened in that moment. He watched his opponent's dark shape running away under the moon; then, feeling as though he had awakened from a bad dream, he thought of that place where he was now—he was in front of the very gate of the Ryûhon Temple.

. . . It had been just one hour before. The group of robbers who attacked the front of Judge Tô's mansion was amazed by the unexpected sally of arrows from inside and outside the carriage shed, and from left and right of the middle gate.

Jûro of Makinoshima, who advanced straight on, was wounded deeply in the thigh, and fell as though he had tripped. Jûro was the first; then, in a breath, two or three people were cut in the face or wounded in the elbows, and hurriedly showed their backs. How many archers there were was not, of course, known. The sharp sound of the colored and white eagle-tailed arrows mingled with the pompous sound of the turnip-tailed arrows; again they came flying. Even Shakin who had hung back was at length shot by a stray arrow through the sleeve of her black hunting dress.

"You'd injure our chief, eh? Let's shoot! Shoot! On our side we've arrows with metal tips."

Heiroku of Katano, beating the handle of his axe, shouted so abusively that some gasped. . . . Instantaneously, from among the robbers the sound of whirring arrows began again. Taking his sword and grasping it firmly, Jirô, who had been hanging back, felt some distress at these words of Heiroku; he was beside Shakin, and he stole a glance at Shakin's face, taking care that she did not observe his interest. In the confusion Shakin was standing aside unruffled; purposely keeping her back to the moon, she leaned on her bow, and, holding the smile at the corners of her mouth, she gazed up at the interchange of flying arrows; then,

Heiroku, raising his angry voice, shouted from aside: "Why do you leave Jûro where he is?–are you so frightened by the arrows that you're going to leave our good friend to his fate out there?"

Jûro, pierced in the thigh, could not rise howsoever he might have wished to do so. He crept along using his sword as a support, wriggling like a crow with the wing feathers plucked; he dodged arrow after arrow. Looking on, Jirô felt himself shudder, and unconsciously he drew the sword at his waist. Heiroku, observing him, stared askance at Jirô's face.

"You stay with the Chief. It's better for a weaker man to look after Jûro," said Heiroku scornfully.

Jirô felt the ironical contempt, and biting his lip, he looked back sharply at Heiroku's face. . . . Just then the robbers who were running over to help Jûro were forestalled by six or seven hunting dogs, who at a signal from a piercing horn came running–from inside the gate into the utter confusion of arrows, raising up the white dust. In the darkness close behind them about ten men and fifteen samurai, each with a weapon in his hands, and striving to be first outside the gate, came thronging. The robbers, needless to say, did not just look on; they let Heiroku, who was swinging his axe among the lines of halberds that bristled like a forest, take the lead; he raised a voice that could have been a man's or a beast's. In contrast to their former disappointment, and rallying their forces in one onslaught, they rushed fiercely forward. Shakin, too, set on her bow a kite's feather arrow; and her face, though menacing, did not cease to smile; hurriedly she took shelter on a bridge of the wall by the roadside and stood guard.–

In an instant the samurai and robbers had become one body; screaming madly, swelling around to the front and rear of the fallen Jûro, they began to fight at random. Among them, too, resounded the voices of hunting dogs starving for blood. For a short while it was uncertain as to which side would be victorious. One man—one of the robber confederates—who had attacked at the rear of the mansion, appeared; he was bathed in a mixture of sweat and dust and appeared to have been wounded slightly in two or three places, as he was smeared with his own blood; judging from the blade of the sword slung on his shoulder, the battle at the rear would seem to have been unexpectedly severe.

"Everybody's retreating there."

The man, looking through the moonlight, and approaching Shakin, had said to her breathlessly:

"Anyhow, the main trouble's that our leader is inside the gate, surrounded by samurai."

Shakin and Jirô, in the dim shadow of the wall, unconsciously looked at one another.

"Tarô surrounded?—What's become of him?"

"I don't know what's happened there, but as it's Tarô, it'll surely turn out all right."

Jirô, turning his face aside, left Shakin's side. But the other fellow felt no concern.

"Besides—the old man and the old woman—they seem to have been wounded. Looking at the situation so far, four or five on our side will surely be killed."

Shakin nodded, and in a stinging voice that pursued him she said:

"Well, we too are pulling out.—Jirô, would you whistle?"

With a change of expression, he put to his mouth the fingers of his left hand, and whistled sharply twice; this signal to withdraw was known to his companions; but the robbers, even after having heard the whistle, still showed no indication of retreating—perhaps because, surrounded by men and dogs, they had no chance to escape. The sound of the whistle, breaking the air of the sultry night, died away along the empty road; afterwards there was the sound of shouting men, of barking dogs and of swords clashing—so much clamor raised as to move the stars in the far away sky.

Shakin, looking up at the moon, moved her eyebrows like a lightning flash.

"It can't be helped.—We ourselves must retreat."

Before she had finished these words, and when Jirô had once more put his fingers to his mouth and was about to whistle, some of the robbers, utterly confused, scattered to left and right of the confusion of men and dogs, approached Jirô and Shakin. At that moment the sound of Shakin's bowstring resounded, and a white dog that bounded in front of one man was pierced by an arrow in the abdomen, and fell on its side, yelping in agony; instantly the black blood from its belly spurted, spotting the ground. Unperturbed by the dog's misadventure, a man followed closely behind it, slashing his sword at Jirô. Almost unconsciously Jirô stopped that sword with his blade. In a moment, in the moonlight Jirô had recognized his opponent by the red beard wet with sweat, and by the formal birch and cherry patterned garments.

Without a moment's reflection he recalled that this man had been the samurai he had seen in front of the Ryûhonji Gate. And with his recollection, fears and doubts suddenly threatened him. Might she have conspired with this man to kill not only my brother but also *me*?—With such doubt crossing his mind, Jirô felt anger darkly before his eyes. Holding his sword firmly in his hands, like a hare on the run, he slipped through under his opponent's sword and stabbed the man in the breast; then with his straw boots he stamped down severely on the face of the man who had fallen.

Jirô felt his opponent's blood spurt warmly over his hands; he felt strong repulsion as the sword-point touched a rib. And he felt his dying opponent beneath the straw boots, gnawing at them. Such circumstances, of course, gave a pleasant stimulus to his revenge; but at the same time he was seized with a certain indescribable fatigue.

If it had not been on the battlefield he would, without fail, have thrown himself down and given himself up to rest. While he was standing on his opponent's face and was pulling the sword from the man's breast, other samurai came from all sides. One man, who unobserved had crept dangerously close to him from behind, was about to level the point of a halberd at his back; but the man suddenly swinging in front of him, and with the point of the halberd tearing the sleeves of Jirô's hunting dress, fell face downwards. An arrow, like a hawk slicing the air, had carved and pierced deeply the rear of his head.

What happened after that seemed to Jirô like something he had dreamed. Amid the swords that descended from right and left, giving forth sounds like a beast's crying, he fought without choice of opponents. Fomenting around him, sounds which came from indiscernible sources—voices, and faces of men with mixed blood and sweat—came and went to the exclusion of all else. As one might expect, the vision of Shakin whom he had left behind, like a spark emanating from a striking sword, from time to time flashed in his mind. Even as the thought would appear, the risk of death coming his way in the same moment would extinguish it. And after that, the sounds of swords and arrows, like the wings of grasshoppers covering the sky, unceasingly clamored by the wall in the narrow side street. Jirô, pursued by two samurai and three dogs, was urged to hew his way little by little along the bystreet towards the south. Having killed one of

his opponents and having driven off the other, Jirô vainly relied
on the belief that he would not be afraid of the dogs. All three
dogs were brown-haired, all three of the same size—no smaller
than calves; all three of them were wet about the mouths with
human blood. As before, they snapped at his feet from right and
left. One of them he kicked under the jowls; another jumped
at his shoulder; and at the same time the other was about to
bite the hand that held the sword. Again, the three encircling
him, whirled about with tails raised high. And as if to sniff the
ground, they buried their jowls in their forelegs and yelped furiously. Jirô, having to some extent relaxed when he had killed
one of his opponents, was not tormented by the persistency of
the hunting dogs.

The more irritated he became, the more his hewing and beating at the air was likely to cause him to lose his footing. Taking
advantage of an unguarded moment, the dogs with hot breaths
gradually and relentlessly closed in on him. As it already had
come to this, there remained only one resort; to rely upon the
last hope and rare possibility that the dogs would grow weary of
chasing him and that he would thus find some chance of escape.
Drawing back his sword, he prepared to strike at any mark, and
risked jumping over the backs of the dogs that aimed at his legs;
relying on the moonlight, he ran off as fast as he could. Rather
than a conscious decision, this was not different from that of a
drowning man who clutches at a straw. The dogs seeing him
run away, with sleek curling tails kicked up the dust, and in one
accord pursued his retreating footsteps.

Not only was such a move hopeless; because of it, he had, it
would seem, entered the tiger's den. Jirô was narrowly able to
turn towards the west at the cross streets by the Ryûhonji, and
in a moment, before he had run two *chô*, the yelping of many

dogs, which were intercepting his path, came to penetrate his ears rather than the barking of the hunting dogs which had been pursuing him. Like black clouds whitened by the moon, from left and right, billowing over the bystreet, a pack of dogs scrambled for their prey. At length, *it happened in a moment.*–One of the hunting dogs swiftly cut in front of him, barking loudly to muster friends, and the pack of dogs became feverishly excited, calling and replying to one another all together; and amid their furor he was whirled instantly into a maelstrom of living, squirming, pungent animal flesh. That so many dogs had gathered through the night in this byway, was not a commonplace event. Packs of fierce stray dogs would gather to prowl triumphantly through the desolate city in tens and twenties, starved for the smell of blood, and they had preyed here since dusk on the plague-stricken women who had been cast out to die.

Jirô, now in the midst of their snapping jowls, had come to the place where the dogs were thus scrambling for the dismembered flesh and bones.

Having scented their prey, the dogs without a moment's passing, like ears of rice being blown by the storm, jumped at Jirô from all directions. One sturdy black beast jumped over the sword; a tailless dog, moving like a fox, coming from behind grazed his shoulder. He felt dogs' whiskers, wet with blood, coolly touch his cheeks; and dogs' legs matted with sand brushed past his eyebrows. He could not choose which adversary to slice or stab; on looking ahead, on looking behind, the innumerable blue-flamed eyes and mouths, filling the road–thronged at his feet.–Jirô, slashing his sword, suddenly recalled the words of the old woman of Inokuma: "If we must die it's better to die and have done with it." With these words crying in his heart, resignedly he closed his eyes, but when the breath of the dogs that would tear his throat breathed hotly over his face, without thinking he would open his eyes and sweep his sword sideways, and how many times he repeated that action he would not know. Meanwhile the strength of his arms was gradually becoming less, for he felt at every strike his sword become heavier; at every step he became dangerously more unsteady. The number of dogs arriving by far exceeded those he managed to strike–from over the pampas grass field and through the breaches in the wall they came continuously.

Raising his desperate eyes, he cast a glance at the moon, small in the sky, and poised with sword in both hands, like a striking flint, his mind recalled his brother and Shakin. He, who would have murdered his elder brother, would now himself instead be slaughtered, and he would be devoured by dogs. No more apt retribution than this! With such thoughts his eyes spontaneously welled with tears. The dogs meanwhile did not spare him. The speckled tail of one of the hunting dogs swept nimbly past, and Jirô in that instant felt in his left thigh the prick of sharp teeth.

It was then that from the bottom of the night, over the twenty-seven streets of both sectors of the Capital, the far-off sound of a horse's hoofs, beating and resounding above the clamor of the dogs, could be heard faintly through the moonlight. Like the wind, the sound began to rise up into the sky. . . .

MEANWHILE, AKOGI, ALONE and serenely smiling, was standing on the parapet of Rashômon, staring at the far-off rising moon. Over Higashiyama, the moon–the slow and lonely moon that looked lean on account of the drought–climbed up into the faint blue of the sky. With it the bridges which spanned the Kamogawa soon began to float darkly in the whitening water.

Beside the Kamogawa, through which until a short time

before an odor as of a dead body had pervaded, spread out before her eyes the Capital, dimly illuminated by a cool light–like the mirage that is said to be seen by the people of Koshi–there appeared the tower with *kurin*–the nine rings–and temple roofs glimmering faintly in the light and shadow; every aspect was vaguely enwrapped. The mountains surrounding the city were, it seemed, yielding up to the night the heat they had absorbed in the day; their own crests were shaded in the moonlight; the peaks, as though in meditation, looked down quietly from above the mist over the desolate city; and within the city there was the faint smell of *nosenkazura*–the red trumpet flower. From various places in the bushes which covered the Gate to the right and the left, the flowers and vines stretched thickly, twining around the pillars of the Gate, now old, and creeping over the loose tiles between the rafters that were spread with spiders' webs. . . .

Leaning on the windowsill and narrowing her nostrils, Akogi inhaled the perfume of *nosenzakura* to her heart's content; her thoughts were incessant and flowed hither and thither, and were mostly of her beloved Jirô, and of the fœtus which moved as though soon it wanted to see the light. . . . She did not remember her parents; even the place of her birth she had already entirely forgotten. She did remember that when a baby, she had been carried, in somebody's arms or on a shoulder under a big cinnabar gate like this Rashômon, but even this she could not feel certain about. But somehow or other she did remember something that had happened after she had attained the age of discretion. And there again, it would have been better, she seemed to think, if she had not remembered. At one particular time, teased by the towns-children, she had been thrown headlong from the crest of the Gojô Bridge onto the river bank. At another time, charged with stealing when she had stolen food because she was starving, she had been suspended naked from a beam of the Jizô-dô; by chance she had been rescued by Shakin and had automatically entered the band of robbers; but even then her misfortunes had not left her. Though almost from her birth she had been an imbecile, she had a heart which was sensitive to hardship. Often she was cruelly beaten when she displeased the old woman of Inokuma; she was subjected to impossible demands by the old man of Inokuma in his drunkenness; even Shakin, when irritable, though normally somewhat kind to her, would grasp her hair and drag her around by it; moreover, the other robbers, hitting at her and bashing her, showed no pity. Akogi, at such times, would always run away to the parapet of this Gate and sob there alone. If Jirô had not then come and sometimes said gentle words to her she would probably have died long before by throwing herself from this Gate.

Something like soot, streaming before the moon, rose up from under the roof into the bluish sky beyond the window; need we say that it was a bat?—Akogi, casting her eyes up into the sky, entranced, gazed on the points of the stars. Again the fœtus moved for a time in her womb; suddenly taking heed, she considered the movements. Even as her heart struggled to escape the pain of being human, her fœtus struggled to suffer such human agony. But Akogi did not meditate on that. Only the joy of becoming a mother—the joy that she herself was becoming a mother—like the smell of the *nosenkazura,* had come wholly to absorb her.

Meanwhile, she began to wonder whether it could not be that the movement of her fœtus meant that she could not sleep. "You are a good child, aren't you? Sleep gently. Soon the day will dawn," she whispered to her unborn child. Though the movement in her womb seemed to stop, it did not stop for long; even the pain came to increase little by little. Akogi crouched down under the window, and turning away from the dim light of the oil-lamp stand, she tried to console the unborn child in her womb; she sang a song in a thin voice:

To thee I shall be ever true–
Until the waves of the ocean
Roll over Matsu Mountain's peak.

The words of the song which she faintly remembered, like the flickering of the light that rose and fell in the quiet parapet– a song that Jirô liked to sing; when Jirô was drunk he would beat time in fun, and closing his eyes, would sing the song many times; Shakin would laugh, would clap her hands, and would say that the melody was queer. Nor should the child in Akogi's womb have not been pleased with the song.

But as to whether the unborn was, in fact, Jirô's, nobody new. Even Akogi was entirely silent on the matter. Should the robbers spitefully question her about the parentage of the child she would fold her arms, and with eyes lowered in shame would obstinately remain silent; at such times, a blush would spread over her dirty face, and on her eyelashes tears would well; observing this, the robbers would make more and more banter about her stupidity in her not knowing the parentage of the child she was carrying. But Akogi believed firmly in her mind that the embryo was Jirô's child; she believed it was a natural thing that the child of Jirô, whom she herself loved, would inhabit her womb. Whenever she would sleep alone on this parapet, without fail Jirô would appear in her dream; so if Jirô were not the parent, who could that parent be?–Casting her eyes into far-off places, Akogi sang a song, and without concern for the mosquitoes that bit her, was lost in reverie. They were beautiful and pathetic dreams that none could dream without the agony of years, yet they were dreams that forgot the agony of mankind. All evils were dispelled. But the sadness of human loneliness was like the moonlight filling the window, and the extent of human grief still more lonely and solemn, was left behind. . . .

. . . Until the waves of the ocean
Roll over Matsu Mountain's peak.

This singing voice, gradually thinning like the flickering light, was extinguished; and then a powerless pining voice, as though to invite the darkness, began faintly to be emitted. Suddenly, in the midst of her song, Akogi felt in her womb a sharp pain.

THE BAND OF robbers had been outwitted by the preparations made by their adversaries; those who had attacked at the rear gate, having been assailed by defending arrows, and those at the middle gate by the samurai who had gone to defend it, had surely met with a bitter counterattack. Despising the ability of the younger samurai, some of the robbers who had gone forward, had shown their backs in desperate confusion; among them, the cowardly old man of Inokuma, in trying to escape ahead of the others, had by some mischance mistaken the direction and had unexpectedly found himself amid a group of samurai with drawn swords. Judging from his fat, wine-soaked body and the pompous way in which he carried his halberd, it might have been thought that he had excellent ability. The samurai, observing him, glanced back and forth at one another; two men, then three men, with swords pointed towards him advanced gingerly from front and back respectively.

"Don't be flurried! I'm a retainer here," the old man of Inokuma shouted frantically and wildly.

"You're a liar. Do you think we're foolish enough to believe that? You're a bad old diehard!"

Abusing him, the samurai swiftly attacked him with their swords. Having come to this, even though he had wanted to run away, there was no way of doing so. At length the face of the old man of Inokuma became like that of a corpse.

"Why should I lie?–Why should I lie?"

Opening his eyes wide and searching ceaselessly, he was impatient to find a way of escape. On his forehead cold sweat oozed; his hands could not stop trembling; wheresoever he looked the cruel life-or-death struggle was being fought out between robbers and samurai. Though under a tranquil moon, the fierce sound of swords, and the shouting voices of the samurai and robbers were raised unceasingly. Eventually he realized he could not escape; resting his eyes on his opponents, as though a different man, he took on an evil attitude, and displaying his upper and his lower teeth, he quickly leveled his halberd, drawing up defiantly, as he abused them.

"What about my lying? Idiots! Vagabonds! Beasts! Come on!"

At these words sparks began to fly from the old man's halberd. One sturdy samurai from among the group had moved closer than the others and from the side had sliced at him at random. As he was old, from the first there was no reason for him to try to match this samurai; before ten clashes of sword and halberd, with the point of his halberd faltering, he retreated gradually. At last, he was chased by his opponents into the centre of the byroad, while the samurai, bellowing, sliced expertly at the handle of the halberd. One thrust–this time from his shoulder tip to his breast—bathed him in a Buddhist cross. The old man of Inokuma, falling on his buttocks, opened his eyes widely as though they would bulge out, and in fear and in pain that was suddenly unbearable, he hurriedly shuffled back, and croaked in a quavering voice:

"Foul play! You've taken me at a disadvantage! Help! Foul play!"

From behind the old man the samurai with the red birth-mark, raising himself, brandished a sword already dyed in blood. If, at that moment, from somewhere, like a monkey running, the hem of its hemp gown fluttering in the moonlight—if some living thing had not run among them, the old man of Inokuma would even then have died a tragic death.

But that monkeylike thing, pushing between the samurai and the old man, had flashed a short sword and in a stroke stabbed the samurai under the breast; in turn, it was cut by the sword swept sideways by the samurai; then jumping up vigorously as though it had trodden on red-hot fire tongs, and holding fast to the samurai's head, it fell down with a thud together with the samurai.

Then, between the two, almost as if they were not human beings, a fierce struggle began. Striking—biting—hair pulling! For some time the two could not be distinguished. At length the monkeylike thing, getting up on top for the second time, flashed the short sword; the face of the man who was held down turned livid in an instant, leaving his birth-mark as red as before. At that moment the monkeylike thing, perhaps losing its strength, slumped over the samurai and fell limp, its face turned upwards; then, bathed in the moonlight, the wrinkled toadlike face of the old woman of Inokuma became apparent for the first time.

Heaving her shoulders, she still clutched her opponent's top-knot in her left hand, and without letting go of it, for some time she continued to moan with pain. At length, goggling once, she moved two or three times and forcibly moaned as many times through dry lips.

"*Ojiisan! Ojiisan!*" she called her husband faintly and longingly. But there was no answer. The old man of Inokuma, as soon as he had been rescued by the old woman, had slipped and fallen in the blood, and having thrown away his weapons and other encumbrances, had hastily run off. Here and there in the bystreets some of the robbers, brandishing their weapons, had for a time continued their fight in the face of death. But all of them, to the dying old woman, like the opposing samurai, were but strangers passing by. Many times the old woman of Inokuma, in a thin voice, called her husband's name; and, more than the pain she was suffering, she felt every time utter loneliness at not being answered. Moreover, her sight having become feeble, moment by moment, the scenery around her gradually became dim. The big night sky spread above her and the small white moon which hung there—beyond these, she could distinguish nothing.

"*Ojiisan!*"

The old woman, accumulating spittle and blood in her mouth, uttering the word in a whisper, lapsed into a trance; at the bottom of her lost consciousness, probably at the bottom of sleep which has no awakening, she sank into a coma. . . .

It was at about that time when Tarô, riding bareback on the chestnut horse, and holding in his mouth his bloodstained sword, took the reins in both his hands and passed by like a storm. The horse, we need hardly say, was the three-year-old from Michinoku—the horse that Shakin had spoken of. The robbers had scattered from the side streets, leaving behind the dead; and the bystreets under the moonlight were thin white as if laden with frost. His hair disheveled, blown by the breeze, Tarô looked triumphantly about him at the crowd of men shouting abuse and clamoring behind him.

It was not unreasonable. . . . Realizing the defeat of the robbers, Tarô had decided that if he could obtain nothing else, he would steal that horse. And, in pursuance of that decision, grasping the handle of his sword, he had scattered the samurai standing in his way and, having entered the gate alone, had no difficulty in kicking down the door of the stable. As soon as he had cut the horse's halter, as though regretting the time occupied in jumping onto its back, he let the horse kick away the samurai who hindered him, and sped off at full speed into the night. There was no time even to count the number of wounds he had suffered in the escapade. The sleeve of his hunting dress was torn, and the *é-bôshi* strings were flying loose, and his *hakama* was stained with the pungent smell of blood. But to think that he had come through the forest of halberds and swords, cutting down *one* man when he met *one*, cutting down *two* men when he met *two*–he was exuberant, far from being regretful. He looked about this way and that, a bright smile spreading at the corners of his mouth, and triumphantly he spurred on his horse.

In Tarô's mind there was Shakin; at the same time there was Jirô. The more he scolded himself for his own deceiving weakness, the more there was depicted in his breast, like a dream, the day when Shakin's heart had first inclined towards him.

On this occasion a horse had been stolen by him, and no other person could have done it. His opponents had been fighting in unison; furthermore, they had occupied the vantage points. If the deed had been performed by Jirô–in his fancy he thought he saw the figure of his younger brother cut down in a moment and fallen beneath the samurai swords. This, of course, was not in the least an unpleasant fancy. Rather something in his mind prayed for that to be true. If, without Tarô's interference, Jirô could be killed, he would not only suffer no conscience, but also, as a result, he could cease to fear Shakin's hating him. As might be expected, such thoughts made him ashamed of his treachery. And taking in his right hand the sword he held in his mouth, he deliberately wiped off the blood.

It happened at the moment when he clapped back his cleaned sword into its scabbard. He had turned at the cross streets, and in his passage under the moonlight he saw a pack of about twenty or thirty dogs, and they were yelping and barking. And among them there was but one man—it was the outline of a man wielding a sword, his back towards the broken wall, vague—dark. In an instant the horse, neighing loudly, whisked its long mane, and, raising clouds of dust with its four hoofs, had carried Tarô like a gale.

"Jirô–?"

Tarô, forgetting himself, frowned sharply when he saw his younger brother. Jirô, too, brandishing his sword in one hand, turned his head and saw his elder brother. And just then it was as if the two had felt something fearful hidden in the depths of each other's eyes. Actually it was but a moment. The horse amid the pack of howling dog would have been threatened. Raising its head in the air, with its forelegs describing a big wheel, the horse galloped on more quickly than it had before. Behind them the dust, whirling whitely in the night sky, for a while became a billowing pillar. In the midst of the pack of wild dogs, Jirô, still suffering from his wounds, stood on the defensive as before. . . .

On the face of Tarô—on the pale face of Tarô—there was no shadow of a smile. In his heart something whispered: "Run! Run!"–in a moment–in part of a moment–even if he would run, all would be over. What he would do, must at some time be done; the dogs would do this instead.

The whisper, "Run! Why don't you run?"—would not leave his ears. Yes, indeed, at some time it must be done. It would not be different then or later. *If my position and my brother's were reversed, my younger brother would not act differently towards me.* "Run!–Rashô-mon isn't far." Tinged in his one eye with the light of fever, half unconsciously he kicked the belly of the horse. Swishing its tail and mane in the wind, the horse scattered sparks with its hoofs and ran straight on. For one *chô*, two *chô* under the moonlight, beneath Tarô's feet the side street like a swift current flowed behind him.

Then, transiently, endearing words sprang up, thrusting themselves onto his lips. They were: "younger brother;" his younger brother he could not forget–his own blood. Seizing the reins hard, Tarô gnashed his teeth in changed expression. In the face of these words, all his reasoning disappeared, swept aside. No longer was he forced to choose between his younger brother and Shakin. Suddenly like a thunderbolt this thought struck his heart. He saw not the sky; he saw not the road; nor did he see the moon. What he saw was but limitless night; he saw the depths of love and hate, like the night itself. Tarô, as if mad, turned his body to utter his brother's name, and with his head thrown back, he drew in with a jerk the reins of the horse. Swiftly the head of the horse changed its direction. Foam–like snow–filled the chestnut's mouth, and its hoofs struck the earth as though they would break it. A moment later, Tarô, his one eye shining like a light from a face that had been dark and grim, galloped his sweating horse back along the way he had come.

From quite near Tarô shouted:

"Jirô!"

As he uttered that name, the storm of emotion which raged

in his heart flowed out sharply. That voice, tinged with an echo of striking white-hot iron, pierced Jirô's ears.

Jirô cast a sharp glance at his brother on the horse. It was not the same elder brother who had galloped away on the horse a few moments before, the brother who had run away. Tarô's brow was tightly knit, and he bit his lower lip firmly, and his one eye fevered strangely; Jirô saw love almost like hate which until now he had not known–a strange burning love.

"Jirô!" snapped Tarô, "Jump up quickly!"–his spirit was like a falling star. Circling across the street he rode into the pack of dogs. It was not a situation in which one could hesitate. Suddenly throwing away the sword he was wielding, taking advantage of the dogs' unguarded moment, Jirô ran after the horse, and nimbly jumped for the smooth neck of the beast. Tarô, too, stretching his monkey-like arm at that moment, snatched his younger brother's collar and lifted him up desperately. The horse's head, sweeping the moonlight with its mane, turned for the third time. Jirô, already on the horse's back, firmly put his arms about his brother's breast.

And in an instant one black dog whose mouth was stained with blood, howling fiercely, churned the dust and jumped at the horse's back. Its sharp teeth were snapping dangerously at Jirô's knees, but, raising his leg Tarô sharply kicked the chestnut's belly. The horse whinneyed and swiftly whisked its tail, and the dog, skimming the tip of the horse's tail, snapped and tore vainly at Jirô's leggings, until it once more fell back into the swirling wave of animals.

But Jirô stared with eyes of ecstasy as though in an enchanting dream. He saw neither heavens nor earth. The face of his elder brother whom he embraced–the elder brother's face half-bathed in moonlight as he stared fixedly at the road along which they sped–that face was gently and solemnly reflected in Jirô's eyes. He felt, filling his heart by degrees, a limitless ease; since he had been separated from his mother's care, this quiet powerful comfort he had not felt through many years.

"Elder brother."

Seeming to forget he was on the horse, embracing his elder brother and smiling with delight, Jirô lay his cheek on Tarô's dark blue hunting tunic and he wept. . . .

Half a moment later the two proceeded quietly through the deserted Suzaku main street. The elder brother still remained silent; nor did the younger brother have anything to say. The quiet night echoed the sound of the horse's hoofs.

In the sky above them there flowed the cool River of Heaven.

8

OVER RASHÔMON the day had not yet dawned. If one were to have looked, one would have seen the moonlight reclining on the peeling cinnabar paint of the balustrade and on the roof tiles laden with cool dew. Below the Gate where the high projecting eaves intercepted the moonlight and the wind, the sultry gloom, unceasingly stabbed by brush mosquitoes, was stagnant–sour. Those of the robbers, who had retreated from Judge Tô's mansion, were standing in the darkness around a faintly glowing pine torch; in groups of threes and fives, some were standing, some lying down and some had stretched themselves out at the base of the round pillars; all were busily treating their wounds.

Among them he who bore the gravest injury was the old man of Inokuma. His face turned upwards, he lay on Shakin's old *uchigi* (silk garment) spread out on the ground, and from time to time half closing his eyes, he groaned in a hoarse threatening voice. In his pained and weary heart he did not know whether he had lain that way for but a short while or for the duration of a year. Various phantoms, as though in scorn of him who was on the point of death, came and went unceasingly before his eyes; so at times these phantoms, merging with the actions being carried out below the Gate, became the entire world to him. In the pit of his illusions he could distinguish neither time nor place, but with a certain exactitude that transcended reason he relived his ugly life.

"Heh!–Obaba!–What's happened to Obaba?–*Obaba!*"

He was threatened by fearful phantoms which, born *of* darkness, disappeared *into* the darkness; his body writhed; he groaned.

Then, Heiroku of Katano, his wounded forehead bound with an undersleeve, brought his face near to the old man.

"Obaba?–Obaba has already gone to Paradise. She's probably on a lotus leaf eagerly waiting for you."

Tossing these words, Heiroku laughed at his own joke and turned towards Shakin who, in a far corner, was attending to the thigh wound of Jûro of Makinoshima. Heiroku said to her:

"Chief, the old man seems in a bad way. It's cruel that he's in such pain. I'm thinking of running him through."

Shakin laughed demurely.

"It's not a joke," she said, "If he must die, then let him die naturally."

"Well–as you say."

The old man of Inokuma, overhearing this exchange, was visited by a premonition–a fear; instantly, his body seemed to freeze. Again he groaned loudly. Though cowardly when facing his enemies, how many times until now had he himself, having reasoned as Heiroku was now doing, fatally stabbed his companions with the point of the halberd?–How many times he had done so, he would not have been able to recall. It was because on such occasions he was interested only in the sport of killing and he wished to exhibit to others his "audacity" in having perpetrated such cruelties.

Then, as though unaware of the old man's agony, somebody sang a nasal song in the flickering light:

The weasel blows a whistle,
The monkey is accompanying
And the locust's beating time.

In response the slapping of mosquitoes could be heard, but some among the company beat time, shouting "Ho!–Yah!" Several of the voices were choked with laughter.–The old man of Inokuma, to make sure he was still alive, shook his body, opened his heavy eyelids and stared at the firelight. The torch, with countless circles emanating from its flame, being attacked by the persistent night, emitted but a thin light. One small golden beetle with a fluttering sound came flying there, but as it entered the inner circle of the flame its wings were burned; it fell, and for a while a strong smell assailed the old man's nostrils.

Soon, like that insect, he too must die, thought the old man; if he were to die, his body, both flesh and blood, would surely be devoured by maggots and flies. *Ah, I myself must die!* His fellow robbers, as though naught of any significance had transpired that night, were clamorous in their singing and their laughter. Throughout such contemplation, the old man of Inokuma felt as though his bones were being smitten with indescribable anger and pain, and along with this feeling, he felt as though a lathe with sparks flying was unswervingly descending before his eyes.

"Beast! Profligate! Tarô–hey–villain!"

From the tip of his tongue that barely moved, the words tumbled falteringly. Jûro of Makinoshima so as not to cause acute pain to his wounded thigh–quietly turned over on his side and whispered in a dry voice to Shakin:

"The old man certainly hates Tarô!"

Shakin frowned, and looking at the old man of Inokuma she nodded her head; then the same voice that had sung the nasal song inquired:

"What happened to Tarô?"

"Perhaps he didn't get away."

"Somebody said he saw him die–who was it?"

"I saw him confronted by five or six samurai!"

"Ah, ah–*tonshô-bodai*–may he rest in peace."

"Jirô, too, is missing."

"It was the same with him."

Tarô dead, Obaba dead! I, too, shall die. To die? What is it to die? By no means do I want to die. But I shall die. Just like the insect I shall die.

Like the cry of brush mosquitoes everywhere in the darkness, such incoherent thoughts pressed his heart. The old man of Inokuma felt that formless undesirable *death* was patiently gazing fixedly at his breathing from behind the cinnabar lacquered pillar; cruelly and composedly it seemed to stare at his agony; little by little it crept along like the waning moonlight. Gradually he felt the dawn close by his pillow. *By no means do I want to die!*

With whom do I sleep at night?
–I sleep with Hitachi-no-sukè,
His flesh as I sleep is pleasant
Like maple on Otokoyama's peak,
–My fame is thus renowned.

The voice singing the nasal song and the old man's pained voice merged. Then somebody, near the pillow of the old man of Inokuma, spat and said:

"I haven't seen the idiot, Akogi, about."

"That's true."

"Perhaps she's sleeping up in the parapet."

"Hah–there's a cat crying up there."

Everybody became silent at the same time. Then a catlike cry was heard above the spasmodically groaning voice of the old man of Inokuma. The wind began to blow hotly between the pillars of the Gate, and faintly the fragrant smell of *nosenkazura* flowers gently assailed the noses of all assembled.

"A cat in disguise. . . ."

"Akogi's companion might well be the old woman transformed into a cat."

Then Shakin interposed reprovingly, making a sound like rustling cloth:

"It's not a cat.–Somebody go and see."

Responding to her voice, as Heiroku of Katano stood up, his sword scabbard struck a pillar. There were twenty or more steps chiselled in the pillar of the parapet. Everybody, for a short time assailed by unreasonable anxiety, became silent. The wind carrying the smell of the *nosenkazura* passed once more faintly among them; then, within a moment, Heiroku, up on the parapet, gave a shout and soon the sound of his footsteps descending the stairs in a scurry, hurriedly disturbed the deep gloom; it was no ordinary matter.

"Would you believe it?–Akogi's given birth."

Heiroku stepped down from the stairway and spiritedly showed them a roundish object enwrapped in cloth. In the soiled cloth, smelling of woman, the baby just born looked more like a skinned frog than a human being. Awkwardly moving its big head, its ugly face frowning, it wailed. The thin, soft hair, slender fingers–everything stirred up dislike and wonder both. Heiroku, looking about him, chatted proudly, jigging the baby in his arms.

"When I went up, Akogi was slumped below the window, groaning as though she were dying; she's mad, but still she's a woman; I thought she was having a spasm when I went near her–so I was naturally astonished. There was something up there in the gloom like a discarded fish's entrails, and it was whimpering. When I touched it, it moved a bit. When I looked at this hairless thing, I wondered if it might not be a cat after all. So, I picked it up and held it to the moonlight to see, and I found it was this newborn baby here. See! It seems to have been bitten by mosquitoes; it has red spots on its chest and belly. Akogi, too, is now a mother."

Fifteen or sixteen robbers surrounded Heiroku who stood around the pine-torch fire; some were standing, some were squatting–each of them stretched their necks as though they were different people and with gentle smiles kept watch over the ugly red lump of flesh into which life had just entered. The baby did not remain still even for a short time but moved its hands, its feet; and then, bending back its head, bellowed powerfully for a short time. And the inside of the toothless mouth could be seen.

The man who had previously sung the nasal song remarked shrilly:

"Ah, it has a tongue."

At that everybody, as though they had forgotten their wounds, guffawed. Then, as if to pursue the laughter, suddenly the old man of Inokuma, in such a voice that they were urged to wonder wherefore the power remained in him, spoke sharply:

"Show me the child. Hey, rogues!–show me the child, won't you?"

Heiroku prodded the old man's head with his foot; in a threatening tone he said:

"If you want to see it, then look at it. Anyway, if there's a rogue among us, it's you!"

Heiroku bent down unceremoniously and displayed the child; the old man of Inokuma opened wide his besmirched eyes and stared at the baby, looking as though he were about to eat it. As he looked, his complexion suddenly paled like wax, and his wrinkled "crow's feet" were beaded with tears. In that moment, around his trembling lips, there was the wave of a strange smile flowing–an innocent expression, that had not been his until then, began to soften the muscles of his face; though he was chattering, his chatter was incoherent. Everyone knew that *death* had at last come to overtake the old man. But nobody knew the meaning of his smile.

The old man of Inokuma, as he lay there, stretched out his hand slowly and softly touched the fingers of the baby; as if pricked by a needle, the baby broke into a pitiful wailing. Heiroku, tempted to scold him, hesitated; it was because he felt that the face of the old man–the wine-soaked, bloodless and fat old man, was at that moment–and only at that moment–brightly shining with a solemnity difficult to disturb. Even Shakin, as if awaiting something, had, with bated breath and without averting her eyes, stared at the face of her parent–at the face of her lover. Still he spoke no word; but on his face there was joy, as if at this juncture there had sprung up the wind that blows at the point of dawn. Then, beyond the dark night, beyond the far sky which was unseen by human beings, he saw coolly breaking, a cheerless, eternal dawn.

"This child," he said, "This child is mine. . . ."

Having spoken this clearly, he touched once more the baby's fingers with the limp hand that had lost its strength; at his side Shakin gently supported him. More than ten robbers, seeming not to have heard these words, each of them remained silent and still. Shakin raised her head and looked up at the face of Heiroku of Katano who was standing with the baby in his arms; she nodded.

"It sounds as if the phlegm has clogged."

To Heiroku nothing in particular mattered. The old man of Inokuma, together with the crying voice of the baby seemingly afraid of the darkness, continued to groan feebly, and like a pine-torch becoming thin, he quietly expired.

"At last he's dead."

"Well, at least we've learned who made Akogi pregnant."

"The body should be buried under that bush, shouldn't it?"

"It'd be a pity to leave it as food for the crows."

In the cool atmosphere the robbers conferred. Far-off was heard the faint crowing of cocks. Dawn began to glimmer.

"Akogi?" solicited Shakin.

"I covered her with a cloth I found, and she's asleep. She's so healthy, I'd say there'd be nothing to worry about."

Heiroku's reply was more gentle than usual.

Meanwhile two or three of the robbers, bearing the corpse of the old man of Inokuma, carried it outside the Gate. Outside, too, it was still as dark. Under the faint dawn moon the upper branches of the dreary *nosenkazura* bush swayed gently, and the smell came floating more and more fragrant. From time to time, barely audible, the sound of dew dripping from the bamboo leaves could be heard.

"Life-and-death is man's lot."

"Birth and death are swift."

"A dead face seems holier than a live face."

"He does seem to have a more honest face than he had before."

Amid these remarks the corpse of the old man of Inokuma, dyed with spots of blood, was carried off into the depths of the bamboo grove and the *nosenkazura* bushes.

9

ON THE following day, in a certain house of Inokuma, the corpse of a woman was found brutally murdered. She was young, plump, beautiful; from the nature of the wounds it would appear that she had stoutly resisted. What ought to have been sufficient evidence was that a sleeve of hunting garb, the color of withered leaves, was jammed into the corpse's mouth.

Again, what might seem strange, was that the woman Akogi, who had been a servant in that household, though present at the time of the crime, was not in the least molested. According to the officers of the peace, these were the general circumstances (we say "general" because Akogi being an imbecile, it would have been difficult to obtain more accurate details).

Akogi had, it happened, been awakened at midnight, and she had overheard Shakin quarrelling with two brothers, Tarô and Jirô. Even while Akogi was trying to discern the reason for the quarrel, Jirô had all of a sudden drawn his sword and cut Shakin down. Shakin had called for help, trying to escape, but Tarô forthwith seemed to add his blade to the scuffle. Then for a short time the abusive voices of the two men and Shakin's agonized voice continued. At length, when the woman had breathed her last, the brothers promptly embraced one another and wept for a long time. Through a crack in the sliding door Akogi had peeped in, but she had not gone to the assistance of her mistress because she thought she must not let her baby—sleeping in her arms—be injured.

"Moreover," Akogi had said, suddenly blushing, "the man called Jirô is the child's father. . . . Then Tarô and Jirô came to where I was waiting and they told me to take care of myself. When I showed them my child, Jirô smiled and stroked its head; what is more, his eyes were brimming with tears. Though I begged them to stay, the two hurried away. They jumped onto a horse that was probably tied to the loquat tree and went off. There were not two horses; holding the child, I looked from the window, and by the moonlight I could see clearly that there were two men riding on the same horse. After that I left my mistress's body where it was and I quietly went back to bed. As I'd often seen my mistress murder people, her own body did not in the least bother me."

The officer of the peace had at length discovered that much. And as Akogi was obviously not guilty, they promptly let her free.

. . . More than ten years later, when Akogi's child had grown up, and she herself had become a nun, she one day saw a man renowned for his bravery pass by; he was one of the escorts of the Governor of Tango, and she said he was Tarô. Indeed the man did have thin pockmarks and only one eye.

"If he had been Jirô I would have straightway run to him and greeted him; but Tarô terrified me so. . . ."

Akogi, in telling of this, acted with the coquetry of a young girl, but whether it were Tarô or whether it were not, *that* nobody knew. Known only was the fact that the man in question had a younger brother who was reputed to serve the same master; that much was discreetly rumored.

THE DOG, SHIRO

Introductory Note:
This story is one of the few contemporary Japanese stories writ-
ten in the lighter vein. It is, however, serious in its assessment of
the place of the individual in society.

In Buddhist belief the soul of a dog or of any other creature
is of equal importance to that of the human being. All souls are
faced with a similar challenge, that of striving through virtue to
attain nirvâna. "The Dog, Shiro" is the simplest of illustrations
of the power of compassion. One must feel at the conclusion of
this naïve but charming story that Shiro has attained the state
of resignation that comes only from enlightenment, and that the
prospects are favorable for the advancement of his soul toward
the desired state.

This story was completed in July of Taishô 12 (1923).

I

IT WAS one spring day in the afternoon. The dog, Shiro, sniffing
the ground, trotted along a quiet narrow street on both sides of
which were long rows of budding hedges; and here and there
among the hedges, cherry was in blossom. Shiro, who had been

skirting the hedges, happened to turn down a certain bystreet. As soon as he had turned the corner he came to a sudden halt as if startled by what he saw.

There was good reason for this. A dogcatcher wearing a figured coat and concealing a net behind him was stalking a black dog; and the dog, unsuspecting, was eating something that might have been bread thrown to him by this dogcatcher. But that alone was not what alarmed Shiro. It was enough to see a dog about to be taken unaware–but the important thing was that the dog was his neighbor, Kuro–indeed, his intimate friend. In the mornings he and Kuro would frequently put their heads together and sniff at one another's noses.

Without hesitation Shiro was about to call loudly, "Kuro, take care!"–but at that moment the dogcatcher cast his eyes at Shiro, and there was no mistaking the threat that flashed from those eyes–"You would warn him, would you?–Beware!–or I'll catch *you* first!" Shiro was so terrified that he forgot how to bark, and he became cowardly all in a moment. Keeping a close watch on the dogcatcher, Shiro began to edge backwards. And, as soon as the dogcatcher was hidden once more by the hedges, Shiro forsook the unfortunate Kuro, and fled.

And just then, the net descended; Kuro's sustained barking rang out; but Shiro showed no sign of stopping, let alone of retracing his steps. Jumping over mud puddles, kicking and scattering pebbles, skimming over "No Thoroughfare" barricades, knocking over garbage bins, he continued on without a backward glance. Just watch him running down that hill! Ach–it seems he has been run down by a car!–Shiro hardly knows whether he is alive or dreaming. Ah, the distressed voice of Kuro still drones like a wasp in Shiro's ears.

"Kyân! Kyân! Help! Kyân! Kyan! Help!"

2

GASPING for breath, Shiro at length returned to his Master's house. Slipping through the dog gate under the black wall, he ran alongside the small lumber shed, till he reached the dog kennel in the back garden. Almost like a gust of wind Shiro ran onto the back lawn. Once he had reached home he was not afraid of being caught in the net. Moreover, his Mistress and Master were playing merrily together on the green grass with a ball. . . . Shiro was happy at what he saw; wagging his tail, he bounded and pranced towards them.

Looking up at the two, Shiro exclaimed breathlessly:

"Mistress! Master!–Today I saw a dogcatcher."

As the young boy and girl did not understand dog language, of course, they heard only 'Wan! Wan!'–But that day, for some reason, they did not even pat him on the head, but rather seemed amazed. Shiro, thinking it odd, tried again to tell them.

"Mistress! Don't you know the dogcatcher? He's a fearsome fellow, isn't he, Master? I escaped, but Kuro from next door was caught."

At that the young girl and boy only looked at one another. Then they began to talk strangely.

"Whose dog is it, Haruo?"

"Yes, I wonder whose dog it is."

–Whose dog? This time it was Shiro who was surprised. Shiro could understand quite clearly his Mistress's and Master's words. But, simply because we cannot understand dogs' language, we assume that dogs cannot understand us. How wrong we are! Because they can understand our language, dogs can learn tricks. But, as we cannot understand dogs' language, to see in the dark, to follow a scent, and to learn generally what dogs might teach us, is not ours to know.

"Whose dog am I?–I?–I'm Shiro, of course!"

But, as before, his Mistress stared at him strangely.

"Could he be a brother of Kuro, next door?"

"Perhaps he's Kuro's brother," the young boy, as he toyed with a bat, pondered deeply over the matter. "This fellow, too, is jet-black."

Shiro suddenly felt as though the hair on his back was bristling. Jet-black? It could not be so! From the time he had been a pup he had been as white as milk. But, to be sure, now as he looked at his front paws–no, not only at his front paws, but at his chest, his belly, his hind legs, his elegant sweeping tail, too–all were as black as the bottom of a pan–jet-black! Jet-black! Shiro, as though crazed, began to leap, frisk and cavort, all the time barking with all his might.

"Ah! Really, Haruo–this dog seems quite mad."

The girl cowered as she spoke tearfully, but her younger brother stood his ground and promptly struck Shiro on the left shoulder with his bat. The next moment the bat came flying at Shiro's head. Evading it, Shiro fled as he had done from the dogcatcher. But this time he did not–as he had done shortly before–run even two *chô*–not even one. Beyond the lawn, under the shade of the hemp palm, there was the cream painted kennel, and when he reached it he turned about towards his little Mistress and Master.

"Mistress! Master! I am Shiro. However jet-black I appear I am still Shiro."

We need hardly mention that Shiro's voice shook with sadness and agitation. But neither of the young people were able to discern Shiro's feelings. As a matter of fact, the young girl said spitefully, "He's still over there barking. He's certainly some cheeky stray dog, eh?"–and she stamped her foot. Haruo, too–Haruo picked up gravel from the path and hurled it at Shiro with all his might.

"Beast! You still hanging about? Take this!–and this!"

The gravel came flying without a break. Blood meanwhile oozed from beneath Shiro's ear. Shiro, his tail between his legs, at length withdrew beyond the black fence. A white butterfly, the dust on its wings bathed silvern in the spring sunshine, fluttered gaily by.

"Ah, from today I shall be a dog without a home."

Sighing as he paused beneath a telegraph pole, Shiro stared dreamily up at the sky.

3

SHUNTED AWAY by his Mistress and Master, Shiro prowled the streets of Tokyo. But, wheresoever he went, he could not forget that he was jet-black. Shiro was startled by a barber's shop mirror that reflected customers' faces; he was startled by the street puddles that reflected the sky just after the rain; he was startled by the glass of the display windows that reflected the young leaves of the trees on the street. Indeed, even the glasses of black beer filled to the brim on the café tables reflected his image. What was to become of him? See that car parked outside the gardens?–that big black car?–The gleaming enamel on the chassis of the car, as he walks alongside it, is reflecting Shiro as clearly as if it were a mirror. Nothing could have reflected Shiro as effectively as that big car. How astounded he was when he saw his reflection! If you could have but seen his face! Shiro whined bitterly and swiftly scampered off into the park.

In the park a light wind was stirring the young leaves of the plane trees. With bowed head, Shiro wandered off among the trees. Apart from the gay pond there, he did not come upon anything that reflected himself. The only sound he heard was that of the bees as they clustered among the white roses. In the atmosphere of the peaceful garden, Shiro was able for a time to forget the besetting misery of having become an ugly black dog.

Yet, he knew that such happiness might last but a few moments. As if in a dream Shiro wandered over to a bench off the pathway. It was then that he heard the yelping of a dog beyond the bend in that path.

"Kyân, Kyân, Help! Kyân, Kyân, Help!"

Shiro trembled instinctively. That sound awakened in Shiro's heart the remembrance of Kuro's last desperate crying. With eyes closed Shiro would have fled in the direction in which he had come, but on a moment's impulse Shiro let forth a weird howl and turned away abruptly.

"Kyân, Kyân, Help! Kyân, Kyân, Help!"

This call echoed in Shiro's ears once more.

"Kyân! Kyân! You're a coward! You're a coward!"

As soon as he had turned round, he began to run in the direction of that voice.

But when he had run to see what it was all about, it was not a dogcatcher who appeared before his eyes. Instead, two or three boys in uniform, apparently on their way home from school, were making a great fuss of pulling a brown pup by a rope tied around his neck. The pup was struggling with all his might in protest against being pulled and was calling repeatedly for help. But the children paid no attention to his entreaty; instead, they laughed and shouted and kicked him in the belly.

Barking vehemently, Shiro flew at the children without the least hesitation. Taken by surprise, the children were both astounded and frightened. As for Shiro–his appearance was ferocious, his eyes were afire, his teeth snapped like chopping knives, as if he were about to bite them. The children scattered and fled in all directions; one of them in his dilemma jumped over the flower bed on the edge of the pathway. Shiro pursued them for two or three *kan* then turned about and returned to the young pup. He raised his voice as if to scold:

"*Sa!* Come along with me. I'll take you home."

Shiro immediately ran off into the trees through which he had just come. The brown pup passed merrily under the bench, kicking the roses as he went and ran on after Shiro, not wishing to be left behind. The long rope still trailed from his neck.

IT WAS TWO or three hours before Shiro and the young pup paused before a modest café. Though it was still daytime, a red electric light glowed in the dim interior of the café, and a tinpot phonograph was playing something like *Naniwabushi* recitative. Complacently wagging his tail, the pup spoke to Shiro:

"This café, the *Taishô-ken*, is where I live.–Where do *you* live, sir?"

"*Sir?*–I?–I come from a street a fair way from here."–And it was with a sad sigh that Shiro said, "Then, I'll be off home now."

"No,–wait, sir! Is your Master strict?"

"My Master?–Why would you ask such a thing?"

"If your Master's not strict, stay here tonight. My mother will be pleased to thank you for your kindness in saving me. At my place we have milk, curried rice and beefsteak—many kinds of tasty things."

"Thank you.—Thank you. I've no time now, but I'll accept your invitation another time.—Then give my regards to your mother."

Shiro glanced at the sky and then went walking off along the pavement. In the sky above the restaurant roof could be seen the crescent moon.

"Sir!—Sir!—Please—if only—."

The pup whimpered plaintively.

"—Won't you just tell me your name? My name is Napoléon—but I'm called both Napoléon and Napo-ko. What might *your* name be, sir?"

"My name's Shiro."

"Oh, Shiro, is it?—That's an odd name for you, sir, isn't it?—When you are black all over?"

Shiro's breast grew heavy with emotion.

"Just the same—I'm called Shiro."

"Then I'll call you Uncle Shiro. Uncle Shiro, do not fail to come again soon."

"Well, Napo-ko—*sayonara*."

"Take care of yourself, Uncle Shiro! *Sayonara! Sayonara!*"

4

AND AFTER THAT?—What became of Shiro?

We shall not recount all the details of his story, as it has already been reported in several newspapers, and perhaps everybody has read of it. It is the story of a black dog that helped certain people whose lives were in danger. Also, at one time there was a popular motion picture called the "The Valiant Dog" based on the experiences of Shiro himself. But in case, by some mischance, you are not familiar with the story, you might care to read the several articles cited below.

Tokyo NICHI-NICHI Newspaper:
ON the morning of the 18th (May) at 8:40 P.M., as the Ôu Express was approaching the intersection of Tabata Station, Sanéhiko–the eldest son of Mr. Shibayama Tetsutarô, a company official at No. 123 Tabata–was standing on the busy railtracks and was in grave danger of being run down and killed. A sturdy black dog ran like lightning to the crossing and rescued the four-year-old Sanéhiko from the wheels of the onrushing train. The authorities greatly regret that this brave black dog disappeared from sight in the milling crowd, and so they have been unable to render it official commendation.

Tokyo ASAHI Newspaper:
THE wife of Mr. Edward Berkeley, a wealthy American, has been summering in Karuizawa. Recently a big snake of over seven *shaku* in length appeared at her villa and attacked her pet Persian cat. A strange black dog suddenly ran to the aid of the cat, and, after a twenty minute struggle, sank its teeth into the big snake and killed it. The heroic dog, immediately after the incident, was nowhere to be found. The lady is offering a five thousand dollar reward in her search for the dog's whereabouts.

KOKUMIN Newspaper:
THREE First High School students, who arrived on 7th (August) at the hot spring resort of Kamikôchi had lost their

way between Mts. Hotaka and Yarigataké while crossing the Japan Alps. Deprived by gales and rain of their tent and provisions, the hikers had almost given up hope of survival. Whereupon, a black dog, which had appeared from some valley into which the party had wandered, walked on ahead of them as if it wanted to act as guide. The party followed this dog, and after more than a day's walk, at last managed to arrive at Kamikôchi. But the students reported that the dog, once the roofs of the hot spring buildings could be seen, barked in delight as it disappeared into the bamboo brush. All members of the party assert that the appearance of the dog was God's providence.

JIJI Newspaper:
ON 13th (September) more than ten persons were burned to death in a fire at Nagoya. In that fire the Mayor of Nagoya, Mr. Yokozeki, almost lost his beloved child. His son, Takémori (3 years) was inadvertently left on the second floor of the burning building and would have been burned to death but for a black dog which brought him out in its mouth. It is reported that the Mayor has issued an order forbidding the destroying of stray dogs within the limits of Nagoya Municipality.

YOMIURI Newspaper:
ABOUT 2 P.M. in the afternoon of 25th (October) a Siberian wolf from the Miyagi traveling zoo, which for several days has drawn crowds of people to the public park inside the Odawara Castle precincts, suddenly broke out of its cage, injured two gatekeepers and escaped in the direction of Hakoné. In view of this, Odawara officials declared a state of emergency and spread a police cordon over the whole town.

The wolf appeared in Jûji-machi at 4:30 P.M. where it fell into a fierce fight with a black dog which eventually overpowered it. The police cordon hastily converged on the spot, and the wolf was soon shot dead. This wolf of the *lupus gigantix* species is said to be of the fiercest breed. Now, however, the Superintendent of the Miyagi Zoo declares that the wolf was shot without just cause; he is angrily contending that he will take action against the Chief of Police at Odawara . . . , etc., etc., etc. . . .

5

LATE ONE NIGHT in autumn, tired in mind and body Shiro returned to his Master's house. His Mistress and Master had, of course, long since gone to bed. Yes, by that time not one person would have been awake. On the lawn of the back garden, the ring of the white moon floated on the tops of the lofty hemp palms. Shiro, wet with dew, settled down in front of his old kennel. There he began this soliloquy to his companion, the dreary moon.

"O Moon! Moon! I left Kuro to his fate. Probably that is why my body has become jet-black. But, in my separation from my Mistress and Master, I have battled against various hazards. In moments, when I saw my body blacker than soot, feelings of shame for my cowardice have been aroused in me. To put an end to this black body of mine I have jumped into fire and even fought with a wolf. Yet, strangely, whatsoever the odds, my life was not taken. Even death has fled from me when I have looked it in the face. At last, full of bitterness, I have decided to take my own life. I feel I should be sad to die if before I kill myself I cannot have one last glimpse of my Mistress and Master. Of course, when they see me tomorrow, they will surely again mistake me for a stray dog. My master might even beat and kill me with his bat, but nothing could be nearer my heart's desire. O Moon! O Moon!–I ask no other favor than to see the faces of my Mistress and my Master. Tonight I have once more ventured all the way home for that one purpose. Please, as soon as it is dawn, let me meet my Mistress and my Master."

His soliloquy at an end, Shiro laid his chin on the grass and lapsed into a sound sleep.

"It's quite astounding, isn't it, Haruo?"

"What is, sister?"

On hearing his Master's small voice, Shiro opened wide his eyes. There were his Mistress and Master standing before his kennel and looking at each other with the oddest expressions. Shiro cast his eyes down at the lawn. When he had become black, his Mistress and Master had been just as surprised as they seemed now. In recalling his grief at that time, he even felt sorry that he had returned home. Then–just then–his Master suddenly jumped up and shouted in a loud voice–

"Father!–Mother!–Shiro has come back!"

Shiro?!–Involuntarily Shiro bounded up. His Mistress, perhaps fearing he might run away, held on to him with both arms and hugged Shiro tightly around the neck; at that moment, Shiro looked into his Mistress's eyes, where the kennel was distinctly reflected in her black pupils. The cream colored kennel in the shade of the tall plane tree–everything reflected in her eyes was as it should be; and, in front of the kennel–as small as a grain of rice, a dog sat. This was serenity–a resplendent feeling.–Shiro was enraptured by the sight of this dog.

"Look–Shiro is crying!"

Holding Shiro in a tight embrace, the sister looked up into her brother's face.–Just look at that patronizing brother as he replies:

"Hmph! Sister–you're crying, too."

THE HANDKERCHIEF

Introductory Note:
"The Handkerchief" ("Hankechi") is not a traditional Japanese commodity. The use of the handkerchief since the early Meiji era is one of the innumerable instances of the Japanese imitation of Western habits and dress from the time of the Restoration (1868). In the Meiji period it was considered fashionable to have a handkerchief, at least for the purpose of waving good-bye to one's friends. The presence of chairs and tables in Prof. Haségawa's house (in this story) is typical of what one finds in well-to-do Japanese residences, most of which have one or two rooms bearing some semblance of Western style.

In this story Akutagawa is wittingly or unwittingly pointing out the dilemma that Japanese still have to face—the dilemma that arises when the mind, accustomed to the esthetic nature of some traditional restraint, is confronted with the tempting abandon of progressive ideas. What Akutagawa, indeed, was aware of—while not being contemptuous of mannerisms—was the inevitable role that the "mannerism" must play in an author's work. He realized that however individualistic an author might be, his style may usually be ascribed to some particular school of writing by virtue of its "manier," and he seemed to fear that his

own work also, must thus fall into some stereotyped character.
"The Handkerchief" was written in September of Taishô
(1916).

PROFESSOR HASÉGAWA KINZÔ of the Law School of Tokyo
Imperial University was sitting in a rattan chair on the veranda,
reading Strindberg's *Dramaturgy.*

His specialty was the study of colonial policy. Consequently,
the fact that he was reading *Dramaturgy* might be something of
a surprise to the reader. But, as might be expected of a professor
who was no less famous as an educator than as a scholar, when
leisure permitted, he made a point of reading through any books
which were concerned with the thoughts or sentiments of the
students of the time, even if such works were out of line with his
special study. Actually, he had taken the trouble to read Oscar
Wilde's *De Profundis* and *Intentions* merely for the reason that
they were favorite books among the students of a certain college
with which he was associated as principal. That being so, it was
not strange that the book he happened to be reading was a discourse on modern European drama and actors. For among the
students under instruction, there were not only some who wrote
critiques on Ibsen and Strindberg, or Maeterlinck, but also some
enthusiasts who wished to follow in the steps of such modern
dramatists and make playwriting their life's work.

As the Professor finished reading each aphoristic chapter, he
put the yellow clothbound book on his lap and glanced vacantly
towards the Gifu lantern hanging on the veranda. Oddly, no
sooner would he do so than his thoughts would depart from
Strindberg. Instead, thoughts of his wife, with whom he had gone
to buy the lantern, would come into his mind. The Professor,

while studying abroad, had married in America; so, his wife was, as you might suspect, an American. But she loved Japan and the Japanese hardly less than *he* did. Especially was she an admirer of the finely wrought objects of Japanese arts-and-crafts. Accordingly, it was safe to surmise that the Gifu lantern, suspended on the veranda, did not so much represent the Professor's taste but rather was an expression of his wife's enjoyment of the things of Japan. . . .

Whenever he put down his book, the Professor thought of his wife and the Gifu lantern and Japanese civilization as represented by that paper lantern. According to his convictions, in the past fifty years Japanese civilization had shown remarkable progress on the material side; but spiritually, it had not made any appreciable progress that was readily discernible; no, rather, in one sense there had been a decline. Therefore, it was the urgent duty of the thinkers of the day to consider what had best be done to remedy this decline. It was the Professor's contention that there was no other recourse but to depend upon the Japanese heritage of bushido. Bushido ought never to be looked upon as simply the moral code of a narrow-minded insular people. On the contrary, its essence might well be identified with the Christian spirit of the peoples of Europe and America. If this bushido could be revived in the existing current of Japanese thought, it would not only revitalize the spirit of Japanese civilization, but it would be advantageous in facilitating mutual understanding between the European-American peoples and the Japanese people. Or, it would be a means of advancing international peace.–He himself had long dreamed of becoming such a bridge spanning East and West. To such a Professor, his awareness that his wife and the lantern–and the Japanese civilization as represented by that lantern–preserved a certain harmony, was ever a pleasant thought.

Then–in his repeated enjoyment of such satisfaction, the Professor gradually noticed that even while he was reading, his concentration continually strayed from Strindberg. A little vexed at this, shaking his head he again began to pore painstakingly over the small type. Thereupon, just where he took up his reading again, the following was written:

> When an actor discovers an appropriate mode of expression for the most ordinary emotion and wins success through this means, then, without due consideration as to its suitability or unsuitability to the occasion, he may–on the one hand because it is facile, and on the other hand because of his success with it–be prone to employ this device. And this is what may be termed a *mannerism*.

The Professor had felt that with art–and especially drama–he had no natural affinity. Even the Japanese theatre he had attended only a few times in his life. Once in a story written by a certain student the name Baikô had been mentioned. The Professor, proud as he was of his encyclopaedic knowledge, had to admit that this name was unfamiliar to him. When it was opportune, he called the student aside and asked him what the name, Baikô, represented.

"–Baikô? Baikô is an actor attached to the Imperial Theatre at Maru-no-uchi; he is currently playing the female rôle of Misao in the *Taikôki Jûdanmé*."

The student, who wore a Kokura *hakama* skirt, courteously had replied in that way.

... The Professor held no opinions whatsoever as to the pertinent criticisms raised by Strindberg. A vague interest was aroused only to the extent to which the comments evoked in his mind an association with the dramas he had seen in the West during his studies abroad. He was, in a way, not much different from the middle-school teacher of English who reads Bernard Shaw's plays in his search for idioms. But, an interest–whatsoever its bent–is still an interest.

The Gifu lantern hanging from the veranda ceiling was still unlit; and, in the rattan chair Prof. Haségawa Kinzô was reading Strindberg's *Dramaturgy*. This is all I need write for the reader to imagine what a long afternoon in early summer it was. But, this does not infer that the Professor was afflicted with a sense of boredom. If a person were to interpret it that way, he would be deliberately and cynically misconstruing what I write.–As it happened, he had to give up reading Strindberg for the time being. This innocent amusement of the Professor's was interrupted by the maid's announcement of a guest. Howsoever long the day, the Professor would never cease to be burdened by life's obligations.

Putting down the book, the Professor glanced at the visiting card that the maid had just brought to him. On the ivory paper in small type was printed *Nishiyama Atsuko*. He could not remember having met such a person. Even so, the widely connected Professor, as he got up from the rattan chair, turned over in his mind the names of his acquaintances. But, still he could not recall a face associated with that name. Then, in lieu of a bookmark, he placed the card in the book which he left on the rattan chair, restlessly adjusted the front of his unlined raw-silk kimono, and again glanced up at the fancy lantern before his nose. It would be so with anyone, in such circumstances, that the host who is obliged to keep a guest waiting is more impatient than the waiting guest. Moreover, it is not necessary to add the explanation that, as the Professor was punctilious in all his affairs, this would have been the case at any time—not only on that day when the caller was an unknown woman.

At last, calculating the proper moment, the Professor opened the sitting room door. A lady of about forty years of age, who had been sitting on a chair, stood up almost at the same time as he entered the room. The guest was elegant beyond the Professor's powers of discernment; her unlined blue-grey kimono was of fine quality, and the black gauze *haori* coat was slightly opened in the front to reveal a jade green clasp with an embossed diamond-shaped design. Her hair was dressed in *marumagé* style as worn by married women; even this detail was noted by the usually apathetic Professor. An intelligent and motherly lady, she had the round face and amber complexion typical of the Japanese. The Professor, after one look at his guest's face, felt he had seen her somewhere before.

–I am Haségawa.

The Professor greeted her cordially. If they had previously met, he thought that she would be thus prompted to offer some explanation of her presence.

–I am the mother of Nishiyama Ken-ichirô.

Having introduced herself in a clear voice, the woman politely returned his greeting.

At mention of the name, Nishiyama Ken-ichirô, the Professor remembered he was one of the students who had written essays on Ibsen and Strindberg. His specialty had been German Law, the Professor believed, but upon entering university he had taken an interest in philosophy and had often come to the Professor with his problems. Then, that spring, he had had an attack of peritonitis and had been admitted to the university hospital. The Professor forthwith had visited him once or twice. It was not without good reason that he had thought he had seen the lady's face somewhere. With those heavy eyebrows, that spirited youth and this woman–as the popular Japanese saying goes–*were as like in appearance as two melons*–so astonishingly alike were they.

–Ah, Nishiyama. . . . Oh, yes.

Nodding to himself, the Professor pointed to a chair on the far side of the small table.

–Then, would you please sit down.

Having excused herself for her sudden visit, and having again bowed politely, she sat down in the chair which he had indicated. At that moment, from her sleeve she took out something white–possibly a handkerchief. The Professor, having noticed this, quickly pushed forward a round Korean fan that was on the table, then sat down in the chair opposite.

–You have a fine home!

The lady deliberately cast her eyes around the room.

–No–it's large enough–but we don't give it very much attention.

Here, the Professor, who was accustomed to this sort of greeting, pressed her to take the iced tea which the maid had brought in, and soon directed the conversation towards her.

–Nishiyama–how is he?–Is there no marked change in his condition?

–Well, . . .

The lady, modestly crossing both hands on her knees, paused a little, then spoke quietly in a caressing self-possessed tone.

–Actually, I came today to talk to you about my son.–In the end, all was useless. While he was alive he caused you much bother. . . .

The Professor had judged that reserve prevented his guest from taking her tea and was just about to take a sip of the black tea himself. Not wishing to be indiscreet in bluntly pressing her, he had deemed it the wiser course to be the first to drink. But the cup had not yet reached his soft moustache when the lady's words suddenly assailed his ears. Should he drink the tea?–or should he not?–such conjecture had for the moment thrust the fact of the youth's death from the forefront of his mind. Certainly he could not hold the teacup in mid-air. Thereupon, the Professor resolutely gulped down half the tea in the cup; and then, with brows knit, he made a stifled exclamation of dismay.

–Even while in the hospital, he often spoke of you, and though I know you must be very busy, I thought I would tell you what had happened and, at the same time, pay my respects. . . .

–That's very kind.

The Professor spoke despondently as he set down his teacup and picked up the blue waxed fan.

–So, nothing could be done? Just at the age when he was about to launch out; but, as I had heard no news from the hospital, I even thought that by now he would have almost recovered.– Then, when did it happen?–his death?

–Just a week ago yesterday.

–At the hospital?

–That's so.

–Well, really it's most unexpected.

–Anyhow, everything was done for him that could be done, so there is nothing to do but to reconcile oneself.–Even so, having brought him up thus far, I cannot help but complain when I think of what *might have been.*

During this interchange, the Professor noticed something extraordinary. In this woman's attitude, in her behavior, there was nothing in the least to suggest that she was talking of the death of her own son. There were no tears in her eyes. She spoke in a normal voice. And, moreover, there was a fleeting smile at the corners of her mouth. Anyone, without hearing her conversation, who might have seen her external appearance, would certainly have thought that this woman was talking of mundane household matters. All this seemed very strange to the Professor.

. . . During the Professor's student days in Berlin long ago, Wilhelm I, father of the Kaiser, had died. The Professor had happened to be in his favorite coffee shop when he heard the report of the royal demise, and at the time it made no extraordinary impression on him. He wore his usual expression of well-being as, his cane under his arm, he returned to his lodgings. But no sooner had he opened the door than the two children from the boardinghouse fell upon him and burst into a flood of tears. One, a girl of twelve, wore a brown jacket, and the other, a boy of nine, was in dark blue short trousers. The Professor, who was fond of children, had no idea of what could be wrong and, stroking the fair hair of the two, eagerly tried to console them.

–What's the matter?–he asked.

The children did not stop crying. And, sniffling, they said:

–Our grandfather, the Emperor, is dead!

The Professor marveled that the death of the Sovereign of a country should bring so much grief to children.

It prompted him to consider problems beyond those associated with the Palace and the people. Since coming to the West, he had many times been distressed by the impulsive Westerners' emotional outbursts which, as at this time, had been a source of astonishment to him who, being Japanese, was a believer in bushido. The suspicion and sympathy he had expressed at that time, he had never forgotten and never could. Even as he had thought the previous situation strange, so now the Professor wondered at this converse situation–a lady who did not weep.

But, this first discovery was immediately followed by a second discovery. . . .

Just then, the conversation of host and guest, having branched forth from reminiscences of the deceased youth to details of his daily life, was once more about to return to the former reminiscences. By some chance, the Korean fan slipped from the Professor's hand and dropped onto the mosaic floor. The tempo of the conversation was leisurely enough to permit momentary lapses. So, the Professor bent forward in his chair and stretched out an arm towards the floor. The fan had fallen under the small table close to the lady's white *tabi* which were concealed in her slippers.

The Professor's eyes then happened to glimpse the hands which, clasping the handkerchief, rested on her knees. Of course, this alone was no revelation. But the Professor had also noticed that the lady's hands were trembling violently. He had noticed that, in her struggle to suppress her agitated feelings, she was grasping her handkerchief so tightly in her trembling hands as almost to tear it. And, finally, the embroidered edge of the crinkled silk handkerchief moved between her supple fingers, as if stirred by a gentle breeze. Assuredly, the lady had a smile on her face, but, in fact, all the while she had been weeping with her whole body.

The Professor's face as he raised himself after picking up the fan wore an expression which had not previously been there. With the feeling of awe at having seen something which he ought not to have seen, came the consciousness of a certain satisfaction; but this, too, was accompanied by an immense complexity—its manifestation more or less dramatically exaggerated.

–Then, I well understand your grief, even though I myself have no children.

The Professor, as though he had seen something radiant, had said those words with a slightly exaggerated inclination of his head, speaking in a lowered, emotionally-imbued voice.

–Thank you. . . . But now, whatsoever we may say, as we cannot have him back. . . .

The lady bent her head a shade. Over her face, serene and unchanged, spread an abundant smile.

TWO HOURS LATER, the Professor, having had his bath and finished his dinner, was picking at some cherries as he sat in the rattan chair on the veranda.

The long summer evening still diffused a thin light; the glass doors of the wide veranda remained open; there was no sign of darkness yet. In the faint light the Professor sat on, his legs crossed, his head resting on the back of the rattan chair, and stared dreamily at the red tassel of the fancy Gifu paper lantern. He seemed not to have read even one more page of the Strindberg he held in his hand. And, it was bound thus to be so. Mme. Nishiyama Atsuko's admirable behavior still filled the Professor's head.

Over dinner the Professor had related the whole story to his wife. And he extolled the bushido of Japanese women. His wife who loved Japan and the Japanese had listened with a sympathetic ear. The Professor had thought it satisfying that his wife had proven such a fervent listener. His wife, his recent visitor, and the Gifu paper lantern–these three–having taken on a certain ethical setting, loomed in the Professor's consciousness.

The Professor did not know how long he had been absorbed in such pleasing reflections when he happened to recall that he had been pressed to contribute an article to a certain magazine. The magazine was soliciting distinguished authorities from various fields to write their general opinions on morality for a col-

umn, "Notes on Modern Youth." He would use this day's incident
for the article; he would send on his impressions right away,
thought the Professor, scratching his head a little.

The hand that scratched his head still held the book. Until
then, the Professor had taken no interest in that book, but he
now opened and gazed at the page he had been reading before,
where he had placed the card as a marker.

Just then, the maid came in and lit the lantern, so even the
small type was not particularly troublesome to read. The Professor, without any real interest, let his eyes fall aimlessly over the
page; Strindberg had written:

> When I was young, I heard a report which probably originated
> in Paris, concerning one Frau Heiberg. While she smiled, she
> would tear a handkerchief in two—a dual performance.—We
> now call it *mätzchen* (slapstick). . . .

The Professor laid the book on his knees. Nishiyama Atsuko's
card was still between the open pages. But, the lady was no longer in his mind. Nor was his wife in his mind, nor the Japanese
civilization. Rather was it something indefinable which jeopar-
dized the peaceful harmony of his soul. The performance which
Strindberg disdained and the problem of practical ethics were, of
course, different. But among the insinuations present in what he
read, there was something which ruffled the Professor's mood of
complacence which he had had since he had stepped out of the
bath. . . . Bushido and its *manier* (mannerisms).

The Professor, as though from discontent, shook his head
two or three times; then, casting his eyes upwards, once more he
began to look intently at the bright Gifu lantern on which were
painted autumn grasses.

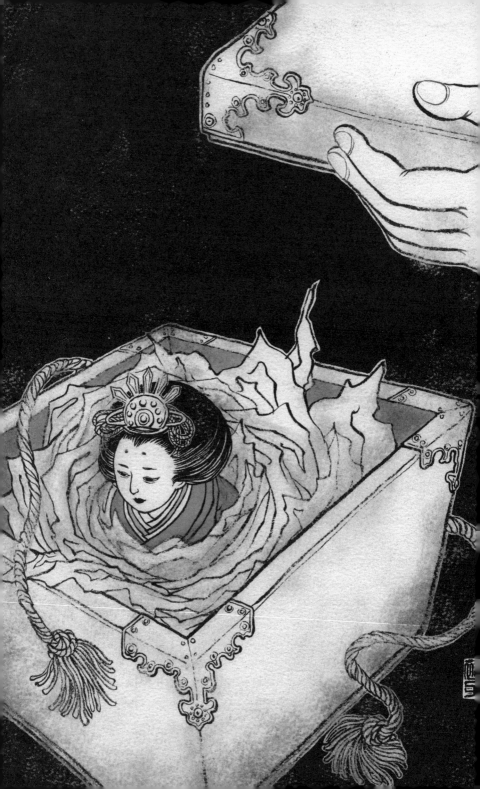

THE DOLLS

Introductory Note:
Those who are familiar with translations of famous "haiku" verse
might remember Buson for his verse about the butterfly on the temple
bell. Buson (1716–1783) was of the middle Edo period.
    It is likely that the Kinokuniya of this story was descended from the
wealthy merchant, Kinokuniya Monzaemon (1672–1734). Today one
of Japan's most prosperous bookshops (at Shinjuku in Tokyo) is called
Kinokuniya.
    An interesting comparison may be made between Akutagawa's
description of the dolls and that of Hatsumi Reiko in her work, "Rain
and the Feast of the Stars" (John Murray, London, 1960). Hatsumi
Reiko's fascinating account of "The Doll's Festival" first appeared in
MADEMOISELLE Magazine in 1958.
    "The Dolls" was completed in February of Taishô 12 (1923).

> Not forgotten, the dolls–
> Their faces until now
> Long hidden away in boxes.
> —*Buson.*

THIS STORY was told to me by an elderly woman.
    . . . It was around November one year when the promise

was made—the promise to sell *the dolls* to a certain American in Yokohama. My family—the family of Ki-no-kuniya—had for generations been moneylenders to the daimyô. Especially, Grandfather Shichiku might be said to have been a man of the world. Though the dolls were mine, I cannot refrain from admitting that they were made with some finesse. For instance, the tiara of the Empress was of coral; and the *sekitai obi* of the *shiozé*, as worn by the Emperor was embroidered with the Imperial crest and other abstract insignia. Such were the dolls.

That my father—Ki-no-kuniya Ihê of the twelfth generation—even considered selling these dolls, could only have happened in the most straitened circumstances—but this you probably have already guessed. Since the fall of the Tokugawa Shogunate, only one hundred *ryô* of the three thousand *ryô* that was owed him had been paid—and that by the Lord of Kashû. The Lord of Inshû, for instance, gave my father an inkstand of Akama-ga-seki in settlement of a loan of four hundred *ryô*. Moreover, we had suffered losses in fires several times. We used to have an umbrella shop, but nothing prospered. So, in those times our valuables were sold to cover our living expenses.

It was Marusa, the curio dealer, who persuaded my father to dispose of the dolls. He is dead now, but I well remember his bald head; nothing could have been more amusing than that bald head of Marusa. This was because in the middle of his bald head there was a tattoo like a black plaster patch. It was said that as a young man he had it tattooed there to hide a small patch of receding hair. It was unfortunate for him that he could do nothing about the tattoo, which remained even as his head became completely bald; Marusa admitted this himself.

At any rate, my father thought I would be distressed if the dolls were sold as I was only fifteen years of age, so, although

Marusa often urged him to sell them, Father hesitated to part with the dolls.

It was my elder brother, Eikichi, who was ultimately responsible for the selling of the dolls. Eikichi, too, is now dead. He was only eighteen years of age at the time the dolls were sold. As a young man he felt the urge for enlightenment in Western culture and so was interested in politics and would not leave aside his English textbooks. He always talked scathingly about the dolls, saying either that the Dolls' Festival was an old-fashioned custom or that it was to no advantage to retain such impractical articles. I do not know how many times he quarreled along those lines with my mother who was of the old world.

Only by selling the dolls, could we, with certainty, pull through to the end of the year. My mother had so far not raised any strong objections, as she knew the predicament in which Father was placed in having to make a decision. . . . As I have said, it was in November when at length we arranged for the dolls to be sold to an American in Yokohama. And I?–I fretted, but being something of a harum-scarum, I was not too distressed by the matter. If he were to sell the dolls, Father had promised he would buy an *obi* of purple satin for me.

The night after Father had agreed to sell them, Marusa visited our house on his way home from Yokohama.

. . . Though I say "our house"–it could hardly be called a *house* after the third fire. We had moved into the storehouse which had survived the fire, and the temporarily repaired house had become a shop. At the time Father was operating an apothecary shop; I can recall some of the names of the medicines embossed in gold letters on the signboard over the medicine chest–medicines such as *shotoku* pills, *ankei* ointment and powder for congenital syphilis.

In the shop was also a *mujintô*. . . . If I say just a *mujintô,* you will probably not understand. A *mujintô* was an old-style lamp in which rape seed oil instead of kerosene was burned. It is a funny thing to say, but even now the smell of the medicines, especially the smell of the dried tamarind skins and rhubarb, never fails to remind me of the *mujintô.*

On the night Marusa called, I can actually recall the dimness of the *mujintô* amid the pervading smell of the medicines.

The bald-headed Master of Marusa sat with my father whose hair was cropped, each on either side of the *mujintô.*

"Then—exactly half. . . . Please be kind enough to check the amount."

Greetings and comments on the weather having been first dispensed with, the Master of Marusa held out the money wrapped in paper. It was evidently the day appointed for payment of the deposit. My father, resting his hand on the *hibachi,* bowed without any comment. In compliance with Mother's instructions, at just that moment, I came in to serve tea. At the very instant when I was serving tea, the Master of Marusa said loudly:

"Please don't—I insist!"

What was this exclamation about? Should I not serve tea? I was a little startled. But then, as I looked at the Master of Marusa, he was proffering another sum of money wrapped in paper.

"It's just a token of gratitude."

"I am already indebted to you. So, please be so kind as to take it."

"Really, you make me feel ashamed."

"No, that's quite absurd—it is I who am ashamed. We are no strangers; so, is it not natural that Marusa should do this for you?—I, who have enjoyed the patronage of Ki-no-kuniya since

your father's time? There is no need to stand on ceremony!–
Please keep the money. . . . Oh, young lady, good evening to you;
indeed, tonight your butterfly hair style is very becoming."

After this bandying of words, I went back into the storehouse
dwelling, feeling no reaction.

The storehouse would have been about twelve mats–rather
large, but it was cluttered with such items of furniture as a cabinet, a long *hibachi,* an oblong chest and a cupboard–and so the
room *seemed* quite small. But the thirty or more paulownia boxes
were what really drew one's attention. It is, of course, quite
unnecessary to mention that these were the dolls' boxes. They
were piled against the wall under the window ready for delivery
at the appropriate time.

That night, as the *mujintô* was being used in the shop, there
was only the dim *andon* lamp standing in the middle of the room.
In the light diffused by that old-fashioned *andon,* my mother
was sewing medicine infusion bags. At a small antique desk my
brother was studying his English readers or something. Everything was as usual. But when I looked into my mother's face as
she plied her needle, I saw there were tears behind the lashes of
her downcast eyes.

I had just served the tea, and it was perhaps a little unreasonable to be looking forward to praise from my mother, but I had
rather expected it. What was the meaning of those tears? It was
embarassment I felt rather than sadness, and so as not to see
my mother, I sat beside my brother as soon as I could. Brother
Eikichi looked up suddenly. He glanced somewhat doubtfully
at both Mother and me, then smiled strangely and again went
on reading the horizontal English text. There was never a time
when I felt greater dislike for that brother of mine on account

of his snobbish interest in enlightenment. He was making light of Mother's feelings, and I felt strongly about it. So, with all my strength, I struck my brother on the back.

"Why did you do that?!" he exclaimed, staring at me.

"I *have* to hit you! I just *have* to!"

Crying, I struck him again. In doing so I had overlooked the fact that my brother was an irascible creature. As I dropped my raised arm, he slapped me across the cheek with the flat of his hand.

"Blockhead!"

Naturally, I began to cry; but at the same time Mother whacked him with a ruler. My brother snapped defiantly at Mother, but even Mother could not bear with him. In a quavering voice, she railed at her son for a long time.

Throughout their dispute I just went on sobbing miserably until father, who had been to see off the Master of Marusa, came in from the shop carrying the *mujintô*. . . . Not only did I stop crying, but my brother, too, on seeing Father, suddenly fell silent. In those days my brother and I were afraid of our taciturn father.

It had been decided that evening that at the end of the month, when we were to receive the balance of the money, the dolls would be handed over to the American at Yokohama. What was the selling price? Thinking about it now it does seem ridiculous. It was exactly thirty yen; but taking into consideration the prices of other commodities at the time, it did seem fair then.

After that, the day when the dolls were to be handed over gradually drew near. As I said before, I had not felt especially upset about it. But, as day by day passed and the appointed time drew nearer, the prospect of parting with the dolls did begin to impress itself upon me. Though I was only a child, I had no expectation that a way would be found to keep the dolls once it had been decided that we should part with them; but I wanted to look at them once more before they would be handed over. The Emperor and Empress, the five musicians, the *sakon* cherry, the *ukon* wild orange, the candle shades, the screen, the lacquered appointments–I wanted to arrange those dolls on display once more in the warehouse; such was my heart's desire. Still, though I pleaded many times with my stubborn father, he would not permit me to do so. "Once we have received the deposit, wheresoever they might be, the dolls belong to others. Other people's property must not be tampered with." So Father told me.

One day near the end of the month there was a gale blowing. Perhaps because she had a cold, or perhaps because she had a swelling on her lip the size of a millet seed and had told us that she was feeling badly, Mother did not partake of any breakfast. After she and I had finished tidying the kitchen, I noticed her pressing her hand to her forehead and looking down fixedly at our large *hibachi*. Then, towards noon, I happened to perceive some change in her condition. The swelling on her lower lip– had it not become puffed up just like a red sweet potato? But, one had only to look at her strangely fevered eyes to see straightway that she had a high temperature. Needless to say, I was horrified; almost beside myself with concern I rushed out to my father who was in the shop.

"Father! Father!–Mother is very ill!"

Father, and with him elder brother who was also at home, came into the living quarters. They were both taken aback when they saw my mother's face. Even Father, who was not easily upset, was lost in thought and said nothing for a time. Meanwhile, my mother exerted all her strength to force a smile, and said:

"It might not be anything serious. It is only that I scratched the swelling with my fingernail. . . . I must soon start preparing lunch."

"Don't be foolish. O-Tsuru will prepare the meal."–Thus almost scolding, Father interrupted. And turning to Eikichi, he said:

"Eikichi!–call Mr. Honma."

In response to Father's order, my brother was already rushing out of the shop into the gale.

Brother always regarded the practitioner of Chinese medicine to be a charlatan and a quack. When the medico had examined Mother, he folded his arms in perplexity. In answer to our question, he ventured the opinion that Mother's swelling was a carbuncle. . . . Generally, if a carbuncle is lanced it does not become serious, but at that time, unfortunately, there was no popular call for surgery. The only treatment in those days was to administer some decoction and have leeches suck the blood. Every day my father, at my mother's bedside, boiled up herbs according to Honma's prescription; and every day, with fifteen sen brother went out to buy the leeches. And I . . . taking care that my brother knew nothing of it, went a hundred times to the Inari Shrine in the neighborhood. Under such circumstances, I was not able to mention anything about the dolls. For some time, then, nobody–not even I–paid any attention to the thirty paulownia boxes which were piled against the wall.

Then, at last came the twenty-ninth day of November–the day before we were to part with the dolls. In view of the fact that it would be my last day with the dolls, I had an irresistible urge to open the boxes once more. No matter how I would implore him, my father would, doubtless, disagree. I decided I would ask Mother to intercede on my behalf. I had thought to ask her first thing in the morning, but somehow Mother's condition seemed to be much graver. She could take nothing except thin rice gruel. At that stage, pus mixed with blood was continuously being discharged into her mouth. Seeing her in such a state, even I, a small girl of fifteen years of age, would not be able to summon the courage to mention my longing to display the dolls. From early morning I was by her pillow, all the while inquiring as to how she was feeling. Three o'clock came at length, and until then I had held my peace.

But, beneath the metal grille of the window, those paulownia dolls' boxes were piled before my eyes. And when the night would finally have passed, those dolls' boxes would be taken to a foreigner's house far-off in Yokohama, . . . perhaps thence to America. Prompted by such thoughts, I could contain myself no longer. Taking the opportunity while my mother was sleeping, I quietly slipped into the shop. Though very little sunshine penetrated the shop, it was more lively if one were to compare it with the storehouse–if only because one could see the people passing by. Father was balancing his books there, and in a corner, my brother was diligently pounding licorice in a mortar.

"Father–I ask you only this one favor in all my life. . . ."

Peeping into Father's face, I approached him with the selfsame request. But Father, as he did not approve, naturally gave hardly any sign of acknowledgement.

"Didn't we discuss that matter the other day?" Then–"Eikichi, before it gets dark, would you go to Marusa's?"

"To Marusa's–Did he ask someone to call?"

"I want you to go to pick up a lamp. . . . If you have anything else to do, call there on your way home."

"But Marusa doesn't keep lamps, does he?"

Ignoring me, Father ventured one of his rare smiles. He said:

"It's no candlestick, or anything like that. . . . I asked Marusa to buy a lamp for us. He has a better eye for bargains than *we* have."

"Then, will we dispense with the *mujintô?*"

"It's time we did."

"All old things should come to an end at some time or other. In the first place, Mother will feel a little brighter when the new lamp is lit."

Father said nothing further. He returned to his *soroban*. But the more my cherished desire was ignored, the more profound it became. Once more, I shook Father's shoulder from behind.

"Father!–Father!"

"Don't bother me!"

Without turning, my father brusquely upbraided me. And, as if that were not enough, my brother, too, was glaring spitefully at me. Thoroughly disheartened, I returned quietly to the storehouse. Hand to her head, Mother raised her fevered eyes, and gazed at me. Then she said with surprising directness:

"Why was your father scolding you?"

At a loss for a reply, I fumbled with the feather beside Mother's pillow.

"Were you being unreasonable again?" . . .

Looking fixedly at me, my mother went on to say bitterly:

"As I have been so ill, and your father is doing everything possible, you must be well-behaved. . . . Though the girl next-door is always going to the theatre. . . ."

"I don't want to go to the theatre. . . ."

"It's not only the theatre–but fancy hairpins and neckbands–you see many things that you want, but. . . ."

Hearing this, I gradually dissolved into tears, whether from vexation or sadness I could not say.

"Mother . . . I . . . I don't want any of those things! Only, before the dolls are sold. . . ."

"The dolls?–before they are sold . . . ?"

Mother stared even closer into my face with wide eyes.

"Before the dolls are sold. . . ."

I spoke a little hesitantly. I had just happened to catch sight of Eikichi standing behind me. I had no idea how long he had been there. Looking down at me, he spoke harshly as always:

"You dolt! It would be the dolls again! Have you forgotten your father's scolding?"

"That will be enough! There's no need for bickering."

Mother closed her eyes in annoyance. But, as if he had not heard, my brother continued to find fault with me:

"You are fifteen years old already, so you should be a little more sensible. To fuss over dolls! You shouldn't begrudge giving up such things!–*should* you?"

"Mind your own business!–they're certainly not yours, are they?" I replied, unabashed. After that, what happened was typical. After an exchange of two or three words brother seized me by the collar of my kimono and threw me down.

"Brat!"

If Mother had not stopped him, my brother would surely have thrashed me. But Mother, half raising her head from the pillow, gasped in rebuke:

"O-Tsuru hasn't done anything to *you*. Why should you want to fight with her?"

"No matter what I said the stupid wench wouldn't understand!"

"It isn't only O-Tsuru you hate, is it? You . . . you . . ."

Mother, her eyes filled with tears, in her mortification, mumbled time and again:

"Don't you hate *me*, too? Here I am ill, and the dolls, . . . you are eager to see the dolls sold, and you tease innocent O-Tsuru. . . . Why do you want to do such things?–It is all so hateful."

"Mother!"

Brother suddenly cried out as he stood beside my mother's pillow, then hid his face in his elbow. (Later, even when our parents died, my brother shed no tears. For a long time afterwards while he was taking an active interest in politics–until the time he was admitted to a mental asylum–he did not show any weakness.) This was the only occasion when I saw my brother weep. This must have been unexpected even to my mother, overwrought as she was. Mother did not proceed with the words she was going to utter, but with a long sigh, let her head fall back on her pillow again. . . .

An hour or so after this argument, Tokuzô, the fishmonger, whom we had not seen for a long time, happened to drop in at the shop. No, he was not a fishmonger; he had once been one, but he had by then become a jinrikisha puller, and Ki-no-kuniya gave him its patronage. I do not know how many funny stories there would be about him. Among them, I still remember the story about his family name. After the Meiji Restoration, he came to use a family name, and in considering what he should call himself, he decided to adopt the name of *Tokugawa*–perhaps to give himself airs; but when he presented his *name* to the Registrar, it was more than a matter of just being reproved; according to Tokuzô's own admission, the Registrar, threatened to behead him on the spot. . . . Tokuzô came to our shop pulling with ease his jinrikisha upon which were decorated Chinese lions and peonies. While I was wondering why he had come, he said he was taking advantage of the scarcity of passengers that day; he wanted to treat me to a ride in his jinrikisha and to take me from Aizuppura to Renga Street.

"How would that be, O-Tsuru?"

My father, in all seriousness, watched me closely as I went out of the shop to see the jinrikisha. These days, it is not much of an adventure for children to ride in a jinrikisha. But it was a great delight for us at that time, just as if the jinrikisha had been a motor car. Because of my mother's illness, and also because it was so soon after our argument, I could not speak out that I wanted to go for the ride without feeling some reserve. Notwithstanding, though still disheartened, I was able to mutter:

"I would like to go."

"Then come and ask your mother—as it was kind of Tokuzô to ask you."

As I had expected, Mother, with her eyes closed, said smiling:

"That's wonderful!"

Luckily, my spiteful brother was absent, as he had gone to Marusa's. As though I had forgotten my tears, I jumped quickly into the jinrikisha; the red rug was wrapped around my knees, and the wheels went *gara-gara* as we moved off. There is no need for me to elaborate on the scenes I enjoyed on that excursion. I shall just mention Tokusô's grievance.

During the ride, we had just reached Renga Main Street when he almost collided with a horse-drawn carriage in which a Western lady was riding. He had a narrow escape, but, clicking his tongue in disgust, he said:

"It's no good! You're just too light, and I was too unbalanced to pull up. . . . Any jinrikisha man who would give you a ride would be unhappy; you had better not ride in a jinrikisha until you turn twenty."

The jinrikisha turned off Renga Street into a side street leading in the direction of our house; suddenly we met up with none other than Eikichi. He walked towards us with hurried footsteps, carrying a lamp stand with a handle of smoked bamboo. On catching sight of me, he raised the lamp, perhaps as a signal for us to wait; but Tokuzô had already wheeled the shafts around and was pulling the jinrikisha in my brother's direction.

"Sorry to trouble you, Toku-*san*–Where have you been?"

"Your sister has been taking a little sightseeing trip around Edo with me."

Smiling sardonically, my brother walked alongside the jinrikisha.

"O-Tsuru–you go ahead of me and take this lamp, while I call at the oil shop."

Mindful of our quarrel of shortly before, I purposely remained silent as I took the lamp. He started to walk on, but quickly turned back again in my direction, and putting his hand on the mudguard of the jinrikisha, he called back to me:

"O-Tsuru!–O-Tsuru, don't mention the dolls to your father again."

I still made no reply. As he had already taunted me, I expected him to do so again, but, with indifference, he continued in a subdued voice:

"Why Father has told you that you mustn't take out the dolls, is simply because he has received a deposit for them. If we look at them, everybody will feel an attachment to them. He is thinking of that. All right? Do you understand now? If you do understand, you should not keep on saying that you want to see them."

I discerned an unfamiliar affection in my brother's voice. But there was no person as strange as Eikichi. As soon as he has spoken thus gently, he once again, all of a sudden, resumed his usual threats.

"If you want to bring up the matter again, you can. But I will make you all the more sorry for it."

Having spoken thus spitefully, without any further word of acknowledgement to Tokuzô, my brother made off somewhere.

In the storehouse that night, we four sat around the dinner table. Mother was there, but with just her head raised above the pillow, she should not perhaps be numbered among those of us around the table. And on that night the dinner did seem brighter than usual. The reason was obvious. In the place of the dim light of the *mujintô*, shone the light of the new lamp. My elder brother and I gazed at the lamp throughout the meal. The glass stand through which the kerosene was visible, the funnel which protected the steady flame—all was so entrancing that our gaze could not but be drawn by that unique lamp.

Turning to my mother, Father said with some satisfaction:

"It is bright, don't you think?–like daylight!"

"Yes, it's very dazzling!"

It was my mother who had replied, and I saw on her face a fleeting expression of uneasiness.

"That's because we are too accustomed to the *mujintô*. . . . But now that we have installed this lamp, we shan't have to light the *mujintô* any more."

"At first everything is exceedingly bright–this lamp, and the Western learning, too. . . ."

My elder brother more than any of us was in a jocular mood.

"It'll be just like everything else after a while. I am sure the day will come when we shall say even this lamp is dim."

"Indeed, perhaps that's so. . . . O-Tsuru, what have you done with your mother's rice gruel?"

"She said she didn't care for it tonight."

I was not particularly concerned as I repeated what Mother had said.

"That's no good. Have you such a poor appetite?"–Father asked.

Mother sighed.

"Yes, somehow the smell of kerosene, . . . it is proof that I am conservative."

After that, we went on manipulating our chopsticks, hardly speaking except for Mother who, seemingly impressed by the brightness of the lamp, spoke in its praise from time to time, even raising a slight smile on her swollen lips.

It was past eleven o'clock when everybody retired to bed that night. Still, though I closed my eyes, I could not easily drop off to sleep. My brother had asked me not to speak of the dolls again. Anyway, I had given up any idea of being able to see the dolls, but my desire to see them had not in the least changed from what it had been a little time before. On the morrow the dolls would finally probably go to a far place. So, there were tears in my eyes as my thoughts wandered in this way. While all were sleeping, dare I quietly take out the dolls by myself and look at them? Such were my thoughts.–Or, should I hide just one of them somewhere? The thought did occur to me!–In any case, if I were discovered in such a venture . . . ! I shrank from putting such thoughts into action. I do not honestly remember ever having contemplated such dread thoughts as I did on that night. I even wished there would be another fire!–If that happened the dolls would be burned before they could be handed over. Or, it would be fortunate, indeed, if the American and the bald-headed Master of Marusa were to be stricken with cholera! If that were to happen we would not have to part with the dolls, but could keep them in our care–such imaginings came floating into my mind. Yet, whatsoever I thought, as I was still a child, before one hour had passed, I had, in the interim become drowsy and fallen off to sleep.

How long after that would it have been? I happened to wake up. I had heard the sound of somebody moving about in the storehouse that was lit by the faint light of the *andon*. Was it a rat?–Or a thief?–Or was it already dawn? Wondering which of these it might be, apprehensively I opened my eyes–just a little. There by the side of my pillow was my father–alone, in his night kimono. I could make out his profile as he sat there. My father! . . . It was not just seeing my father there that astonished me. Set out before him were the dolls, which I had not seen since the Doll Festival.

It might have been at a time of night when people say they see reality in a dream. Almost catching my breath, I looked on this strange scene. By the dim light of the *andon,* I could see the Emperor doll holding an ivory scepter, the Empress doll–its tiara bedecked with jewels, the *ukon* wild orange, the *sakon* cherry, the porter carrying a long-handled umbrella, the Court Lady holding up a food tray a little below the level of her eyes, the small gold-lacquered mirror and chest, a small folding screen decorated with shell, the rice bowls, the decorated candle shades, the balls of colored thread, and again, my father's profile. . . .

As if I were seeing them in a dream, . . . ah, that is what I have already said. But were the dolls of that night really a dream? Were they an illusion that I had created in my subconscious mind because I so urgently wanted to see the dolls once more? Still now I am at a loss to know whether or not it were true. But in the depths of that night, I saw my elderly father gazing on those dolls. Of this alone I am sure. Even if it were but a dream,

I doubt that I would have any regrets about it, as, in any case, I saw before me my father who was not in the least different from me in spirit—my father who, awe-inspiring as he *could* be, was sensitive as a woman.

Many years ago I had intended to write the story of *the dolls*. I have written it now because Mr. Takita persuaded me to do so, and also because four or five days ago I met a little foreign girl playing with the heads of some old dolls in the guest room of a certain Englishman's house at Yokohama. The dolls of which I have told you, are perhaps by now discarded with leaden soldiers and cheap rubber dolls in some toy box and are possibly suffering the same grief.

GRATITUDE

Introductory Note:

"Gratitude" ("Ho'ôn-ki") is set in one of the most entertaining periods of Japanese history–the turn of the 16th/17th centuries when the Japanese, especially in the south of Honshû and Kyûshû, were turning their interest towards foreign trade. Christian missionaries were tolerated at the time only because of their close association with foreign merchants. They were, for the most part, honest intermediaries between Japanese and foreign traders. Although some may doubt the sincerity of Japanese converts of the time, it must have been gratifying when daimyô would order all their retainers, on pain of displeasing their lord if they were to disobey, to become "Christians." This did facilitate the task of the missionaries, for there would have been some who were honest enough, nevertheless, like Hôjôya Yasoêmon of this story, to embrace Christianity with sincere devotion. By the beginning of the 17th century there were, it has been estimated, about one hundred and thirty thousand Christians in Kyûshû and southern Honshû.

Except for the "confessional" technique of this story, it matters little whether it were God or the august ancestors who were offended by the characters' misconduct. In Japan, where a wrong has been done, some act is deemed vital for the redemption of the miscreant's honor and for the salving of his conscience. In contemporary Western society the word "honor" has for many come to be regarded as archaic. Here is one instance where the dignity of feudalism may be superior to the freedom of the individual in the modern social welfare community, where one is "free" from traditional family obligations, and where one has not the same fetters of conscience as, for instance, in circumstances such as those which provide the movement of this story. The Christian atmosphere of the story does, however, evoke among Westerners some depth of understanding of the principles involved in this tale.

"Gratitude" was completed in March of Taishô 11 (1922).

THE CONFESSION OF *AMAKAWA JINNAI*

I AM a man called Jinnai. My complete name—well, for a long time now the world has known me as Amakawa Jinnai.—Do you, too, know this name? You probably know me as the renowned robber. Do not be surprised that my reason for coming tonight is not to steal. So, by all means feel secure.

I have heard that among the Christian padres of Japan you are known for your exalted virtue. So, the fact that—if only for a brief time—you will be in the company of a notorious robber will not be pleasant for you. Though it might come as a surprise to you, I am not always committing a theft. One of the retainers of Sukégaêmon of Luzon, who was summoned to the Juraku Palace at one time, called himself Jinnai. Again, the tea-ceremony water receptacle called *Akagashira*, a vessel prized by Rikyû—I have heard it said that the master of *renga* verse who presented it to Sen-Rikyû might have been Jinnai. Come to think of it, the name of the interpreter of the Dutch language from Ômura city who translated the *Amakawa Diary* just two or three years ago–was he not Jinnai?–There was, besides, the itinerant priest who in a quarrel on the river bank at Sanjô saved the Capitão Mardonedo; and there was the merchant who traded in foreign medicines in front of the Myô-koku-ji in Sakai–if we look into the question of what was the real name of each, we would unmistakably find it was Jinnai. Indeed, of even greater significance than this, is that last year the person who offered to the Church of St. Francis the pagoda-shaped gold relic case which contains the finger parings of the venerable Mother Maria–was he not also Jinnai?

But, tonight, regrettably, I have not time to tell you more about such deeds. Only, please believe that Amakawa Jinnai is not too different from all the world's people.–Is that not so?– Then, I shall be as brief as possible, and I shall confine myself to business. I have come to ask you to say a mass for the soul of a certain man. No, he is no relative of mine. And, though I say so, it is not *my* blade that is stained with his blood. His name?–The name–well, whether it be wise to reveal his name is not for me to judge. For a certain man's spirit–for this Japanese Paul, I am beseeching a requiem. Should I not be doing this?–Indeed, as it is Amakawa Jinnai who asks this of you, you should not take it lightly. In any case I want to reveal to you only the circumstances. But, regardless of whether it means life or death to you, it is vital that you promise not to divulge to others what I am about to tell you. As you have a cross suspended from your breast, you can surely keep a promise, can't you? Well then–forgive my rudeness. (He smiles) To me who is a thief, it would be conceit to doubt you–a padre. But, if you do not keep this promise (suddenly he is earnest)–even if you do not burn in the fires of the inferno, you will have your punishment in this present existence.

This is already a story of two years' duration. . . . It was just midnight, and there was a piercing wind. I was wandering through the Capital disguised as a traveling monk. It was not my first night of wandering the streets. For over five days or thereabouts, always after eight in the evening, when the eyes of the world were not abroad, I would spy out the houses. Of course, why I was thus engaged it is not necessary to mention. At that time I had made up my mind on the spur of the moment to go to Malucca, and so I had to have ample money. At the time there were no passers-by, but in the sky in which only the stars twinkled, there was the agitation caused by a wind with never a lull. Passing the dark houses and making my way down Ôgawa Road, by chance I turned at the crossroads where I came upon a spacious squarely-built mansion. This was a landmark in the Capital–the headquarters of Hôjôya Yasoêmon. Though engaged in similar shipping ventures, the House of Hôjôya would, after all, not have been able to compete with the House of Sumi-no-Kura. But, at any rate, as he had one or two ships leaving regularly for Siam and the Luzon Islands, he was unmistakably a man of some substance. I had not been harboring any particular designs on that house but was happy that I had happened to stray there–and that chance aroused in me the feeling that I wanted to do something about it. As I said before, the deep night was breathing a wind–and this house was of the right dimensions for me to carry out my business. Hiding my bamboo umbrella-hat and stick behind a rain-water tank by the roadside, I quickly climbed over the high fence.

Bear in mind the rumor that has been passed about.–It is common belief that Amakawa Jinnai uses the *art of invisibility*. But, being different from ordinary people, you would not hold that there is any truth in this. I do not use *invisibility;* nor is the

devil on my side. It is only that I, Amakawa, was taught phys-
ics by a surgeon on a Portuguese ship. If I put that knowledge
into practice, the breaking of a massive lock, the drawing of a
weighty bolt are not especially difficult tasks. (He smiles) Even
to this underdeveloped land of Japan has come such knowledge,
the unprecedented way of the thief, taught by the West as it has
taught the Way of the Cross and the use of firearms.

Before another moment had passed, I was entering Hôjôya's
house. But, still keeping to the shadows cast by the light, I was
making my way through the dark corridor when I was surprised
to hear voices in a room of small dimensions. The whole appearance of the room in no way differed from that of a *cha-shitsu*
(tea-ceremony room). Would it be the Ceremony of *Tea When-
the-Cold-Wind-Blows?*–smiling bitterly at this thought, I quietly
drew nearer. Actually, to have come across people talking at
this time, instead of looking upon it as a hindrance to my work,
rather was I lost in wondering what refinements these people–
the Master of the House, and the companion who was perhaps
a guest–might be enjoying in the spiritual confines of that tea
room. Such were the idle thoughts provoked in me.

Quickly I moved to the outside of the sliding paper-doors;
as I had expected, my ears informed me that an iron kettle was
at the boil. But, together with that sound, I was surprised to
hear talking and weeping. I did not have to listen twice to know
it was a woman. That in the *cha-shitsu* of such a great house a
woman was weeping in the depths of the night was no insignifi-
cant thing. I held my breath, and looking through the crack that,
conveniently for me, had been left between the *fusuma* doors, I
peeped into the *cha-shitsu*.

The light from the *andon* lantern shone on the antique paper
scroll hanging in the alcove; there were frostbitten chrysanthe-

mums arranged in a hanging vase.–An elegant atmosphere pervaded the room. His back to the alcove, the elderly man directly facing me would be the Master, Yasoêmon; in ivy-patterned *haori* coat, both his arms folded firmly, to the casual observer he would have appeared to have been listening to the sound of the boiling kettle. Beside Yasoêmon, on the side nearer the *fusuma*, sat a refined elderly woman, her hair dressed in *kôgai-magé* style.

As the woman wiped her tears from time to time, her profile was revealed to me.

Unfettered as they must have been, here seemed only adversity. At such a thought, I could not refrain from smiling. In saying *I smiled*, it is not that I bore any ill will towards Hôjôya or his wife. Throughout my forty years of notoriety whenever I found that seemingly happy people were not happy, naturally there came a smile to my lips. (A cruel expression on his face) So, at that time, too, I experienced as much pleasure from observing the grief of husband and wife as if it were a *kabuki* drama that I was watching. (A cynical smile) But this trait is not confined to me. If we look into the *sôshi* tales which are enjoyed by everybody, it seems almost a matter of course that they are sad.

Soon it seemed that Yasoêmon sighed as he said:

"At this stage, neither crying nor wailing can alter the situation. It has already been decided that from tomorrow the employees must be dismissed."

Just then, a stern gust of wind shook the *cha-shitsu*, drowning the voices. I could not hear what reply Yasoêmon's wife made. But the Master, hands clasped on his knees, nodded and raised his eyes towards the wicker ceiling. His brushy eyebrows, his prominent cheekbones, especially his piercing eyes–all these which I took in all at one time as I looked into his face, convinced me I had met him once before.

"Lord Jesus Christ!–in our matrimonial hearts implant the strength of thy grace. . . ."

Yasoêmon, with eyes closed, began to mutter the words of a prayer. The woman, too, was begging the divine protection of the Lord God. Unblinking, I continued to study Yasoêmon's face. Then, when another strong gust came again, in my heart flickered a memory of twenty years before; I could clearly place Yasoêmon in my memory.

Twenty years before–no, there is no need for me to tell of it.

I shall mention only the brief facts.–One time when my life had been in danger in Amakawa (Macao), I was assisted by a ship's captain. At the time we parted without introducing ourselves; but this Yasoêmon who was before me was unmistakably that same skipper. Surprised by the coincidence, I stared all the harder at this elderly man's face. The smell of sandalwood seemed to permeate the air about his majestic shoulders, and like the spraying of the tide on a coral reef, it curled about him.

Yasoêmon, finishing his long prayer, said quietly to the elderly woman:

"I believe everything is in the Lord's hands.–Then, the kettle is boiling, so would you care to make tea?"

But the elderly woman, curbing her still surging tears, replied in a voice that seemed to fade away:

"Yes–even so, the regrettable thing is. . . ."

"Hm, it is idle to complain. The sinking of the *Hôjô Maru*; the total loss of the silver–."

"No, it isn't that. If only our son, Yasaburô, were here. . . ."

While I was listening to this conversation, the smile again rose to my lips. But this time, it was not because I felt happy at Hôjôya's ill-luck. It was the pleasurable thought that the time had come to return an old favor; and this prospect delighted me. To me–the wanted Amakawa Jinnai–the pleasure of being afforded such a splendid opportunity to requite that favor–it was now within my power to know this pleasure. (Ironically, the good people of the world are to be pitied. For one thing, they work not any evil, but are strangers to the satisfaction that arises from doing good.)

"Well, to be without such a wastrel as Yasaburô–this is surely our good fortune."

Yasoêmon turned eyes of shame away from the *andon*.

"If we had even the money he has spent, perhaps we would have been able to survive this crisis. That is what I had in mind when I renounced him."

Just as he had said this, Yasoêmon stared at me, startled. His surprise was not without reason, for, without stealth, I had opened wide the dividing *fusuma*. As to my appearance–in my disguise of a wandering monk–having cast off the straw umbrella-hat, I wore a foreign head-scarf.

"Who?–Who are you!?"

Although Yasoêmon was old, he rose quickly from his knees.

"Ah, you must not be so surprised. I am known as Amakawa Jinnai–well–please be at ease. Amakawa Jinnai is a thief, but tonight my sudden visit is for a slightly different reason."

Thrusting back my head-scarf, I sat myself down in front of Yasoêmon.

You could well guess, without my telling you, what happened after that. To help deliver Hôjô from impending disaster, I bound myself in a pledge of gratitude to supply him with six thousand *kan* of gold within the space of three days and no longer.

"Ah–there is someone outside the door!–Don't you hear footsteps? Then excuse me for tonight. . . . Either tomorrow or the night after, I will sneak here again."

The light of the stars of the Southern Cross glittering in the sky over Amakawa Port cannot be seen in the skies of Japan. If I, too, had not at that time vanished from the skies of Japan, this night I would not be here to do honor to the spirit of Paulo by coming to beseech a Mass.

Well–and my manner of flight?–It is not a matter to cause undue anxiety. Even through that high skylight, even by way of that big fireplace, I can be gone unmolested. Therefore, I beseech you, for the sake of the spirit of my benefactor, Paulo, take care not to reveal anything of this confession to others.

THE CONFESSION OF HÔJÔYA YASOÊMON

PADRE!–Do listen to my confession. As you know, of late there have been many rumors about Amakawa Jinnai. The man who lived in the pagoda of the Negoro Temple, the man who stole the sword from the Supreme Lord and again, the man who attacked the Viceroy of far-off Luzon Islands–all were he, I have heard. It is rumored that he was at length arrested, and his head has been held up to public contempt in the vicinity of the Ichijô Modori Bridge; that much you might have heard. I owe a boundless debt of gratitude to Amakawa Jinnai. But for that man's benefaction I by now would have met with indescribable disaster. Let me relate the circumstances, and, for the sinner, Hôjôya Yasoêmon, please bespeak the compassion of Almighty God.

It was the winter of two years ago. The cargo vessel, *Hôjô Maru*, had been wrecked in persistently stormy weather, and all the money I had lent on the security of the vessel became irrecoverable; with this and other unfortunate complications, it seemed that the disintegration of the House of Hôjôya could not be averted. As you would realize, I had business associates among the townspeople–but I would not have called them friends. So it was that our family business, just as the big ship had been sucked into the swirling current, seemingly had foundered beyond redemption. Then came a night–a night I graphically remember. There was a sharp wind blowing when in the *cha-shitsu* tea room with which you are familiar, myself and my wife, unaware of the lateness of the hour, had been talking together. There, suddenly in the guise of a priest, except for the foreign-style hood he wore, appeared that Jinnai. I was, of course, not only surprised, but angered. Yet, I heard from Jinnai himself that he had furtively entered my house to steal, but, attracted by the flicker of light from the *cha-shitsu* and the murmur of the voices, he had gone to the *fusuma* and peeped in, and had seen me, Hôjôya Yasoêmon–I who had been his benefactor and saved his life twenty years before.

Indeed, it was twenty years ago that I was Master of a small chartered vessel plying between Amakawa and Japan. One time while anchored in port I had, in truth, given assistance to a yet sparsely bearded Japanese. According to his story at the time, he was being sought for having killed a Chinese drinking-partner in a quarrel. That young Japanese subsequently became Amakawa Jinnai, the notorious robber. At any rate, as I knew Jinnai's words were no lie, I was content in that the rest of the household was sleeping; I asked the purpose of his errand.

Then, Jinnai told me that, if it were within his power, he wanted to assist the House of Hôjôya in its crisis–in gratitude for the favor of twenty years before. He asked the total sum required to meet my current needs. I smiled scornfully. For my monetary needs to be furnished by a thief–was it not whimsical? And if Amakawa Jinnai did have such money, he would not have entered my house for the purpose of stealing. But, though Jinnai inclined his head in an attitude that suggested it might be difficult to obtain such a high sum, he readily promised that if given but three days he would provide the whole amount. Still, whether or not he could supply it–since my need was for such a large sum as six thousand *kan*–he could surely not be relied upon to do so. I decided it was hopeless to depend on such a rare chance.

Together we partook of ceremonial tea administered by my wife before Jinnai retired into the sharp wind. On the next day the promised money was not delivered; nor did it come on the second day; on the third day, snow fell–and even after the night had descended there was still no word. I had previously contended that Jinnai's promise could not be relied upon. But, the fact that I had not dismissed my employees and was rather committed to the turn of events, was at least an indication of the fact that I was waiting. Again, in fact, on that third night, as I sat facing the *andon,* I listened keenly at every snapping of a twig under the weight of piled-up snow.

Then, when it had just passed midnight, suddenly from the garden outside the *cha-shitsu,* would it not be the sound of some scuffle that I heard? My heart was, of course, dwelling on the fate of Jinnai. Had Jinnai, by some mischance, been caught by the authorities?–Quickly, in the face of such thoughts, I thrust aside the *shōji* that opened onto the garden, and raising the *andon* lamp, peered out. Around the bent and broken *Ta-Ming* bamboo, deep in the snow that lay about the *cha-shitsu* two men were in a scuffle!–Swiftly, one of them broke away from his opponent and fled towards the fence, through the shadows cast by the shrubbery. There was the sound of dislodged snow, the sound of the man clambering over the fence–then, with the man's dropping to safety somewhere on the other side of the fence, there was quiet once more. The man who had remained behind made no especial effort to pursue him, but, brushing away the snow from his body, quietly walked over to me.

"It is I, Amakawa Jinnai."

Taken aback, I gazed at Jinnai. That night, too, with the habit of a Buddhist monk Jinnai wore the foreign head-scarf.

"Ah, I regret the outrageous scuffle. I shall be happy if nobody has been awakened by the noise."

Jinnai's smile was sardonic as he joined me in the *cha-shitsu*.

"Well now–as I was sneaking in I espied somebody crawling right below this floor. I grabbed hold of him to get a look at his face, but he, at length, got away."

As a little while before I had been anxiously considering the possibility of his being captured, I asked Jinnai as to whether or not the intruder could have been an official. But Jinnai said that far from being an official the fellow was surely a thief. For a thief to catch a thief–a rare coincidence! This time the sardonic smile floated on my own face rather than on the face of Jinnai. But, in any case, having heard nothing of the success or failure of the monetary venture, my spirits were low. Then Jinnai, before he spoke again, had surely read my heart; gradually unfastening his money-belt from about his abdomen, he set down a parcel of money beside the fireplace inset in the floor.

"Be at ease!–I have contrived to provide the six thousand *kan*. Actually, I had almost acquired it by yesterday, but, as two hundred *kan* were still wanting, I waited until this evening to bring it all. Please accept this package. Unbeknown to your good wife and yourself, the money I had accumulated until yesterday, I hid under the floor of the *cha-shitsu*. Perhaps the thief who came tonight was here because he had smelled out that money."

As if in a dream I heard these words. I was receiving money bestowed on me by a thief!–Without my asking, I know you would surely tell me it was not right. On the boundary of half-believing, half-doubting as to whether or not he could supply the money, I did not think of *right* or *wrong*. As I see the matter now, I had not actually said I would accept it; but if I were to refuse, my entire household would be reduced to beggary. As I was faced with that, I clasped my hands respectfully before Jinnai and wept, without saying a word. . . .

I heard nothing further of Jinnai for two years. Released from the threat of insolvency, in my security I was able to say farewell to those days of tribulation, and because my rescue had been entirely owing to Jinnai's assistance, unbeknown to others I prayed even to the Holy Mother Maria for the man's welfare. Then, what should happen, but hearkening to recent rumors, I heard it said that Amakawa Jinnai had been captured and piked on the Modori Bridge–I was horrified. Secretly I wept. In considering the recompense due for the accumulation of his wickedness, I could not help but weep. It is phenomenal that over long years he did not suffer the retribution of heaven. But, in *gratitude*, I wished at least secretly to arrange for a requiem mass to be said for him. Today, with this thought in mind, I hastened unaccompanied to the Ichijô Modori-bashi to see that piked head.

When I had reached the vicinity of Modori-bashi, there were many people already gathered in front of that pike. As is always the custom on such occasions, a low-ranking official stood guard near the white wooden board upon which was inscribed the record of his crimes. But the head, set on a tripod of three bamboo poles–that head which was shockingly smeared with blood–

what should I say?–As soon as I saw that sallow head in the midst of the clamorous mob, I involuntarily staggered. This was not that man's head; it was not the head of Amakawa Jinnai! Those heavy eyebrows, those pointed cheekbones, the sword wound on the brow–that head was not in the least like the head of Jinnai. But, suddenly the sunlight, the crowd hustling around me, the piked head there on the bamboo–such was my fierce surprise that *all*, I felt, had flowed away to the farthest reaches of the world. This was not Jinnai's head! This was *my* head. This was myself of twenty years before–of the very time when I had helped Jinnai. Yasaburô!–If I could have moved my tongue, I do not know whether or not I would have shouted that name. But, far from being able to raise my voice–as though my body were sickened with malaria, I could only tremble.

Yasaburô!–I stared at that piked head of my son as though it were a phantom. From under half-opened eyelids in the head that was sloped back a little, the eyes stared fixedly at me. What could be the reason for this? Was it that my son by some mistake had been thought to be Jinnai?–But, if there had been proper investigation, such a mistake could not have occurred. Then, would my son have been Amakawa Jinnai?–The masquerade monk who had come to my house–that man who went by the name of Jinnai–could *he* have been someone else? No, that would not have been the case. Throughout the whole length of Japan, he who had contrived to obtain six thousand *kan* of gold within an appointed time–could *he* have been any but Jinnai? Recalling the night of two years before when the snow had been falling, the form of the stranger who had fought in the garden with Jinnai came clearly into my consciousness. The figure of that unknown man–whom did it put me in mind of? Could it not have been my son? From my one glance that man's shape had somehow reminded me of Yasaburô, my son. But, was my mind only meandering? If it had been my son. . . !–As if awakening from a dream, I turned gloomily towards the piked head. On those strangely slack purplish lips, something approximating a smile lingered.

A piked head with a smile!–Hearing such a thing, you might be inclined to laugh; when I first observed it, I thought my eyes might have been deceiving me. But, though I looked many times, there was, to be sure, a brightness as of a smile floating on those parched lips. At that strange smile I gazed for a long time. And, indeed, at some time on my own face, appeared the glimmer of a smile. Yet, even as I smiled, my eyes naturally began to ooze hot tears.

"Father, forbear–!"

That wordless smile said this.

. . . Father, forgive me for being an unworthy son. I had come quietly and unobtrusively to your house on that snowy night two years ago–just to beg forgiveness for that which moved you to renounce me. It would have been shameful for me even to have been seen by any of your employees in the daytime, so I purposely waited until it was well into the night, and knocked on the door of my father's sleeping quarters for the purpose of attracting your attention. Then, I had the fortune to see a light shining on the *shôji* door panels of the *cha-shitsu*, and timidly I made my way over to them. All at once, from behind without a word of challenge, somebody confronted me.

My father–from then on, what happened is known to you.

. . . Because it had all been too unexpected, as soon as I saw your figure, disengaging myself from that undesirable fellow, I fled beyond the high fence.

The figure of the fellow I had seen in the snow light was strangely like a Buddhist monk; so, after making sure that I was not pursued, I crept over and hid once more outside the *cha-shitsu*. Through the *shôji* of the *cha-shitsu* I heard all the conversation.

Father–Jinnai who helped Hôjôya had become the benefactor of our House. I decided that if Jinnai were ever in peril, I would requite the favor even at the cost of my life. If I had not been a vagabond cast off from my family, there would have been no opportunity for me to achieve this. Throughout the intervening two years, I was awaiting my opportunity. And–that chance came. So, please forgive an unworthy son. Born an outlaw I have requited the honor of my House. That, at least, is consolation. . . .

Weeping and laughing as I made my way home, I praised my son's gallantry. You would probably not know, but from the time my son, Yasaburô, and I became Christians, as a profession of religious faith, Yasaburô assumed the name of *Paulo*.–But– but, my son met with ill-fortune. And, *not only* my son. I, too–if I and my House had not been saved by Amakawa Jinnai from downfall–I would not be aggrieved like this. Was it good to have escaped bankruptcy?–Or, would it have been better to have my son alive? (Suddenly with bitterness) Please help me! If my life continue on in this way, I do not know whether I shall not come to hate my great benefactor, Jinnai. . . . (Sobs for a long time)

THE CONFESSION OF YASABURÔ (PAULO)

AH, Holy Mother Maria!–With the coming of dawn I shall be decapitated. Even if my head fall to earth, my soul, like a little bird, will be flying to your side.–No, I who have perpetrated only bad actions, instead of being received into the magnificence of Paradise, will surely fall headlong into the fierce and fearful fires of the Inferno. But I am satisfied. In twenty years, no such happiness has dwelt in my heart.

I am Hôjôya Yasaburô. But, my piked head will be called Amakawa Jinnai. I will be that Amakawa Jinnai.–Is that not the most pleasant of thoughts? Amakawa Jinnai!–how does it sound?–Is it not a fine name? Even behind these dismal bars, only that name on my lips gives me a feeling as though this cell were filled with the roses and lilies of heaven.

One unforgettable night of heavy snow in the winter of two years ago. . . . Having entered the Capital, in search of money for gambling, I sneaked into my father's house. Then, as a light shone through the *shôji* of the *cha-shitsu*, I went on tiptoe to investigate; it was then that without a word somebody grabbed me by the collar. Though I struggled free, I was seized again; who it was that had seized me I did not know; but his stolid strength indicated that he was no ordinary fellow. It was after we had had two or three encounters that the *shôji* doors of the *cha-shitsu* were slid open, and there, clearly outlined as he held up the *andon* lantern towards the garden, was my father, Yasoêmon. I exerted all my might to break loose, and I fled over the high fence.

But, having run about half a *chô*, I hid under some eaves, and peered up and down the street. Other than occasional drifts of powdery white snow, there was no movement in the darkness. My opponent had apparently given up the pursuit. Yet, that man–who would he have been? Though I had seen him only for an instant, I felt sure that he was a monk. But, in thinking over those recent events, if I were to consider his strength and especially the intricacies of his strategy, he was like no ordinary priest. To begin with, on such a snowy night, that there should come some priest into the front garden–was that not odd? After briefly reflecting in that vein, though it might be a hazardous venture, I decided to return and hide myself outside the *cha-shitsu.*

Barely two hours afterwards, that suspicious-looking monk, taking advantage of the break in the snowstorm, went off down Ôgawa Road. It was Amakawa Jinnai! Samurai, *renga-shi,* merchant, mendicant priest–in whatsoever guise he appeared, still he was the thief notorious throughout the Capital. Furtively I followed Jinnai. Never before had I known such strange delight. Amakawa Jinnai! Amakawa Jinnai! In my dreams, how I had longed to see that man! This was Jinnai who had stolen the sword of the Supreme Feudal Lord. It was the Jinnai who had cheated Shamuroya of the coral, who had felled the aloes-wood of the feudal Lord of Bizen–who had seized the clock from Capitão Pereira, commander of the Portuguese mercantile fleet–who had broken into five warehouses in one night–he who had cut down eight samurai at Mikawa–he who was responsible for the phenomenal exploits that would be talked about by future generations was none other than Amakawa Jinnai, the man who was at that moment before me; his wicker hat tilted down over his face, he walked along the dimly-lit snowy road. That I was able to gaze on such a figure, was not *that alone* happiness?–But there was further happiness to come.

When we had reached the rear wall of the Jôgon Temple, I hastened my pursuit of Jinnai. As there was a long earthen wall where no houses stood, this was a most suitable place to avoid observation even in daylight hours. Jinnai, on perceiving me, did not betray any especial surprise but quietly stopped at that place. Leaning on his stick, he did not utter any word but waited for me to speak. In fear and awe I knelt with my hands on the ground before Jinnai. And as I looked on his complacent face, I could not find my voice.

After an interval, my face flushed, I at length spoke up:

"Please forgive me. . . . I am Hôjôya Yasoêmon's son; my name is Yasaburô. . . . It is, in fact, to ask of you a favor that I have pursued your footsteps."

Jinnai just nodded. I, in my timidity–how thankful I felt! Having thus audaciously thrust myself upon him, pressing my hands even deeper into the snow, I briefly related the fact that I had been cast out by my father and that I had entered the fraternity of the unemployed. These circumstances had prompted me to go to my father's house to steal, where having unexpectedly encountered Jinnai, I had, moreover, returned and overheard in full the clandestine conversation between my father and Jinnai. Jinnai still said nothing but looked at me bleakly. So, having told all, I shuffled forward a little and peeped up at Jinnai's face.

"The favor you have bestowed upon the House of Hôjô lies on my shoulders. I have decided to become an adherent of yours, as a sign I have not forgotten that favor. Do what you will with me. I know how to steal. I am skilled in the devices of arson. Beyond that, not in one aspect of villainy am I inferior–."

Jinnai was silent. With mounting earnestness I continued to plead.

"Please find some use for me! I will not fail you.–Kyô, Fushimi, Sakai, Ôsaka–there are no areas unbeknown to me. I can walk fifty *ri* in one day. My strength is such that I can lift four or five rice bales with one hand. I have killed two or three men. Please *use* me somehow! For you I will do anything. Even if you ask me to steal the white peacocks in Fushimi Castle, I shall do so. The belfry of the Church of St. Francis–if you say, *Burn it!*, I will go to burn it down; if you command, *Abduct the Lady of the Minister of the Right!*, I will go to abduct that Lady. If you say, *Decapitate the Chief Officer-of-the-Peace!*, I–."

Even as I prattled on in that way, I was kicked aside in the snow.

"Idiot!"

Jinnai shouted this at me; then he began to walk on as before. Almost out of my mind I clutched at the hem of his habit.

"Please *use* me somehow! Surely no circumstances would force me to leave you! For *you* I will brave water–fire. In *Aesop's Fables*, was not even the King of the Lions saved by a mouse?–I would become that mouse. I–."

"Be quiet! Jinnai has no use for the favors of such as you."

Shaking himself free of me, Jinnai once more kicked me aside.

"Leper! Learn your filial duty!"

When he had kicked me this second time, suddenly I spoke in chagrin:

"All right, then–there will surely come a time!"

But, without turning around, Jinnai hurried with all possible dispatch along the snow-covered road, his wicker umbrella-hat glimmering in the moonlight which at some time or other had begun to shine. For two years, I did not see Jinnai. (Suddenly he laughs) *Jinnai has no use for the favors of such as you!* . . . That was what he had said. But I–as soon as it is dawn, I am to be put to death in place of Jinnai.

Ah, Holy Mother Maria!–in my striving to return Jinnai's favor over these two years, I cannot gauge the extent of my suffering. Favor?–No, rather than say *favor,* I should say I am returning *resentment.* But where is Jinnai?–What is Jinnai doing?–Is there anybody who would know that?–Above all, what kind of man is Jinnai? Even *that* none would know. The fake monk I met was a short man of more or less forty years of age. But, he who is in the prostitute quarter of Yanagimachi would not be more than thirty years old–and is not that florid-faced, bearded man a *ronin?* The foreigner, bent from the waist with age who created the disturbance in the Kubuki Theatre–the young samurai who allowed his hair to hang in front of his head–the same who plundered the treasure of the Myôkoku-ji–if one is to believe that all such persons are Jinnai, then that man has, after all, powers beyond those of any ordinary man; while I myself, since the end of last year, have been inflicted with hemorrhaging.

Desiring only the satisfaction of resentment, every day while wasting away, I have dwelt only on this matter. On a certain night, therefore, a plan suddenly began to take form in my mind. Maria! Maria! It was unmistakably Thy grace that revealed this plan to me. Only by discarding my body, wasted with consumption, by throwing away my body of just bone-and-flesh–in just the fulfillment of that deed–my hopes are accomplished. My joy was so great on that snowy night that I kept on laughing to myself, and repeating those same words: *To be beheaded in place of Jinnai!* . . . *To be put to death in place of Jinnai!*

To be beheaded in place of Jinnai.–Isn't that a glorious thing?–With my death Jinnai's crimes will, of course, be expunged.–Throughout this broad land of Japan, Jinnai walks with great pride. In place of *him* (he laughs a second time)–instead of *him,* in one night I shall become the *thief of thieves!* He who was Ruson-suké Zaemon's assistant; he who chopped down the aloes-wood of the Lord of Bizen Saishô; he who was intimate with Sen-

Rikyû; he who cheated Shamuroya of the coral; he who looted the treasury of the Castle of Fushimi; he who cut down the eight Mikawa samurai–everything that was the so-called *notoriety of Jinnai* will wholly be taken away from him. (He laughs a third time) Indeed, in helping Jinnai, I am killing Jinnai's name, and at the same time as I return the favor bestowed on my House, I requite my *resentment;* there is no reprisal so delightful! It is natural that tonight's happiness affords me endless mirth. So now– behind these bars, ought I not to laugh?

After I had formulated this plan, I penetrated the precincts of the Imperial Palace–under the evening's shallow cover, beneath the night's darkness, I went to steal. Light filtering through the slits in the bamboo blinds, the flowers among the pines glimmering where the light was scattered–that much I seem to remember having seen. But, on jumping from the roof of the long circular corridor, in a trice I was surrounded by four or five samurai guards. Just as I hoped, I was seized and bound. The bewhiskered samurai who had overpowered and bound me with rope as tightly as he could–did he not mutter: *This time we've taken Jinnai himself! . . . ?* Yes, he said that. Who but Amakawa Jinnai would steal into such a place as the Palace? When I heard these words, even while I squirmed frantically, unconsciously I emitted a smile.

Jinnai has no use for the favors of such as you! . . . Those were his words. Yet, as soon as it is dawn I shall be put to death in place of Jinnai. What an excellent retribution! When I am but a piked head, I shall await the coming of that man. On seeing my head, Jinnai will surely feel my voiceless roars of laughter. *How about it now? Has Yasaburô returned the favor?* Such will be the burden of that laughter. You are no longer Jinnai. Amakawa Jinnai is this head, the most notorious on earth, Japan's greatest robber–! (He laughs) Ah, I am content. Such contentment occurs only once in a lifetime. My father, *Yasoêmon*, when you see my piked head– (With regret)–please forgive me, my father!–Wasted as I am with consumption, even if I were not put to death, I could not go on living for more than three years.–Please pardon your unfilial son. I was born an outlaw, but, in any case, I have been able to return the *gratitude* of my House. . . .

THE FAITH OF WEI SHÊNG

Introductory Note:
Wei Shêng appears in ancient Chinese literature as the epitome
of faithfulness. Although one does suspect some satirical atmo-
sphere about the theme in Chinese literature, we feel that Akuta-
gawa was in a serious mood when he adapted this story.

This seriousness derives, one suspects, from Akutagawa's
spiritual affinity with the faith of Wei Shêng. Akutagawa
pursued Lady Enlightenment and self-detachment through the
creation of literary works, but the ardently desired Lady eluded
him just as she failed Wei Shêng. As Wei Shêng calmly accepted
his destiny when the Lady did not come, so Akutagawa, hav-
ing gone as far as he felt he could go in his pursuit, chose self-
annihilation at the age of thirty-five.

According to Buddhist teachings, the soul is not immortal,
but desires pass on from one living being to another until they
are conquered; the soul is then set free and is no longer bound
by the mutations of nature.

This story was completed in December of Taishô 8 (1919).

WEI SHÊNG, lingering under the bridge, had been waiting for his
Lady to come.

Above him there was the high stone bridge rail with ivy crawling about it here and there. The white robes of people passing hither and thither shone clearly in the setting sun and billowed gently in the breeze. But still the Lady did not come.

Quietly blowing on his flute, Wei Shêng looked down at the sandbank beneath the bridge–only that small strip of the yellow sand was not yet invaded by the water of the stream. There among the reeds perhaps many crabs dwelt, as there were many round holes; and there he could hear the faint sound of lapping water.–But still the Lady had not come.

For some time Wei Shêng, having crossed to the water's edge, looked out over the quiet water line where no boat moved.

Along the water's edge fresh reeds grew densely, and rounded willows were growing in abundance among the river reeds. So, the water weaving among the reeds and willows did not seem broad compared with the river's breadth from bank to bank. Like an *obi* sash gilded with a mica-colored cloud, the water was quietly undulating among the reeds. But the Lady–the Lady had not yet come.

By degrees the evening's dusk deepened. Turning his footsteps from the water's edge and meandering to and fro on the narrow sand, he listened for sounds in the evening quiet.

For some time the footsteps of passers-by had ceased. The sound of neither shoe nor hoof, nor the roll of carriage could be heard from the bridge. The sound of wind, the sound of reeds, the sound of water–then from somewhere shrilly came the cry of a green heron. Pausing to think of it, it would seem that the tide was intruding, and from a little time before, the hue of the water washing the yellow sand had begun to glisten close by. And yet the Lady did not come.

Wei Shêng–sternly frowning–enlivened his pace more and more over the vague sand beneath the bridge. Meanwhile, gradually came the water—one *sun*, one *shaku*—climbing over the sand; and at that time, too, from the river, the smell of protruding reeds and the smell of water clung coldly about his skin. Looking up at the bridge he could see only the balustrade—blackly, sharply silhouetted against the sky—the clear light fading as the sun set.

Wei Shêng then stood still.

Under the bridge, the river was wetting his shoes—brimming with light colder than steel, it was swelling up. Quite soon, he was sure, his knees, his breast, would be hidden by the swell of unrelenting water; indeed, even then both of Wei Shêng's shins were covered by the swell of the gradually rising tide. But still—his Lady had not come.

Wei Shêng, standing in the water, still embraced some hope as he cast up his eyes many times at the sky above the bridge.

The meager twilight crept over the water that immersed his abdomen; through the evening mist the cluttered reeds and willows sent only the sad sound of rustling reeds and leaves. Then, grazing Wei Shêng's nose, a fish that might have been a perch lithely frisked its tail. In the sky into which for one moment that fish had jumped, the starlight was so thinly diffused that even the shape of the ivy twining the balustrade was indiscernible in the darkness of evening.—And still the Lady had not come.

At midnight, when the moonlight spilled into the river reeds, and the willows, the waters, and the breeze were communing in whispers, the body of Wei Shêng was gently borne from beneath the bridge towards the sea. But Wei Shêng's spirit, in the lonely moonlight from heaven, would probably have reflected longing thoughts; and stealing away from the corpse, Wei Shêng's departing spirit, just like the smell of weeds and water rising from the soundless river, rose up towards the faintly glimmering sky.

Thousands of years thence, this spirit, having traversed in its time countless transmigrations, has surely again been entrusted to life in human form. This spirit is the spirit that dwells in *me*; and I–born in these modern times–cannot do work of any worth. Day and night, at random, I live a life that is apt to be desultory and dreamy, awaiting the coming of something inconceivable; and like that Wei Shêng beneath the bridge at dusk, I seem to live awaiting always a beloved who never comes. . . .

THE LADY, ROKU-NO-MIYA

Introductory Note:
The theme of this story is derived from "The Renunciation of the
World by the Lady Rokunomiya" (Vide: Book 19 of the "Kon-
jaku Monogatari"). In the original version, the suitor becomes
a monk after the death of the Lady. In this story the Lady's
restless spirit must wander; as for the Lady's spirit being able
to find neither heaven nor hell, at least the circumstance that
the fiery carriage and the lotus faded from her vision coincides
in both versions. But the story about the child who fell from a
tree does not appear in the original.
The location of "Rokunomiya" is unknown.
"The Lady of Rokunomiya" ("Rokunomiya-no-Himegime")
was completed in July of Taishô 11 (1922).

I

LADY ROKU-NO-MIYA's father was sprung from royal lineage.
But, formal in manner, he was unadapted to the spirit of the times
in which he lived and so did not rise above the rank of *Hyôbu-no-
daifu*. The Lady lived with her parents in a mansion situated on

a hill in the environs of Roku-no-Miya. And the Lady, we should mention, had been attributed the name of the area.

The father and mother doted on the young Lady, but, disinclined to arrange a marriage for her according to the custom, they waited in expectation of someone coming forward to make a proposal. The Lady's demeanor was at all times modest, in conformity with the training she had received from her parents. It was a life in which there was no awareness of sadness, nor yet of happiness; and, although the Lady was secluded from the world, she did not feel any marked discontent. Her parents' well-being was all that really mattered to the Lady.

The cherry that drooped into the pond opened its meager blossoms every year. And, as the years went by, the Lady blossomed into adulthood. But the father on whom she depended, suddenly died as a result of years spent in over-imbibing. And that was not all, for the mother within the space of six months, inconsolable in her grief, finally pursued the footsteps of the father. The Lady herself was far too bewildered to be overcome with grief, for, protected as she had been, there was in fact none to communicate with her other than the wet-nurse who had cared for her from childhood.

Without sparing herself, this same governess labored continuously for the Lady. As time went by the mother-of-pearl caskets and the silver incense bowls that had been family heirlooms were disposed of, one by one. Likewise, the menservants and maidservants were gradually dispensed with. Even the Lady became increasingly aware of the hardships of life. But the Lady was unable to remedy the situation. Yet in the lonely residential quarters of the Mansion, the Lady carried on the monotonous diversions of her earlier existence–her *koto* playing and her poetry writing.

Then, at sunset one autumn day, the governess came to the Lady and said reflectively:

"My nephew, a priest, begs leave to introduce to you a certain lord—the former *Lord* of Tamba. Besides being handsome he is said to be kindhearted, and his father, though a provincial governor, was the son of a *courtier* and is closely linked with the highest of families. What are your feelings about meeting him? . . . It might be somewhat of an improvement on this circumscribed life which you live."

The Lady began to whimper. To yield to a man's nakedness in order to relieve her straitened circumstances would be the same as selling her body. That in society such affairs were numerous, she was, of course, aware. But, in reviewing her existence at the time, the Lady was consumed with grief, and the atmosphere as she confronted her governess was as when wind revives the withered leaves, and all the while she hid her face in her sleeve.

2

SOONER or later it came about that every night the young man would call on the Lady. True to the words of the governess, the man had a gentle heart. His appearance, too, was genteel. It was apparent to everybody that he was intrigued by the Lady's beauty. The Lady was not, of course, indifferent to the man. Oftentimes she would place her trust in him. Nevertheless, she did not experience one night of joy when, as they consorted together, they were shaded from the dazzling light by the butterfly-and-bird screen.

Little by little during that time, the Mansion began to disport an air of elegance. The black shelves and the rattan blinds were

new, and the servants increased in number. Naturally, compared
with previous times, the governess' life became more active, but
the Lady, in spite of such change, seemed just as lonely.

One night when it was raining, as the man sipped his saké he
told the Lady an unpleasant story from the Tamba countryside
about a traveler who, while making his journey to the province
of Izumo, lodged at an inn on the foothills of Oé-yama. Quite
unexpectedly during the night the mistress of the inn gave birth
to a baby girl. The traveler saw some big fellow, a stranger to
the place, who, coming out from where the baby had been born,
exclaimed: "At the age of eight years–*death*!," and disappeared
from sight. In the ninth year after that, the traveler was on his
way to the Capital when he sought lodging at the same inn. The
little girl had, indeed, died in her eight year when, as she fell from
a tree, she had been pierced in the neck by a reaping hook.–That
was the general tenor of the story. When the Lady heard the tale,
she felt intimidated by the force of destiny. To live out her life
relying on this man was a fate no more fortunate.

There was no way in which to defeat the course of events;
and, she smiled wanly at the thought.

Many times the pines about the Mansion eaves were bent
with the weight of the snow. As in old times, the Lady played
the *koto* and enjoyed, also in the daytime, the game of *sugoroku*.
At night, as she lay on the bedding with the man, she could hear
the sound of the water-fowl flapping onto the pond. Though she
was never distressed, at the same time she was never happy. But,
usually the Lady, amid this leisurely existence, was able to enjoy
a transitory satisfaction.

Sooner than one would have expected, even that comfort
came to an end. One night when at length spring had come
around again, and the Lady and her lover were together, the

young man had something distasteful to convey. "Our times together are now in their twilight," he told her. It seemed that the man's father would, at the forthcoming session for annual appointments, be elevated to the Governorship of Mutsu; in view of that, the young man was obliged to go with him into the deep recesses of the snow country. The man certainly felt immeasurable remorse at parting from his Lady; but, as he had concealed from his father any knowledge of his union with the Lady, it would have been difficult for him to reveal the affair at this time. Sighing, the man spoke for a long time about this recent turn of events. . . .

"But, in five years the term of office will be completed. Until that time, please be content to wait."

The Lady gave herself up to weeping. Even if it were not from *love*, the thought of severance from a man upon whom she depended made her miserable beyond words. Caressing the Lady, the man comforted her with many consoling words. But, all his words were choked with tears.

The governess, who had had no inkling of the matter until then, brought the young couple a flask of saké and a tray of food. They were remarking that the cherry which drooped over the pond was in bud.

3

IT WAS springtime, six years later, but the young man, who had gone to the provinces, had not returned to the Capital. Meanwhile, the Lady had lost all her servants as, one by one, they had retired and left her service. The east wing in which she had been living, gave way one year before a gale; so, since that time the

Lady had taken up her residence in the vacant samurai quarters, even though the samurai quarters were restricted in area, and so dilapidated that she could barely be sheltered from the rain and dew. At the time when they had moved to those quarters, the governess could not withhold the tears as she looked on her mistress in such a miserable plight; but, at other times she was–for no reason for which she could specifically account–only angry.

It was, of course, a life of hardship. Before the miniature shrine on the shelf, rape had long since been substituted for rice. By then the Lady no longer owned any formal attire apart from that which she wore. If they needed firewood, the governess would strip off the rotting boards of their former residence. But still the Lady, as in old times, maintained her spirits sufficiently to play the *koto* and to sing; and she persisted in waiting for her lover.

One moonlight night in the autumn of that year, the governess went to the Lady and said pensively:

"The Lord will not now return. How would it be if you, also, were to forget your affair with the Lord. In fact, lately, a certain Tenyaku-no-suké has been earnestly wishing to meet you. As we are in such a plight. . . ."

When she heard what the governess had to say, the Lady recalled the affair of six years before. Six years!–then she was so stricken with grief that she was distraught. But now, both her body and her mind had become too weary. "I just want to wither quietly with age. . . ." Beyond that, she had no desire. When the governess had finished her intimation, the Lady–gazing at the white moon–shook her head; her face had become thin and lethargic.

"I do not want to embark on any further venture. . . . I don't care whether I live or die."

AT THAT SAME hour, her lover in a far-off mansion in the Hitachi district was taking some saké with his bride—a Lady who had won favor with his father, a Lady who was the daughter of the Governor of that part of the country.

As if startled, the man looked up at the moonlit eaves.

"What was that sound?" he said.

At that moment, the figure of the Lady had for some reason come floating before him. . . .

"It was probably only a chestnut falling."

—As she replied, the Hitachi wife clumsily poured the saké.

4

WHEN THE MAN returned to the Capital, it was late autumn, in the ninth year.

He was making his way to the Capital in the company of his wife's household of Hitachi. In order to avoid the inauspicious days for traveling, he lodged at Awazu for three days. He purposely chose to enter the Capital at nightfall to escape the daytime gaze of the public. He had sent his compliments two or three times by letter to his former mistress in the Capital; but as the messenger had not returned—or if by chance he had indeed returned it was after failing to locate the Lady's house—not once had the Lord obtained a reply. For that reason, on his entering the Capital, his affection was once more revived in him. Having installed his Hitachi wife safely in her father's house, without even a change of habit, he set out for Roku-no-Miya as expeditiously as he could.

Arriving at Roku-no-Miya, he inspected the Mansion and found that the four-post gate and the main residential quarters with its thatch of cypress bark, which he remembered of old, had entirely disappeared; and thereabouts all that remained were the ruins of the mud wall. Pausing for a while amid the undergrowth, he stared vacantly at the garden. Onion weed was growing in the half-buried pond. In the light of the new moon the onion weed glimmered faintly amongst the desolate mass of leaves.

In the environs of the administrative quarters, which were still as he remembered them, he saw a tilting shingle-roofed building. On his approaching, it seemed there was someone's silhouette in this structure. Peering through the darkness, the man softly raised his voice to the silhouette. Thereupon, the form of an old nun, somehow familiar, came tottering into the moonlight.

When he divulged his name, the nun was speechless. She wept. Then, after a while, in a faltering voice, she spoke of the Lady:

"Although you might not remember me, I am the mother of a maid who was once in service here. She served the Lady for five years even after your Lordship left for the provinces and then she retired to Tajima with her husband. I, too, took my leave of the Lady and departed with my daughter; but, as I was deeply concerned for the Lady's welfare, I came up alone to the Capital, and found—just as you see—there was nothing left of the Mansion. And I am perplexed about her whereabouts. My Lord would not be aware of this, but while my girl was in service here, the Lady's wretchedness was far beyond my power to describe. . . ."

After having listened to all that was spoken, the man stripped off one of his robes, and handed it to the infirm old nun. Then, with bowed head, he tacitly retired, treading heavily on the grasses.

ON THE following day, the man set out in search of the Lady, making his way here and there about the Capital. But, wheresoever he went, the people he encountered glibly denied any knowledge of her.

Many days hence, as he was passing the Suzaku Gate one evening, he stood under the eaves of the west *magaridono* to avoid a sudden shower of rain. A mendicant monk was also there, weary of waiting for the rain to cease. The rain continued to pelt down drearily on the vermilion lacquered Gate. Looking askance at the priest, he paced hither and thither over the stone pavement to divert himself from his vexatious thoughts. Quite soon the man's ears happened to catch, through the thin lattice of the window, an indication that somebody was inside. Almost without purpose, he glanced through the window.

Through it he caught a glimpse of a nun, clad in tattered matting, attending a woman who was apparently ill. In the dim evening glow, the woman's wasted appearance was indeed ominous. But, a single glance was enough to satisfy him that this woman was the Lady whom he sought. On the point of raising his voice, he looked closely at her emaciated form and, for some reason, did not let his voice go. Unconscious of his presence as she lay on the threadbare matting, the Lady chanted, as though in pain:

While I lie dozing, bleak
the wind through apertures—
yet I no longer care. . . .

When he heard the voice, in spite of himself, the man uttered the Lady's name. She naturally raised herself from her pillow. As she caught sight of the man, muttering faintly, she sank once more face downwards on the matting. The nun–that loyal governess–with the help of the man who hurried to her assistance, raised up the Lady. But, looking into the raised face, the governess–and even the man, of course–were all the more disturbed.

In her distraction, the governess rushed to the mendicant monk of whom we have spoken and begged him to recite a sutra for the dying Lady. In response to the request, the monk knelt by the Lady's pillow. But, instead of reciting a sutra, he addressed the Lady thus:

"We have no power over transmigration. Without effort on your part we cannot invoke the name of Amida Buddha."

In the man's embrace the Lady faintly murmured the name of Buddha. In a moment of terror she gazed at the parapet of the Gate.

"Ah–I see a blazing carriage over there. . . ."

"That must cause you some misgivings, but if you concentrate your mind on Buddha, all will be well."

The priest lifted his voice. After a pause, the Lady again began to mutter, as though in a dream:

"I see a golden lotus. It is large, like a canopy. . . ."

The priest was about to speak, but this time the Lady strained even more than before to express herself.

"I see no lotus now. Where it was there is only darkness, and wind is blowing. . . ."

"Beseech Buddha–with all your heart. . . . Why is it you do not call on Him with all your heart?"

The priest spoke almost in rebuke. Yet, as though her heart were crumbling, the Lady repeated:

"Nothing!–I see nothing. . . . Only the wind in the darkness–only the cold wind comes blowing."

The priest, too, with hands clasped, assisted the Lady in her invocation. . . .

The man and the governess stifled their tears and continued their praying to Amida. Her voice mingled with the sound of the rain, the Lady stretched out on the ragged mat and gradually assumed the face of death.

6

THEN, one moonlight night some days later, the monk, who had assisted the Lady in her devotions to Buddha, was clasping his torn robes about his knees before the Suzaku Gate as a samurai, chanting some song, ambled along the moonlit highway. On perceiving the monk, the samurai's *zôri*-clad feet came to a halt as he raised his voice indifferently.

"I have heard that recently in the precincts of Suzakumon the weeping of a woman can be heard.–Is it so?"

Crouched on the flagstones, the monk replied with the one word:

"Listen!"

The samurai listened intently for a while. But he could hear nothing other than the faint sound of insects. In the vicinity, only the smell of pines was wafted on the night air. The samurai was about to speak when, amid the silence, suddenly from somewhere, a woman's voice was heard faintly giving expression to its grief.

The samurai put his hand to his sword. But the voice from the window of the *magari-dono*, after one protracted wail, gradually faded.

"Invoke the Buddha!" demanded the monk, lifting his face to

the moonlight. "–That is a spirit which knows neither heaven nor hell. It is a woman's fainthearted spirit.–Invoke the Buddha!"

But the samurai held his silence as he stole a glance at the monk. But a moment before he had clasped his hands as though in fear. He ventured:

"Are you not the Father Superior Naiki?–Why are you in such a place. . . ?"

His secular name was Yoshishigé-no-Yasutané; in society he was known as the Father Superior Naiki; and even among the disciples of the Superior, Kûya, he was known as a priest of eminent virtue and exalted rank.

THE KAPPA

Introductory Note:
Since Kappa are described in the story in some detail directly and indirectly, we do not wish to confuse our readers by recounting the many contradictory opinions of the Kappa's appearance–especially since the translators have never had the good fortune to see a Kappa for themselves. Kenkyûsha's standard dictionary describes the Kappa as a water imp, a river monster with bobbed hair. It was referred to as being like an ugly child and as having greenish-yellow skin–"especially to be found in Kyûshû near Arima." Some referred to them as being like monkeys: they have "long noses and round eyes, auburn hair on the chin, grayish skin, five fingertips and five toes and have an odor like that of the fish." Others have mentioned the Kappa's preference for melons, eggs, apples and human livers, and how knives cannot cut Kappa, as well as how one becomes insane after wrestling with them. It is said that many country girls have blamed Kappa for the loss of their virginity. More precisely, the Kappa have been described as being about three feet in height and about a hundred pounds in weight. Offend Kappa and it is said they cry like babies; please Kappa and they will show their gratitude in some way. Those wishing to include Kappa in their sightseeing visits to Japan should go to

the coast of Mito or swim in the Oisé River near Nagoya. One should be cautious when the prankish creatures are about.

Some country children are still in the habit of throwing cucumbers into the river before swimming to woo the Kappa's tolerance and divert him from his pranks.

Because the Kappa are "not of this world," this story has been compared favorably by some with Jonathan Swift's "Gulliver's Travels," Samuel Butler's "Erehwon," and Anatole France's "Penguin Island." Perhaps Akutagawa was influenced by these works.

"The Kappa" was completed by Akutagawa on February 11th of the Second Year of the Showa era (1927).

PREAMBLE

THIS IS THE STORY of a patient of a mental asylum—Patient No. 23's story which he will tell to anybody. He is over thirty years of age, but for some reason, at a glance, he seems to be rather a younger lunatic. The experiences of his early life—well, let them be, whatsoever they might have been. Clasping his knees firmly, from time to time looking out of the window—outside the iron-barred window there is an oak tree, with not even a withered leaf, which spreads its branches into the snow-clouded sky—he went on for a lengthy time telling his story in the company of myself and the Superintendent, Dr. S. He did not really remain still all the time; for instance, when he spoke of surprise, suddenly he would jerk back his head. . . .

I would like to portray rather accurately what he told me. If, however, any cannot bear with what I write, it would perhaps be worth his while to visit S. Mental Hospital at X Village in a

Tokyo suburb. The youthful looking Patient, No. 23, will lower his head in the utmost politeness and will indicate a cushionless chair. Then, with a melancholy smile lingering on his face, he will quietly repeat this tale. Finally, I remember his demeanor when he ends his story. Ultimately, with a swift movement of his body, all in a moment he will brandish his fists at anyone and bellow: "Get out!–You rogue!–You idiot!–You jealous, obscene, impudent, self-conceited, cruel, selfish animal!–Get out! You rotter!..."

I

IT HAPPENED in the summer of three years ago. Carrying a rucksack on my back, like most people do on such occasions, I set out from the Kamikôchi hot-spring inn with the intention of climbing Mt. Hotaka. To climb Mt. Hotaka one must follow–as you know–the Azusa River. As, of course, I had previously climbed Mt. Hotaka and also Yarigataké, I went off alone, without a guide, along the Azusagawa Valley upon which the morning mist had descended. As the mist did not lift, the splendid views were concealed. The mist was actually deepening. After I had walked for only an hour, I half decided I would make my way back to Kamikôchi Inn. But, even if I were to return to Kamikôchi, I would, at any rate, have to wait for the sun to break through; but, the mist continued steadily to deepen. "Then–I must go on with the climb!" With this in mind, I waded through the bamboo grasses, careful not to stray from the Azusagawa Valley.

Though my vision was thwarted by the density of the mist, I could make out the fresh green and leafy branches of the thick beech and fir trees. Horses and cows turned out to graze, suddenly thrust their faces before me. Though at one instant I could see them, at the next they were lost in the abundant mist and completely hidden from me. By that time my feet were becoming tired and my hunger increasing. The mountaineering clothes I wore had become wet from the mist and were even heavier than they were normally. At length I abandoned the climb, and, guided by the sound of the water on the rocks, I began my descent down Azusagawa Valley.

Then, seating myself on the rocks by some trees, I lost no time in taking my meal—having cut open a can of corned beef and put a fire to the withered branches I had gathered. I suppose this would have taken me about ten minutes; meanwhile everywhere the malicious fog began somewhat to lighten. Biting into a piece of bread, I looked at my wristwatch. It was already after one-twenty; yet, rather than that, what surprised me was some strange face whose shadow fell for a moment onto the round face of the wristwatch. It was then for the first time, in fact, that I saw a Kappa. Behind me on one of the rocks there was a Kappa like those I had seen in illustrations; with one arm embracing the trunk of a white birch, and the other holding its hand over its eyes, it looked down on me with curiosity.

I was astonished, and for some time I did not move. The Kappa, also, seeing me surprised, did not even move his hand over his eyes. Then, in a moment, I quickly jumped to my feet and leapt at the Kappa on the rock; but at that same moment the Kappa fled. Had it indeed run away? I saw it for a moment, then, in a twinkling, it had disappeared. Increasingly surprised, I looked about in the bamboo grasses. And, I saw the Kappa crouching, ready to escape and looking back at me from two or three meters distance. There was nothing odd about that, but to me what was extraordinary was the color of the Kappa's body.

On the rock the Kappa had been gray, but now the color had changed entirely to a vivid green. Calling out, "Damn you!" I once more ran at the Kappa. Naturally, again the Kappa fled. For as long as thirty minutes I beat the bamboo grasses, clambering over rocks, recklessly pursuing the Kappa.

The Kappa was fleet of foot, by no means inferior to a monkey. Chasing it as if in a dream, I lost sight of it many times. Many times I stumbled when my feet slipped. But, coming to where a large Chinese horse chestnut spread its branches thickly, a grazing bull luckily stood blocking the Kappa's progress. Moreover, the bull's horns were thick; its eyes bloodshot. When the Kappa saw the bull, raising a kind of scream, it appeared to somersault into the midst of especially tall bamboo grass. As for me, I was delighted and charged in to seize it. It was then that I fell into a hole I had not noticed, without my having even touched with my fingertips the slippery back of the Kappa; I fell, plunging head over heels into deep darkness. Our human minds at moments of crisis think of the most inconsequential things; as I fell, I recalled that the name of the bridge near the hot-spring inn at Kamikôchi was called "Kappabashi."—Then, what happened immediately after, I do not remember. Only, before my eyes, I was aware of something like lightning, just before I lost consciousness.

2

I HAD fallen face upwards, so the moment I regained consciousness I saw that I was surrounded by many Kappa. One who wore a pince-nez on his thick beak, knelt beside me and put his stethoscope to my chest. That Kappa, when he saw me open my eyes, said to me with a gesture, "Be quiet, please;" then to some

Kappa at the rear of the crowd he called out, "Quax! Quax!" And, from somewhere two Kappa walked up bearing a stretcher and put me on it. They proceeded quietly through some street that was crowded with Kappa. On both sides the street was not in the least different from the Ginza. In the shade of the beech avenue, striped shop awnings projected here and there. And countless vehicles moved down the street, on either side of the avenue.

I seem to recall that the litter on which I was borne at length turned down a narrow side street, and I was carried on Kappa shoulders into some house. According to facts I learned later, it was the house of the Kappa who wore the pince-nez–the physician called Chakk. Chakk had me put into a quaint little bed and made me drink a measure of some transparent liquid medicine. I lay on my side on the bed while Chakk was attending to me. In fact, as I ached in every joint, I was quite incapable of movement.

Chakk came without fail to examine me two or three times a day. Also, about once in every three days the Kappa on whom I had first set eyes–a fisherman called Bagg–came to visit me. Compared with what humans know of Kappa affairs, the Kappa are quite conversant with the affairs of humankind. This would probably be because the Kappa capture more human beings than humans capture of the Kappa, although the word "capture" might be inappropriate. Before my time, at least, our people had often gone to the Kappa country. Not only that, there have been plenty who have lived their whole lives in the Kappa country. Let us examine the reason for this. Just because we are not Kappa–because we enjoy the privilege of being human beings, we are given food there without working for it. Actually, according to Bagg's story, a certain young road-construction worker, after going by chance to that country, took a female Kappa for a wife; and, it is said, he lived there until his death. On top of the fact that his wife was that country's foremost beauty, she had the utmost talent for deceiving her navvy-husband.

After a week had passed, by virtue of a legal decree of that country, I came to live next to Chakk as an "Especially Protected Inhabitant." However small the dimensions of my house might have been, it was well set up. Of course, that country's standard of living is not much different from that of the Japanese. In the corner of my guest room, nearest the thoroughfare, there was a small piano; and, on the wall hung an etching in a frame. But, as for the essentials of the house, the measurements of the tables and chairs being suited to Kappa, I felt as if I had been put into a nursery room. That was the only inconvenience I experienced.

During the evenings I received Chakk and Bagg in this room, the drawing room, and I learned the Kappa tongue. Well, there were not only Chakk and Bagg. As I was "an especially protected citizen" everybody was curious. There was Gaël who used to call on Chakk every day to have his blood pressure checked; Gaël was manager of a glass company; he used to drop in on me, too. During the first fortnight, however, the most friendly of my visitors was the fisherman, Bagg.

It was dusk one sultry day. I turned towards Bagg who was seated opposite me at my table. Thereupon, whatever it was he was thinking about, not only did he fall silent, but opening wide his big eyes, he stared fixedly at me. If I remember correctly, I asked, "Quax, Bagg, quo quell quam?" which translated means, "Ah–Bagg, what is it?" Bagg did not reply. He suddenly stood up, thrust out his tongue, and as if he were a frog, showed some indication of leaping at me. Just then, fortunately, Dr. Chakk happened to put his head into the room.

"Heh! Bagg, what are you doing?"

Chakk, putting on his pince-nez, stared at this Bagg fellow. And Bagg, seemingly abashed, put his hand to his head several times and apologized to Chakk:

"You must really excuse me. But the fact is, as this gentleman's discomfiture was interesting, I was carried away. What I did was out of mischief, sir, so do be patient with me."

3

BEFORE I proceed with my tale, I must offer some explanation as to the beings called *Kappa*. It has been doubted until now as to whether these animals really exist, but since I myself have lived among the Kappa, there ought to be no room for doubt. But if we ask what kind of animals they are, then it must be explained that they have short hair on their heads, and, of course, they have webbed hands and feet. These facts are authoritatively set down in "A Short History of the Water Tiger." The average height of the Kappa would be, more or less, a meter. According to Dr. Chakk, their average weight is from twenty to thirty pounds. Right in the middle of their heads they have an elliptical dish; this dish, according to the age of the Kappa, gradually hardens. In fact, the dish of the old Kappa, Bagg, is quite different to the touch from that of the younger Kappa, Chakk. But, the strangest attribute is the color of the Kappa skin. The Kappa have no definite color as do human beings; their color changes in sympathy with their surroundings; for instance, when they are in grass, their color changes to green, and when they are on rocks they become as gray as the rocks themselves. This, of course, is not limited to the Kappa; it is also the case with the chameleon. Whether or not the Kappa has a close proximity to the chameleon in skin type, I would not know. When I discovered this color-changing quality, I remembered that–according to folklore–the west country Kappa were green and the north-eastern Kappa were red. Furthermore, I recalled that when I was chasing Bagg, I could not understand how he had eluded me. Moreover, beneath the Kappa skin they seem to have an abundance of fat; although the temperature in this subterranean country is low–the average temperature being at all times fifty degrees Fahrenheit–such things as clothes are unknown. Naturally enough, some Kappa wear spectacles, some carry cigarette cases and wallets. But the Kappa, like the kangaroo, has a convenient abdominal pouch, in which they can carry accessories not in use. Only, what was queer for me was that they were not concealed even by a loin cloth. At one time I inquired of Bagg why it was that they had this habit of going naked. Then Bagg, throwing back his head, laughed and cackled in reply: "We think your hiding yourself is amusing."

4

GRADUALLY I came to learn the everyday language of the Kappa. Also, I came to understand the Kappa customs and mannerisms. What was most strange among these customs was that the Kappa laugh at things we humans regard as serious; at the same time, what we regard as funny, they take to be serious; in that way, they are incongruous. Humans, for example, regard "righteousness" and "humanity" as serious, but when Kappa speak of such entities they laugh uproariously. In the aggregate their outlook on what is amusing is quite different from our human outlook. At one time I was talking with the physician, Chakk, about birth control. At that time, Chakk, opening his big mouth, laughed so much that he dropped his spectacles. I was vexed, of course, and asked him what was so funny. In a general way I remember Chakk's answer, though I am not sure that I might not be more or less mistaken about the details; also, at the time, I was not altogether proficient in my comprehension of the Kappa language. "–But it's queer for parents to consider their own convenience only. It's too selfish–don't you agree?"

If we look, as humans, at Kappa childbirth, that too is odd. Actually, to observe for myself, I soon went to a little place where Bagg's wife was in confinement. Even the Kappa on the point of giving birth are the same as humans. Of course, the physician and the midwife assist at the birth. But when the child is about to be born, the father, as if at the telephone, puts his mouth to the mother's uterus and inquires in a loud voice: "Think well in replying as to whether or not you wish to be born into this world." Of course, Bagg, on his knees, many times repeated such words. He then gargled with the antiseptic which was on the table. On this occasion the child in the wife's womb, more or less speaking with restraint, soon replied in a small voice:

"I don't want to be born. First, the fact that my father would hand down his mental aberrations is a terrible thought, and apart from this, I believe that a Kappa's existence is not good."

When Bagg heard this reply, he scratched his head as though in embarrassment. The midwife on duty quickly thrust a thick tube into the wife's uterus and injected some fluid. Then the wife, as though immensely relieved, let escape a deep sigh. At the same time her belly–which had been swollen–decreased little by little like a balloon giving off hydrogen.

As such a reply was made, you may understand that Kappa children can, of course, walk and chatter soon after they are born. From what Chakk told me, there was once a child who, on his twenty-sixth day after birth, lectured on the existence or nonexistence of God; it is said, however, that the child died in its second month.

Leaving aside the subject of childbirth—in the third month after I had gone to that country, I happened to see what was written on a huge street-corner poster. On that poster Kappa were depicted—about a dozen or so Kappa—wearing swords and blowing trumpets. Also, at the top, spiral ideographs just like clock springs were drawn. If I were to translate these spiral characters, I could arrive at the general meaning; but, here again, I could not be sure that I was not mistaken as to the details. At any rate, a Kappa who was walking with me—a student named Rapp—clearly read it to me, and I made a note of each item.

Enlist in the Heredity Voluntary Corps!!!
Healthy male and female Kappa!!!
To eradicate the errors of heredity
Marry unhealthy male and female Kappa!!!

Of course, I told Rapp at the time that such a situation was impracticable. Then, not only Rapp, but the whole group of Kappa around the poster started to laugh heartily.

"Impracticable? From what you have told me, I think you humans, too, do the same as we do. Your sons fall in love with servants, your daughters fall for chauffeurs!—Why do you think that is? It's because they are unconsciously eradicating hereditary evils. First, compared with the human Volunteer Corps you were speaking of lately—those volunteers who kill one another to seize a railway line—our volunteer corps is noble, don't you think?"

While he spoke earnestly in this way, only his fat belly was shaking incessantly with amusement. Yet, I was in no mood for laughing, as I was hurriedly trying to catch hold of one of the Kappa. He had taken the opportunity to catch me off my guard in order to steal my fountain pen. Yet, the slippery fleshed Kappa was not easy to catch. Without effort, that Kappa swiftly gave me the slip and got away. His body, thin as a mosquito, was bent forward as he lurched away.

5

IT HAPPENED that the assistance rendered me by Rapp was not inferior to that rendered by Bagg. But I must not forget that I was introduced to a Kappa named Tokk. Tokk was a poet among the Kappa. Kappa poets are not different from human poets in that they grow their hair long. To relieve the boredom I would some-times go to Tokk's house. Tokk lived a life of some ease, writing poetry and smoking in his small room in which were arranged alpine plants in pots. Moreover, as Tokk was a free lover he had no legal wife, but there would be a female Kappa in a corner of the room engaged in such pastimes as knitting. Tokk always had a smile for me; a Kappa smile, however, is not so pleasant, and at first I felt rather uneasy about it.

"Ah! I'm glad you're here. Well–do sit in that chair," Tokk would say.

Tokk would speak authoritatively on the life of the Kappa and about Kappa art. According to what Tokk believed, there was nothing more absurd than the normal lives of Kappa. Parents and children, husbands and wives, brothers and sisters lived, gaining their only pleasure from inflicting hardship on each other. There was no greater foolishness than "the family system."

"Just take a look at the extent of their foolishness!" Tokk

once exclaimed, pointing out the window. Outside the window a Kappa, who was still young, was carrying on his shoulders not only Kappa who were apparently his parents but also seven or eight female and male Kappa, and he was struggling along, gasping for breath. But as I felt sympathy with the young Kappa's dutiful spirit, I–on the contrary–lauded his gallantry.

"Hm, you have the quality to become a citizen of this country, too. . . . Incidentally, would you be a socialist?"

I replied, of course, *"Qua"*–this apparently means "Yes," in the language used by the Kappa.

"Then, you would not look askance at sacrificing a genius to console a hundred mediocre people."

"Well then, what are *your* leanings? Someone has said that Tokk's beliefs are anarchical, but. . . ."

Tokk exclaimed proudly:

"Me? I am a superman"–which, if translated precisely, means "super-Kappa."

This Tokk had his own peculiar ideas about art. From Tokk's standpoint, art should have no control but should be art for art's sake. Consequently, he contended that, before anything, artists must be "supermen" who transcend good and evil. It must not, however, be assumed that this was only Tokk's opinion; it would seem that all of Tokk's poet colleagues had similar attitudes. Actually, I often went with Tokk to the "Superman Club," for amusement. Regarding those who congregated at this poet's club–there were poets, novelists, playwrights, critics, artists, musicians, sculptors and dilettantes. There were all manner of "supermen." They always conversed briskly in a salon brightly lit with electric light. Whereupon, Tokk would, by the way, triumphantly draw attention to their "superman" qualities. For example, there was the sculptor who was clasping a young Kappa among the devil-fern pot plants and was eagerly practicing sodomy. Again, a certain female novelist, climbing onto a table, bade us watch her as she imbibed sixty bottles of absinthe; but, what is more, when she had finished the sixtieth, she immediately tumbled off the table and was reborn in Paradise.

On one splendid moonlight night I was walking arm in arm with the poet, Tokk, as we returned from the Superman Club. Tokk was unusually crestfallen and not inclined to say a word. Soon we passed before a small window from which a light was shining. And, inside, facing the window, a husband and a wife Kappa were seated at a table with several children, having their evening meal. Tokk sighed and suddenly said to me:

"You know, I believe I am a super lover, but when I see such a family, I do nevertheless feel envious."

"But, if you really think about it, don't you think you are contradicting yourself?"

And Tokk, under the moonlight, with his arms folded firmly, gazed from outside that small window at the evening dinner table of the five Kappa. After a time, he replied:

"Whatsoever we say about those fried eggs, they are more nourishing than love affairs!"

6

REALLY, Kappa love affairs and human love affairs are, in large measure, different in purport. As soon as a female Kappa discovers a Kappa worthy of her, she does not pause to reflect on what measures she must take to ensnare the male Kappa; the guileless female Kappa recklessly runs in pursuit. I have actually observed a female Kappa running madly after a male Kappa. Not only that, the parents and brothers and sisters of the young female Kappa, of course, assist in the chase. The male Kappa has a wretched existence. Even after he has rushed hither and thither and has by good fortune managed to escape, he might even be confined to bed for two or three months afterwards. At one time I was reading Tokk's poems in my house when who should run in but the student, Rapp. He came stumbling into the house and fell onto the floor; gasping for breath, he said:

"Terrible! I've been ensnared at last!"

Instantly throwing down the book of poems, I locked the door, and peering through the keyhole, I found a short female Kappa—her face powdered with sulphur, still prowling outside the door. From that day, for some weeks, Rapp rested on my bed. Not only that, his beak entirely rotted and fell away.

And we cannot say that the male Kappa will not at times fervently chase a female Kappa. I also saw such a male Kappa who was wildly chasing a female; while the female Kappa was escaping, sometimes she would purposely stand and stare, or she would scramble on all fours and would just at the appropriate time—as if exhausted—allow herself to be caught. The Kappa I saw, embraced the female Kappa and for a while lay still. But at length, when I saw him stand up—was it despair?—was it remorse?—At any rate I cannot find the epithet to use—he did make a pitiful face. Still, that was not so bad. On another occasion I saw a small Kappa chasing a female Kappa; the female Kappa, according to custom, was making her enticing flight. Then, from the opposite side of the street, a big male Kappa came snorting. When the female Kappa saw this Kappa, she shouted in a shrill voice: "Help! Help!—this Kappa's going to kill me!"

Of course, the big male Kappa, immediately catching the little Kappa, pinned him to the middle of the roadway. The little Kappa, two or three times clutching at the sky with his webbed hands, ultimately expired. But while this was going on, the female Kappa was mewing and clutching tightly at the big Kappa's neck.

Of the male Kappa, each and every one of those I knew had been chased by female Kappa. Even Bagg, who had a wife and child, had also been chased. Only Magg, the philosopher–this was the poet Tokk's neighbor–had not been caught even once; perhaps this was because there was hardly a Kappa who was as ugly as Magg, for one thing; or, again, another reason might have been that Magg made a point of staying indoors and did not put his head into the thoroughfare. Sometimes I went to this Magg's place to talk. Magg, in a dimly lit room, where there was a seven-colored lantern, would be seated at a high-legged desk, with one of the bulky books it was his custom to read.

Once I discussed with this Magg the love affairs of Kappa.

"Why does the government not supervise more strictly the female Kappa's chasing of the male Kappa?"

"One reason is because there are few female Kappa among the government officials. As you know, the female Kappa, being the more jealous of the sexes, is the stronger; if only there were greater numbers of female government officials, then there might be a law against male Kappa being chased. But we are aware of how useless such a law would be. Why I say this is that even in official government circles, the female Kappa would chase male Kappa, you know."

"But to live as *you* do is happiest, isn't it?"

Then Magg, moving off the settee, clasped both my hands and said, with a sigh:

"As you are not like us Kappa, it is natural that you do not understand. You know, even I, for some reason, have the feeling that I want to be chased by those dreadful female Kappa."

7

OFTEN I went out to music recitals with Tokk. And I still have not forgotten the third music recital which I attended with him. Indeed, the appearance of the auditorium was not much different from those in Japan; and in the gradually sloping rows of seats three or four hundred Kappa–male and female–every one of them holding a program, were quite absorbed in listening. On the occasion of this third recital I was sitting in the front row with the poet, Tokk, his female Kappa and the philosopher, Magg. When the cello solo was finished, one odd narrow-eyed Kappa, a score-book indifferently clasped in his hand, jumped onto the platform. This Kappa, according to the printed program was the renowned composer, Craback. Craback was a member of the Superman Club to which Tokk belonged, so I knew him by sight.

"Ein *lied*–Craback," the program stated. Generally, even as is the custom in our country, the Kappa programs were published in German.

Craback, after just the one bow, went over and sat before the piano amid a storm of applause; nonchalantly he began to play his *lied*. If we are to believe Tokk, Craback had neither then nor before him a genius to match him among the country's natural musicians. As for me–as I was interested also in his hobby of writing lyrical poetry–I was inclined to listen enthusiastically to those reverberations from the grand piano. Both Tokk and Magg were even more enthralled than I. Only the beautiful female Kappa–

at least "beautiful" by Kappa standards—grasping her program tightly, stuck out her long tongue just as though she were out of temper. According to Magg, it was said that because she had missed capturing Craback about ten years previously, she probably still harbored resentment against this musician.

Craback, becoming impassioned, proceeded to play the piano as though he were fighting it. Whereupon, throughout the music hall, a thunderous cry echoed: "Performance prohibited!" I was startled by this voice, and unconsciously I looked behind. The owner of the voice was obvious to all—an imposing policeman in the far back row; as I turned around, the policeman, calm and relaxed, once more bellowed in a voice still louder:

"Performance forbidden!"

Then—

Then, from that point onwards there was utter confusion. "Police despotism!"—"Play, Craback! Play!"—"Idiot!" "Beast!" "Clear out!" "Don't be beaten, Craback!" Seats were upset amid the ferment of such shouting; programs flew everywhere; in addition empty cider bottles and stones and chewed cucumber came raining from all sides. Astounded, I tried to ask Tokk what it was all about. But even Tokk seemed to have grown excited; he had climbed up onto his chair and was calling out repeatedly: "Craback, Play!—Play!" And had Tokk's female Kappa meanwhile forgotten her enmity?—She was no less fervent than Tokk as she shouted: "Police tyranny!" In desperation I turned to Magg and inquired:

"What's it all about?"

"This?—In this country we often have this kind of thing. Fundamentally art and literature. . . ."

—When anything came flying Magg's way he would draw in his head a little.—

He continued:

"Fundamentally, whatsoever is expressed in painting and in literature, can be understood clearly; so, in this country their sale or exhibition is never prohibited. We do, however, ban performances of music that a Kappa with no ear cannot appreciate, *né?* It is not a question of whether or not music corrupts the people."

"But has that policeman an ear for music?"

"Well now—that's doubtful, isn't it. Perhaps while listening to the musical arrangement he was reminded of the beating of hearts when in bed with his wife."

In the interim the great tumult had increased all the more. Craback, seated at the piano, looked back at us arrogantly. But, in spite of his pride, he could not proceed, as he had no protection from the various objects that came flying at him. Consequently, every second or two he had to duck. Yet, with his narrow eyes flashing fiercely he did manage to preserve his pride as a great musician. In my case, of course, wishing to protect myself, I took advantage of Tokk as a shield; but as I was still curious, I continued to inquire of Magg:

"Such censorship is surely outrageous?"

"Eh?—No—it is more advanced than the censorship of any country. However, consider XX—actually only a month ago. . . ."

Unluckily for Magg, at the very moment he said this an empty bottle had fallen on his scalp; he let out a "Quack!"—this is only an interjection—and suddenly lost consciousness.

8

STRANGE as it seems, I had a liking for Gaël, chairman of the glass company. Gaël was an investor among investors. In all probability there was no other in the whole Kappa country who had such an outsized paunch as Gaël's. But with his litchi-like wife and cucumber-like children about him, seated in an easy chair, he looked almost a happy Kappa. I sometimes went out to Gaël's house for dinner, taking along Judge Pepp and the physician, Chakk. Taking with me Gaël's letter of introduction, I went to inspect a variety of factories which more or less had some connection with Gaël's associates.

What was of especial interest for me in those factories was the publishing house workshop I saw. A young Kappa engineer escorted me around this factory which I observed was operated by hydroelectric power. Gazing on the gigantic equipment, I admired the present-day advance in machinery in the Kappa country. I was informed that the total annual production of books was seven million volumes. In the publishing of so many books, not the least effort was expended. To produce books in that country, ash-colored powder and paper and ink were fed into the funnel-shaped mouth of the machine; about five minutes after these raw materials had been introduced into the machine, books in octavo, quarto, demi-octavo and other sizes were discharged in countless numbers. While I stared at the various books as they came flowing down like a cascade, I asked the Kappa engineer, who was proudly looking on, what the grey powder might be. And the engineer, standing in front of the glistening black machine, nonchalantly replied:

"Oh, that? That's asses' brains, you know. Well, to put it briefly, after they are dried they are ground into powder. The market price for one ton is two or three sen."

There was no reason, of course, why such industrial miracles should occur only in book publishing. Even picture book publishing and sheet music publishing functioned in the same way.

In fact, according to Gaël, a monthly average of seven to eight hundred different machines were invented; it is said that more and more heavy industry which does not require Kappa-power is being developed. As a consequence they say that it is not unusual for forty or fifty thousand workers to be dismissed at a time. Though I read the morning newspapers every day giving special attention to this matter, I did not even once encounter the word "strike." As I thought this was odd, I inquired about it on one occasion when I was invited to dinner at Gaël's house with Pepp and Chakk.

"They are all consumed, you know," said Gaël somewhat indifferently as he puffed at his after-dinner cigar. But I did not comprehend just what "consumed" referred to. Therefore, observing my obvious perplexity, Chakk, putting on his pince-nez, turned towards me and added a word of explanation.

"All those workers are killed off to provide meat. Have a glance at this newspaper. This month exactly sixty-four thousand, seven hundred and sixty-nine workers have been dismissed. For that reason alone the price of meat has dropped."

"And don't they offer any resistance to being killed?"

"It's of no use for them to cause a fuss, as we have the Workers' Slaughter Law."

These were the words of Pepp whose face looked pained behind the potted wild peach. To be sure, I felt uncomfortable. But, of course, Gaël the host, as well as Pepp and Chakk, thought that such situations were natural. Chakk actually laughed at me and said as if in ridicule:

"At least there is the fact that countless numbers are prevented by the State from dying of starvation or committing suicide. We simply administer a little poison gas to them, and they feel no great pain."

"But what you said about eating their flesh, . . ."

"We mustn't joke about it, although if you were to ask Magg, he would just laugh heartily. In your country, don't the low class women become prostitutes? To feel resentment about eating the meat of workers is mere sentiment."

Gaël, who was listening to this exchange, looked at the plate of sandwiches on the table and said coolly:

"Well, what about it?–Won't you take one? They're made of worker's meat."

I was, of course, nonplussed. That was not all; with Pepp's and Chakk's laughter behind me, I fled from the drawing room of Gaël's house. It was such a wild night that there was not even the light of stars shining in the sky above the houses. Returning to my dwelling in the midst of the darkness of the night, I vomited incessantly. My vomit glistened white in the darkness. . . .

9

But, without error, Gaël, the glass company chairman, was a kindhearted Kappa. Often I went with Gaël to his club where I would pass a pleasant evening. For one thing, unlike the style of the Superman Club to which Tokk belonged, it was certainly a comfort to go there. Furthermore, although Gaël's conversation, in contradistinction to that of the philosopher, Magg, did not have depth, it opened a new wide world to me. His sundry comments were spirited, and he always stirred his coffee with a spoon of pure gold.

One deep foggy night, I was listening to Gaël's chatter–a vase of winter roses between us. The whole room, I clearly remem-

ber, was in secession style, and there were slender gold borders
on the white upholstery of the tables and chairs. Gaël, a smile
beaming on his usually complacent face, talked about the Quorax Cabinet which had just at that time assumed power. The
word, "Quorax," had no meaning except as an interjection, so I
shall not go beyond translating it as "Oya!". At any rate, before I
proceed, I should mention that it was the political party which
had pledged itself to promote "The Welfare of the Kappa."

"The statesman who controls the Quorax Party is the famous
politician, Roppé. 'Honesty is the best foreign policy,' was what
Bismarck said, wasn't it? But Roppé extends honesty even to
internal affairs. . . ."

"But Roppé's policy speech . . ."

"Oh! Listen to what I have to say. His statements are, of
course, entirely false. But since everybody *knows* such to be a
lie, after all it's not dishonest, is it? To say that it's all a down-
right lie would be only prejudice on your part, don't you agree?
We Kappa, like you, . . . anyhow that's beside the point. What
I want to tell you is about Roppé. Roppé controls the Quorax
Party. Then again, Roppé is in turn controlled by the 'Pou-Fou'
newspaper. The term 'Pou-Fou,' is an interjection with no meaning, and if a translation is insisted upon, the closest we can get to
it is 'Aa!'.–The newspaper's General Manager, Quiqui, controls
Roppé. But even Quiqui cannot say he is his own master; he who
controls Quiqui is this very Gaël who is before you."

"But, if you will pardon me, the 'Pou-Fou' newspaper supports
the workers. If the Manager, Quiqui, also receives his instructions
from *you*, . . ."

"The journalists of the 'Pou-Fou' newspaper are, of course,
supporters of the workers. But the control of the journalists is in

the hands of Quiqui, and *he* can have no control that Gaël does not invest in him."

Gaël was laughing as usual and was toying with his pure-gold spoon. As I studied this Gaël, I did not hate Gaël himself, but my sympathy was aroused for the 'Pou-Fou' newspaper journalists. Gaël, from my silence, seeming rapidly to sense the direction of my sympathy, expanded his bulbous paunch and said:

"But, the 'Pou-Fou' newspaper journalists do not support all workers, you know. That is, we Kappa, before supporting anyone, support ourselves, you see. . . . But what makes the matter more troublesome is that Gaël himself is subject to another's control. Who do you think exercises that control? I am controlled by my wife–the beautiful Mme. Gaël, you know."

Gaël laughed loudly.

"That is rather fortunate, isn't it?"

"In any case, I am satisfied, but this is a fact I would reveal only to you–only to you who is not a Kappa can I be so frank."

"Therefore, the Quorax Cabinet is ultimately controlled by Mme. Gaël?"

"Just as you say, *né?* And the war we had seven years ago was caused by a female Kappa."

"War?–Did this country have a war?"

"We had! It could happen again at any future time–since we have neighboring countries. . . ."

This was the first time I had any inkling as to whether or not the Kappa country was an isolated nation. According to Gaël's explanation, the Kappa always regard the Otters as potential enemies. Moreover, the Otters are equipped with armaments not inferior to those of the Kappa. I felt profound interest in that war against the Otters.–Indeed, the novel information that the

Otters were a bitter enemy of the Kappa was known neither to the author of the work, "Of the Water Tiger," nor, it is certain, to Yanagida Kunio, author of "An Anthology of the Folklore of Mountains and Islands."

"Before the War broke out, both countries were, of course, patiently and surreptitiously spying on each other, with the result that each was equally fearful of the other. This was the existing state of affairs when an Otter visited a Kappa and his wife in this country. At the time the female Kappa intended murdering her husband, as the husband was a wayward fellow, you see; in addition, his life insurance policy might more or less have been a temptation."

"Were you acquainted with the husband and wife?"

"Well, not exactly. I knew only the male Kappa. My wife, too, had remarked that this Kappa seemed to be a rogue. But, rather than think him bad, there are—in my opinion—numerous insane Kappa who are victims of the obsession that they are being chased by female Kappa. . . . It was at this juncture that the female Kappa put potassium cyanide into her husband's cocoa; but, by some mistake, she presented it to the Otter guest to drink. The Otter, of course, died. Then . . ."

"Then war broke out?"

"Unfortunately the Otter was of some distinction, you see."

"Who won the war?"

"This country, naturally. Three hundred and sixty-nine thousand five hundred Kappa died heroically in battle. Yet, those losses were nothing at all compared with those of the enemy country. The furs in this country are almost all Otter furs."

"During the war, apart from manufacturing glass, I was sending cinders to the battlefield."

-"What is done with cinders?"

"They are used for provisions, of course. When Kappa are hungry, they are prepared to eat *anything*."

"Now–don't be offended, but the Kappa at the Front–well, in our country it would be a scandal."

"Even in this country it's not much different. Still, if we admit to it, nobody regards it as a scandal. You know, the philosopher, Magg, says, 'If the evil be confessed, of itself it is expunged.' What is more, apart from enjoying the profit, I was burning with patriotism."

Just then, the Club waiter came in. Having bowed to Gaël, as though reading from a book, he said:

"Next door to your house there's a fire!"

"Fire?–a fire?"

Gaël sprang up in surprise. Of course, I too rose to my feet. But the waiter added complacently:

"–But it's been extinguished."

As he watched the waiter retreating, Gaël's expression was between tears and laughter. Looking closely at his face, I felt the hate I had been harboring for this glass company manager. Now, Gaël–no longer the capitalist, but only an ordinary Kappa–was standing there. I plucked from the vase a winter rose and handed it to him.

"Even though the fire has been put out, your wife must surely have been scared. Then, take this with you and go home."

"Thank you."

Gaël grasped my hand. Then, suddenly grinning, he said quietly:

"The neighboring property is mine, you know. I'll at least get back the fire insurance money, I suppose."

I remember vividly Gaël's smile at that time—a smile I could neither despise nor hate.

10

". . . WHAT'S the matter?—again today you are looking a little strange, aren't you?"

It was the day after the fire. I was puffing at a cigarette and speaking to Rapp, the student, who was slumped in my drawing room chair. Actually, his right leg crossed over his left, Rapp was looking down at the floor, hanging his head so low that I could not see his rotting beak.

"Rapp—if I may ask—what is the trouble?"

"Ah, nothing—a trifling matter—really."

Rapp, raising his head at last, expressed himself in a sad nasal voice.

"While I was looking out of the window today, for no particular reason I happened to whisper, 'Ah, the insect-catching violet is in bloom.' Then, my younger sister, all of a sudden seeming to change color, said crossly, 'Well, I *am* the insect-catching violet, anyway. . . .' In addition, my mamma with whom my sister is favorite, snapped at me."

"Why did it make your sister unhappy when you spoke about the insect-catching violet blooming?"

"Oh, perhaps she took it to mean that it was time she caught the male Kappa, don't you think?—At that stage, Aunt, who is on bad terms with Mother, entered the argument; so it developed more and more into a great fracas. Then Papa, who is drunk the whole year round, overhearing the quarrel, came to blows with everybody irrespective of who they might be. That was not all, for before we had settled the matter, my younger brother ran off with my mother's purse and went to see a film or something. I ... truly, I too. . . ."

Rapp, burying his face in his hands, fell silent and wept. Naturally I was sympathetic. Notwithstanding, I was contemptuous of Tokk who was against the family system. Tapping Rapp on the shoulder, I did my best to console him:

"You shouldn't be defeated by such a situation. Do show some courage."

"But . . . but, if only my beak weren't rotting."

"You'll just have to resign yourself to that. Well, let's go to Mr. Tokk's house."

"Mr. Tokk holds me in contempt as I can't cast off my family as fearlessly as Mr. Tokk does."

"Then let's go to Mr. Craback's."

Since the musical recital I mentioned, I had been friendly with Craback, so I took Rapp to the musician's home. Craback–compared with Tokk–lives far more extravagantly. That is no reason, however, to think he lives like the capitalist, Gaël. He displays various curiosities, and seated on the Turkish-style settee beneath his own portrait, inside a room filled with Tanagra dolls and Persian-patterned ceramics, he was always playing with his children. But on that day, his arms folded over his breast, he just sat there with a pained expression on his face. What is more, discarded papers were scattered on the floor at his feet. Rapp, too, who with the poet, Tokk, had often met Craback, seemed surprised at his appearance and on that day, after bowing politely, silently sat down in a corner of the room.

"What's the trouble, Craback?"

Barely having paused to greet him, I thus questioned the poet.

"What's the trouble?!–those blockhead critics–they say my lyrics are not in the same class as Tokk's."

"But as you are a musician. . . ."

"If that were all, I would be tolerant. They even say I am not worthy of the title, 'musician,' as compared with Rokk."

The musician, Rokk, was often compared with Craback. Unfortunately, since Rokk was not a member of the Superman Club, I had not once spoken with him. But, his face–with its peculiarly turned-up beak–I had often observed in photographs.

"Even Rokk, without doubt, is a genius. But Rokk's music has not your overflowing modernistic fervor."

"Do you really think that?"

"I do, indeed."

Thereupon, Craback, getting quickly to his feet, grabbed a Tanagra doll and abruptly threw it onto the floor. Rapp seemed to be astonished beyond measure, and letting out a gasp, appeared as if he were about to run off. But Craback made a sign both to Rapp and to me not to be alarmed and then remarked coolly:

"Even you, too–just like those vulgar Kappa–have no ear! I am terrified of Rokk."

"Eh?–you are?–Do stop pretending to be modest."

"Who's pretending to be modest? If, in the first place, I am pretending to you, I am pretending before the critics. I–I am Craback, the genius. So, from this standpoint I am not afraid of Rokk."

"Then, of *what* are you afraid?"

"Perhaps it is some unknown entity–possibly the star which guides him."

"I don't follow you."

"Then, let me explain so you will understand, eh?–Rokk is not influenced by me, but, I have been subject to Rokk's influence at some time or other."

"As for that–your sensitivity. . . ."

"Ah, listen.–It's not a problem of sensitivity. Rokk works contentedly as only *he* can; whereas I get irritable. Well, looking at it from Rokk's point of view, I am not sure whether or not there is any difference. But to me there is ten miles of difference."

". . . But your masterly compositions?"

Craback narrowed his already narrow eyes and stared at Rapp in vexation.

"Don't say another word!–Have you any comprehension of such matters? I know all about Rokk. Even more than the dogs that prostrate themselves before him, do I know Rokk."

"Ah–you should calm yourself."

"If I were to calm down. . . . I always think in this way–some unknown nobody has cast Rokk before me to deride me. The philosopher, Magg, understands something of such problems, but he is always sitting under his colored lamp, forever reading battered old books."

"How so?"

"Take a look at this recent book written by Magg–'An Idiot's Words.' "

Craback handed me a book–or rather he threw it at me. . . . Then, folding his arms again, he suggested gruffly:

"Then please excuse me for today."

Rapp, whose dispirited mood had returned to him, accompanied me onto the thoroughfare. We walked along the street with its thronging traffic, and its variety of shops, and stood in the shade of the beech avenue, not saying a word. Whereupon, who should come by but the long-haired poet, Tokk. Looking closely at us, Tokk extracted a handkerchief from his belly pouch and wiped his forehead many times.

"Well, it's a long time since we've met; I am thinking of going to see Craback since I haven't been to see him for quite a while."

Thinking it unfortunate for artists to quarrel, I tactfully made mention to Tokk of Craback's ill-humor.

"Really?–then I'll dismiss the idea since Craback is in a state of nervous prostration. As I haven't slept for two or three weeks myself, I am feeling weak, too."

"How would it be if you took a stroll with us?"

"No, today I'll forego the pleasure if you don't mind.–Look!"

No sooner had he spoken than Tokk quickly and firmly grasped my arm. His body was suddenly bathed in a cold sweat.

"What's wrong?"

"Yes, what is it?"

"I thought I saw what could have been a green monkey poking its neck out of the window of that car!"

As I was more or less anxious, I recommended that he proceed to the residence of the physician, Chakk, for medical advice. But Tokk, no matter what I said, was in no mood to concur. Moreover, as if suspecting something, he looked from one to the other of us and even ventured to say:

"I'm never an anarchist, you know. That, at least, be sure not to forget.–Then, goodbye–excuse me with respect to Dr. Chakk."

We sank into reverie as we bade farewell to the departing Tokk.–"We"?–No! I should not write "we," for at some time or other the student, Rapp, having stretched his legs apart right in the middle of the street, was staring through his "thigh spectacles" at the unceasing flow of vehicles and pedestrians. I was astonished, thinking that this Kappa was daft as well; and I pulled him aside.

"Is this a joke?–What are you doing?"

But Rapp, rubbing his eyes, replied with unexpected composure:

"No, as I feel so gloomy, I was looking at the world upside down. But it is, after all, the same place."

11

THESE ARE excerpts from the text of Philosopher Magg's "An Idiot's Words:"

"A fool always believes that all are fools but himself."

"It is certain that our love of nature springs from the fact that nature is neither jealous of us nor hates us."

"The most intelligent way of life is to be contemptuous of the customs of the time, but still to live without in the least breaking them."

"What we want to be most proud of is what we do not have."

"Nobody has any objection to smashing idols. At the same time nobody has any objection to becoming an idol. But those who are the most idolized of gods–sitting cautiously on the pedestals of idols–are fools, rascals, and heroes."

(Craback had marked this paragraph with his fingernail.)

"According to our history, *thought* of any consequence possibly reached its zenith three thousand years ago. We would now but add a new flame to old kindling wood."

"It is one of our characteristics that we are in the habit of transcending our own awareness."

"If happiness be accompanied by pain, and peace be accompanied by boredom–?"

"To plead for oneself is difficult compared with pleading for others. People who doubt should be mindful of the lawyer."

"Pride, lust, suspicion–from these, various sins have sprung up for the past three thousand years; at the same time, too, in all likelihood, all manner of virtues."

"To diminish material desires does not necessarily bring peace. To gain peace we must even decrease spiritual desires." (Craback had left the trace of a fingernail on this, too.)

"We are not as happy as human beings! Humans have not reached as advanced a state of evolution as have Kappa." (When I read this paragraph I laughed involuntarily.)

"*To do* is to be able to do. . . . *To be able to do* is to do. After all, our lives cannot avoid this circular reasoning–that is, our lives are contradictory from beginning to end."

"After becoming insane, Baudelaire expressed his opinion of man in one word: 'Woman!' But we cannot judge the man himself simply by what he said. Rather, let us say that in relying on his poetic genius to be sufficient to support himself, he forgot the one word 'stomach.' "

(On this passage also, Craback had left the mark of his fingernail.)

"If we care to live a rational life from beginning to end, we must naturally deny our own existence. Voltaire, who made a god of reason, ended his life contentedly; this points, we may say, to the fact that human beings are not as advanced as Kappa."

12

IT WAS a comparatively cold afternoon. As I had become weary of reading "An Idiot's Language," I went out to visit the philosopher, Magg. Then, at a certain lonely street corner, I espied a Kappa as thin as a mosquito, leaning dreamily against the wall. And besides, it was, without mistake, the Kappa who had at one time stolen my fountain pen. As I thought this was a splendid chance, I called over a sturdy "policeman," who happened to be passing by.

"Please question that Kappa,—as just a month ago that fellow stole my fountain pen."

The "policeman" raised his truncheon in his hand.—In that country, police officers instead of carrying swords, carry truncheons made from yew branches.

"Hey, you!" he called to the Kappa. I thought perhaps that the Kappa might run away, but he walked quite composedly towards the "policeman." What was more, with arms folded, he stared rather arrogantly up into my face and at the police officer's. The officer, however, was not angry; taking his notebook out of his abdominal pouch he rapidly interrogated the Kappa.

"Your name?"

"Grukk."

"Occupation?"

"Until two or three days ago I was a 'postman.'"

"Good. According to what this man says, you stole his fountain pen."

"Hm—about a month ago I stole it."

"Why?"

"I thought it might make a good children's toy."

"And the child?"

At first the police officer poured sharp eyes over the fellow Kappa.

"Died a week ago."

"Have you the death certificate?"

Then the thin Kappa took a document from his pouch. When the police officer had scanned the paper, he suddenly burst into laughter and tapped his fellow Kappa on the shoulder.

"All right then, sorry to have troubled you."

As I was amazed, I stared at the police officer. And the thin Kappa, murmuring complaints to the officer, moved on behind us, and went his way. Finally taking myself in hand, I said to the police officer:

"Why didn't you arrest that Kappa?"

"He is innocent."

"But the fact that he stole my fountain pen—."

"It was for a child's toy, wasn't it? Now the child is dead. If you doubt my judgment, take a glimpse at Clause 1285 of the Crimes' Act."

After this exchange with the policeman, I abruptly left. As there was nothing I could do, I went off towards Magg's home, repeating to myself, "Clause 1285 . . . Clause 1285."

The philosopher, Magg, likes having guests. Actually, that day, there were also congregated in the dim room, Judge Pepp, Chakk the physician, and the glass company chairman, Gaël; tobacco smoke rose up from under the seven-colored glass lantern. The fact that Judge Pepp was there was most convenient for me. As soon as I had sat in a chair, in lieu of consulting Clause 1285 of the Crimes' Act, I forthwith questioned Pepp.

"Pepp, my friend, it's very rude of me, but in this country are criminals not punished?"

Pepp, calmly puffing forth the smoke from a gold-tipped cigarette, made a somewhat flippant reply.

"Not only do we punish them—there is even the death penalty."

"But only a month ago, I–."

After I had given all the particulars I asked about Clause 1285 of the Crimes' Act.

"Hm, this is what is written–'Howsoever a prisoner may have acted, after the circumstances which prompted the crime with which he is charged have ceased to exist, the said prisoner will not be convicted.'–At least, in considering the situation in which you were involved, there is the fact that the Kappa culprit was previously a parent and is now not a parent, so the crime is naturally expunged."

"That's quite irrational."

"You mustn't treat the matter lightly–eh? It is itself unreasonable to treat with the same consideration the Kappa who *was* a parent and the Kappa who is *now* a parent. Under Japanese law, however, both cases are considered in the same way. That to us is very funny."

Pepp threw aside his cigarette and gave an expressionless

laugh. Chakk, who had only the vaguest idea of legal matters, interrupted, adjusting his pince-nez a little. He directed the question to me:

"In Japan, too, do you have the death penalty?"

"We have—in Japan people are hanged."

As I more or less felt antipathy towards the coolly indifferent Pepp, I had taken the chance to be ironic.

"This country's death penalty is more civilized than Japan's, isn't it?"

"Of course it's more civilized."—Pepp was even more non-chalant—"In this country there is no hanging. On rare occasions we use electricity. Usually we just pronounce the name of the criminal."

"And that causes the Kappa's death?"

"Of course. The Kappa nervous system is delicate compared with that of humans."

"The method is not only for criminals. Murderers use it, too."

Manager Gaël's face, dyed purple under the colored glass lantern, showed an amiable, smiling countenance.

"I had a heart seizure because a certain socialist said I was a thief."

"Such cases are unexpectedly numerous, né? A certain lawyer I knew, even died after a similar experience."

I turned to the Kappa who had interjected—to the philosopher, Magg, who continued to disport an even more cynical smile, speaking the while without looking at anybody's face.

"Somebody called that lawyer Kappa a frog. You know, of course, that in this country to call a Kappa a frog is to insinuate he's a brute of a Kappa. Day by day, wondering if he really were a frog, he gradually pined away."

"After all, that's suicide."

"To be sure, the fellow who called that Kappa a frog, said it for the express purpose of killing him. Yet, if we look at it from your point of view, it is suicide. . . ."

Suddenly, just at the very moment that Magg uttered these words, from the far wall of that house—from the house of the poet, Tokk, it seemed—a pistol shot echoed, reverberating in the air.

13

WE RUSHED to Tokk's house. Tokk was clutching a pistol in his right hand, and from the bowl on his head blood poured out. He was slumped on his back, face upwards in the midst of the pot plants. And beside him, a female Kappa, her face buried in Tokk's breast, was loudly weeping. While holding up the female Kappa in spite of the fact that I did not relish touching the Kappa's slimy skin, I asked:

"What happened?"

"I don't know. . . . He was just writing something, and then for some reason he shot himself in the head.—Ah, what shall I do?— qur-r-r-r qur-r-r-r!"—she made the sound Kappa make when they weep.

"Tokk was rather selfish, wasn't he?"

It was glass company chairman Gaël, who, shaking his head sadly, said this to Judge Pepp; but Pepp was lighting a gold-tipped cigarette, not saying anything. Whereupon Chakk, who until then had been kneeling to examine Tokk's wound, struck an attitude worthy of a medico, and communicated to us five people (—in fact, to us four Kappa and one person):

"It's no use. . . . Tokk had chronic stomach trouble, and that alone would be reason enough for him to be melancholy."

"He was writing something?"

Philosopher Magg, as though apologizing in soliloquy, took up the paper on the desk. With stretching necks, all, with the exception of myself, stared over Magg's shoulder at the sheet of paper:

As for me, I shall arise and go,
To the valley far beyond this world
Where the walls of rock rise up sublime
And always is the mountain water clear–
To the fragrant valley with flow'ring herbs.

Looking back at us, with the wisp of a bitter smile, Magg said:

"This is taken from Goethe's 'Mignon.' . . . Tokk's self-immolation was the result of his weariness."

The musician, Craback, then happened to drive up in his car. Craback, observing this scene, paused in the doorway for a moment, and then walking over to us, called to Magg and said:

"Is that his Last Will and Testament?"

"No, it's his last poem."

"Poem?"

But then, Magg, without ceremony, handed the manuscript of Tokk's poem to Craback whose hair was topsy turvy. Without looking around, Craback read the manuscript with fervor. He hardly gave answer when Magg inquired:

"What do you think of Tokk's death?"

" 'As for me, I must arise!'–I, too, might also die at any time. . . . 'To the valley far beyond this world. . . .' "

"You were surely one of Tokk's friends?"

"Friends?–Tokk was always solitary."

" '. . . To the valley far beyond this world,'–only Tokk, unfortunate as he was, '. . . where the walls of rock sublime. . . .' "

"Unfortunate?"

" '. . . Mountain water clear. . . .' *You* are all fortunate. '. . . the walls of rock . . . sublime. . . .' "

I was sympathizing with the female Kappa who was still crying; gently embracing her shoulders, I took her to the settee in the corner of the room. Nearby was a Kappa of two or three years of age, laughing at I know not what. For the sake of the female Kappa I caressed the child Kappa; at sometime I know not when, I felt the tears welling up. While I was living in the Kappa country I shed tears neither before nor after that time.

"But to belong to the family of such a selfish Kappa is pitiful, eh?"

"He didn't even give a thought to what would happen afterwards."

Judge Pepp, lighting a fresh cigarette, made that characteristic reply to capitalist Gaël. Then we were startled by the musician Craback's loud voice. Craback, grabbing the manuscript of the poem, called out to nobody in particular:

"Superb! I can write a wonderful requiem!"

Craback, his slender eyes shining, seized Magg's hand for a moment, then suddenly dashed out the door. Of course, by this time, a great multitude from the neighborhood had come crowding around the door of Tokk's house, and were staring curiously into the room. Craback pushed aside the crowd as he made his exit. Thrusting the Kappa throng to right and left, Craback hastily drove off in his car. At the same moment as his engine was heard, he seemed to disappear.

"Hey, there! Really!–You mustn't stare like this!"

Judge Pepp, in the absence of a police officer, pushed out the Kappa crowd and slammed Tokk's door; and so, the room became suddenly hushed. In such quiet, amid the smell of Tokk's blood mixed with the perfume of the alpine flowers, we discussed the winding-up of Tokk's affairs. But the philosopher, Magg, only stared at the corpse of Tokk, in dreamy contemplation. Tapping Magg's shoulder, I asked:

"What are you thinking?"

"About the life of Kappa, *né*. . . ."

"What about it?"

"Whatsoever Kappa might say–Kappa life to be perfect. . . ."

More or less embarrassed, Magg added in a small voice:

"At any rate, we Kappa do believe in some power outside ourselves."

14

THIS UTTERANCE of Magg's reminded me of religion. As I am, of course, a materialist, I had not even once given any serious thought to religion. But, at this time, feeling the impact of Tokk's death, I pondered what the general concept of Kappa religion might be. I straightway asked the student, Rapp, about this problem.

"We have Christianity, Buddhism, Mohammedanism, Zoroastrianism, and others. The strongest religion, whichever way we look at it, would be the modern teaching–the 'Life Religion' as we call it."

–I do not know that 'Life Religion' would be a good translation. The original word is *Quemoocha*. *-Cha* gives the idea of the English suffix *-ism*. *Quemoo,* in its fundamental form, *quemal* would be translated by 'to go eating and drinking convivially and uniting sexually' rather than be translated simply by 'living.'"

"Then, have you churches and temples in this country?"

"Are you joking?–The modern sect's Temple is the largest in this country. How about us going there just to take a look at it?"

One cloudy, sultry afternoon, Rapp went with me for the sole purpose of visiting that Grand Temple. In truth, it was a building ten times the size of the Church of St. Nicholai in Tokyo. Furthermore that huge building combined into one style a miscellany of architectural features. As I stood before this Grand Temple, gazing on its lofty steeples and domed roof, I felt overawed. In fact, the towers pointing into the sky, seemed like countless feeling fingers. We stood still in front of the portal.–Compared with the porch itself, we were but tiny beings!–We remained for some time gazing up at that Temple that was an atrocious monster rather than a building.

And within, the Grand Temple was spacious. Among its Corinthian-style domes, several worshippers were meandering. And, like us, they looked tiny. Before long, we met a Kappa who was bent with age, and Rapp, nodding his head, politely addressed him:

"Aged sir, it is pleasing to see you're well."

With the utmost politeness, the fellow Kappa, bowing, replied:

"Thank you, Mr. Rapp.–You too, as usual–." He paused a moment in the course of his reply as he observed Rapp's rotten beak. "–In any case, you look well enough, eh? Then today, what is the purpose . . . ?"

"I came here today to bring this visitor. As you perhaps might know, this gentleman–."

From then onwards, Rapp chattered on about my affairs. This was probably because he was anxious to provide an excuse for his rarely having visited the Grand Temple.

"–So, I would be honored if you would do this gentleman the favor of guiding him around a little."

The old man, with a broad smile, first greeted me, and then pointed gently to the front of the altar.

"Though you ask for 'guidance,' I am no expert. . . . We believers worship that 'Tree of Life' on the altar. As you see, the 'Tree of Life' bears golden and green fruit. We say the golden fruit is 'Good Fruit,' and that the green fruit is 'Evil Fruit.' "

While this explanation was in progress, I had some feeling of boredom; the words of this bent old man even sounded like an old parable. Actually I pretended to be listening zealously. But, from time to time I did not forget to cast my eyes gingerly about the interior of the Grand Temple.

The Corinthian style columns, the gothic vaults, the arabesque chequered floor, the complex secession prayer stand–the harmony with which all was arranged presented a strange savage beauty. But what attracted my vision beyond all else were the marble busts within the tabernacle. I had a feeling those images were somewhat familiar to me, and I was not wrong in this. The decrepit Kappa, having completed his explanation of the "Tree of Life," walked over with Rapp and me to the front of the tabernacle and added a word of explanation about the busts.

"This is one of our saints–St. Strindberg who combated various evils. It is said that this saint, after a life of terrible suffering, was saved by the philosophy of Swedenborg. But actually, he was not saved. This saint, like us, believed in Life Religion. Otherwise he would have found nothing to believe in. you should read the book, 'Legender,' which this saint left to us; in it he has confessed the fact that he once attempted suicide."

Feeling a little gloomy at the turn of the conversation, I cast my eyes at the next niche. The bust in the adjacent niche was that of a fat moustached German.

"This is the poet-author of 'Thus Spake Zarathustra;' this is Nietzsche. This saint sought salvation in the 'Superman' which he himself had created. Yet, after all, he became insane without being saved. Probably, if he had not become insane, he would not be accounted a saint."

The old Kappa, after a short silence, guided us to the third niche.

In the third niche was Tolstoi. "This saint practiced greater self-denial than any. The reason for this is because this man—since he was of aristocratic origin—did not want to show his suffering to the curious mob. This saint endeavored to believe in Christ in whom we cannot really believe. He contended that he believed. But time and again in his later years he could not bear his tragic lies, it would seem, and it is true that this saint would often gaze with trepidation at the crossbeams in his study. But, he is numbered among the saints, though he did not, of course, commit suicide."

In front of the fourth niche the bust was that of a Japanese. When I looked on that Japanese face, as one might expect, I felt a nostalgia.

"This is Kunikida Doppo. He was a poet who clearly knew

the heart of the laborer who is run down and killed. But you undoubtedly need no further explanation.–Then, look in the fifth alcove."

"Isn't this Wagner?"

"It is! He was the revolutionary who was the colleague of a king. St. Wagner, late in life, even said grace before meals. But, he was a devotee of the Religion of Life rather than a Christian. According to the correspondence left by Wagner, he had to endure such terrible suffering in this world that many times over he came near to committing suicide."

Even at that moment we were standing before the sixth niche.

"This is a friend of St. Strindberg. He was a French painter– a one-time banker–who left his wife and children and took, instead, a Tahitian girl of thirteen or fourteen years of age. This saint had a sailor's blood in his coarse veins. But, look at his lips; arsenic or some such substance leaves its trace. And in the seventh alcove? . . . Already you are tired, *né*? How about coming this way?"

I was, in fact, tired, and so Rapp and I followed the old man as he passed through a corridor perfumed with incense to enter a room. In a corner of the small room there was an offering of a bunch of wild grapes before a black statue of Venus. Having imagined that it being the priests' quarters, this section would be totally unadorned, I was somewhat surprised. And, the old man seeming to sense my sentiments, before counseling us to take a chair, elaborated somewhat remorsefully:

"Do not overlook the fact that ours is a Life Religion. Our god–the 'Tree of Life' teaches us to 'live a full life.' Rapp, have you introduced this person to our Scriptures?"

"No, . . . the fact is, I myself have hardly read them."

Rapp, scratching the dish on his head, had replied with honesty. But the old man, unperturbed, quietly smiled as he continued his discourse.

"Then, perhaps you would not know of this. Our god created the world within a day—the Tree of Life is, in fact, a tree, and it is all-powerful; moreover, the Tree of Life made a female Kappa; the female Kappa found life tedious and sought after a male Kappa. Our god, pitying her misery, took the female Kappa's brain, and from it made a male Kappa. Our god gave his blessing to the two Kappa, 'Eat, copulate, and live a prosperous life!' "

Listening to the old man, I remembered the words of the poet, Tokk. Unfortunately, Tokk, like myself, had been an atheist. As I was not a Kappa, it was not unreasonable that I was not acquainted with the Life Religion. But Tokk, who had been born in the Kappa country, ought, of course, to have had a knowledge of the Tree of Life. As I pitied the fate of Tokk who had rejected this teaching, I interrupted the old man and spoke of Tokk's problem.

"Ah, the unfortunate poet, *né*?"

As he listened to what I had to say, the old man let out a deep sigh.

"The deciders of our destiny are Faith, Circumstance, and Chance.—You might, furthermore, add Heredity to these.—Unfortunately, Tokk did not have Faith."

"Tokk would have envied *you*. Yes, I also envy you. Rapp is still young. . . ."

"If only my beak were all right, I would probably be more of an optimist."

The old man sighed deeply and with tearful eyes, glanced over at the black Venus as he spoke to us.

"I, too, in fact–and this is my secret, so please do not divulge it to anybody!–I, too, in fact, cannot believe in our god. But, at some time or other, my prayers–."

The old man had hardly spoken.–Suddenly, the door of the room sprang open, and a big female Kappa thrust herself at the old man. Naturally, we tried to seize the female Kappa, but she had in the same instant thrown the old fellow onto the floor.

"You old rogue! You went off again today, with drinking money from my purse."

After ten minutes had transpired, keen to be away in fact, we left the old couple and descended the steps of the Grand Temple porch.

We had walked for a long time when Rapp said to me:

"There's reason enough for the old fellow not to believe in the Tree of Life, *né*?"

But, rather than reply to that, I unconsciously turned towards the Temple rising into the clouded sky–above all to the high towers and domed roof stretching up like countless feelers. Somehow the Temple floated like a weird mirage in a desert of sky.

15

ABOUT A WEEK after that episode I listened to some interesting information casually supplied by Chakk, the physician. There was talk that a ghost had appeared at Tokk's house. By then, Tokk's female Kappa had already gone somewhere else, and our poet friend's house had been converted into a photographer's studio. According to Chakk, it had been suggested that every time photographs were taken in the studio, Tokk's form emerged obscurely from behind the image of the person photographed.

Chakk is a materialist and does not believe in such things as life after death; as he told me this there was, indeed, a contemptuous smile floating over his face. "The spirit does seem, after all, to have a materialistic existence, *né?*" He added this by way of annotation. I did not differ from Chakk in that I did not believe in spirits, but, as I had had some affection for the poet, Tokk, I quickly ran off to a bookseller's and brought back the newspapers and magazines which had published articles concerning Tokk's ghost and carried photographs of the ghost. To be sure, on my examining the photographs, a Kappa very much like Tokk appeared, hovering behind old and young, male and female Kappa. But, rather than the photographs, what astounded me was an *article* concerning Tokk's ghost—a report by the Spiritualist Research Society dealing especially with Tokk's spirit. Having made a rather literal translation of the report, I shall present you with a summary of it. The assertions in parenthesis, however, have been added by way of explanation.

REPORT concerning the spirit of Mr. Tokk, the Poet, (Published in Journal No. 8274 of the Spiritualist Research Society). At No. 251 YZ Street, the former residence of Mr. Tokk, the Poet, who committed suicide some time ago,—which place has since become the studio of Mr. XX, the Photographer—our Spiritualist Research Society recently opened a provisional investigation. The members present were as recorded below. (Names omitted.)

Our seventeen members, together with the Spiritualist Research Society Chairman, Mr. Pekk, accompanied by our most reliable medium, Mme. Hopp, assembled at 10:30 A.M. on 17th September, in a room of the studio. Mme. Hopp, as she had felt the psychic atmosphere immediately on entering the studio, sustained convulsions throughout her whole body and happened to vomit several times. According to Madame, as a result of the Poet Tokk's extreme addiction to tobacco, the spiritual atmosphere, also, contained nicotine.

Our members were seated silently around the table with Mme. Pepp, who had abruptly fallen into a state of trance. After three minutes, twenty-five seconds, the spirit of Tokk took possession of Madame. As recorded below, our members, in order of seniority, began to question the spirit of Mr. Tokk which was appearing through Madame.

QUESTION: Why do you come forth in spirit?

ANSWER: To know of my posthumous fame.

QUESTION: Do you—that is, do spirit beings still desire fame after death?

ANSWER: I certainly wouldn't mind it. But one Japanese poet whom I have encountered is contemptuous of fame.

QUESTION: Can you tell us that poet's name?

ANSWER: Unfortunately I have forgotten. I remember only one seventeen syllable verse which he wrote and was fond of.

QUESTION: Then how about the poem?

ANSWER: "Furu iké ya
kawazu tobikomu
mizu no oto."
(An old pond,
A frog leaping,
—the sound of water!)

QUESTION: Do you believe it to be a masterpiece?

ANSWER: I think it's really not bad at all. Only, if he had selected a Kappa instead of a frog, it would have been still more dazzlingly brilliant.

QUESTION: Why so?

ANSWER: Because it is a poignant fact that we Kappa seek Kappa even in art.

The Chairman, Mr. Pepp, addressing us at this time, reminded us seventeen members that this was an extraordinary investigation meeting of the Spiritualist Research Society and not a convention of critics.

QUESTION: How about life as a spirit?

ANSWER: Spirit life is not different.

QUESTION: Then, do you regret your having committed suicide?

ANSWER: Really, I have no regrets. If I get tired of this spiritual life, I shall take a pistol and suicide back to life.

QUESTION: Is it easy for a spirit to suicide back to life?—or is it difficult?

Mr. Tokk's spirit matched this question with a question from his own side. To those who had known Tokk it was a strikingly natural repartee.

ANSWER: Is suicide easy or difficult?

QUESTION: Is your spirit life eternal?

ANSWER: There are so many differing opinions concerning the nature of our life that it is impossible to tell you which one is the right one. It should not be forgotten that, fortunately, there exist among us, Christianity, Buddhism, Mohammedanism, and Zoroastrianism, and various other dogmas.

QUESTION: In what do you yourself believe?

ANSWER: I am, as always, a sceptic.

QUESTION: Though that be so, you could hardly doubt the existence of spirits?

ANSWER: Unlike you, I do not entirely believe in them.

QUESTION: How large is your circle of friends?

ANSWER: My friends range from ancient to contemporary, Oriental and Occidental–not less than three hundred souls. If I were to mention the eminent ones, they are von Kleist, Mainläender, Weininger, . . .

QUESTION: Are your friends only those who have taken their own lives?

ANSWER: Not really. There are those, like Montaigne–who advocates suicide and is one of my respected friends. Only, there is a pessimist who did not commit suicide–Schopenhauer–I have no fellowship with *him*.

QUESTION: How is Schopenhauer doing?

ANSWER: He has established, for the present, spiritual skepticism, and is going on to discuss the advantages and disadvantages of suiciding back to life; but, he does appear awfully relieved that it has been proven that cholera is caused by bacteria.

Our members asked tidings of one soul after another–Napoleon, Confucius, Dostoyevsky, Darwin, Cleopatra, Buddha, Demosthenes, Danté, Sen no Rikyû and other spirits. Mr. Tokk was unable to reply in detail. On the contrary, he asked various items of gossip about affairs relating to himself.

QUESTION: How about my reputation after my decease?

ANSWER: A certain critic is asserting that you are one of the many minor poets.

QUESTION: He would be one who harbors enmity because I did not present him with a copy of my poems. . . . Have my "Complete Works" been published?

ANSWER: Your "Complete Works" have been published, but, it seems, the sales are not spectacular.

QUESTION: My "Complete Works" three hundred years from now—that is, after the author's rights have expired, ought to be in extremely high demand. . . . How about the woman who used to live with me?

ANSWER: She has become the wife of Rakk, the bookseller.

QUESTION: Unfortunately she would not know yet that Rakk has a false eye. And my child?

ANSWER: We have heard it is in a national orphanage.

After Mr. Tokk had been silent for a while he renewed his questioning.

QUESTION: How about my house?

ANSWER: It has become the studio of so and so.

QUESTION: What has happened to my desk?

ANSWER: We don't know anything about that.

QUESTION: I—I left a bundle of confidential letters in a drawer, but fortunately they have no connection with you very busy people. Now, in the spirit world, it is by degrees sinking into nightfall. I ought to take my leave of you. Farewell!—all. Farewell, my good people!

Finally, with these words, Mme. Hopp was suddenly aroused again.

WE seventeen members, swearing before the Almighty, do guarantee the authenticity of this interrogation. (Memorandum: We paid our reliable medium, Mme. Hopp, according to the remuneration to which, as an actress, she had at one time been accustomed.)

16

SUBSEQUENT to my reading that article on Tokk's ghost, as I became gradually depressed by the affairs of that country, I felt I wanted to return to the world of human beings. But, no matter how I searched, I could not locate the hole into which I had fallen. Some time afterwards, while chatting with the fisher-Kappa, Bagg, I heard from him of a certain elderly Kappa who spent his hours reading, and playing the flute; he lived quietly in this way on the outskirts of the Kappa country. As I thought I would never of my own accord find the way to escape from that country, I went speedily to the suburbs to make some inquiries of this Kappa. But when I reached the small house, I found no old Kappa, but only a tender-bowled Kappa–a Kappa of twelve or thirteen years of age, playing softly on a flute. Of course, I thought I had mistaken the house, but to make certain, I asked his name, and discovered that this was, without error, the same old Kappa to whom I had been directed by Bagg.

"But you are like a child. . . ."

"Would it be that you have not heard? It was my destiny that when I came from my mother's womb, I had white hair. Then, gradually becoming younger, I have now become the child that you see. But if I were to estimate my years, I would have been about sixty years old when I was born, so, by now I would be a hundred and fifteen or a hundred and sixteen years of age, or thereabouts."

I looked around the room. Amid the plain chairs and tables there was a prevailing air of chaste happiness.

"You seem to live more happily than any other Kappa?"

"Hm, that might be so. When I was young, I was old; and now I have become young. Consequently I do not thirst with greed like an old man; I am not even steeped in lust like a young man. At any rate, though throughout my life I might not exactly have found great happiness, I have, without doubt, been contented."

"Really?—that is comforting."

"No, that alone would not have been sufficient. I have enjoyed good health and have had ample property to provide a comfortable living for myself. But I think the happiest thing was, at least, that I was old when I was born."

For some time I talked with this Kappa about the poet, Tokk, who had committed suicide, and we talked of Gaël, who consulted his physician every day. It seemed from his demeanor that, for some reason, the old Kappa had little interest in what I was saying.

"You have no exceptional attachment to life compared with other Kappa?"

When the old Kappa had studied my face, he quietly replied:

"I, too, like other Kappa, was asked by my father if I wanted to be born into this country, whereupon I was delivered from my mother's womb."

"But in my case, by an impulse of chance, I fell into this country.–Now I want you to show me some way out–"

"There is only one road out–"

"What did you say?"

"–That is the road by which you came here."

When I heard this reply, my hair stood on end.

"Unfortunately I can't find that road."

The old Kappa, with youthful eyes, stared fixedly at me.

Then, at last, raising his body, he crossed over to a corner of the room and pulled on a rope that hung from the ceiling. Whereupon, a skylight–which I had not previously noticed–opened. And, outside that round skylight, branches of pines and oaks stretched up to the serene sky. Yes, like a huge arrowhead, Yarigataké peak reared up there above me. I was truly overjoyed, like a child who glimpses an airplane.

"Well!–you can go up through there."

As the old Kappa said this, he pointed to the rope dangling before us, and what until then I had thought to be a rope was, instead, a rope ladder.

"Then, I'll take my departure."

"Only, I warn you beforehand not to repent your leaving."

"It's all right. I shan't regret it."

As quickly as I had spoken, I clambered up the rope, and at the top I peeped down at the far-off bowl of the venerable Kappa's head.

17

HAVING RETURNED from the Kappa country, for some time, I was disturbed by the smell of human flesh. Compared with us humans, Kappa are clean skinned. Furthermore, the shape of human heads–to me who had long seen only Kappa–seemed somewhat unpleasant. I doubt if you will understand this, but human eyes and mouths, let alone the human nose, strangely aroused feelings of discomfort. Of course, as soon as I could, I devised ways and means to avoid meeting people, but I gradually seemed to become accustomed to my fellow humans, and within only six months I began to go out anywhere without concern. The only thing that troubled me was that, when I talked with anybody, the Kappa language came to my lips.

"Will you be home tomorrow?"

"Qua."

"What?"

"Ah, yes, I'll be home."

That was the general tenor.

But, after about a year had passed since my return from the Kappa country, I failed in certain business affairs. . . . (When the man broached this subject, Dr. S. cautiously told him to leave that topic aside. According to the Doctor, when the fellow talks about this subject he becomes so violent that the nurses cannot handle him.)

Then, I shall bring my story to its conclusion. . . . On account of certain business failures I decided I wanted to return to the country of the Kappa. That's the truth. It was not just that I would *go* there, but rather that I wanted *to return* there, as I had come to feel while I was there that the Kappa country was my home country. . . .

I quietly stole out of my house and took the Chûô Line train, but I was unlucky enough to be caught by a policeman, and at length, I was admitted to this institution. Even though I have been dragged off to this hospital for the time being, I continue to think about the Kappa country. . . . What is Dr. Chakk doing?– As usual, the philosopher, Magg, will probably be engrossed in thought under his seven-colored glass lantern. As for the student, Rapp, who happened to be my good friend–Rapp, whose beak had become rotten. . . . Then one cloudy afternoon like today, while I was absorbed in such reverie, I all but gasped. Howsoever it had come about, there poised before me was the fisher-Kappa, Bagg, his head nodding over and over again. After I had calmed myself, I do not remember whether I laughed or wept. But, in any case, after a long interval, what is certain is that I felt moved to use the Kappa language:

"Oi, Bagg, why have you come here?"

"Oh, I came to visit you. As it seems you have some ailment–"

"How did you know that?"

"I heard it on the radio news."

Bagg laughed exultantly.

"But how did you get here?"

"Nothing could be easier. The Tokyo rivers and canals serve us Kappa as high roads."

This put me in mind of the fact that Kappa, like frogs, are amphibious creatures.

"But there are no rivers in these parts."

"I managed to reach here through the iron pipes of the water supply. Then, getting out through the fire hydrant . . ."

"The fire hydrant?"

"Aren't you forgetting, sir?–there are mechanics among the Kappa, too."

Since then, every two or three days I have received visits from

Kappa. According to Dr. S. I am suffering from dementia praecox; but Dr. Chakk–this is certainly not being very polite to you–says I do not have dementia praecox, but that it is Dr. S. who has dementia praecox–and you people, too. Chakk, the physician, comes to visit me; also the student, Rapp, and the philosopher, Magg, have been here. But nobody comes in the daytime except Bagg, the fisher-Kappa. Especially if two or three come together, it is always at night–on moonlight nights. Just last night in the moonlight I talked with the glass company chairman, Gaël, and the philosopher, Magg. And that's not all, for the musician, Craback, has even played for me on his violin. Look at that bunch of black lilies on that desk over there–*né?* Craback brought it to me last night."

(I turned to look, but, of course, there was no bunch of flowers on the desk.)

"Then this book here, the philosopher, Magg, brought especially for me. Just take a look at the first poem.–Ah, no–you would not know the Kappa language. Then, I'll read it to you instead. This is a volume of Tokk's recently published 'Collected Works.' "

Spreading open an old telephone directory, he began to read in a loud voice the following verse:

–Among the palm flow'rs and the bamboo
Buddha is forever sleeping;
By the roadside's withered figs
Christ also, it would seem, is dead. . . .
But in the end we all must rest–
Sleep before the theatre scene.
(And if behind the scenes we glance,
there we find but patch'd-up canvas?)

"But, I am not skeptical like this poet. As long as Kappa keep visiting me—ah, one thing I have overlooked. You remember my friend, Judge Pepp?—after losing his post, he really went off his head. I have heard that in all probability he is now in the Kappa country's mental asylum. If Dr. S. will approve, I would like to go to visit Pepp, *né*?"

SAIGÔ TAKAMORI

Introductory Note:
When the Emperor Komei died of smallpox in 1867, the fifteen-year-old Mitsuhito, through the militant efforts of court nobles and the most powerful clans such as the Chôshi and Satsuma, succeeded to the Imperial Throne as the one hundred and twenty-second Emperor. Under the style of Emperor Meiji, partly as a reaction against the unreasonable treatment of the Imperial Household throughout many centuries, and largely because of the Emperor's progressive spirit, he set about winning the confidence of his subjects and reconstituting Japan as a democratic nation.

The most vehement opposition to extensive reforms came from the Satsuma Clan with headquarters at Kagoshima in Kyûshû, the Castle town of the Shimazu family. Already foreign powers had found the Satsuma clan aggressive in its determination to resist all foreign influence in Japan. Through his personality and courage and determination, Saigô Takamori became the leader of the Satsuma, and for some years served his country faithfully as a member of the progressive government.

At length Saigô became more and more disgruntled by the many instructions from Tokyo transmitted swiftly and effectively by a newly established postal service. It was irksome for samurai throughout Japan to subdue centuries of family pride when ordered by the Government to assume non-militant occupations or, alternatively to enter the newly constituted National Army, Navy or Police force.

Saigô had some two hundred cannon cast, using a Prussian cannon as a model, and bought rifles from European merchants. He armed over twenty-two thousand men. Although one can never be sure of anything in history, as this story– "Saigô Takamori" aims to expound, Saigô discovered a kinsman's (Okubo Toshimichi's) plot to assassinate him. At least what is certain is that General Yamagata received "orders" under Imperial Seal, though the Seal, it is said, might have been a forgery, to lead some sixty-five thousand men against Saigô. Prince Arisugawa was in supreme command of maneuvers to suppress the rebellion. (Curiously enough, Okubo himself was assassinated in the following year, 1878.)

During the battle of Shiroyama in the early morning of September 24th, 1877, Saigô was struck in the thigh by a bullet. History books record that he committed "seppuku" (suicide) and, at his own request, was simultaneously decapitated by one of his officers. Saigô's samurai retainers followed their master in suicide. (Seppuku is vulgarly referred to as harakiri–belly slitting.)

The posthumous honors which the Emperor bestowed upon Saigô Takamori were indications both of the honesty of purpose of Saigô who was known to have a deep understanding of bushidô, and of the wisdom and tolerance of the Emperor Meiji– for which qualities he remains, in the minds of the Japanese, Japan's most popular Emperor.

"Saigô Takamori" was completed on December 15th, Taishô 6 (1917).

THIS IS the story as told by Honma–by Honma who graduated two or three years before me from the Department of History at my University. Many would know him as the author of several intriguing discourses on the Meiji Restoration. When Honma and I were having a meal together, just a week previous to my removing my place of residence to Kamakura last winter, he happened to relate this story.

I do not know why, but I can recall the whole story vividly even now, so, in placing it on record, I shall here be fulfilling my assignment for the Editor of SHISHÔ-SETSU Magazine. I might add that, according to what I have since heard, this story of Honma's about Saigô Takamori is well-known among his various associates, and I have no way of knowing whether or not it is now known in even wider circles.

When Honma told me the story, he said: "You are free to hold your own view as to its authenticity." And, there is no need for embellishment of Honma's version. So, even if readers just glance through this article as though they have come across it in an old newspaper, I shall be content.

IT WOULD HAVE been perhaps seven or eight years ago. It was towards the end of March, when the first blossoms of the single-petaled cherry of Kiyomizu were gradually appearing. A little sleet would still have been falling with the rain and the nights bitter-cold. Honma, who was a university student at the time, sat in the dining car of the express which had left Kyôto at some minutes past nine; he had a glass of white wine before him and was dreamily smoking a M.C.C. cigarette. Having passed through Maibara shortly before, the train would undoubtedly be approaching the borders of Gifu Prefecture. As he looked through the windowpane, he saw that everything outside was enveloped in darkness. From time to time there would be a flickering light left behind as the train sped along; perhaps it was a light from a far-off house, or perhaps a spark from the funnel of the engine. Meanwhile, the sound of rain that had turned to ice, striking the windows, mingled with the resonant and monotonous echoing of the wheels of the train.

Only the previous week, Honma had taken advantage of the spring vacation to go alone to Kyôto to gather historical background leading up to and subsequent to the Meiji Restoration. But, on his arrival in Kyôto, he had become so absorbed in the various places he had wanted to visit, he had suddenly realized that there was not much time remaining before the next term's lectures were due to commence. He had visited the *Miyako Odori* (Kyôto dance), had been to shoot the rapids of Hozugawa, had gazed idly at Mt. Higashi and had come to feel ashamed of having thus spent his days. Honma had at last bestirred himself to pack hastily, and, because it was raining, the spruce figure in student uniform and cap took a jinrikisha from the entrance of the Tawara-ya Inn to the bus stop at Shichijô.

On boarding a second-class car of the express, he found it so crowded that he could barely move; through the good graces of the steward he was eventually able to find a space in which to squat but where it would be impossible to sleep. In such congestion, all the sleeping berths would undoubtedly have been reserved. For a long time Honma squatted–awake–between an army officer reeking of saké who had loins the size of ten bales of rice, and some woman who ground her teeth as she slept. With hunched shoulders he had given over his mind as best he could to youthful fancies, but even these had little by little been exhausted as the strong adjacent pressure had seemed to increase. It was then that Honma had been forced to get to his feet and, having left his cap in the empty space, had taken refuge in the adjoining dining car.

The dining car was deserted but for one customer. Making his way to a far table, Honma ordered a glass of wine. It was not that he really wanted a drink; he simply wished to fill in the time until he became sleepy. Thus, when the curt waiter had left before him that amber glass of wine, he let it pass his lips sip by sip and lit a cigarette. The tobacco smoke rose gently in little blue rings to hover about the electric lighting. Honma stretched his legs to full length under the table; for the first time that night he gave a sigh of relaxation.

Still, only his body was relaxed; his spirit was strangely sunken. For some reason, as he was sitting there, he suddenly felt the darkness beyond the windowpane closing in upon him. And soon, he felt that the plates and cups, well-arranged on the white tablecloths, were sliding in the direction in which the train was traveling. Gradually the sound of the teeming rain began to press heavily upon him. Feeling somehow insecure, Honma raised his eyes and involuntarily looked about the interior of the dining car. The cupboard with its mirror, the many burning lights, the rape blossoms in the glass vase–all these swaying things crowding in upon his vision, cried out to him inaudibly. But his attention was drawn to the table opposite, where, resting chin on hands, sipping a glass of whiskey, was the only other passenger in the car.

He was an old gentleman, somewhat grey, with flushed cheeks; his sparse beard gave him something of a Western appearance. On the bridge of his prim pointed nose, he wore metal-rimmed spectacles. The impression he created was altogether a graphic one. He wore a black lounge suit, and at a glance it could be seen that his clothing was by no means stylish. The old gentleman happened to raise his eyes at the same time Honma had raised his. Without precisely looking at Honma, those eyes did rove towards him. At that, Honma on an impulse called out a greeting.

Honma had acted in this way because of a feeling that he had seen the old gentleman's face somewhere before. Had he really seen the man?—or had he seen a photograph? He did not quite know. But he was certain that he remembered having seen the face before. Consequently, Honma turned over in his mind the various names of his acquaintances.

Then, while Honma was still preoccupied with these reflections, the old man rose, and struggling against the swaying of the train, strode over to him. Casually he sat down on the other side of the table and addressed Honma in a deep frank voice.

"Pardon me. . . ."

Honma's smile as he nodded in reply was noncommittal.

"Do you know me?—Perhaps you don't?—Anyway, it doesn't matter. You're a university student, aren't you?—an arts student?—I'm a similar kind of *merchant*. Perhaps we might even be in the same trade?—What are you specializing in?"

"History."

"Ah—history. You also are of the breed despised by Dr. Johnson.—Or, to quote Johnson's own words, 'Historians are no better than almanac makers.' "

As he spoke, the old gentleman threw back his head and laughed loudly. He seemed to be considerably intoxicated. Honma merely grinned without replying as he thoroughly surveyed his companion. The old gentleman wore a dark tie with his lounge suit. His waistcoat was threadbare in several places, but, suspended over it imposingly, he wore a thick silver watch chain; his clothing was by no means that of a poor man. This was evidenced by his collar and shirt cuffs which—freshly white—sat stiffly on his soft flesh. Possibly he belonged to the upper strata of scholars, and so was quite indifferent to his mode of dress.

"Yes, almanac maker!–There's much truth in it. To my way of thinking it poses an immense problem. However, be that as it may– And what is your particular field of research?"

"Restoration history."

"So the subject of your graduation thesis would be within that scope."

Honma rather felt he was undergoing a viva voce examination. In his own dreary mood it was as though he were being cross-examined by his companion's compelling manner of speaking and that he was caught up inextricably in this situation. Taking up his glass of white wine, he answered as though giving the matter some thought:

"I intend to make a study of the South-West Rebellion."

At that point, the old gentleman interrupted the discussion; he half turned about and ordered in a thunderous voice:

"Oi! Bring me another whiskey!"

And immediately again, he turned back to Honma and resumed his chatter–his eyes somewhat mocking behind his pince-nez.

"The South-West Rebellion?–That's interesting. I've done some research on that theme, too. Since I had an uncle who joined the rebel army and died in battle, I have done some excavating of facts on the basis of that association. I don't know whether or not you have conducted your research following the historical data, but the erroneous accounts of that skirmish are legion; and those erroneous accounts are widely-accepted as authentic historical data. When there is no great caution exercised in the accepting and discarding of material, one is inclined to commit unthinkable blunders. You, too, should be careful about this above all else."

Considering the other's attitude and manner of address,
Honma could not quite decide whether or not to thank him for
his advice. Feeling unsure as to what he should do, he sipped
the wine, and contented himself with obscure replies such as a
simple "Yes." The old gentleman, however, took no heed of the
replies. At this juncture, the old man moistened his lips a little
with the whiskey the waiter had brought, and extracting a porcelain pipe from his pocket, he packed it with tobacco.

"Please pardon me for saying so, but even for the cautious
researcher, the historical material about that conflict is, of all
historical data, the most unreliable."

"Really?"

Silently nodding, the old gentleman put a match to his pipe.
The foreign aspect of his face was accentuated by the red glow;
as the dense smoke curled about his sparse beard, there was a
pervading odor of Egyptian tobacco.

As he watched, Honma felt suddenly that for some reason
or other this gentleman provoked him. He was, of course, aware
that the man had been drinking and was inclined to talk at random. But as he had acquiesced to everything the man had said,
he was feeling ashamed for what the gold buttons on his uniform
represented.

"But I–I cannot believe the necessity for special caution. What
reasons do you have for thinking so?"

"Why?–it's just common sense, you know. In attempting to
compare–one by one–all available sources on the South-West
Rebellion, I have discovered a great many errors. Well, surely
that's enough.–Don't you think it's enough?"

"True. But, I want to hear those facts which you have discovered. A person in my position might find himself tremendously
assisted if made aware of them."

The old gentleman, puffing on his pipe, held his peace for a long time, as he stared out into the darkness beyond the windowpanes. He grimaced; then, out of the darkness and the rain, a station, where a number of people waited, dimly flitted past his vision. As he studied the face opposite, Honma felt like grumbling to himself, "Serves you right!"

The old man said:

"If only there would be no political consequences, I would be happy to talk—but in the event of this secret leaking out, Prince Yamagata would come to know of it. And, this would mean trouble not only for me—"

Engrossed in his thoughts, the old gentleman spoke without haste; then adjusting his pince-nez, he stared closely into Honma's face, and with searching eyes the old man was quick to detect the expression of disdain which floated there. Draining, with relish, the dregs of his whiskey, he suddenly moved his bearded face and thrust his liquor-smelling mouth beneath Honma's ear. His accent was almost biting as he whispered:

"If you promise not to divulge this, I'll give you an instance of what I mean."

Now it was Honma who frowned. The conviction flashed through his head that the old fellow was mad. But, having pressed the matter thus far, he thought it a pity not to hear the whole story. Though oppressed by the challenge, he was prepared to stand unflinchingly before it, with the dauntless spirit one finds in a child. Stubbing his cigarette butt in the ash tray, he squared his shoulders before saying clearly:

"No, I shan't divulge the secret, so you can tell me what is on your mind."

"All right, then."

The old gentleman puffed a dense screen of smoke from his

pipe, and his narrow eyes looked directly into Honma's face. Until then he had not paid sufficient attention to observe that they were not the eyes of an imbecile. Actually, though they differed from the eyes one is normally accustomed to, they betrayed a certain gentleness, and a smile forever lurked in their depths. From his silent observation, Honma felt a strange contradiction between those eyes and the speech and behavior of his companion. But the old man was, of course, quite unconscious of all this. The blue tobacco smoke weaved about and obscured the pince-nez, and as though following the progress of the vanishing smoke, the old gentleman threw his head back a little, and quietly severing his eyes from Honma, let them wander off into the distance while–as if muttering to himself–he poured forth these extraordinary facts.

"There is no limit to the various points which could be raised, so I shall mention one of the most significant errors–the fact that Saigô Takamori was not killed at the battle of Shiroyama."

On hearing this, Honma suddenly was overcome with mirth. He lit another cigarette, and with pretended earnestness he chimed in:

"Oh, really?"

There was little point in taking an interest in what the man would say after that. This one wild statement had revealed the real character of the old man's contentions. He was unconcernedly placing among the score of *misinformation* a fact well-accepted in the various historical references–the death in battle of Saigô Takamori at Shiroyama. This was absolutely crazy–one might as well make Yoshitsuné and Genghis Khan the same person or suggest that Hidéyoshi had been the illegitimate child of a nobleman. Here was a naïve old country bumpkin! Honma felt strangely irritated, and at the same time somewhat despairing of the issue, decided to terminate the discussion with the old man as soon as possible.

Then the old gentleman said:

"Not only did he not die on that occasion at Shiroyama.– Saigô Takamori lives to this day!"

Proud of what he had said, the old gentleman glanced at Honma who, as might be expected, had merely chuckled by way of reply to such a statement. His companion then, an ironic smile momentarily fleeting across his brow, deliberately questioned him in a quiet measured tone.

"So you don't believe me? No, we shan't argue. I can see you do not believe what I say. But–but it is true. Why do you doubt that Saigô Takamori lives to this day?"

"As you already have a special interest in the South-West Rebellion and have assessed the facts you would not, perhaps, wish to hear them from me, but, since you have asked me, I would like at least to tell you what I know."

Honma was gradually becoming indignant, and he resolved to make a drastic move to put an end to this farce. It was all so immature. Leaving aside any prefatory remarks, he certainly disputed the assertion about Saigô's fate at Shiroyama. It is hardly necessary to give a full account of the discussion which followed; let it suffice for me to state that Honma's citations were, as usual, factual and fairly thorough and logical. Simply to state that his facts were *conclusive* is enough. All the while drawing on the chinaware pipe–the smoke puffing, puffing–the old man took a keen interest in the argument but showed not the least indication of giving way. Behind his iron-rimmed pince-nez his small composed eyes overflowed with a tender brightness, though his smile was ironic. Again, those eyes strangely blunted the force of Honma's argument.

"Naturally, according to some suppositions, your contentions are correct, but–"

Having admitted defeat on this point, the old man conceded it calmly.

"–but those suppositions are, without doubt, based on Tsunéki Kajiki's 'Investigatory Records on the Seige of Shiroyama.' So I, who deny from the beginning such historical sources, strongly assert that your arguments are utter nonsense. But wait–one can argue from various angles about the truth of historical data. But I have proof which transcends the various historical contentions. What do you think that could be?"

Behind the twirling smoke, Honma had hesitated somewhat before replying, so the old gentleman leaned forward as he said solemnly:

"It is that Saigô Takamori is with us now riding on this train."

The imperturbable Honma was, as one might have expected, really amazed this time. Though his reason was threatened, still he did not lose his equanimity. Astounded, Honma took the cigarette from between his lips, and once more blowing out the smoke–though he spoke no word–stared with suspicious eyes at his companion's high-bridged nose.

"If we compare the 'facts'–as presented in your historical material–what do they amount to? Every scrap is worthless. Saigô Takamori did not die at Shiroyama. The proof of this is that he is riding at this very moment on our express in a first-class berth! Why is this not possible? Would you rather rely on what is set down on paper than rely on a living human being?"

"Ah–though you say he's still living, since I myself have not seen him I cannot believe."

"Since you haven't seen him?"

The old man, in a proud tone, repeated Honma's words, and he leisurely knocked the ash from his pipe.

"That's right–since I haven't seen. . . ."

Having recovered his self-assurance, Honma deliberately and coolly thrust forward his doubts once more. Yet the old man did not attribute any consequence to these doubts. As he listened, his attitude was one of confidence, and it was evident as he squared his shoulders.

"As he is riding on the same train, you can see him even now if you so wish. Still, by now Nanshû (Saigô) might be asleep. As he is in the first-class compartment adjoining this one, you have nothing to lose by going along to see."

As he said this, the old gentleman poked his pipe into his pocket and stood up wearily. With his eyes he signaled to Honma to follow. There was nothing for Honma to do but to accompany him. Then, a cigarette in his mouth, he thrust both hands into the pockets of his trousers and reluctantly left his seat. He strode behind the staggering old gentleman, between the two rows of tables, in the direction of the car door. The wineglass and the whiskey glass threw a thin semi-translucent shadow onto the white tablecloth; amid the sound of the rain beating on the window-pane, that lonely shadow trembled.

IT WAS ABOUT ten minutes later. The wineglass and the whiskey glass had been filled once more with amber liquid by the hand of the surly waiter. And that was not all. The old gentleman with the pince-nez and Honma in his student's uniform, sat around the two glasses as before. A fat man in *hakama* and a woman with the air of a geisha had entered earlier, and had sat down at the table opposite. They chattered on in Kamigata (Kansai) dialect, over the endless clack of cutlery as they picked at what looked like fried shrimp.

But Honma was happy and took not the least interest in the couple. This was surely because Honma's head was filled with the scene which he had just witnessed–a scene which must have astonished him when he had observed it. In the first-class compartment with its nightingale-brown seats and curtains to match, he had seen a corpulent mountain-like man, with a white beard, asleep there; and –ah! in that lofty countenance, surely enough– could it be by some mistake?–he had perceived the form of Nanshû–? Was it mere fancy that the electric lighting there was not as bright as it was in the dining car? But the lines about the eyes and mouth were clearly characteristic and demanded no closer examination. Yes, indeed, it was Saigô Takamori whom he had visualized since his childhood.

"Well then?–Do you still maintain your belief in his having been killed in the Shiroyama Battle?"

The old man's red face, with its flickering smile, called for Honma's reply.

Honma was perplexed. What was he to believe? Should he believe the countless historical records acknowledged by everyone? Or should he believe the countenance of that imposing elderly man he had just seen? To doubt the former would be to doubt his own head; to doubt the latter would be to doubt his own eyes. There was ample reason for Honma's perplexity.

"Do you actually–although you have now seen Namshû with your own eyes–do you still want to believe the historical data?"

The old gentleman, taking up his whiskey glass, continued in the tone of a lecture:

"First, ask yourself what are the historical references for which you have a predilection; then, examine them. For a while let's set aside the assertion of Saigô's death at Shiroyama. Generally the more critical our approach to history, the more we find that nowhere is there any reliable historical data. Anybody, recording certain facts must naturally, of his own accord, accept or reject, and having made his choice, proceed with his dissertation. Even when there is no *intention* to select, we cannot help but do this very thing. The significance of this is that, by such action alone, we have removed ourselves from our objective approach. Granted? In every trustworthy opinion there exists a host of untrustworthy aspects. There is the story that, for this very reason, Sir Walter Raleigh once threw away a manuscript on world history that he had written; this well illustrates what I mean. You, too, should appreciate that! In practice we cannot even judge the facts of something that has happened before our eyes."

To speak truthfully, Honma had no prior knowledge of this story about Sir Walter Raleigh; but from his silence, the old gentleman seemed to decide that Honma *did* know.

"–So, with regard to the compilation of certain records on Saigô's death at the Battle of Shiroyama, there is plenty of room for doubt. Still more, the Twenty-fourth day of September in the Tenth year of Meiji (1878 A.D.) at the Battle of Shiroyama was, according to the historical data, the day upon which Saigô died, but all they make clear is that a man *believed to be Saigô* died. Whether or not that person was the real Saigô Takamori is, naturally, another problem. Moreover, if we take the story that the head and headless body were located–as you said before, differing opinions are never scarce. If you do doubt this, then doubt!

While entertaining such doubts, you have met on this train Saigô Takamori, or else a person of striking resemblance to Saigô Takamori. Then, do you still believe the records of history?"

"But, *né*–it must certainly have been Saigô Takamori's corpse. Therefore–"

"There are under heaven many people resembling one another. To have a scar such as an old sword wound on the right arm is not peculiar to one person. Do you know the story of Ti Ching's examining the corpse of Nung Chih Kao?"

Honma then openly confessed that he did not know. Indeed, he, who had been perplexed all this while by his companion's strange logic and close familiarity with the various aspects, was gradually feeling something approximating respect for the pince-nez. The old gentleman then, taking from his pocket the chinaware pipe, leisurely puffed at the Egyptian tobacco.

"Ti Ching having pursued Nung Chih Kao for fifty *ri*, upon entering Ta Li, saw his enemy's dead body clothed in a golden dragon robe. Inferiors all said it must be the corpse of Nung Chih Kao, but Ti Ching alone would not listen. 'How can I be certain of this? Even though we find no further trace of Nung Chih Kao, I dare not curry favor by announcing his death at the Imperial Court!'–Not only was this worthy from an ethical standpoint; in his attitude as a seeker after truth those words are valuable. It is regrettable, however, that at the time of the South-West Rebellion, the general in charge of the Government Army lacked the prudence to be meticulous. So far as the details are concerned– 'possibilities' have been substituted for 'absolutes.'"

At length, Honma, who had had nothing to say, out of desperation made a last puerile confutation.

"But would there be people having such a striking likeness?"

Whereupon, for some reason or other, the old gentleman took

from his mouth the chinaware pipe, and choking with tobacco smoke, burst into laughter. His laughter was so loud that the geisha at the table opposite turned around and looked in their direction with a bewildered expression. Yet, the old gentleman did not stop laughing. With one hand supporting his pince-nez that was likely to fall off, and holding the lighted pipe in the other, he kept on laughing–deep gurgling laughter. As Honma had no idea of the reason for the outburst, he set down the wineglass and only stared blankly at his companion's face.

"There are!" replied the old man, taking his time to regain his breath.

"–You have just seen the person sleeping there. That man is like Saigô Takamori, isn't he?"

"Then–that man, who is that man?"

"He?–That's my friend, *né*. He is a medical practitioner by profession; besides that, he paints *namga*."

"Then, he isn't Saigô Takamori?"

Speaking with such seriousness, Honma's face suddenly reddened. The humorous role that until then he himself had played suddenly appeared in a new light.

"If you are offended, do forgive me for talking to you; as you have so many youthfully honest thoughts, I was inclined to be a little mischievous. It was indeed a practical joke; but what I have *said* has been no joke–that's the sort of person I am."

The man, after searching in his pocket, presented his card to Honma. There was no degree printed after the name; but Honma, after just a glance at the card, was at last able to associate the old man's face with the name on the card. The old gentleman beamed at Honma–his smile one of satisfaction.

"I did not dream who you were, Professor. I have said many rude things, for which I am put to shame."

"A while ago, we were discussing authoritative references to Saigô's death at Shiroyama. If you were to adopt a tone of doubt in your graduation thesis, it can be made worthy of interest, eh? Even at my own university, there is one student this year specializing in the Restoration.–Mah!–let's leave this discussion aside and have another drink."

The rain and sleet seemed by then to have eased off, as there was no sound on the windows. The fat man and his lady companion had left the car, and the only thing remaining to attract Honma's attention was the glass vase with its rape flowers disseminating their faint perfume through the brightly lit dining car. Honma drained the wineglass with obvious enjoyment; his cheeks were tinged with color when suddenly he said:

"Professor, are you not a sceptic?"

The old man's eyes behind the pince-nez indicated assent. But all the while there was a bright smile behind the assent.

"As an ardent disciple of Pyrrho, I am satisfied that we cannot really be sure about anything, even about ourselves. One such vagary is Saigô Takamori's survival or death. So, in compiling a history, I do not think I could write a history which would be altogether truthful. Therefore I must be satisfied to write the most probable account of history. When I was young, I thought I wanted to be a novelist. If I had become one, I would naturally have written novels. It might even have been a better proposition than my being an historian. At any rate, I *am* content to be a sceptic. You think so, too, don't you?"

THE GREETING

Introductory Note:
The setting of "The Greeting" is Yokusuka, a Japanese naval
base until the end of World War II, and now an antarctic whal-
ing base and one of Japan's most prosperous fishing ports. Now
the train travels the distance between Tokyo and Yokusuka in
an hour and a half and provides the first stage of travel on a
tour of the Miura Peninsula.
  The author completed the story in September of Taishô 12
(1923).

YASUKICHI has just reached his thirtieth year. Like most other
literary journeymen, he lives in a whirl. So he thinks of *tomorrow*
but seldom of *yesterday*. But, while walking along a street, while
working on his manuscript, or while riding on an electric train,
it sometimes happens that he vividly recalls a past scene. His
experience has been that almost always such scenes have been
awakened in his mind by some stimulus upon his sense of smell.
The stimuli to the sense of smell, for those who regrettably live
urban lives, are invariably offensive odors. For example, nobody
ought to care for the smell of soot or smoke from steam loco-
motives. In his case, however, whenever he smells such an odor,
the memory of a certain young lady, with whom he came face to

face five or six years ago, flashes upon his mind like sparks of fire shooting up from the chimney.

It was on the station platform at a summer resort that he used to see this young lady. At the time he was living at the summer resort; and, whether rainy or windy, he used to catch the down-train at eight o'clock and alight from the up-train at four-twenty in the afternoon. The reason for his taking these trains daily is a matter of little concern. Riding on the same train every day, he very soon became familiar with a dozen or so faces. The girl was one of these. But from the afternoon of the seventh day of January to the twentieth day of March or later, he does not remember having seen her once. In the mornings the upbound train on which the girl rode had no connection with that on which Yasukichi rode down.

The girl would have been between sixteen and seventeen years of age. She was always dressed in a silver-grey suit and a matching hat. Though she was short of stature, she was slender. Particularly her legs, in their silver-grey stockings with which she wore high-heeled shoes, were as slight as those of a deer. Her face was not that of a beauty, but—Yasukichi had still to find a paragon of beauty in the heroines of modern novels whether of the East or the West. In portraying women, authors almost always make some excuse, such as: "She was not beautiful, but . . ." The acknowledgement of flawless beauty apparently hurts the dignity of modern man. Therefore, even Yasukichi added the proviso, "but—" as he repeated over to himself his opinion of the girl: *the face was not that of a beauty,* but *she had a winsome round face* with the tip of her nose turned slightly upwards.

Yasukichi, at the sight of her, did not remember his heart having throbbed as is written in love stories. He thought only that it was natural for her to be there, as was the case when he saw the familiar face of the Commandant of the Naval Base or the cat from the newsstand. Nevertheless, her familiar face attracted him. So, when he did not see the girl, he felt somewhat disappointed, even if it were not a keen sense of loss. Actually, he felt much the same disappointment when the newsstand cat had been missing for a few days. If the Commandant had suddenly died or something of the sort–well, then it might have been a little different, but again not much different from when the cat was missing, though surely he would have felt that such an event would be a little out-of-the-ordinary.

It was a humid cloudy afternoon about the twentieth day of March when it happened. That day as usual Yasukichi, having fulfilled the day's commitments, took the four-twenty train. As far as he vaguely remembers, he was probably too tired after poring over his work, to do any reading on the train as he would normally do. He does remember that while leaning against the window frame, he was looking out at the hills and fields which were beginning to take on the genial array of the coming spring. A certain Western novel which he had read described the sound of a train running across plains as "Tratata . . . tratata . . . tratata," and that of a train crossing an iron bridge as "Trararach . . . trararach." Indeed, as he listened listlessly, could he not hear such sounds? He recalls that such was the trend of his thoughts.

After a weary thirty minutes Yasukichi at last alighted at the summer resort station. The downward train had pulled into the station a little earlier. Caught up in the crowd, he happened to be staring at the people getting off the other train.–There, unexpectedly, he saw the girl. As I have already mentioned, Yasukichi had never come across her in the afternoon. Like a cloud filtering the sunlight, or like the blossoms of the pussy willow, her silver-grey figure appeared unexpectedly before him. *Oh dear!*–he thought.

At the same instant the girl also appeared to have caught sight of *him*.

Quite spontaneously Yasukichi bowed to the girl!

The girl to whom he had bowed must have been surprised. Unfortunately he no longer remembers how she had looked then. He was too flurried to observe the look in her eyes. *I've done it!*– he thought and was conscious of his ears burning. But this only he remembers–that the girl had acknowledged his greeting.

At last, after he had left the station, he felt annoyed at his own stupidity. What had prompted that rash bow? It was purely a reflex action. It was just like blinking one's eyes at a flash of lightning. He could not be held responsible for a deed which was beyond his control. But the girl–what would *she* think? Well, she had returned his greeting. That too, however, might have been a reflex action at the moment of her surprise. Very likely she might now be thinking of him as a ne'er-do-well. Instead of swearing to himself he should have been apologizing to her for his grossness, but he had not thought of it at the time.

Instead of going back to his boarding-house, Yasukichi went to the deserted beach. This was not a unique thing for him to do. Whenever he became bored with his humdrum existence–his five yen per month lodgings and his fifty sen lunches–he would often sit on the sand, smoking his Glasgow pipe. This day, looking out over the sea under the cloudy sky, he put a match to his pipe. There was nothing he could do about the day's episode. But, on the morrow he would be sure to come face to face with her again, and what would the girl do then? If she thought he was a rake, naturally she would not even glance at him. But, if she did not think so, on the next day, again, as on this day, she would perhaps respond to his bow.–His bow? Would he– Horikawa Yasukichi–nonchalantly bow again to that girl? No, he would not feel like bowing. But now that he had bowed the one time, some chance might occur for them to greet each other again, and if they did so, . . . Yasukichi happened to recall that the girl's eyebrows were beautiful.

Today, after a lapse of five or six years he remembers with a strange distinctness only the balmy calm of the sea on that occasion. Yasukichi remained looking vacantly out over the sea for a long time, holding in his mouth his pipe, unlit. His thoughts were not on the girl alone. For instance, he thought of the novel which he was going to set about writing soon. The hero of that novel was to be an English language teacher imbued with a revolutionary spirit; renowned for his inflexibility he would be unbending before all authority, except there would have been one time in his life when he had absent-mindedly bowed to a girl whose face seemed familiar. Perhaps that girl had been of short stature; but seemingly she had been slender–especially about the legs in their silver-grey stockings with which she wore high-heeled shoes. At any rate, it was probably true enough that his thoughts had been conquered by that girl. . . .

The next morning at five minutes to eight, Yasukichi was pacing up and down the crowded platform. While on the one hand he was full of the expectation of seeing her, on the other hand, he was of half a mind to try to avoid her. But he knew that he really did not wish to avoid meeting her. Perhaps his anticipation was not different from that of the professional boxer when he is about to face a strong opponent in a match. But, what could not be forgotten was his sickening fear that, when he did come face to face with the girl, he might do something which would exceed the bounds of common sense. Once Jean Richepin had audaciously kissed Sarah Bernhardt, who happened to be passing by. As a Japanese, Yasukichi would surely not attempt a kiss, but he was afraid he might commit some other breach of courtesy, such as winking. Feeling nervous, at least he half-tried to look for her and half-hesitated.

Then suddenly, his eyes discovered the form of the girl walking leisurely towards him. In his encounter with fate, he kept on walking straight ahead. The two came close together in no time–ten steps–five steps–three steps–until she was just before his eyes. Raising his head, Yasukichi looked her full in the face, while she, too, looked steadily at *him*. The two, having come face to face, tried to pass by without incident.

It was just at this instant that he perceived some quavering in her eyes, whereupon he was seized with an overpowering impulse to bow. There was no premeditation in this–it had happened within a moment. The girl passed quietly onwards, leaving behind a startled Yasukichi. Like the clouds which filtered the sunlight or like the flowering pussy willow. . . .

Twenty minutes later found him jolting in the train, his Glasgow pipe in his mouth. Not only did the girl have beautiful eyebrows–the pupils of her eyes were of a cool blackness; her somewhat tilted nose, . . . but, to be thinking of such things– might that be called *love?* He does not even remember what he answered in his mind to this question. All that he remembers is the glimmer of sadness that assailed him at the time. While watching a curl of smoke rise from his pipe, he continued to think about the girl in this melancholy strain. Meanwhile, the train was running through a gorge in the mountains, one wall of which was bathed in the morning sunlight. . . .

–*Tratata . . . tratata . . . tratata . . . trararach.*

WITHERED FIELDS

Introductory Note:
This story is not so much concerned with Bashô, the poet, him-
self as with Bashô's disciples. The disciples and samurai who
witnessed his last moments were all preoccupied with their own
affairs throughout their vigil, so it was not much different for
Bashô than if he had died a lonely death in withered fields.

Bashô had felt the onset of illness since he had left Edo on
May 11th, and had become considerably weaker during his
subsequent travels through Nagoya and the Kansai district,
visiting his disciples here and there. News of his illness was
widely bruited about the countryside, so it is not surprising that
so many disciples could journey from far off provinces to Osaka
to pay their "respects."

At least they had the intention *of paying their respects,*
but were to discover in "the fleeting moments" before Bashô's
passing, that to mourn for another is not much different from
mourning for one's self. Is this, then, a story of the conscience
of honest souls? Rather, we ourselves have read it as a story of
Bashô's triumph in art even at the moment of death. It could
be said that all the haiku written by Bashô were mirrors of
life as he actually saw it passing, except for this one "farewell"
haiku, which was written in anticipation of his experience at

*the moment of death. It was an accurate prophecy which, when
fulfilled, moved each disciple according to his own character.*

*In pursuit of such a theme, Akutagawa has bequeathed to us
one of the most profound stories ever written.*

*"Withered Fields" ("Karénoshô") was written in September
of Taishô 7 (1918).*

LAST NIGHT when I slept not, having turned over in my mind a
verse, I summoned Jôrô and Kyorai, dictated the verse to Don-
shû, and had them recite it.

> Ill while traveling,
> My dreams go wandering
> in the withered fields.
> *–the Hanaya Diary*

The Twelfth day–the Tenth month–the Seventh Year of the
Genroku era (A.D. 1654) .... Far-off above the tiled roofs, the
passing glow of morning sky, as if it threatened wintry showers,
drew the drowsy eyes of the merchants of Osaka. But fortunately,
there was no rain to mist the tops of the denuded willows, and
with the thinning of the clouds, the quiet winter's day bright-
ened. And the river, though it flowed betwixt the rows of houses,
seemed still–the floating onion waste not moving on its waters–
and its pale color was somehow not cold. And the people passing along the banks–round-hooded people–people wearing
leather *tabi*–all moved lightly as though unmindful of the chill
movement in the air. The color of *noren* (the shop-curtains), the
traffic of vehicles, the sound of a distant samisen from a puppet
theatre–were so peaceful in the glimmer of that quiet winter's

day, that the city dust reposing on the bridge's ornamental posts was undisturbed.

On that day at Midomae Minami-Kyûtaro-machi in a rear room of the house where Hanaya Nizaemon lived, the respected Matsuo Tosei widely known as Bashô–*haiku* Master of the time, lay prostrate on his back, attended by disciples who had come from far and near. His years but fifty-one, quietly he would soon withdraw his living breath, "even as the warmth of buried coals declines." The hour did barely exceed four-thirty in the afternoon. The dividing *fusuma* had been removed from the commodious room where blue smoke rose up in one long streak from incense being burned at the pillow-head. Only in this room, filtering through the paper on the newly pasted *shôji* (sliding papered screens) which shut out the winter reigning in the garden, was the light gloomy, chilling our bodies, piercing our bones. Ranged about Bashô who lay peacefully on his side by those *shôji* doors was, first, Mokusetsu–physician–with one hand thrust between the coverlet to feel the fluttering pulse–a frown upon his rigid brow. And crouched behind, feebly calling Buddha as he prayed, was Jirobê–the old servant who had come journeying from Iga with the Master. Also quite near Mokusetsu, one well-known in the eyes of all, was Shinshi–big, burly Shinshi Kikaku swelling the bosom of his pongée coat as he watched over the Master, together with Kyorai, dignified, square of shoulders in his *kempô*-dyed coat. Behind Kikaku, was Jôsô, looking like a Buddhist priest, linden rosary entwined about his wrists, and his posture appropriately constrained. Next was Osshû who was unable to refrain from sniffing as his grief surged forth; and keenly watching Osshû's grief, as he adjusted the sleeves of his old priestly garments, was one, small like a child in build, his unsociable chin turned to one side. This was Inenbo, who sat facing Mokusetsu, and abreast of swarthy, obstinate Shikô. As well as these, however, there were many disciples sitting to the right or left of the Master's bed—all were breathless, loath to take their leave. There was only one at that time who, kneeling in a corner of the room, lamented in a voice too feeble to disturb the faint flow of incense at the pillow-head. Not long before, in a hoarse and spluttering voice, Bashô had uttered his quavering last words; then, his eyes half-opened, he seemed to lapse into a coma. On his lightly pockmarked face, the cheekbones were sharply drawn, and his wrinkled lips had paled long before. But it was the color of his eyes that was especially sad—eyes dreamily glazed; and it was as if they aimlessly sought beyond the ceiling of the room the limitless cold sky.—"Ill while traveling, my dreams go wandering in the withered fields." And now he, too, perhaps—as in his last *haiku* of but several days before, was aimlessly wandering in moonless dreams through those vast twilit fields.

"—Water," said Mokusetsu and quietly turned around to Jirobê. The old servant had the bowl and *hanéyôji* (feather brush) in readiness, and he gently pushed the two utensils towards the pillow of the Master; then, as if reminded of it, once more he swiftly began to yield up his undivided mind to fervent prayers for Bashô's soul. In his guileless country-bred heart, this man, Jirobê, would have keenly sensed his obligation to seek the Mercy of Amida Buddha for Bashô and for all who passed to Nirvâna—so deep was his belief.

At the very moment he had asked for the water, Mokusetsu, the physician, had begun to doubt, as always, that he had fulfilled his rôle, but soon again Bashô rallied, and with no word, gestured to Kikaku who sat by his side. The feeling of strain which had flickered in the sympathetic hearts surrounding Bashô's bed,

WITHERED FIELDS

deepened then. At the same time, however, into that tense atmosphere crept also a sense of relief that this unavoidable moment of destiny had come. Still, none acknowledged it–so delicate that feeling of relief that even the forthright Kikaku was taken aback at reading the same feeling of relief in Mokusetsu's eyes when he and Mokusetsu had happened to exchange glances. Hurriedly he averted his eyes, as he took the *hanéyôji* with composure.

"Allow me," he said, with a bow to Kyorai seated beside him, and then, dipping the *hanéyôji* into the bowl of water, he edged forward on his fat legs and peered down at the Master. If we speak the truth, Kikaku must have imagined that to bid farewell to the Master would surely be a sad affair, but as he took the water to perform this last rite, contrary to his expectation of the dramatic nature of this act, his actual feeling was one of indifference. Furthermore, when he saw how strange beyond expectation his Master appeared, he was aroused to abhorrence and wished only to turn his eyes from that deathbed–so enfeebled were the Master's bones and flesh. Though we say it was *abhorrence*, that still does not explain it, for as an unseen toxin exerts power over the functioning of the body, so it was a type of repugnance difficult to bear. Was it then through this whim of chance that he poured forth upon the Master's dying flesh his own antipathy to all forms of ugliness?–But here–in his own sweet joy of *living*, here was death–and by its very nature menacing his thoughts. In any case, such was his inexpressible discomfort that no sorrow lurked in his heart for the wan face of the dying Bashô; so, Kikaku, when he had moistened those thin purple lips, hastily slid back–a grimace on his face. And in that moment of retreat, a feeling as if of self-reproach shot through his heart, but too intense, no doubt, was his abhorrence of Bashô for him to heed the ethics of it.

299

It was Kyorai, already wavering, his self-composure lost it seems, who next to Kikaku took the *hanéyôji* in response to Mokusetsu's signal. For him who had ever earned a modest name, after discreetly nodding to them all, there must have been an unsavory taste as he looked on the face of the prostrate and emaciated old *haiku* poet—a strange mixed feeling in him of satisfaction and remorse. But that satisfaction and remorse, like shade and sunlight, bore with them a destiny that had entangled him; since some days before he had felt it humbling him. That is, as soon as he had news the Master lay so ill, he had straightway come there from Fushimi, hastening to Hanaya's place, irrespective of the depths of night, and knocking on the gate, had all day long not once neglected to attend the Master's needs. Besides, he had entreated Shidô to assist him and had sent a man to the Sumiyoshi Daimyojin Shrine to beseech prayers for the recovery of the Master. And he had conferred with Hanaya Nizaemon concerning the purchase of various requisites; he became in every way almost like a cartwheel, assisting where he could. And, of no account was it, as he had thus given of himself, that others were obliged to him. And yet, in his absorption in his care of the Master he had sowed warmly and deeply in his heart some satisfaction. Indeed, that alone in the background of his conduct, as a latent source of satisfaction, gave to him the impetus of natural movements not once impeded; and were that not so, this man would not have gossiped as he had done when he and Shikô had been keeping vigil by the light of a paper lamp; fleeting and indulgent chatter it had been, when he had stressed what filial duty really meant, and that his loyalty to the Master was in a sense like that he bore towards his parents—so had he long reminisced. But in the midst of his elation he perceived on the perverse Shikô's face, a derisive smile, and this smile which had

flickered once awakened discord in his heart. And he discovered
the root of this discord was that very satisfaction with himself
which he had begun to criticize. And still, on the following day
as he took care of the Master, so gravely ill with an unknown ailment, his very anxiety for that condition gave him cause to look
upon his own efforts with satisfaction. Truly then, in him–an
honest man–such satisfaction with himself must doubtless arouse
feelings of shame. Since then, Kyorai's every action was inhibited
by the incompatibility of this *satisfaction and remorse*. And when
by chance he had seen his own smiling face reflected in Shikô's
eyes, Kyorai became all the more conscious of his self-satisfaction
and consequently felt even deeper disgust with himself. Many
days, however, it had been thus. Fastidious in morals as he was,
and also frail of nerves, this day while beside the Master's pillow,
administering those last rites, he lost all composure; in the face
of such a contradiction in his heart, not without some reason did
he feel regret. Therefore, when taking up the *hanéyôji*, oddly his
whole body stiffened; and, as he touched with the moistened tuft
the lips of Bashô, his agitation was so strange that he trembled in
his eagerness. But, happily, just then beads of tears spilled from
his eyelashes as the disciples watched; so all of them, even caus-
tic Shikô, would have thought that his agitation stemmed from
his grief.

At length Kyorai, once more squaring the shoulders of his
kempô coat, shuffling, went back to his place–the *hanéyôji* he
passed to Jôsô who was behind him. This old and faithful one,
with eyes modestly cast down, murmured indistinctly as he gently moistened Bashô's lips; there was a solemnity about Jôsô. But,
at this austere moment, suddenly from the corner of the room,
laughter–galling laughter–burst forth. Ah, no!–from the belly's
pit a loud laugh rose up, rose up, was damned at the throat and

lips, until, unable to be suppressed, it broke piecemeal through the nostrils. But, we need hardly say, there was no real laughter. Curbed until it burst overflowing from his breast, it was the lamentation of Seishu who had been given up to tears. Unmistakably it was the expression of tragic grief. And there would have been scarcely one among the disciples there who was not reminded of the Master's famous *haiku*:

The grave moves—
our weeping
like autumn winds.

Affected by the grim atmosphere climaxed by Seishu's lamentation, Osshû, who was similarly stifled by tears, felt his displeasure arising towards exaggerated emotion—or, if this is not an apt expression, then, towards his own lack of will-power to restrain himself from breaking into loud weeping. Such an unpleasant state could occur only when emotion was tempered by intellectual reasoning. So, his intellect, and not his heart, being moved by Seishu's sudden display of grief, his eyes began to brim with tears. But even while he looked down on Seishu's lamentation as a sign of weakness, and his own tears as shameful, he was forced to acknowledge his *own* weakness as he gave way to emotion. Hands on his knees, the tears welled in his eyes and he began to sob. But, by that time not only Osshû had given way to tears. Simultaneously, it seems, from among the disciples drawn up about Bashô's bed, intermittent sniveling disturbed the chill gloom of the room.

Amid these sounds of distress, Jôsô quietly moved back to his place; his linden rosary was wound about his wrists. Then, after him, Shikô, who had been facing Kyorai and Kikaku, made his way up to the Master's pillow. Shikô Tôkabô was well-known as a cynic, and so it was not to be expected that the surrounding atmosphere would tempt him to tears. As always, the expression on the face of the dark-complexioned man was a mocking one; and when he bent artlessly to touch with the *hanéyôji* feather the Master's lips, that strange perverseness was still in evidence. But even *he* made no attempt to combat the deep emotion of the moment. "In my mind my wind-pierced bones exposed in weatherbeaten fields."–Some days before, the Master had expressed his gratitude to us: "Lying on the grass, making the earth my pillow, I expected to die; but now on such *futon,* soft as this, that I can gain this way my dearest desire–that is more wonderful than any other thing." But it did seem that room of Hanaya's was not so different from the *withered fields*. And, he thought: as *I* was moistening the Master's lips I recalled that I had felt, when he had uttered those words, that they would be his last. And even but the day before I had been planning in my mind a posthumous collection of the Master's *haiku*. And finally until this day, until this very moment, I had watched–my eyes investigating as though I had an interest in his progression towards death. And now it was ironic for me to find that I was not beyond taking the further step of contemplating that some day I would write of the dying moments of the Master. While attending upon the Master, the anxiety in my mind impinged, not directly on the Master's death, but on the consequences of that death–the repute of other schools–the interests of the other disciples there–and, too, my own self-interests. And, as from time to time, Bashô had contemplated the boundless withered fields of human life, so now the field in which he was himself exposed was just as desolate.

We, his followers, did none of us mourn the Master's passing, but mourned *ourselves* who lost a master. Not grieving that our Master met his death in *withered fields*, we grieved only for ourselves who had lost our Master in the dusk. But, as for moral blame–how can we attribute any blame to those of us who are by nature heartless? And thus, submerged in such pessimism even while he was exulting in it, his task of moistening the Master's lips completed, Shikô returned the *hanéyôji* to its place beside the water bowl and then glanced scornfully around at those disciples who were choking with their tears; and by easy movements he went back to his place again. Just as the amiable Kyorai, when confronted by Shikô's indifferent attitude, had been overwhelmed by insecurity, so, the fact that Kikaku's face effected a strangely enigmatic expression seemed to indicate that he was somewhat bothered by Takabô (Shikô) whose nature it was to look on all things with indifference.

After Shikô it was Inenbo who trailed the hem of his black Buddhist robe over the tatami mats. He crawled forward slowly, too scared to look, for the Master's dying moment was imminent. The pale complexion of the Master was even further drained of blood, and sometimes no breath was expelled from between the moistened lips–as if he had forgotten how to breathe. And then, as if remembering once more, his throat would expand to let pass his feeble breath. Then, from deep down in his throat several times there was a faint gurgling of phlegm. His breath, all the while became more sluggish. So, Inenbo, who was about to touch those lips with the white tip of the *hanéyôji*, was suddenly seized with dread. The groundless fear, which was unrelated to his sorrow at the leave-taking of his Master, that *next to die* might be himself, pressed close. But, inasmuch as it was unreasonable, once thrust forward there was scarcely sufficient self-control to resist the fear. This man had an ingrained fear of death, and even when he made his customary pilgrimage, he had always been abnormally sensitive to this dread; and at such time he would experience a strange fear, and his whole body would be bathed in sweat. So, when he heard of others' deaths–in that it was not *he* who died he felt somewhat secure. But, again, if he dwelt on what would transpire when he did die, conversely this man would feel anxiety. The circumstances surrounding Bashô provided no exception. While Bashô had not been so near to death, . . . but when a bright winter's sun had beamed upon the *shoji*, and the narcissus, a gift from Sonojô, had poured forth its fragrant odor, and all then present had crowded around the pillow of the Master, there to compose *haiku* to console the Master in his illness–he, too, according to the circumstances, had composed *haiku* while balancing between the twofold feeling of relief and fear. He had not forgotten the first cold wintry day of rain, when Mokusetsu had anxiously inclined his head as he had observed that the Master would not even eat the pears he so favored; then, relief had merged with uneasiness, and soon uneasiness had spread its somewhat chill and gloomy shadow of terror throughout Inenbo's soul–as if he were to be the next to die. Therefore, sitting by the pillow while he faithfully moistened the Master's lips, Inenbo was cursed by the evil spell of such a fear; almost, it seemed, he could not look upon the Master's face in that last moment. No–only once it seemed he was about to look straight at him; in that same moment in Bashô's throat there was the faint sound of clogged phlegm, and even as he glanced it seemed–halfway–his courage fell away.–"Next to the Master it is *I* who'll die!" His eardrums were inflicted constantly with that premonitory voice; and his slight body cowering as he resumed his place, Inenbo's harsh face was even harsher in avoiding others' eyes as he turned his own eyes upwards.

Following Inenbo–Osshû, Seishu, Shikô, Mokusetsu–and all others present made their way in turns to wet the lips of the Master. But, as the number dwindled, so Bashô's breathing grew fainter and fainter. The throat no longer moved; the thin pockmarks, somewhat like wax on that small face, the faded color of the eyes gazing into distant space, the silvern beard extending from the chin–all was frozen into lifelessness, and his soul was dreaming, so it seemed, of the heaven whither it was bound. And then, in the place behind Kyorai, Jôsô, that old and faithful Zen devotee hung his head as he felt flowing within his heart unlimited sadness and unlimited comfort–flowing by degrees as Bashô's breath became fainter. We need waste no explanation on the sadness, but the comfort–it was, so to speak, a strange serenity like the cool light of dawn spreading in the darkness; moment by moment, worldly thoughts were cast off, and as might be expected, even his tears changed to a chaste sadness which did not in the least afflict his heart. Was it that he rejoiced that Bashô's spirit had transcended the vain desires of life and death and was returning to the supreme bliss of the eternal Nirvâna? Nay, there was a further reason which he could not acknowledge. If so, was there any person who should hesitate long enough that he dare commit the folly of deceiving himself? Jôsô's comfort was in the joy of release. With the resurgence of his unfettered strength, which gradually spread through its confines, his spirit was free of that vain submission to Bashô's strong personality. And in the rapture of that ambivalent joy and sadness, as though by then unaware of the other disciples sobbing around him, on his lips a faint smile curled as if all grief were vanished; fingering his rosary, reverently he paid homage to the passing of Bashô.

In such a way it happened that Bashô, the greatest *haiku* master, unprecedented in ancient or in modern times–Matsuo Tosei– enveloped in "the boundless grief" of followers who mourned his passing, suddenly began his journey towards death.

ABSORBED IN LETTERS

Introductory Note:
Takizawa Bakin (1767–1848), author of "Yomihon" and "Kusasôshi," is one of the few Japanese classical authors known among Western readers. His works have been widely translated into English, French, Italian and, to a lesser extent, several other languages. He was a prolific writer and became the nucleus of culture and education of his time. He died in his eighty-second year (November 6th of Kaèi 1) leaving some two hundred and twenty-eight volumes which still have a substantial following among the Japanese. His works might be compared with the "ukiyo-é" of art–the "floating" or "fleeting" style which must surely have provided his illustrator, the renowned Hokusai, with boundless inspiration.

Bakin's early life was difficult. His father, a steward to the Matsubira family, died when Bakin was nine years of age. Bakin had two elder brothers and two elder sisters. Because of obduracy, Bakin's attempts to serve his father's master were fruitless. Earlier he pursued interests in medicine, teaching, professional fortune-telling and satirical poetry, but without any success. He married the daughter of a shoe merchant and for a time, to relieve him from the rigors of his poverty, earned a meager living as a scribe. Having inherited his mother's fancy for literature, he devoted long hours to reading fairy tales, fiction, "jôruri" (ballad-drama), military annals, and "haikai" (verse). In the autumn of his twenty-fourth year (Kansei 2 –1790) he begged assistance from Santô Kyôden (1731–1816), an illustrious fiction writer, and in the following spring was admitted to Kyôden's house as assistant and apprentice.

The balance of Bakin's career is evidenced by the catalog of his many masterpieces, the most popular of which is believed to have been "Nansô Hakkenden" ("The Eight Dogs of Nansô") written between Bunka 11 and the closing year of Tempô (1814–1841) through twenty-eight years–a work consisting of some three thousand pages.

Even in his old age when beset with blindness, when his daughter-in-law, O-Michi, was obliged to act as his amanuensis, he persisted in his fervor for being "absorbed in letters."

"Absorbed in Letters" was completed in November of Taishô 6 (1917).

I

IT WAS a certain morning in September of the Second year of Tempô. From early morning at the Matsu public bath in Dôbôchô, Kanda, there had, as usual, been many customers. Shikitei Samba, in a humorous book published several years earlier had written, "deities, Buddha, love, heartlessness–all are visitors to the public bath," and a description of such a spectacle would, even today, remain unchanged. In the bath, the *kakâtabané* (merchant) who sings popular songs, the *honda* style (high top-knot) coiffure who wrings out his towel on the landing stage of the bath, the round forehead of the *ô-ichô* (samurai) who pours water over a tattooed back, the *yoshibéyakko* (low top-knot) just now wash-ing her face, squatting on her buttocks before the water trough, the bald head who pours an incessant stream of water over him-self, the *abuhachi-tombo* (dragonfly) lad absorbed in playing with a bamboo pail and ceramic goldfish–in the narrow confines of the bathing room these various wet bodies glisten like glass as the morning sunlight pierces the window and shines obscurely through the dense morning vapor. There are many noises con-tributing to the clamor. First, there is the splashing of hot water in the bath, and there is the sound of the moving of pails; there is chattering, and there is singing. Sometimes the wooden clappers sounded by the bathkeeper can be heard. So, inside and outside the bathtub screen, all is quite noisy, like a battlefield. Stooping to pass under the *noren,* opulent merchants come–beggars come. There are always customers going in and out. In that confusion–.

Having modestly sought out a corner away from that confu-sion, an elderly man all of sixty years was quietly washing away the dirt. Sixty?–he would have been well over sixty. Between his unbecoming yellowed side-locks, his eyes even seemed a little faded. Though he was sturdy, his bones were accentuated by his thinness; and, on his hands and feet the skin had slack-ened; everything about him indicated a strong resistance to the decline of age. His face matched his body; from the prominent cheekbones to the tightly drawn jawbone, around the line of his somewhat large mouth, the abundance of animal virility, still amazingly apparent, indicated his lingering prime.

The man scrupulously cleaned the dirt from the upper parts of his body and not pausing to sluice himself with water from the wooden pail, proceeded to wash his lower limbs. The silkiness of the black washcloth, with which he had rubbed himself over and over again, cleansed the greasiness from his exceedingly wrinkled skin, though the dirt that he wiped from his body could hardly be called such. Perhaps he was suddenly aware of autumn's loneliness, for having washed each leg–as though he had wiped away his strength, the hands that held the towel came to a standstill, and he let his gaze fall into the soiled hot water of the pail in which the sky from beyond the window was clearly reflected. A sparse branch of red persimmon, revealed under the projecting tiled roof, was also captured in the reflection.

In this aging man's heart hovered the shadow of *death*. But *death* having once threatened him seemed to have nothing formidable to conceal. Rather it was that the sky in that pail quietly stirred in him a longing for the comfort of Nirvâna. Released from all soil and toil, if he could sleep in that *death*–if he could sleep, dreamless, like an innocent child–that would be a wondrous thing, so weary was he of living. Over many decades he had come to feel the ennui of unceasing creative work. He was tired. . . .

In his dejection, the man raised his eyes. Quite near him were the animated voices of many naked people moving about in swirling steam. Inside the bath gate a voice swelled into a popular theatrical song. Not a shadow of the image of eternity that was reflected in his heart was to be discerned in the mirth and singing in the bathhouse.

"Ah, *Sensei*–little did I realize I would meet *you*. Somehow, I would not have dreamed that Kyokutei Sensei (Bakin) would be here for a morning bath!"

The elderly man was suddenly jolted by the voice that called his name. He saw beside him a fine-complexioned *hosoichô* (merchant) of medium stature; the man set down a wooden pail, and a wet towel hung over his shoulders. He broke into a hearty laugh as he climbed out of the bath and was about to give himself a final sluice with clean water. Smiling, Bakin Takizawa Sakichi answered somewhat cynically:

"It is good to see you in your usual good spirits."

2

"THANK-YOU, but I'm by no means in good spirits. Still, to revert to something that *is* good, your 'Tale of the Eight Dogs' is becoming more and more interesting, *Sensei;* and, what is more it's quite an achievement...."

The *hosoichô* proffered this opinion in a loud voice as he dipped his towel into the tub.

"... Funamushi, disguising herself as a blind street singer, has it in mind to kill Kobungo but is finally apprehended and tortured; but she is rescued by Sosuké from ill-treatment! The plot is, in fact, an exquisite one. And, again, as Sosuké and Kobungo chance to meet a second time—well, although I'm only Heikichi of the fancy-goods shop, I am still a tolerable connoisseur of *yomihon* fiction. Even I—even I am sure that your 'Tale of the Eight Dogs' is beyond criticism. In fact, it is extraordinary!"

Bakin again washed his feet and deigned no comment.... Towards the readers of his works he had always felt goodwill, but that goodwill did not influence his evaluation of the people who read his works. To Bakin in his wisdom, this was natural, but it was strange that, on the contrary, his estimation of people had hardly any *influence* on the goodwill he might feel towards them. Hence at the one time he was able to feel both contempt and goodwill towards the same person. The fancy-goods man, Heikichi, was just one such reader.

"To have written the great work would surely have been no easy task. To begin with, *Sensei*, you could be said to be the contemporary Lo Kuan Chu of Japan. . . . Excuse me for expressing my humble opinion."

Heikichi had again spoken loudly, laughing with alarming boisterousness.

A slightly-built man pouring hot water over himself—a squint-eyed *koichô* (top-knot) turned around to look from Heikichi to Bakin. Screwing up his face, he spat into the stream of water.

Bakin adroitly changed the course of the conversation.

"You would be absorbed as usual in writing *haiku* verse?"

It was not that the squint-eyed man's expression had influenced Bakin, as Bakin's eyesight was fortunately (?) weakened to such a degree that he could hardly see his squint eyes.

"I am deeply grateful for your interest in just a clumsy side line of mine.—Today a *haiku* gathering, tomorrow a *haiku* gathering—at several places here and there I do brazenly—impudently—compose verse—but, what should I say?—versification is by no means an easy task for me. At times, *Sensei*—well, how is it with *you*?—don't you have any especial interest in composing lyrics and *haiku*?"

"No, I have no special aptitude for such pursuits. Nevertheless, I used to compose them at one time."

"Ah—you are joking!"

"No, *haiku* verse is uncongenial to my temperament—it's like trying to see through a fence."

In saying it was *uncongenial*, Bakin had spoken with emphasis. It was not that he thought he *could not* compose lyrics and *haiku*. Rather he was confident of his understanding in that field and sure that he was not lacking in dexterity; but he had had for such various forms of expression a long-standing contempt. This was because, in order to pour one's whole self into the composition of lyrics and *haiku,* too much formality was required, and he felt such media insufficient for adequate expression. Howsoever cleverly one might compress one's thought into verse, such a medium could express but a part of one's feelings and descriptive powers. Such art was, in his opinion, of an inferior quality.

3

BENEATH his emphasis on the word *uncongenial* lurked his contempt. But, unhappily, the sundry goods vendor did not seem to be in the least aware of Bakin's deeper meaning.

"Ah ha!–that would be so. According to the convictions of such as me–I know that such a school of writing as *Sensei's* abides no restrictions, but–it is well said that *one man is not twice gifted."*

After this show of deference, Heikichi wrung out his towel and rubbed his body until the skin became red. But to Bakin, in whom the spirit of pride was a dominant one, the fact that he suffered those words with humility was wholly unsatisfactory. Besides, Heikichi's tone of seeming deference displeased him more and more. He half raised his body and threw his towel and washer onto the floor; he grimaced as he spoke up boastfully:

"It is not that I haven't the ability *to become* an exponent of contemporary poetry and *haiku. . . ."*

But, even as he spoke, his childish pride aroused him to sudden shame. When a little while before Heikichi had been praising "The Tale of Eight Dogs" in the most sophisticated terms, Bakin had not felt any great satisfaction; but turning over the whole conversation in his mind, he felt he was inconsistent in being annoyed that he was looked upon as lacking the ability to compose lyrics and *haiku*. Moved on the whim of the moment by such introspection, he began to feel that it was as if he were hiding his inward shame. He poured the pail of hot water awkwardly over his shoulders.

"Yes, of course, if it were not so, you could never create such masterpieces. Since I judged that you could be no less of a poet than a writer, I might flatter myself that I have keen insight. Excuse me, Sir, for making too much of myself."

Again, Heikichi laughed loudly. The squint-eyed man had by then moved away, but his spittle left on the floor flowed away with the hot water which Bakin had poured over himself. Bakin was conscious of increasing embarrassment.

"Well—I fear I have spoken thoughtlessly. I shall take my bath now."

Feeling a strange dissatisfaction in his own behavior, he acted upon this dismissal and leisurely stood up by way of indicating his retirement from this amiable reader. But Heikichi had been encouraged by Bakin's boasting and seemed to take some pride in the mere fact of being one of the readers.

"Then, I would be much obliged, *Sensei,* if you would write a lyric or *haiku* for me some time soon. Would you do this?—Please don't forget!—Then exuse me, if you will; though you must surely be busy, when you are passing, would you drop in on me?—Well, I will do myself the honor of calling on *you.*"

Heikichi's eyes, as he said this, had been half pursuing Bakin who, once more having rubbed himself with his wet towel, had turned his back on Heikichi and was walking through the bath gate. On returning home, Heikichi thought he would perhaps acquaint his wife with the way in which he had spoken to Kyokutei *Sensei.*

4

BEYOND the bathtub screen it was as obscure as night. The steam there was denser than fog. Nearsighted Bakin pushed gingerly among the people, seeking out a corner. At last he was able to soak his wrinkled body. The temperature of the water was so hot, he felt the heat penetrating to the tips of his nails. Drawing a long breath, he peered around leisurely. There were seven or eight heads floating in the bath within the gloom; everybody around him was talking or singing. The misted light from the bath gate reflected the glassy surface of the hot water which dissolved the human oil; the water lapped monotonously; and the nauseating odor of the public bath assailed the nostrils of the bathers.

Bakin's reverie had long tended towards the romantic. Amid the steam of the bath, the background of a novel presented itself to him. He visualized a ship's heavy canvas, and on the sea beyond the canvas the wind seemed to rise with the evening; the ponderous sound of the waves beating on the bulwarks, altogether like the lapping of oil, could be heard. Over that sound was the flapping of the canvas, like the sound of bats' wings; as though keenly aware of it, a seaman stared out over the bulwarks towards the sea upon which a fog was descending; the new red moon hung beshadowed in the sky. Whereupon . . .

Having progressed thus far his reflections were rudely shattered. He could hear some voice close by raised in criticism of his *yomihon* works–but the tone of voice seemed to suggest that it was deliberately meant to be overheard by Bakin. Bakin, who had apparently been on the point of emerging from the bath, lingered on, intent on listening to the criticism.

". . . In *Chosakudô Shujin*, Bakin certainly opens his big mouth, but what he writes is but a rehash. Suppose we take a plain example; in 'The Tale of Eight Dogs,' he closely draws from the *Suiko-den,* doesn't he? But, suppose we grant that it doesn't matter about his not being original, we can at least say it has an exciting plot because it was previously a famous *Chinese* story, wasn't it? And he gives it a flavor of originality. On the other hand, his reheated Kyôden is quite disappointing! . . ."

With his weak eyes Bakin peered through the steam towards the man who was abusing his name, but the density of the steam clouded his vision, and Bakin could not make him out clearly. It did seem, though, that it could indeed be the squint-eyed *koichô* who had been beside him shortly before. If so, obviously irritated by Heikichi's praise of Bakin, the man was purposely finding fault.

". . . First, it can definitely be said of all Bakin's works that in writing them he uses only the tip of his brush. His works have no substance. When his works do have anything to convey, it is just as if he were a master of a temple school merely interpreting the *Shisho-gokei.* Thus he has no knowledge of current affairs. As proof of this, there is very little portrayed in his writings which is outside the affairs of olden times. There is the incident of his novel about O-Somé and Hisamatsu; he disguised the source under the title, *Shôsenjôshi Aki-no-nanakusa.* This is typical of Bakin—one example of many. . . ."

Bakin, somewhat conscious of his own superiority, could not be aroused to antagonism, even had it been his wish. Though irritated, strangely enough, Bakin could not hate this ill-spoken man. Instead, he had the desire to turn his contempt on himself in all honesty. That he made no move to retaliate was probably because of his advanced age.

". . . In that regard, Ikku and Samba were great writers. In their works they portrayed quite normal people. Never did they use their skill to invent from superficial knowledge. There, largely, Bakin is different. . . ."

As Bakin well knew from experience, such adverse criticism of his *yomihon* was not only something unpleasant, it also carried some danger. That is to say, he realized that if he were to assent to that derogatory criticism there need be no disparagement of his own self-assurance, but to refute it would mean that he would feel compelled to react against it in any further creative activity. And, under the stimulus of that discreditable inducement, he perhaps would at some time create literary work which was bizarre. The author who draws his themes only from the prevailing taste of the times–if he were in the least inclined towards this mode of writing–would unexpectedly fall into peril. Until that time Bakin, therefore, had felt he should not read adverse criticism of his own works. Although this was the principle he followed, it was not that he did not feel tempted to read such adverse criticism. There in that bath, listening to the abusive *koichô,* he had half succumbed to its fascination.

Since these were his beliefs, he readily admitted the folly of wasting all this time immersed in the hot water. Then, leaving behind the flow of words of that very petulant *koichô,* he strode through the bath gate. Beyond the window, the blue sky was visible through the steam, and against that blue sky there was the outline of the persimmons basking in the warm sunshine. Returning to the water trough, unperturbed he raised it and poured hot water over his body.

". . . At any rate, Bakin is a sham. He is nothing more than a Japanese imitation of the Chinese Lo Kuan Chu."

Thus, the man who had been talking in the bath, probably presuming Bakin to be still there, continued to proclaim his fervent philippics. Perhaps the squint-eyed one had not seen Bakin's figure climb out of the bath and stride through the bath gate—perhaps he had not seen because he was unfortunate enough to have squint eyes.

5

BUT AFTER he had left the bathhouse, Bakin's feelings sank. The squint-eyed one with the tongue of venom had at least been as successful as he could have expected to be. As Bakin strolled along the street under the autumn sun, those derogatory comments he had heard in the bath recurred to him one by one, and he dissected them minutely. Examining each point, he was at once able to establish in his mind how foolish and valueless were the man's views. In spite of this, however, his feelings had been aroused, and they were not easily subdued.

His displeased eyes looked up at the houses on both sides of the street. There was no bond between the houses and his feelings—all those houses were testimony to the way of life of the day. There was the tobacco shop of *Shokuni-meiyu* with its persimmon-colored curtain; alongside it was *Honstugê,* the comb shop with its yellow arched signboard; next was the *Kago* Restaurant with its hanging lantern; and there was a flag with a picture of the divining rod of *Bokuzei,* the fortune-teller—the meaningless line of buildings was a passing blur.

"Why am I irked by such malicious remarks which hold me up to ridicule? . . ."

Bakin continued to think in this vein.

". . . In the first place, the fact that the squint-eyed man bore me some ill will has made me disgruntled. That a person has a grudge against me is enough to upset me regardless of the reason for it—so it can't be helped. . . ."

Pondering over the affair in this manner, he felt ashamed of his own feelings. As it was rare to find people with such an overbearing manner as himself, so it was also rare to find people as sensitive as he to the ill will of others. And, in analyzing these two traits of character which might be thought to be altogether paradoxical, it was apparent that they did, in fact, spring from one source—he had long felt, indeed, that they sprang from the same nervous process.

". . . Besides, my displeasure is the result of yet another stimulus. I am placed in a state of conflict with those squint eyes. I have never enjoyed being placed in such a position; that is why I have never liked being involved in games of skill."

Having come to analyze this matter thus far, he proceeded to skip further in his reasoning when an unexpected change occurred in his mood, as might have been visible from the sudden relaxation of his lips which had hitherto been tightly closed.

". . . Finally, the fact that the man, who has placed me in this position, is a squint-eyed one is truly upsetting. If he had been a man of somewhat better class, undoubtedly I would have some power to resist such a distressing spectacle. Somehow, on account of his squint eyes, I cannot help but be annoyed. . . ."

With a bitter smile Bakin's eyes searched the sky. Out of the sunlit sky the clear cry of a kite fell like rain. He was conscious that his feelings, submerged until then, gradually lightened.

". . . But, howsoever adverse is the criticism raised by those squint eyes, the worst they can do is cause me some displeasure; howsoever the kites may cry, they cannot stop the motion of the universe. My 'Tale of Eight Dogs' will be completed, and *then* there will be no epic in Japan, written in any age, to rival it!"

While endeavoring thus to bolster his retrieved self-confidence, he turned quietly into the narrow road that led to his house.

6

HE WENT INSIDE, and looking about him, as he became accustomed to the dim light of the porch, he saw on the shoe rack a pair of thonged snow *geta*. Whereupon a vision of the blank-faced guest floated before his eyes. He was disgusted at the thought of what a bother it was to have to squander further time with a guest.

"Today," he thought, "the whole morning will have been wasted."

As he crossed the threshold, Sugi, the maid, appeared sympathetic as she greeted him at the door, her hands lowered onto the floor to bow; and looking up at him, she said:

"Mr. Izumiya is in the drawing room awaiting your return."

Nodding, he handed his wet towel to Sugi, but was in no haste to enter his study.

"O-Hyaku?–where is O-Hyaku?"

"She's gone to the Temple."

"With O-Michi?"

"Yes, and with the boy, too."

"And my son?"

"Gone to Mr. Yamamoto's."

All the members of his family were absent from the house. As there was nothing to be done about it, with a feeling of disappointment he opened the *fusuma*–decorated paper doors–of his study which adjoined the vestibule.

Looking in through the opened doorway, he perceived the shiny fair complexion of an oddly smug face. The man, biting on a slender silver *kiseru* pipe had settled himself precisely in the middle of the room. In the study, except for the screen upon which was pasted a monument tracing and the contrasting scroll-painting of red maple and yellow chrysanthemums, there was not one decorative ornament. Fifty book chests, the color of paulownia wood, were ranged along the wall. A winter would already perhaps have passed since the paper of the *shōji* sliding doors had been replaced; across the white patches–which had been cut and pasted on to mend the fractures in the paper–the shredded banana leaves, beaten upon by the autumn sun, threw their agitated shadows. The fashionably dressed visitor was not in keeping with his environment.

"Ah, *Sensei,* it's good to see you!"

As soon as the *fusuma* paper doors had slid open, the visitor with courteously lowered head, spoke in a smooth tone. This was Izumiya Ichibé, the bookseller, who had undertaken the publication of Bakin's *Shimpen Kimpeibai* which was, at the time, next in popularity to "The Tale of Eight Dogs."

"You have presumably been waiting a while. Though not my usual habit, I went to take a morning bath."

Bakin, with his usual scowl, sat himself down decorously.

"Oh–a morning bath?–indeed?"

Ichibê gave vent to the comment as though he had been greatly affected by Bakin's disclosure. There are few people who, like this man, become easily awed by somewhat trifling circumstances. No, rather one should say that people who appear so easily impressed are a rarity. Bakin soon settled down to take a puff on his pipe and rapidly, as always, directed the talk along business lines. He did not especially like this affectation of Izumiya's.

"Then, you have some business to discuss?"

"Well, yes, I have come about another manuscript."

Ichibê, twirling his *kiseru* with his fingertips, turned and looked at Bakin, as he spoke in his soft effeminate voice. This man had a strange disposition. That is to say, his outward behavior and inner intentions were almost in all circumstances incompatible. The outcome of his professed intentions was always entirely opposite. Whenever he had a very strong intention, he emitted an effeminate voice.

As he listened to that voice, Bakin instinctively scowled a second time.

"Your request for a manuscript is out of the question."

"Yes, would it be something of an inconvenience for you?"

"More than an inconvenience. This year, as I have accepted many contracts for *yomihon* fiction (complete stories), I have no time to venture into the field of *gôkan* books (serial stories)."

"Indeed you are busy."

As he said this, Ichibê's face took on its blank expression, and he tapped his *kiseru* on the ashtray as if to signal that he had completely forgotten the subject of conversation. Suddenly his conversation switched to Nezumi-kozô Jirôdaifu.

7

Nezumi-kozô Jirôdaifu, captured that year in the beginning of May, had his head piked by the middle of August. He had been a truly renowned robber!–He would break into only the daimyô residences and would later distribute to the poor the money he had stolen. At that time, the term *gizoku*–chivalrous robbers– strangely enough became quite a byword for this thief, and he had become a giant among the people.

"Indeed, *Sensei*, Nezumi-kozô broke into seventy-six houses of the daimyô and stole money amounting to three thousand one hundred and eighty-three *ryô*, two *bu*. It is too terrible to think about. Although he was nothing better than a *thief,* he surely could not have been an ordinary human being."

Bakin's curiosity was naturally aroused. Behind such talk Ichibê would all the time secretly conceal his conceit of the fact that he was supplying inspirational material to his writers. Of course, this very self-conceit keenly provoked Bakin to vexation; but this same provocation moved him to further curiosity. His abundant ability as an artist made it easy for him to succumb to the fascination of the theme, especially at this point.

"Hm–there, indeed, was a really notorious fellow!–I had heard various rumors about him, but never did I imagine that his exploits had extended thus far."

"There, in truth, we have the robber of robbers, eh?–It is said that in his earlier days, he had been a retainer or something to Aro-Tajima-no-Kami; so it happened that he was well-informed about the various mansions. Listening to the talk of those who witnessed his hanging and the parade beforehand, I have heard that he was a corpulent man, and of an amiable nature. At the time of his hanging he was wearing a dark blue garment of grass linen, and, it is said, a white silk undergarment–altogether like a character from one of your own works, *Sensei*–eh?"

Making some vague reply, Bakin puffed on his pipe. But Ichibê was no more surprised than previously, it would seem, by his vague answer.

"How would it be?–Would you not do me the favor of writing a story about Jirôdaifu to follow on in the tradition of *Kimpeibai*?–I know you are extremely busy, but–but, whether you would oblige–one word of agreement?–"

Having used Nezumi-kozô's story as an inducement, Ichibê drifted, at this point, towards pressing on with the manuscript–the dominant idea in his mind. Bakin, accustomed as he was to Ichibê's habitual measures, continued to refuse his compliance. Not only that, he was becoming all the more cross. That his curiosity had been aroused even for a moment by Ichibê's stratagem made him feel that he had been duped. Still puffing clumsily at his pipe, he reasoned in this way:

"To begin with, writing–as I would be–under pressure, I could not produce anything satisfactory. As I cannot assure you of a good seller, it would be a trifling venture for you. Taking this into consideration, I think my reply should, in the ultimate, be satisfactory to us both."

"That might be so, but please do make an effort just this once!–How would it be, then? . . ."

As he spoke, Ichibê "turned a placating face" into Bakin's line of vision. (This is how Bakin himself describes a certain aspect of Izumiya's glance.) And, as he turned his face he breathed smoke, between long pauses, through his nose.

"I can by no means write it! Even if I wanted to attempt it, I haven't the time, so it can't be helped."

"Then, I am put to some trouble, aren't I? . . ."

After this comment, Ichibê suddenly spoke of contemporary writers, all the while holding between his thin lips the mouthpiece of the slender gold pipe.

8

"ANOTHER THING—it is said that Tanéhiko's new book about something or other has appeared. His works could be said to place an emphasis on urbanity and are somewhat melancholy. If they were not written by Tanéhiko, they would not be written at all, would they?"

Ichibê, somehow, had the habit of overlooking terms of respect when referring to the various writers. Whenever Bakin heard him speak so familiarly, he felt that behind his back Ichibê would refer to him, too, simply as "Bakin . . ." Insofar as a fickle writer's name was tossed without terms of respect from the mouth of a person who was classing him with his own artisans—wherefore was there the need to write a manuscript for such a man?

It was not unusual for Bakin's peevish pride to be aroused over some irritation such as this. That day, too, when he heard Ichibê use the name of Tanéhiko, there was good reason for the expression of bitterness he gradually assumed. But Ichibê seemed not to care in the least.

"Even I myself am thinking of publishing Shunsui's work. I know you don't like him, but still, for the vulgar reader, he is suitable enough."

"Is that so?"

To Bakin there came a fleeting memory of the exaggerated vulgarity in the face of Shunsui he had seen at some time or other. The rumor that Shunsui had said, "I am not an author, but, catering to the tastes of my readers, I am simply a hack-writer who writes love stories," even Bakin had heard long before. Therefore, he had contempt from the bottom of his heart for this writer who was not much of a writer. But, while having no connection with this writer, as he heard Ichibê bandy Shunsui's name with such familiarity, as usual he could not suppress a feeling of distaste. "But, in any case, in dealing with a piquant theme, he is splendid–a writer worthy of his name."

As he spoke, Ichibê stole a glance at Bakin's face, then once more turned his gaze to the gold pipe that he held in his mouth. The sudden glance, which held something of the man's concealed vulgarity, was distressing to Bakin. Anyhow, that is how Bakin felt.

"Shunsui will write two or three instalments at a stretch while the brush does not leave the paper.–By the way, have you such a rapid pace?"

To Bakin's displeasure was added a knowledge that he was being coerced. As his self-esteem was boundless, he did not, of course, care to be compared with Shunsui and Tanéhiko. But he himself was inclined to be slow in writing, and that fact, seeming to indicate a certain incompetence, was always sufficient inducement to him to feel crestfallen. But, on the other hand, if he were to estimate his own artistic conscience, there were many times when he could place his work at high value. Such being his nature, he felt he could not rely on the tastes of the average man and permit him to deliver judgment. At that point, gazing upon the *red maple-and-yellow-chrysanthemum* in the alcove before his eyes, he said, as though he almost spat out the words:

"There are times and circumstances, aren't there?–There is the time to be swift and the time to be tardy."

"Ha–there are times and circumstances, it is true."

For the third time Ichibê appeared to be deeply impressed, but that this impression of his was not a genuine one, it is needless for us to mention. Soon afterwards, he again cut in:

"Then, about the manuscript, I have repeatedly mentioned–would you give it your consideration? Shunsui, too. . . ."

"There is some difference between Taménga (Shunsui) and me."

When irritated, Bakin had the habit of drawing his lower lip a little to the left. This time he drew aside his lip with fierceness.

"Well," he said, "I would incur your pardon.–Sugi . . . Sugi! . . . Did you put Mr. Izumiya's shoes around the right way?"

9

AFTER HE had chased Izumiya Ichibê from the house, Bakin crossed to the veranda pillar and gazed out at the narrow garden scene; he still had to exert all his efforts to conquer his wrath.

In the garden that was quite bathed in sunlight, the leaves of the banana tree were in shreds, and the sultan's parasol had been shorn of leaves; there were also the Chinese black pines and the green bamboo. Bakin was the possessor of a liberal area of warm sunshine. The lotus near the hand-basin was already bearing sparse blooms, and the fragrant olive growing beyond the low fence still retained its sweet odor. From far up in the blue sky, descended the intermittent calls of a flock of kites, like the sound of flutes.

In contradistinction to nature his thoughts dwelt on the lower-class order. The unfortunate circumstance that human beings were living such inferior lives was an inevitable spur to him. Being afflicted by their vulgarity, he reacted in a coarse way himself in word and deed. He himself had actually chased away Izumiya Ichibê. The fact that he had *chased* him was not an act worthy of one from the higher classes; but on account of the vulgarity of his companion, he had been pushed to the point where he, too, had performed a low-class action. That is why he had done it. The significance of his action was that he had degraded himself to the same level as Ichibê.

As his thoughts wandered on, he discovered in his memory of the immediate past, a similar incident. It was in the previous spring that a man called Nagashima Masabé of Kuchiki-kami Shinden in Sôchû had sent him a letter asking if it might not be possible for him to become a resident disciple of Bakin's. according to the letter, the man had become deaf in his twenty-first year, and since that time until the time of writing the letter—when he was twenty-four years of age—he had had a mind to study to become a writer of renown—and he had assiduously applied himself to writing stories. Needless to say, he was an avid reader of Bakin's "The Tale of Eight Dogs" and "Travels around the Islands." . . . That he lived in the provinces had become somewhat of a hindrance to him. . . . *Therefore could you not permit me to be a resident disciple at your house?* There was also the fact that he had six *yomihon* manuscripts of his own authorship. . . . *When these have been corrected and revised by you, I would like them to be duly published.* . . . Such was the general tenor of the letter. Naturally, to make such demands of Bakin was asking too much altogether. But that the man was hard of hearing, while Bakin was afflicted with indifferent sight, had possibly been a wedge which pierced an inlet to Bakin's sympathy. Although Bakin had replied that he could not meet with his demands, he had been urged to send a more gracious reply than was usual for him. The subsequent letter that Bakin received by return mail from the young aspirant expressed little that was beyond the scope of fierce censure.

"Speaking of your works, 'The Tale of Eight Dogs' and 'Travels around the Islands,' though they are rather lengthy, I have had the perseverance to read through these clumsy *yomihon*, but you have refused even to glance at my six *yomihon*. This reveals that you are a person of low-class background, does it not . . . ?"

Beginning with such an invective, the letter concluded with: "That you have no resident disciple, is an indication of your stinginess."

Bakin, in his irritation, had written an answer which was couched in words expressing his opinion that it was a matter of some disgrace to him for his *yomihon* to have been read by such a shallow youth. After that, there was no further communication from the applicant for discipleship–but, would the youth still proceed with his *yomihon* manuscripts? And was it fanciful to consider that the boy's *yomihon* might at some time be read by people throughout Japan? . . .

Out of such reverie, a heartless attitude was stirred in Bakin both for Nagashima Masabê, and at the same time, heartlessness towards himself. And again, it led him into inexpressible loneliness. But the sun was innocently dispelling the scent of the fragrant olive, and on neither the banana nor the sultan's parasol did the becalmed leaves stir. Even the calls of the kite were not as sonorous as they had been. Nature and man! . . .

When ten minutes later Sugi, the maidservant, came to inform him that his midday meal was prepared, he was leaning vacantly against the veranda post, still altogether enwrapped in a dream.

10

LEFT TO HIMSELF after he had finished his midday meal, he at length withdrew to his study where, wishing, in some way or other, to tranquilize his restlessness and disquiet, for the first

time in a long while he opened *Suiko-den*. The place at which
he had by chance opened the book was the part where Hyûshi
Tôrinchû, at Sanjin-byô, was looking on at a burning haystack
one windy, snowy night. As usual his interest was aroused by this
dramatic setting. But when this customary interest had reached a
certain point, it habitually changed to uneasiness.

Those of Bakin's family who had gone to pay their respects to
the ancestral graves had not yet returned home. The interior of
the house was quiet like a forest. His face in repose was gloomy
as he drew on his unpalatable tobacco; and with the *Suiko-den*
open in front of him, a certain question, which all the while had
been in the back of his mind, came to the fore.

There had always existed the insoluble problem of the reconciliation of *himself as a moralist* and *himself as an artist*. From his
early years he had not doubted the "Way of the Sages of Old"—
the *Sen-Ô-no-Michi*. His novels were, as he had himself avowed,
an artistic expression of the *Sen-Ô-no-Michi*. In that, there was no
contradiction; but between the value which the *Sen-Ô-no-Michi*
attributed to art and the value attributed to it by his own emotions, there was an unexpectedly great gap. Consequently he was
a combination of the moralist who affirmed the former, and the
artist who naturally affirmed the latter. Of course, it could have
been a cheap conciliatory idea that hewed a way out of this contradiction. In practice in the background of this insipid compromise with the public, he had tended to hide his equivocal attitude
towards art.

But, even if he deceived the public, he was not himself
deceived. Though he were to deny the value of fiction unless
it exalted good and suppressed evil—when this did not parallel
the artistic inspiration which ordinarily overflowed in him—he
instantly felt insecure. This was the reason why, in fact, one para-

graph of *Suiko-den* had by chance evoked in him a reaction far beyond his conjecture.

At this point, as he tacitly smoked his tobacco, Bakin tried to divert his thoughts towards his absent family, because he had not the courage to be introspective. But *Suiko-den* lay open before him. His insecurity focused on *Suiko-den* was not easily erased from his mind. It was opportune, then, that Kazan Watanabé Noboru came to visit him. As Kazan held under his arm a parcel wrapped in a purple cloth and was wearing a formal kimono and coat, he had come presumably to return some books which he had borrowed.

Bakin, with revived spirits, went out to the porch for the express purpose of greeting this friend.

"The reason for my calling today is partly to have the pleasure of seeing you and partly to return some books I borrowed from you."

Kazan spoke thus directly as he entered the study. On closer observation we might have seen that, apart from the purple bundle, he carried something rolled in paper–something that looked as if it might have been painted silk.

"If you have time, won't you take a look?"

"Ah–quickly, *do* let me see!"

His smile was forced as, concealing his excitement, he unwrapped the silk from its paper and displayed it before Bakin. The picture depicted a scattering of stark, denuded trees, and standing among them were two men with clasped hands, talking; yellow leaves were strewn about the forest, and crows flew in confusion over the treetops.–As Bakin looked over the picture, it could be said that he experienced a faint chill as of living autumn.

As Bakin's eyes had alighted on this thinly-colored *Kanzan and Jittoku*, they gradually sparkled with a delicate moisture.

"As always," he said, "this is an exquisite piece of work. I am reminded of the Wang Wei–

The evening drum is sounding–
And leaving behind their food
The nesting crows return.
–In the desolate forest,
As I walk I hear
The cry of fallen leaves."

II

"I FINISHED painting this yesterday, and I have brought it with the idea of presenting it to you if you wouldn't mind–"

Stroking the traces of beard on his young chin, Kazan's tone was one of satisfaction.

"In weighing the merits of the pictures I have painted, this is about the best I can do. Still, howsoever I try, I have not yet been able to paint an absolutely satisfying picture."

Bakin continued to scrutinize the picture as he muttered his thanks. By chance there flashed in the depths of his mind at this time the thought that his own work was being neglected. But Kazan, for his part, seemed able to think of nothing but his own painting.

"Every time I see pictures executed by the old masters I long to be able to paint as they did. Wood, stone, people–all become *real* trees, *real* rocks, *real* people–in them the emotions of the old painters live on eternally. That alone is true greatness! Towards that end I am still but a child."

"The old masters remarked that future generations ought to be feared."

Bakin amused himself with such unwonted pleasantry as he looked on with envy at Kazan's complete absorption in his painting.

"We should also," he said, "be fearful of posterity! Therefore, if we–jammed between the old masters and posterity, do not make some move of our own, we are only jostled about. Moreover, this has not been our problem alone. The old masters were in the same plight and posterity, too–eh?"

"Somehow, we must go forward, or we will soon be pushed aside. Therefore, it seems vital that every craftsman take at least one step forward."

"Yes, that's fundamental."

Both host and guest, moved by their own words, fell silent for a short while. And the two strained to hear the quiet sounds of the autumn day.

" 'The Tale of Eight Dogs,' as usual, makes good progress?"

At last Kazan had approached a different subject.

"No, but it can't he helped if it makes little headway. The work of the old masters is beyond my attainment."

"If *you* find it so, then it is hopeless for everybody."

"And I would say I am more hopeless than anyone else. But, by all means, having come thus far, there's nothing one can do except to continue on. With that in mind, I have resolved to die in battle with 'The Tale of Eight Dogs.' "

As he spoke, Bakin, as if ashamed of himself, smiled bitterly.

"After all, we must certainly not think that the writing of mere fiction is easy to achieve."

"My painting is the same. Once having made a start and having proceeded to a certain point, I am anxious to finish it as best I can."

"We'll die in battle together, *né*?"

The two laughed heartily. But in that laughter flowed a certain loneliness that both would have understood. Simultaneously, host and guest, from the bond of their mutual sadness, felt strongly agitated.

"But, in the matter of pictures, there is something to envy, *né*? More than anything else, it is good that the artist does not receive any censure from the government."

This time it was Bakin who had changed the subject of conversation.

12

"THAT'S NOT entirely so.–I hardly think you would have such worry with your writings."

"No, I have a great deal!"

Bakin quoted as an example of the baseness and narrowmindedness of the officials responsible for book censorship, the fact that he had been ordered to revise part of the text of one of his novels because he had written of an official receiving a bribe. And, following that explanation, Bakin continued to criticize.

"And isn't it interesting that the more the censorship officials find fault the more the tail pokes out? As the censors themselves take bribes, they are displeased if there is any mention about officials taking bribes and insist on a revision of the text. Again, as their minds are prone to obscenity, they will brand as obscene any publication that makes any mention of tender affection between man and woman and yet, they are under the impression that their own moral sensitivity is on a higher plane than the author's–which is an absurdity. One could say they are like monkeys who look into a mirror and bare their teeth; their own vulgarity serves to irritate them."

As Bakin's simile was over-enthusiastic, unthinking he burst into laughter.

"It would be largely as you say–but if your work be altered, it is not to your own disgrace, whatsoever the censorship officials and others might say about it; your work has its own excellence and so its own literary value."

"In behaving as they do, the officials often go to the excess of tyranny. On an earlier occasion I wrote about sending food and clothing to a prison, and five or six lines of my text were deleted."

As Bakin spoke, both he and Kazan chuckled.

"But in fifty or a hundred years from now, when the censors cease to exist, 'The Tale of Eight Dogs' will still continue to be read."

"Whether or not 'The Tale of Eight Dogs' will survive, I am afraid that there will always be censors."

"That could be so–but I doubt it."

"Even if the censors be non-existent, society will never be free from censor-like people. When we look back over the burning and burying of books and scholars in China in ancient times, your opinion is hardly feasible."

"You say that, *Sensei,* only because you are discouraged."

"I am not discouraged–only, a world rife with censors is forlorn."

"Then all you can do is to keep on working."

"At any rate, that's all one can do."

"There again, we can die in battle together."

This time the two did not laugh. Not only did they not laugh, but Bakin's face hardened a little as he looked at Kazan. In these words of Kazan's, passed off as a joke, there was a curious sharpness.

"But, before anything, youth should have the discretion to survive—as death in battle can be achieved at any time," said Bakin, after a pause.

But, as Bakin was aware of Kazan's political views, this time he would perchance have been aware that this was touchy ground. Nevertheless, only laughing, it seemed that Kazan would ignore the remark.

13

WHEN KAZAN had left for home, Bakin, with the enthusiasm that had been bequeathed to him, again turned to his desk with the idea of resuming work on his manuscript of "The Tale of Eight Dogs." Before proceeding, it had been a longstanding habit of his to look over and peruse briefly what he had written on the previous day. Even on that day, with vermilion brush he corrected between the columns, reading over slowly and carefully many sheets of the manuscript.

Then came the realization that what he had written, for some reason, did not please him. Between ideograph and ideograph, discords were lurking, marring the entire harmony. At first he construed it as the result of his own irritation.

"I'm not in the right mood for this. As my writing has reached a deadlock, I should not try to force myself on."

In the wake of such thoughts he returned once more to his

manuscript reading, but the discordant tone was no different from what it had been. The fact that he did not enjoy the complacency of a man of advanced years disconcerted him.

"I'll just look over some of the previous work."

He let his eyes rove to the section of his manuscript prior to what he had previously written. In this too, he again found a disorderly confusion of aimless rough phrases. He reread the part even previous to that. And, again, he read what he had written prior to the previous material.

But, pursuant to his reading, there developed a growing awareness of the clumsy plot and chaotic composition. There was the instance of a descriptive passage which impressed no image. There was an exclamatory passage which lacked the element of any deep emotion. And again, there was an argument which groped along with no rational development. This manuscript to which he had given several days of writing, when examined with new eyes, he could but regard as useless chatter. Suddenly he felt a pang of pain as though his heart were pierced.

"There is nought else to do but to rewrite it from the beginning!"

As this screamed in his mind, he pushed aside the manuscript vexatiously and relaxed, lolling on one elbow. But, even in his anxiety, he did not sever his eyes from the desk. At that desk, where he had written "The Crescent Moon" and "Dream of Namka," he was now writing "The Tale of Eight Dogs." On that desk lay the Chinese Tuan Ch'i ink-slab, the dragon paperweight, the toad-shaped paulownia water bowl, the varicolored porcelain screen upon which lions and peonies were drawn and the brush-stand of bamboo root on which orchids were carved—these accessories had all become familiar from long before, along with the agony of creative writing. In the present feeling of fail-ure in a whole lifetime of laborious toil–as if it cast over him a deep shadow–as if it thrust mysteriously to the root of his self-confidence–he could not look at those familiar objects without feeling some irritating anxiety.

"Until a short while ago, it had been my aim to write a great work which had no rival in this land. But there again, in that, too, perhaps there existed the kind of vainglory common to all men."

Such consuming trepidation was hard for him to bear and wrought upon him a dreary solitariness. It is not that he forgot his customary modesty in the face of the Japanese and Chinese geniuses for whom he had profound respect; but he did not restrain his arrogance before the fussy contemporary writers and was haughty even unto the end. How could he realize that he was inclined to laud himself out of ignorance of the world when he had, after all, the same capacity as they? His strong *Ego* was filling him with passion too ardent to allow him the refuge of *enlightenment* and *resignation.*

Leaning his body on the desk in front of him, while gazing on his own foundering manuscript, he saw the sinking of a junk through the eyes of the shipwrecked captain–he tranquilly set about combating the exigencies of despair. If at this time the *fusuma* behind him had not been noisily slid open, and a voice had not called–"*Ojiisama*–I'm back!", if tender arms had not embraced his neck, he would have been ensnared forever in fear-ful gloom. But, his grandson, Tarô, had opened the *fusuma* with the boldness and naïveté that only children have, and without ado sprang onto Bakin's knees.

"Grandfather–I'm back!"

"Ah, it's good that you're back so soon."

With these words, on the wrinkled face of the author of "The Tale of Eight Dogs" shone a joy as of a different man.

14

FROM THE direction of the living room the voices of his spirited wife, O-Hyaku, and of O-Michi, the retiring girl who was his son's wife, could be heard in animated conversation! Sometimes the thick voice of a man could be heard over theirs, so it was apparent that his son, Sôhaku, had returned and joined them. Tarô, bestraddling the knees of his grandfather, concentrated his gaze on the ceiling while he appeared to be listening keenly to the chatter outside. His cheeks were red from his outing in the open air, and about his tiny nostrils there was a movement every time he breathed. He was wearing a chestnut-and-plum colored kimono with small family crests.

"Hey, Grandfather–!" exclaimed Tarô, as though straining to collect his thoughts, and at the same time restraining a laugh; his dimples many times appeared and vanished.–It induced in Bakin, too, a spontaneous temptation to laugh.

"Every day, . . ." began Tarô.

"Uh?–every day . . . ?"

". . . Work hard!"

Bakin erupted into flowing laughter; but even as he laughed he went on to say:

"Then–?"

"Then–ah, then, you mustn't be cross."

"Well, well–is that all?"

"There's more yet–."

As he spoke, Tarô himself burst into laughter; his topknot jerked as he lifted his head, his eyes narrowed, his pure white teeth were revealed, and his tiny dimples appeared. Watching and laughing, Bakin could by no means imagine that when this boy would grow up to adulthood he would wear on his face woes like the rest of humanity. Bakin was steeped in the bliss of the moment; then, once more he felt a qualm in his heart.

"There is still something?"

"A few things."

"What things?"

"Well, Grandfather–as you are becoming more famous–."

"Becoming famous?"

"–As you're becoming famous, it would be good if you'd be more patient."

"I *am* patient, aren't I?" asked Bakin earnestly, without thinking.

"More!–You must be *more* patient!"

"Who's been telling you that?"

"Well–."

Tarô mischievously peeped at his grandfather's face and laughed.

"Who?"

"Yes, who?–You went to the Temple today. Was it something the priest said?"

"No."

Tarô shook his head emphatically. Half raising himself on Bakin's knees, he thrust forth his chin a little.

"Well,–" he began.

"Um?"

"–The Kwannon at Asakusa said so!"

He laughed gleefully as he spoke in a tone that suggested he had been listening to his grandmother. As if afraid that his grandfather might restrain him, he suddenly leapt down. Very pleased with his fooling, he clapped his tiny hands and almost tumbling over, ran in the direction of the living room.

In Bakin's heart, something solemn, whatsoever it might have been, flickered for a moment; on his lips lingered a serene smile, and his eyes filled with tears. Whether this was a joke that Tarô himself had invented, or whether it was something passed on to him from Tarô's mother, made no difference. That he had heard such words from the lips of his grandchild at this very time was strange indeed.

"But, had Kwannon really said so?–I should work hard! I *should not* be so irascible!–And I *should be* more patient!"

This elderly man of letters–of sixty or so years of age–laughing in the midst of his tears, nodded as would a child.

15

THAT NIGHT. . . .

. . . That night, Bakin, by the light of a dim round lantern, began further work on "The Tale of Eight Dogs." When he was writing, the members of his household did not enter his study. Within the quiet room he could hear the oil gurgling in the lamp, and from outside the chirping of crickets spoke vainly of the long night's loneliness.

When at first he had lowered brush to paper, some faint spark had glimmered in his mind. And, when he had written ten columns–twenty columns–and had gone on to further writing, gradually the spark grew into a flame. From experience Bakin knew what it was and took infinite care with every movement of his brush. His inspiration burned brightly like a fire; once it had been kindled, if he did not take care to feed it, it would soon be extinguished.

"Don't be too hasty!–but, as swiftly as possible think as deeply as possible!"

As if to restrain his rapid brush, which was inclined to escape from him, many times he whispered those words to himself. Light, powerful as shattered stars, was flowing more swiftly than a river through his mind, infusing him moment by moment with strength, urging him onwards whether he would or not.

He no longer heard the voices of the crickets. The thin light of the cylindrical lantern now did not strain his eyes in the least. Zealously slipping down the pages, his brush sped of itself, as though it were desperately writing in veneration of some god.

Flowing through his head–even as the silvern River of Heaven flowed through the sky–came a dynamic overflowing of his thoughts in unbounded torrents. In dread of this strange power, he felt then that the weak confines of his body could not endure its intensity. And, grasping his brush stiffly, many times he called to himself thus:

"To the utmost limits will I go on to write. If what I am writing I do not write now, I do not know whether I shall ever write it!"

But, flowing on like a light piercing a fog, his speed did not in the least slacken. On the contrary, drowning his inhibitions in the dizzy torrents, he let those torrents come cascading to sweep him away, until at last he became their captive, and forgetting all else in the course of that flow, he let his own brush sweep on like a flood.

That which was reflected in his princely eye at that time was neither advantage nor disadvantage, neither love nor hate. Moreover, his misgivings about adverse criticism had already vanished. But what remained was only strange rejoicing, and, too, there was profound emotion, enchanting and heroic. Strangers to this feeling cannot savor the mental state of being *absorbed in letters,* nor can they comprehend the stern spirit of the man of letters. In this very thing there was *life*–and the dregs having been washed away, did not life gleam resplendent before the eyes of the author, like a new ore?

MEANWHILE, AROUND THE lamp in the sitting-room, the mother-in-law, O-Hyaku and the daughter-in-law, O-Michi, were seated facing one another, busily sewing. Tarô had already been put to bed. In a place a little aside, the ailing Sôhaku had for a short while been preparing his medicine.

"Father has not gone to bed yet?"–O-Hyaku had at length muttered, as though in grievance as she smeared her needle with hair oil.

"As he is most likely absorbed in his writing, he'll be unconscious of anything else," replied O-Michi, without lifting her gaze from the needle.

"He's an incorrigible fellow, isn't he?–he can't make any worthwhile money, it seems."

At this remark O-Hyaku looked at her son and her daughter-in-law, but Sôhaku pretended not to be listening and made no reply. O-Michi, too, went on silently plying her needle. The crickets there and by the study, as always, were chirping to acclaim the autumn.

THE GARDEN

Introductory Note:

One must not think of a Japanese garden as one does of an "English" or "French" or "Italian" garden in which orderliness and symmetry prevail to impress the eye either with the spaciousness of the landscape or the deftness of the human mind in disciplining nature. The object of the Japanese garden is rather to avoid the impression that man has had any part in the arrangement. Apparent irregularity of trees, shrubs, rocks, ponds, rivulets, and mounds assists in this illusion.

One of the attributes of an artistic Japanese garden is antiquity. The garden may be a link with the moods of one's ancestors; it is surely a satisfying feeling for the sons and daughters of old families to feel they walk on garden paths that have been trodden for generations by their ancestors.

When nature has its way, the garden becomes a wilderness. This wild growth is of divine inspiration but would require divine understanding to appreciate it. It would be too complex for the human mind to appreciate such scenery without some fourth dimensional vision. There must, therefore, to satisfy man's esthetic sense, be a compromise—a mutual understanding—between man and nature in the garden, as there should be in every aspect of life. To effect this compromise man must tax his imagination sufficiently for him to be able to preserve the rhythms of nature.

If man succeeds in creating such a garden, its serenity will never fail to have some spiritual impact upon the human soul.

It should be remembered by those who read this story that a garden still embodies its infinite spiritual quality–the expression of its creator–whether it be enjoyed or ignored, whether it decay or endure for a myriad years; in this there is an absolute, and absolutes are of God.

"The Garden" ("Niwa") was written in June of Taishô 11 (1922).

I

THIS IS A story about the garden of Nakamura's old-style house that had been a stage inn.

For as many as ten years after the Meiji Restoration the garden had somehow been preserved in its original condition. There had been a clear pond, shaped like a gourd; and where pines leaned on an artificial mountain, there were the summer houses, the *Seikaku-ken*–the House of Cranes, and the *Senshin-tei*–the Pure Spirit Cottage. Over the cliffs of the "mountain" to the rear, a waterfall had cascaded a white spray into the farthest reaches of the pond. A memorial to Princess Kazu-no-Miya's journey to this province–a stone lantern–was, year by year, overwhelmed by the spreading yellow roses. And this feeling of devastation had eventually become apparent everywhere, especially in early springtime when the young shoots would all sprout at the same time on the high treetops inside and outside the garden. In the background of this picturesque artificial scenery, a gradually expanding atmosphere of savage strength could be sensed, disturbing one's presence of mind.

The retired master of the Nakamura family–an old man with a chivalrous disposition, lived out his life without undue concern, his legs dangling in the *kotatsu* of the main building where he would play *go* and cards with his old wife who was laid up with head ulcers; and sometimes after his old wife had had five or six wins in a row, he would fly into a rage. The eldest son, who had succeeded to the family headship, lived with his new wife, a cousin, in a small semi-detached section connected by a corridor with the main house. Eldest Son–known by his nom-de-guerre, Hyôtoku Bunshitsu–had an irascible temperament. His ailing wife and younger brothers, and even the retired master, were afraid of him. . . . At that time there was living in the town a mendicant, Seigetsu, who often came to visit. Even Eldest Son, oddly enough, gave saké to Seigetsu, and urging him to compose verse, was good humored in his presence–

. . . Still the mountain has the scent of flowers
–and there is the cuckoo; . . .   –Seigetsu
. . . here and there
the cascades are sparkling.   –Bunshitsu.

–Such was the association they left behind. Of the remaining brothers–two of them–the next in line was adopted by a rice dealer relative, and the other was working at a substantial saké distillery in a town five or six *ri* distant. As though by mutual agreement they rarely appeared at the head family's residence.

347

Not only was the third son residing at some distance, but from early in life he and the Eldest Son had not been of a like mind. The second son, as a result of his having fallen into debauchery, hardly ever returned to his family.

Over a period of two or three years, the garden gradually became drearier; duckweed began to float on the pond. In the thickets there seemed to be a mingling of withered trees. Soon the retired old man—one summer when the drought was severe—dropped dead of a cerebral hemorrhage. Four or five days before his sudden death, when he was drinking *shôchû*, a noble in white Court costume had repeatedly entered and come out of the *Senshin-tei* over by the pond; at least the old man had reported having seen such a phantom in broad daylight. In the late spring of the following year, Second Son, absconding with his foster parent's money, eloped with a bar hostess. Then, in the autumn, Elder Brother's wife had a miscarriage.

Eldest Son, after the father's death, went to live with his mother in the main building. The subsequent lessor of the detached section was a local preparatory school headmaster. And the headmaster, a believer in the principles of the venerable Fukuzawa Yukichi's dissertation on utility, had sooner or later persuaded Eldest Son to grow fruit trees in the garden. Thenceforth, when spring came, the miscellaneous colored blossoms of peach, apricot and plum began to flourish amid the familiar pines and willows. The headmaster, when walking sometimes with Eldest Son in the new fruit garden, reviewed the situation: "As you see, we can now have an excellent *flower-viewing*. This way two things are accomplished at the same time." But, the artificial mountain and the pond, and the summer houses, fell further into dilapidation. There was an artificial wilderness added to a natural one.

That autumn there was a forest fire on the mountain behind, such as had not occurred in recent years. After that fire the waterfall, which until that time had fallen into the pond, ceased its splashing. Soon afterwards, from the time of the first snow, Eldest Son fell ill; according to the physician's diagnosis, it was what was formerly called consumption, currently tuberculosis. Throughout the time he was in and out of bed, he became irritable and peevish. In fact, in the January of the following year, while Third Son was at home for New Year, Eldest Son in the heat of a quarrel had thrown a small brazier at his brother; Third Son, having left the house again, did not bother to be present to witness Eldest Son's death. Eldest Son, after more than a year of illness, while his wife was keeping vigil, had breathed his last in the shadow of a mosquito net. . . . "The frogs are croaking, eh?– What's Seigetsu doing, I wonder?" These were his last words. As for Seigetsu, perhaps he had long before grown tired of the scenery in that place and so had ceased to go there, even to beg.

Third Son, after a week of mourning for Eldest Son, married his master's youngest daughter. And, the schoolmaster who had leased the detached building, having fortunately been promoted elsewhere, Third Son brought his bride to live there. The black lacquered cabinets that came to the detached dwelling were decorated with red and white cloth. But in the main quarters, Eldest Son's widow soon became ill; her illness was the same as her late husband's had been. Her son, Renichi–as the mother was constantly coughing up blood–was put to bed every night with his grandmother. Without fail, the grandmother, before going to bed, wound a towel around her head; attracted by the smell of the discharge from her head eruptions, the rats would come near in the night; if she were to have forgotten the towel she would surely have been bitten on the head by the rats. At the end of that same year, Eldest Son's widow died, as an oil lamp is put out. Then, on the day following the burial, the summer house in the shadow of the artificial mountain was crushed by a heavy snowfall.

When spring came round once more, of the garden there was to be seen only the thatched roof of the *Senshin-tei* and, in the copse, the trees in bud.

2

IN THE evening on one cloudy, snowy day, after an absence of ten years, Second Son returned to his father's house. His father's house?–actually it then belonged to Third Son. Third Son's attitude could hardly have been said to be especially disagreeable, though again, it was not especially welcoming; that is to say, he accepted his rakish brother without incident.

Ever since, Second Son lay prostrate, hardly stirring from the *kotatsu* in the room that housed the Buddhist altar in the main building. In the big altar there were the memorial tablets to both his father and elder brother; and, as if wishing to ignore these memorials he left the shrine doors closed. He hardly ever appeared, other than to take his three meals with his mother and younger brother's wife. Only the orphan child, Renichi, sometimes went to his room to play. Second Son would draw mountains and ships on Renichi's lithographic paper...

The flowers are blooming on yon Mukôjima
Come, wile away the time, O tea-house girl!...

Somehow he managed to illustrate such old songs, with an uncertain hand.

Soon spring came again. The meager peaches and apricots blossomed throughout the vegetation which spread through the garden, and even the pond which shone with a leaden light, reflected the shadow of the *Senshin-tei*. But Second Son, shut off by himself in the Buddha room, dozed almost the whole day long. Then, one day the faint sound of a samisen was borne to his ears, and at the same time snatches of a voice in song:

> ... This time in Suwa skirmish, Yoshié
> Of the Matsumoto Clan, was charged
> With the burden of the cannon defense ... !

Second Son, reclining on his side, raised his body curiously. Without doubt it was his mother in the guestroom, singing and playing the samisen. ...

> ... That day, so elegantly–so bravely did he advance
> That there was witnessed magnificent heroism. ...

Was his mother singing and playing to her grandchild? She went on singing the *otsu-é* popular ballad. It had been said that her rough-and-tumble husband had learned it from a courtesan; it was a song that had been popular twenty or thirty years before:

> ... Under enemy cannon fire,
> On the battlefield of Toyohashi–
> Dissolved inevitably with dew on grass–
> To future ages and generations
> He bequeathed immortal fame.

On the expressionless and bearded face of Second Son, the eyes began to shine strangely.

Two or three days after that, Third Son discovered his elder brother digging in the shade of the artificial mountain where the butterburs flourished. Second Son, out of breath, wielded the mattock awkwardly. Acting with such earnestness, he cut a somewhat comical figure.

"Brother—what are you doing?" came the voice of Third Son from behind, as he puffed on a cigarette.

"Doing?"

Second Son looked up, his face radiant as he said to his younger brother:

"I'm thinking of building a stream *here.*"

"Why build a stream?"

"I'm thinking of making the garden as it used to be."

Third Son, laughing, said nothing further.

Second Son swung his mattock every day and continued feverishly to construct the stream. But, weakened by illness as he was, it was not easy for him to work. He became tired and worn, indeed. Even beyond the fact that it was unaccustomed toil, his hands blistered, his nails were torn at the quick; but somehow he felt compelled to carry on. Sometimes he threw the mattock down on its side, and lay down as if he were dead. Under the simmering heat the flowers and the young leaves were enveloped in vapor. But, after relaxing for a time, he would stagger obstinately to his feet to resume his mattock-swinging.

Even so, after many days, the garden still showed little change. The weeds flourished as usual in the pond, and the thickets stretched forth their branches. Especially after the fruit trees had shed their blossoms, the garden seemed even more unkempt than it had previously. And it did not help matters that neither young nor old were sympathetic with Second Son's toil. Third Son, who was enterprising, was absorbed in speculations in silkworm raising and the rice market. Third Son's wife felt a womanly repugnance to Second Son's illness. Even the mother— on account of his ill-health, was apprehensive about his over-exertion in the garden. Notwithstanding, Second Son stubbornly turned his back on man and nature and obstinately went about the task of changing the face of the garden.

Soon, on one rainy morning when he went out to look at the garden, he saw Renichi laying stones along the edge of the stream that trailed among the butterburrs.

"Uncle!"–Renichi gleefully called, "I shall help you from today."

"Hm, yes, by all means!" said Second Son with a bright smile.

From that time onward Renichi did not leave the premises but assiduously helped his uncle. Second Son, to divert his nephew, would listen, as they paused for breath under the shade of the trees, to Renichi's questioning chatter about the sea, about Tokyo, about the railways, while Renichi munched fresh plums, and with absolute absorption would listen to what his uncle told him.

The rain season that year was an empty one. Both the invalid and the child–undaunted by the fierceness of the sun and the stuffiness of the grasses–dredged the pond and lopped the trees, gradually expanding their work. Whatsoever the external difficulties they had to bear–all were conquered; only the inner difficulties they could do nothing about. The garden of old times appeared in Second Son's imagination like a vision. But, in demarcating the position of the trees, or when marking out a path, he found it difficult to recall the details. Sometimes in the midst of his work he would lean on the mattock handle, and he would look vaguely about the area.

"What is it, uncle?"—Renichi, uneasily searching his uncle's face, would usually proffer this same question.

"How was it here before?"

Second Son, sweating profusely, would always mutter something to himself in this vein:

". . . I think this maple was not here."

And Renichi, with his muddy fingers, would do nought else but kill ants.

There were, however, as time went on, not only the inner difficulties to combat. Gradually when summer deepened, Second Son became repeatedly confused, probably from his state of exhaustion. He would fill up portions of the pond he had already dredged, or he would replant the pines where he had rooted them out. Such occurrences were frequent.

Renichi was especially angered once when, to make stakes for the pond, his uncle had cut down a willow tree by the water's edge. He said to his uncle:

"This willow was only just planted there!—why cut it down now?"

As Renichi stared, his uncle replied:

"Ah, yes, nowadays I really don't know what's what."

Second Son, with gloomy eyes, looked down over the pond in the heat of the noon sun.

Then, when autumn came, from among the thronging grasses and trees, the garden floated in haze. It was not, it is true, quite the same when compared with the garden of old times, because the *Seikaku-ken* was no longer there, and no water flowed from the falls. Ah!—though created by a famous landscape gardener, the elegant old world charm that the garden had expressed was almost nowhere apparent. But *the garden* was there! The pond in clear water reflected the rounded artificial mountain. And once more, pines leisurely thrust forth their branches even in front of the *Senshin-tei*. But, in the throes of his work of restoring the garden, Second Son was again taken to his bed. His body ached in all its joints, and the fever did not abate.

"You are too foolish—irrational!"

—His mother who sat by his pillow repeated those same grumbling words. Still, Second Son was happy. There remained many corners in the garden that he wished to restore; but, at any rate, his struggle had not been in vain. In *that,* he was satisfied. His decade of pain having taught him resignation, his resignation comforted him.

At the end of that autumn, unheeded, Second Son drew his last breath. It was Renichi who discovered him! Raising his voice, Renichi went running to his kin in the detached dwelling. Straightway the family members crowded around the dead man, alarm on their faces.

"Look!—Brother appears to be smiling."

Third Son turned to his mother and continued:

"See there, today Buddha's doors are open!"

Turning her attention to the family altarpiece, Third Son's wife did not look at the dead man.

After the burial of Second Son, there were many times when Renichi would sit alone in the *Senshin-tei*. With bewildered expression, looking out on the water and the trees of late autumn. . . .

3

SUCH WAS THE garden of the old-style house of the Nakamura family, which house had once been an official post-station inn. Not yet have ten years passed since the garden's restoration; and now the house has been demolished. On the site of the demolished house, a railway station has been erected, and a small refreshment room now stands in front of the station.

There is no member of the Nakamura family left at the place. The mother, as we might imagine, has long since been numbered among the dead. Even Third Son, it is said, having failed in his enterprises, has perhaps gone off to Ôsaka.

The steam train pulls into the station every day, then leaves again. There is a young station master who, in his moments of leisure, from behind his big office desk, stares at the green hills; he talks with the station hands; but in that talk, there is no mention of matters touching on the Nakamura family. It goes without saying that there is no one in the place who thinks about matters pertaining to the summer house on the artificial hill.

Yet, meanwhile, at a certain Academy of Western Art at Akasaka in Tokyo, Renichi sits before an easel. The light from the skylight, the smell of the oil paint, a model with her hair dressed like a cleft peach–the atmosphere of the school has nothing in common with that of his village home. But, as he moves his brush, sometimes as his spirit dreams, there is before him the face of a sad, aging man. And that face, smiling at him when he is weary in his work, surely murmurs to him:

"When you were but a child you helped me. . . . Now, allow me to assist *you!*"

Renichi, in his present poverty, continues day by day to paint in oils.

And Third Son?—Nobody knows or cares about Third Son.

THE BADGER

Introductory Note:
Bewitchment by the badger is benevolent and not the mali-
cious fox-bewitchment; so one should not be perturbed about
being bewitched by a badger. The badger ("mujina") is of the
carnivorous dog family, similar to the fox in appearance though
somewhat fatter; the top of its head is broad, its mouth sharp,
and its eyes round; its limbs are short, and its tail is a tuft; its
fur is usually dark grey; it lives in burrows, and is said to be
Asian in origin. In Japanese folklore the badger often assumes
the form of a mirage.
"The Badger" was written in March of Taishô 6 (1917).

AS RECOUNTED in the *Nihon Shoki*, the *Chronicles of Japan*, it was
springtime in the second month of the Thirty-fifth Year of the
Empress Suiko (circa 627 A.D.) that a badger first assumed the
shape of a man. This event occurred in Michinoku. According
to another source, the badger did not really assume the shape of
a man but only mingled with men; but, irrespective of whether it
was transformed into a man or only mingled with men, it would
at least seem to be true that it sang after its transformation, as this
fact is recorded in both sources.

If we look at the *Suinin-ki*, an even earlier source, it is written that in the Eighty-seventh Year a dog belonging to a man called Mikaso from the district of Tamba ate a badger, and the Yasakani curved gem was found in this badger's stomach. Bakin borrowed that curved gem story in writing of Yao-bikuni Myôchin in his novel, "The Tale of Eight Dogs." But the badger of Suinin only stored the precious jewels in its belly, and did not go to the extent of changing its form as did the badgers of later generations. Well then, let us conclude that badgers, from the second month of the spring of the Thirty-fifth Year of the Empress Suiko, adopted the habit of changing their form.

Of course, the badger has from ancient times—from the time of the Eastern Conquests by Jinmu—lived in Japanese mountains and fields. And, in the Year 1288 of the Foundation of the Empire (628 A.D.) the badger began to bewitch people. In reading this you might perhaps be quite astounded at first, but probably it all would have come about in this way—

ABOUT THAT TIME a girl living in Michinoku, a water drawer, fell in love with a saltmaker of the same village. But the girl lived under the supervision of her mother. So, to meet night after night in secret, they had to exercise extraordinary care.

Every night the boy would cross the sandhills to hover about the girl's house, whereupon the girl, heeding the appointed time, would quietly steal forth from the house. But the girl, who had to take every precaution not to arouse her mother's suspicions, was often late. One time the moon was already setting when at length she came to her beloved; at another time the first cocks were crowing far and near, and still she had not come.

Then, when the affair had gone on for some time, there was a night when the lad, crouching in the shadow of a rock shaped like a screen, began to sing in a loud voice to divert his loneliness;

mustering his impatient feelings in his brackish throat, he sang with all his might in an endeavor to be heard above the ferment of the seething waves.

The mother, hearing the voice, asked her daughter who was lying beside her what it might be; and the daughter, questioned by her mother twice—even three times—pretended to be asleep, yet when questioned so persistently she could not but venture an answer: "It was not a man's voice!"—Confused, the girl deceived her.

Then, what could it be if it were not a man?—persisted the mother. To which the girl showed her resourcefulness by replying that it might be a badger.—*Love* from antiquity has many times taught woman such tact.

After daybreak, the mother told an old mat-weaving woman, who lived nearby, of how she had heard the voice; the old woman, too, had been another who had heard the singing. Though she had said she doubted that badgers really sang, the old woman repeated the story to a reed-cutter.

Thus, the story was related here and there till it reached the ear of a mendicant priest who happened to be in the village. The priest explained in some detail the plausible reasons for a badger's singing. In the Buddhist teaching there is the matter of transmigration of souls; so the badger's spirit, had in a former life, perhaps, been the spirit of a man. If that were so, what men could do, so could badgers. The fact of a badger's singing on a moonlit night was not especially strange.

From that time, numerous people in this village reported having heard the badger sing. And, eventually a man came forward who had even *seen* the badger. He had gone to look for sea gulls' eggs one night, he said, and on his way back along the seashore, there in the light from the moon on the snow that still lingered,

he saw clearly a badger skulking in the shadows of the dunes–
and the badger was singing.

So, by this time, even its form had been seen. Thereafter, to
hear that voice, for almost all villagers–young and old, men and
women–came to be somewhat of a natural phenomenon. The
badger's song was heard on occasion from the mountains, sometimes from the sea; sometimes, too, it was heard here and there
from the thatched roof tops scattered between mountain and sea.
And not only that, ultimately even the young girl–the saltwater
drawer–was one night surprised by that singing voice.

The girl, of course, thought it was the voice of her lover.
Glancing at her mother's breathing, it seemed to her that her
mother was sleeping soundly; sneaking out of bed she opened
the door and peered outside. But, outside there was only the thin
moon and the sound of waves; and nowhere was there any sign
of the man. For a long time the girl looked about. Then suddenly,
as she felt the breath of a chill spring wind of evening, she stood
petrified with her hand on her cheek. At that moment she had
vaguely discerned in the sand before the door, the footprints of
a badger.

The story swiftly found its way to the Keiki district beyond
many hundreds of *ri* of mountains and rivers. Then the Yamashiro
badgers began to change their form; the badgers of Ômi began
to change. When the Tokugawa Era came, there was Dansaburô
of Sado Island, a creature who, though defined as neither badger nor racoon, began to bewitch people in Echizen Province
beyond the sea.

It was not that the badger came to *bewitch* people, but,
you might say, my friends, that it was *believed to bewitch*. Yet–
between *bewitchment* and *belief in bewitchment* there is not much
distinction.

Not only is this confined to badgers. After all, is not any *existence* but what we believe it to be?

In "The Celtic Twilight" Yeats wrote of the story of the children of Lough Gill who were convinced that a little Protestant lass, robed in blue and white, was St. Mary of ancient times. In this way, if we judged from the facts that exist within men's minds, St. Mary on the lake would not be different from the badgers in mountain and marsh.

We also, just as our ancestors believed in the transformation of badger people, should believe—should we not?—in what abides within our minds?—and should we not live according to the bidding of these beliefs?

It is for this reason that we should not be contemptuous of *badgers*.

HERESY

Introductory Note:
The dominant theme of "Heresy," as the name implies, is religion. The classical literature of the Heian era has given inspiration to the author—a circumstance that we cannot be critical of, without condemning Shakespeare for his pilfered themes.

"Heresy" has been included in this volume because of the magnificent portrayal it provides of Japanese aristocratic elegance. Contemporary Japanese, unfortunately, often boast proudly that their country is no longer "feudal," but is "free" and "democratic." Yet this story should indicate to those who are convinced that "liberty, equality, and fraternity" are heavenly ordained and natural human rights, that the further we progress towards such an "ideal" state, the less our civilization can provide of the elegance and gentility of the feudal ages.

Chronicles on the progress of mankind have universally provided us with ample evidence of the character of sons being the antithesis of the character of uncouth parents. The corollary is that there is normally a reaction among progeny against the vulgarity and cruelty of ancestors.

Since both vulgarity and cruelty have become characteristics of the twentieth century, one can, therefore, hope for some natural relief in future years against the heresy of materialism which has even been acknowledged by the Christian Churches in their battle for survival.

In this story, the young Lord of Horikawa represents the dignity and honor of the Japanese Court of the Heian era. The story must end with the expectation that such dignity and honor is self-sufficient without any foreign imposition. Upon the young Lord falls the onus of challenging the foreign "religion." It is left for the reader to decide which of the two dynamic characters of "Heresy" should be triumphant.

Throughout this story one may compare the grace and restraint of Court elegance and feudal honor with the abandon and gaudiness of this unrestrained democratic age.

"Heresy" ("Jashûmon") was written in November, Taishô 7 (1918) but never completed.

I

PREVIOUSLY I have told of the origin of the "Hell Screen"–the astounding incident which occurred during the lifetime of the Lord of Horikawa; and now I want to tell you of the one strange event in the life of the young Lord, his son. But, first I will tell you, in outline, of the passing of the old Lord who died from an unaccountable illness.

The young Lord was about nineteen years of age at the time. In speaking of this sudden illness, I should mention the fact that only six months or so previously, there were falling stars in the sky over his mansion; there was the untimely blossoming of the red plum in his garden; the white horses in his stables became black overnight; and the multi-colored and silver carp lay gasping in the mud of the pond, the waters of which had evaporated before one's eyes. Among such evil omens, what was considered especially terrifying was that a certain lady, on her dreaming pillow, saw a carriage fiercely blazing like that in which the daughter of Yoshihidé had ridden. Drawn by beasts with human faces, it descended from heaven, and from inside the carriage a gentle voice said: "Please fetch the Lord to this carriage"–such was the tale that went about–and, it was said, that at that moment the beasts with human faces groaned weirdly, and even in the darkness of her dream, she saw the beasts rise up, and their lips were blood red. Shrieking in her sleep she was at length awakened by her own voice, her entire body in a clammy sweat, her heart thumping as if to beat out an alarm. So, not only the lady, but all of us from the Lord's wife down, being anxious for the safety of the Lord, affixed talismans to the gate of the mansion and summoned priests of renowned experience that they might pray, each in his own fashion, but, in truth, the presaged fate was surely inevitable.

One day, with snow hovering about, and the cold hanging heavily, while riding in his carriage on his way back from the mansion of the Dainagon of Imadegawa, the Lord suddenly ran a high fever; by the time he had reached home his body had become an unpleasant purple, and he could only gasp: "It's hot! . . . It's hot!" It almost seemed that even the white twill covers of the bedding would be scorched. From that moment onward, priests, physicians, augerers beside his pillow–all of them–made desperate efforts on his behalf; but his fever rose higher and higher until at last he rolled over onto the floor, and in a distraught voice, unlike his own, he roared: "Aô!–There is a fire in my body!–The smoke–where does it come from?!" He died after six hours of agony so cruel that it defies description. The sadness, terror, awe at that time–even as I recall it now, I can distinctly see floating before my eyes the smoke from the holy invocation seeping through the shutters, the red skirts of the weeping Court ladies wandering about in distraction, the absent-minded fortune-tellers and magicians; even as I tell the story in passing, I cannot restrain my tears. Yet, pervading those recollections is the figure of the youthful Lord who, without appearing in the least perturbed beyond the overcast expression on his pale face, sits stiffly besides the pillow of the Lord, his father. At the thought of him a strange feeling—as of a tempered sword-edge well-burnished—coldly permeates my body; but, for all that, we thought him the more reliable of the two.

2

BETWEEN father and son, never could there have been so much that was contrary—from appearance to disposition—as between the Lord and the young Lord. The Lord, as you know, was a tall and sturdy man, but the young Lord was of medium stature—frail since his birth; unlike his manly heroic father, the young Lord was gentle of countenance. It could be said that the young Lord and his mother, the beautiful *kita-no-kata* (Lady Horikawa), were as alike as two melons. Closely-set eyebrows, cool eyes, the curl of the sensitive mouth—it was a womanly face he had, but there was a concealed depth in him. Not only did he appear splendid when arrayed in his Court dress—I would prefer to say that he was a figure worthy of veneration, such quiet authority did he possess.

If, however, I were to suggest where lay the most marked difference between the Lord and the young Lord, I would say it would have been in their dispositions. The Lord was grandiose and valiant in his actions; he had a spirit which, it was said, never ceased to intimidate people; but the young Lord who chose to be delicate on every point was, I remember, elegant in every way. As we can discern the Lord's disposition from the style of the mansion of Horikawa, so from the small Tatsuta-no-In at Nyakuôji, built by the young Lord can we gauge something of his elegant taste. The maple garden of the Tatsuta-no-In was just like the one in the poem by Kanshôjo; the clear stream running through and embroidering the garden, the countless white herons which were released onto the stream—in everything there was apparent the young Lord's grace and refinement.

The Lord showed preference for the martial arts; but the young Lord found his enjoyment in poetry, song and music and associated indiscriminately with those renowned for their skill in those arts. As though he were unmindful of his own status, he mixed freely with them. It was said that not only did he enjoy such pastimes, but that he had been absorbed for years in the intricacies of the various arts. Although he did not play the reed pipes, people asserted that since the time of the renowned Shichinominbu there was no other as worthy as the young Lord to ride in the Three Boats. To this day many poems by the young Lord remain in the verse collection of the Lord's family; the most praised of his poems is one he composed and recited on hearing the question and response of two Chinese at a Buddhist mass at the Ryugai Temple which had commissioned Yoshihidé's painting of the Five Phases of Transmigrations of Life and Death. As the two Chinese were examining the molded design on a Buddhist gong—of an eight-petalled lotus dividing two peacocks—one of the Chinese pronounced the words, *Shashin sha-ka-shi,* and the other replied with, *Da-fu-ryû-chô.* As the meaning was obscure, those congregated there began to discuss the words, and the young Lord overhearing the discussion, fluently and delicately wrote this poem on the back of a fan he held and passed it around:

Though struck, the birds take not to wing,
—In their enjoyment of the flowers
They are imperiling their lives.

3

As THE Lord and the young Lord were so completely different, the two were incompatible, it seemed, and the circumstances gave rise to a variety of rumors. One rumor was that father and son were competing for the same Court Lady, but I am sure such a foolish thing never could have happened. As far as I can remember, when the young Lord was fifteen or sixteen, the seeds of disharmony had already sprouted. This was in some way connected with the reason why the young Lord did not play the reed pipes, for, as I have already mentioned, he did not play them.

At one time, the young Lord showed an exceeding fondness for the reed instruments, so he became a disciple of Naka-mikado no Shô-nagon, a distant cousin. The famous reed instrument called the *Garyô* had been handed down to each succeeding generation of that man's family, together with musical scores—the *Daijiki* and *Nyujiki* tones; so Naka-mikado no Shô-nagon had a unique technique of his own.

The young Lord had, in the hope of being initiated into the *Daijiki* and *Nyujiki* tones, long applied himself assiduously to the Shô-nagon's instructions, but for some reason unknown to him Shô-nagon would not heed the young Lord's plea.

Not receiving any satisfactory reply on the several occasions he had pressed the Shô-nagon, the youthful Lord was naturally disappointed, and one day when he was playing a game of *sugoroku* with the Lord, he happened to voice his dissatisfaction. The Lord laughed heartily as usual but gently soothed him: "Don't be disturbed!–A time will come when the score will come to hand." Within two weeks it happened that Naka-mikado no Shô-nagon, on returning from a drinking bout at the Horikawa mansion, suddenly began hemorrhaging, and died. There seemed nothing out-of-the-ordinary about this event; but on the following day, when the young Lord went to the living quarters for no especial reason, there on his desk, inlaid with mother-of-pearl, lay the *Garyô* pipe and the *Daijiki* and *Nyujiki* scores, deliberately left there, so it was said, by some unknown hand.

Subsequently, when once more the Lord and the young Lord played *sugoroku* together, the Lord said with some emphasis:

"Are you making some progress on the reed pipes?"

The young Lord quietly stared at the checkerboard as he replied complacently:

"No, I have made up my mind that during the rest of my life I will never play the reed pipes."

"Why have you made such a decision?"

"It is just that I want to pray for the soul of the Shô-nagon."

As he spoke, the young Lord stared fixedly at his father's face. But the Lord, as though entirely oblivious of his voice, spiritedly shook the dice tube and remarked:

"Again, it seems, I have a straight win!"

–He continued with unconcern to follow through with his victory. This discussion proceeded no further, but, I remember that from that time there was a certain constraint dividing father and son.

4

FROM THEN up to the time of the Lord's demise, father and son watched each other as would two falcons hovering in the sky, each wary of the other at every instant. Yet, the young Lord disdained all forms of quarreling, and no matter what his father did, there was hardly a time when he would show his hostility, but rather would he, on the occasions he disapproved, smile ironically, a curl at the corners of his mouth, and utter but one or two sharp words of criticism.

When it was bruited throughout and beyond the Capital that the Lord had met with the night procession of the hundred demons of Nijô Omiya and had come to no harm, the young Lord turned to me and said facetiously:

"The demon has met demons! That my father was unharmed is not strange."

On a later occasion, at the Kawara-no-In at Higashi Sanjô, when even the nocturnal apparition of the spirit of Tôru, the deceased Minister of the Left, was exorcised by the Lord's authoritative command, I remember the young Lord saying with a similar curl on his lips:

"Tôru, the Minister of the Left, was a man of refined taste, was he not? So, quite out of tune with my father's mode of conversation, it is natural that he should vanish."

And, by chance, the Lord overheard these words uttered by his son; beneath the contemptuous smile there could be discerned on his face traces of the anger within his heart. Again, returning from a plum-viewing in the precincts of the Imperial Palace, the Lord's ox carriage happened to swerve and injure an old man on the road; the old man clasped his hands and gave thanks to Providence for having been run down by the oxen of the mighty Lord's carriage, and on that occasion also, in the presence of the father, the young Lord turned in the direction of the ox keepers:

"What simpletons they are! If they must swerve the carriage–why was the churlish fellow not run down and killed? If a mere injury causes him to clasp his hands–the old man would have been in ecstasy if he had met with his death under the carriage wheels and would have been be grateful for having been given such an opportunity to be greeted by the saints in Paradise. My father's fame would surely have been boosted. They are indeed dull-witted fellows."

I can recall the ill-humor of the Lord on that occasion as he raised his fan, and we–wondering if perhaps he would strike the young Lord in reproof–felt chilled, but the young Lord flashed his fine teeth as he said smiling:

"Father! Father! Such temper! Even the ox keepers are in a quandary! With this in mind, next time they run over a victim they will be sure of killing him, and my Lord's fame will be noised about as far as Shintan (China)."

Such was the guileless expression on the young Lord's face that his father became conciliatory and with pained expression could do nought but proceed on his way.

And so it was that, as he kept vigil at the passing of the Lord, his father, the set figure of the young Lord seemed most mysterious to us. But even now, as I recall that time–I feel the same reaction as though contemplating the keen edge of a well-tempered sword. Yet, for all that, strangely enough, we placed our trust in him. We were sharply conscious of the succession of authority at the time. Not only did we have this feeling with the mansion itself; it was as if the shadow which overcast the whole realm had suddenly swung from south to north, evoking a restlessness in us.

5

FROM THE day, therefore, that the young Lord succeeded to the headship of his House, never had there been an atmosphere of such serenity throughout the mansion; it was a genial as a spring breeze. It is hardly necessary to mention that poetry gatherings, contests in floral verse and exchanges of love verse have been constantly held there ever since. Also dating from the young Lord's succession, the attire of the Court ladies and of the samurai became as gay and colorful as to be almost a re-creation of the old pictorial scrolls. Another of the changes was in the personnel of those who frequented the Mansion. Even Ministers of State and great Generals who did not excel in some art or accomplishment were hardly ever received in audience by the young Lord. Or, if ever they were received, they felt ashamed of their own lack of refinement, as might be expected, and naturally rarely came to visit the young Lord.

On the other hand, those who excelled in poetry and music, even though they might be samurai without any rank or office, were likely to receive praise beyond their deserts. For example, on a certain autumn evening when the moonlight was shining through the lattice work and the grasshoppers were chirping, he summoned an attendant, and it was a newly appointed samurai who came. Whatever he was thinking of, he suddenly turned to the man with the demand:

"The grasshoppers are chirping–listen to them!–Compose a verse about it!"

The samurai at his feet, inclined his head for a time, then at length began to recite:

"The young willow's . . ."

–So far he had not made the customary reference to the season, and as this seemed odd, some tittering arose among the ladies; but the samurai continued:

> The young willow thread
> the grasshopper spins
> through the summer–
> In the autumn weaves his song.

A sudden silence fell after this eloquent recitation, and a clover-patterned ceremonial Court robe was thrust towards him into the moonlight seeping through the lattice. In fact, the samurai who had spoken was the only son of my elder sister and the same age as the young Lord. Beginning thus his public service, he afterwards was a frequent recipient of the Lord's patronage.

This incident, then, gives a general idea of the Lord's mode of living. Meanwhile, having taken a wife, year by year his official rank was raised; but as this fact is well known I shall not dwell upon it. Rather I shall hasten to fulfill my promise and shall recount the one strange event in the young Lord's lifetime. I would say that though he enjoyed the reputation of being "the most gallant man throughout the land"–in truth, he differed from his father in that his life was an uneventful one. Besides this one incident, I remember no other anecdote of importance which would be widely known.

6

OUR STORY begins five or six years after the former Lord's passing. Around that time the young Lord was writing letters to a young Lady celebrated for her beauty–the only daughter of Naka-mikado no Shô-nagon to whom we have previously referred. Even now when anyone inadvertently refers to his infatuation at that time, the young Lord always passes it off lightheartedly.

"The universe is vast," he would say, "those were the days of dreams, and love moved me to write clumsy songs and verse. When one thinks of it, it is the same madness as trampling on a fox's mound, is it not?"

He was quite without restraint in openly deriding himself. But at the time the young Lord had been completely absorbed in his attachment, which was quite exceptional for him.

Yet, he was not the only one affected in this way. I would not be far wrong in saying that every young courtier of the day was infatuated by the Lady. About the family mansion of Nijô Nishi-no-Tôin there was a constant stream of suitors arriving by carriage or on foot. It was rumored that on moonlight nights it would not be out-of-the-ordinary to hear beneath the pear blossoms the flute music of not one but of two admirers in their *taté-yé boshi*.

It was a fact that the renowned genius, Sugawara Masa-hira, when his passion for this Lady was unrequited had, in his despair suddenly renounced this world and had gone to Tsuku-shi (Kyûshû) or had perhaps even braved the Eastern Seas and crossed to China. No one was quite sure of his whereabouts. He had been one of the young Lord's close associates, a companion in verse; he used to refer to the young Lord as Rakuten and to himself as Tôba. For so highly talented a person–irrespective of how beautiful the Lady Naka-mikado was–for him to exile himself because of one rebuff cannot be regarded as anything but heedless.

But, in thinking it over, perhaps it was not without reason. As I have said, the Lady Naka-mikado was beautiful. I once saw her attired in a resplendent garment, a brocade of a willow and cherry pattern studded with jewels; with downcast languorous eyes, she was a glittering figure under the oil lamp; the charm of her figure is an unforgettable memory. But this Lady–quick to discern human character, readily perceived the shallowness of the indiscreet courtiers, and so she teased them unsparingly even as she would a pet cat that she would not allow to return to her lap.

7

So, MANY amusing situations arose among those who paid court to this Lady–situations quite reminiscent of the *Takétori Tale*. There is a most pathetic incident involving Kyôgoku no Sadaiben whom the urchins of the capital used to refer to as Sadaiben the Crow on account of his swarthy complexion; but this was no hindrance to his passionate feelings, and he was very much enamored of the Lady of Naka-mikado. Though keen-witted, this Sadaiben had a rather timid disposition, so he could not bring himself to declare his passion for the Lady; and even within his own circle of friends he was most reticent in this matter. He was unable to conceal entirely, however, his secret adoration, and there were times when those of his own group would tease him and would entangle him with their questions. On such occasions Sadaiben the Crow would desperately sidestep them with various devices.

"It's not just a matter of my being in love. As the Lady herself has shown some response, I am indeed becoming more confident of success." He would even quote various phrases from the letters and even poems which he hinted had been sent to him by the Lady; thus he endeavored indirectly to instill the idea that the Lady was consumed with love for him. His friends, always mischief bent, half-believing, half-doubting, lost no time in forging a letter from the Lady and inserting it in a sprig of wisteria and arranged for it to be delivered to Sadaiben.

There was a ringing in his heart as Kyôgo no Sadaiben hastily broke the seal of the letter, and learned that though the Lady had yearned for him to return the love she bore him, she had waited in vain and in her grief had written to inform him that, reconciling herself to the burden of her love, she had decided for the remainder of her life to take holy vows. Even in his dreams he would not have dared imagine that the Lady returned his love; so now, Sadaiben the Crow did not know whether to be sad or happy. With the letter spread open before him, after a time, he sighed and decided he would declare the longings with which his eyes abounded–longings which until then he had concealed in his breast. It was towards the end of the May rains, so taking along a serving boy to hold up his big umbrella, he made his way to the gate of the Nijô Nishi-no-Tôin Mansion. The gates were heavily barred, and, although he knocked loudly, there seemed no likelihood that they would be opened. Meanwhile, night came, and, as the walled road was an unfrequented one, he heard only the frogs croaking; rain fell, soaking his clothes. He gradually became numb and his eyes hazy.

This was his plight when at length the gate bolts were drawn, and forthwith an aging samurai like myself, one Heidaiyu, handed over a letter enwrapped as was the previous letter in a wisteria branch, and firmly replaced the bolts on the gate.

He returned home weeping, and when he perused the letter, there was but one stanza of an old song scrawled across the page, and beyond this, it did not communicate one word:

Though I have pined for love
thou dost requite it not!
No longer would thy Lady
bear vain love for thee.

Needless to say, the Lady had learned the details, from the mischievous young Lords, of the constraint of Sadaiben the Crow.

8

IN COMPARISON to the young ladies of society of the time, it might seem that I have been exaggerating the Lady's conduct, but as my purpose is to reveal something of the affairs of the young Lord in whose service I am, it would surely be pointless for me to stray from the truth. There was, in fact, another Lady much under discussion in the Capital at the time—a very strange Lady, indeed, in that she had a great liking for insects and creeping forms of life; it is said that she even kept snakes. But, to tell more about her here would be entirely irrelevant. . . . Upon the death of her parents, the Lady Naka-mikado had appointed Heidaiyu as head retainer over the various men- and maidservants. Benefitting from hereditary wealth, she was able to lead an unrestrained existence, and, endowed with natural beauty and intelligence, deigned to live without fear of censure.

In a society in which rumors were rife, even among her kinsmen, there were some who said she was actually the daughter of the wife of the Shô-nagon and the former Lord Horikawa, and that the Lord had poisoned Naka-mikado, out of jealousy. But the circumstances of his death were as I have recounted them, and there was no foundation of truth in that rumor. If the circumstances had been actually as others suggested, never would the young Lord have considered giving his heart to that Lady.

According to all I have been told, the Lady had at first been curt in her rejection of the young Lord's fervent advances. At one time even, when my nephew had been entrusted with the young Lord's letter, just as with Sadaiben the Crow, the gates were not opened for him. Indeed, Heidaiyu, hating to the point of revenge the House of Horikawa, on that occasion thrust his white head among the late spring pear blossoms that projected above the wall, and rolling back the sleeves of his drab hunting garb, snarled at my nephew who was trying to force open the gates.

"Ah, a thief!–and in daylight I have no pity for thieves!!–If you take even one step inside this gate, Heidaiyu will take his sword and cut you in two and cast you outside again."

If it had been myself who was thus threatened, we would surely have come to blows, but my nephew only pelted Heidaiyu with ox-dung from the roadside before returning home.

From that time, even if the young Lord did contrive to have his letters delivered safely, he received not even one reply. Yet, he ignored his failure, and for over three months continued to dispatch to her letters, songs, and splendid painted scrolls. What the young Lord says is no less than the truth:

"Those were days of dreams, when love moved me to write clumsy songs and verse."

9

AT THIS time a grotesque priest–the like of whom had never before been seen–appeared in the Capital preaching the Mary Religion. As he was much talked about, there will be some of you who did come to hear him. He was compared with the *tengu* which are depicted in books and come from the land of Shintan (China), or with the devil that haunted the palace of one of the royal princesses.

If my memory be reliable, the first time I saw that priest was on a certain hazy day in springtime. Returning from an errand, I happened to pass by the Shinsen Gardens. Clustered by the wall outside the gardens were twenty or thirty people wearing *momi-é* and *tatéyé* hats, and, also, the popular *ichimé* headgear–and there were even a scattering of children propped on stilts, all railing and clamoring; I thought it might have been some mad dancer under the curse of a powerful god, or a stupid Ômi merchant who had had his goods snatched by a thief. With no particular interest I was nevertheless tempted, by virtue of the commotion to keep to the rear of the crowd.

I was surprised to see this priest–in appearance much like a beggar–letting forth a steady flow of language. The pennant on the pole he was holding aloft bore the likeness of some unfamiliar bodisâttva. I would place his age at about thirty. Swarthy, with uplifted eyes, the expression on his face was somehow frightening; and for clothes he wore a tattered black robe. His hair fell in a whirl around his shoulders, and the queer charm in the shape of a cross that hung about his neck surely marked him as being no ordinary priest. As I watched, a gust of wind blowing through the gardens scattered cherry petals about his head, and I gained the feeling that, rather than priest, he was surely one of the *chira-eyu* demons; and his weird appearance sparked the imagination to believe that his kite's wings were hidden beneath his robes.

Just then, a stalwart man beside me–possibly a blacksmith–as quick as thought, wrested a stilt from the hands of one of the children, and gnashing his teeth, yelled:

"How dare you call Jizô-Bosatsu a *tengu!*"

He struck out at the priest's head; whereupon, the priest bared his teeth in an unpleasant smile, and, as the wind blew the petals about the portrait of the female bodisâttva, the priest upbraided him:

"Even if you attain glory in this life, but violate the commands of the Heavenly Emperor, when the time arrives for you to pass life's barrier, you will fall headlong into the agonizing torments of hell, and your flesh, tumbling into hell's furnace, will groan to the extremity of time. Moreover, even before you face death, you who would persecute a priest of Mary, will within the day merit severe retribution from the angels of heaven. You will inhabit a leprous body!"

We were overawed by such vehemence; and even the blacksmith, balancing the stilt like a halberd, stared amazed at the priest's frenzied outburst.

10

ON THE spur of the moment, the blacksmith once again raised the stilt and lunged at the priest.

"Haven't you finished your babbling, yet?" he railed; and at the same moment we saw the blacksmith severely strike out with the stilt at the priest's face, and it seemed that another inflamed weal would be left on those sunburned cheeks. But, sweeping aside the fallen petals that lay scattered over the bamboo, it was the blacksmith and not the priest who had suddenly collapsed on the ground.

All winced on seeing this and instinctively prepared for flight. The *momi-é* and *tatéyé* hats, with a show of cowardice, suddenly moved back from around the priest. The blacksmith, still grasping the stilt as he lay sprawled on his back at the feet of the priest, frothed at the mouth as though he were epileptic, while the priest looked on at the man's breathing.

"You see! Do you still think me a hypocrite! The host of angels have, on the instant, struck down with unseen swords this wayward fellow. He is fortunate that his head is not broken and his blood not flowing over the roads of the Capital," announced the priest arrogantly.

Then suddenly, from among this group of people become so silent, arose the wild crying of one of those children who had had stilts; his unbound hair awry, he ran stumbling to the side of the fallen blacksmith.

"Father, Father, yô! Father!"

Over and over the child cried thus, but the blacksmith showed no sign of regaining consciousness; and the whiteness of the foam from his lips, blown by the restless spring wind, was scattered over the breast of his hunting jacket.

The child repeated:

"Father, yô!"

–But when he saw that the blacksmith made no reply, with a grim threatening look, he jumped to his feet, and with both hands he seized the stilt from his father's grasp and struck out impetuously. But the priest warded off the blows with the flagpole, and with a show of unconcern laughed again unpleasantly. Then he said gently to the boy:

"This is absurd. That your father has lost his senses is not the work of the Mary Priest. But injuring me," he said in reproof, "will not revive your father."

Needless to say, it was not such logic that halted the child who, in any case, had not really expected to overcome the priest in such an engagement. The blacksmith's small son, flourishing the stilt five or six times, broke into sobs and stood cowering in the street.

II

GRINNING at this development, the Mary Priest went over to the boy.

"Well now, you are a reasonable boy, intelligent beyond your years. If you calm yourself, the many angels of heaven will reward you and will come down and revive your father's spirit. I shall assist you to pray; follow my example and we shall beseech the mercy of the Heavenly Emperor."

Having thus spoken, the priest, clasping the flagpole in both hands, knelt in the middle of the road and lowered his head in reverence. Closing his eyes, he began to recite loudly what sounded like a weird *dhârani*. It must have been for about an hour that he continued in this way while we, in a circle about him, listened to his strange incantation; at length, opening his eyes, from where he knelt the priest stretched his hand over the blacksmith's head; instantly the face began to regain its normal color, until eventually a long groan spilled forth from between the frothy lips.

"Ah! My father has come back to life!"

Discarding the stilts the child, joyful once more, ran to his father's side. But, before he had been able to assist in any way, the blacksmith groaned as he gradually began to raise himself, his movements unsteady like those of a drunken man. Apparently satisfied, the priest stood up quietly, and, as if to shield them from the sun, he held the banner of the female bodisâttva over the heads of parent and child, then spoke with sternness.

"The grace of the Heavenly Emperor, like this vast sky, is broad and infinite.–Can you not believe?"

The blacksmith and his child were still kneeling on the ground embracing one another. In dread of his priestly powers their souls would surely have whirled off into the sky. With eyes raised to the female bodisâttva, trembling they joined their hands in praise and worshipped. Then, all of a sudden, two or three of those among us doffed their broad hats, while others adjusted their smaller *é-boshi* and seemed to join in the worship. But feeling repelled, without knowing why, I felt that the priest and the female bodisâttva's image were somehow imbued with the wind from the world of evils. Taking advantage of the blacksmith's recovery, I hastily got to my feet and left that place.

I learned afterwards that this priest's teaching had come over from Shintan (China) and was called the teaching of Mary. Nothing definite was known about him, although it was even said that although born in this country, he had grown up in China; others said he came not from Shintan or Japan, but from Indian climes, and that though he walked the streets by day, by night he converted his black dyed robe into wings and would fly up into the sky about the pagoda of the Yasaka Temple. But there was no foundation in such lies. Nevertheless, so numerous were the miraculous deeds attributed to this Mary Priest that there did seem to be some truth in the reports.

12

THE MOST outstanding of such feats was that this Mary Priest, through the mysterious powers of his *dhârani*, instantly cured many sick people. He gave eyes to the blind, legs to the lame and tongues to the dumb. It would be a task to enumerate all such accomplishments. But, the most renowned of his cures would surely have been the cure of the boil with human face with which the Governor of Settsu was afflicted. The Governor had assassinated his nephew, then had stolen the nephew's wife; whereupon, it is said that in punishment the nephew's face appeared on the uncle's left kneecap in the form of a strange boil. Day and night he suffered great pain as though his kneecap were being whittled. Upon subjecting himself to the priest's incantation, "the face" softened in color in a moment, and from the place where the mouth appeared to be, the word, "Namu!" was uttered; then it disappeared leaving no trace. In every case where people had been possessed by foxes or by *tengu* or by some strange unfamiliar demons, once they had received the cross talisman, just as vermin are shaken off the foliage of trees during a gale, those demons were dislodged.

Nevertheless, these widely talked of powers of the Mary Priest had another aspect. It has been my own experience to witness in the streets that priest pronouncing fearful punishments on people who denounced the Mary Religion or persecuted Mary believers; resulting from such curses, well water changed to foul-smelling blood, rice on the stalk was devoured overnight by grasshoppers, the vestal virgins of the Hakushu-sha, in retribution for their having prayed for the death of the Mary Priest, had become unsightly lepers. In the aftermath of such events, rumor that the priest was a *tengu* changeling strengthened. But, a hunter from furthest Kurama, having averred that he would shoot the priest with an arrow were the man really a *tengu,* was suddenly blinded, perhaps pierced by the swords of those heavenly angels; he consequently became a believer in the Mary Religion.

Such was the influence of the priest that old and young, men and women, gradually were converted to his beliefs. When a person became a believer, there was a *kanchô*-like ceremony in which, it was said, devotees were wet on the head with water. There was no other way of proclaiming conversion to the new God except through this ceremony. One day when my nephew was passing over the big Shijô bridge, he saw a crowd on the bank under the bridge, and taking a look to see what it was about, he saw that it was the Mary Priest administering his mysterious ceremony to a samurai who seemed to be from the east country. They were on the bank of the Kamo River. The warm water on which cherry petals were reflected, the shadow of the erect samurai kneeling reverently with a long sword at his side and the strange priest holding up the cross: my nephew said that the spectacle of this unfamiliar ceremony was a most intriguing one.

In speaking of all this, I have forgotten to mention that, when he first came there, the Mary Priest had constructed a small straw hut among the outcasts' dwellings on the Shijô bank, where he lived a completely isolated existence.

13

But to return to the young Lord. . . .

It was an unexpected chance that brought him to more intimate terms with the lady of his heart—the Lady Nakamikado. The

event of which I speak happened one night whe
of orange blossoms and the voice of the cuckoo b
rain to come, though, oddly enough, the moon wa
bright to distinguish faces. The young Lord was on h
from a clandestine affair, and in order to escape noti   , instead
of his usual conspicuous retinue, he had taken along only one or
two servants. The carriage proceeded at a leisurely pace under the
bright moon. On account of the lateness of the hour, there were
no others abroad–the only sounds came from the voices of frogs
and the carriage wheels. Outside the lonely Bifuku-mon, especially
since many fox fires burned there, there was an indefinable atmosphere of foreboding; even the pace of the soulless oxen seemed
to hasten. Then, suddenly from the shadow of the wall nearby,
there was a strange coughing; white blades flashed brightly in the
moonlight. Six or seven masked men–apparently robbers–fiercely
bore down from left and right on the young Lord's carriage.

The ox-keepers and servants took fright; in this confusion, at
the very first moment of peril they fled as fast as they could in the
direction in which they had come. The robbers ignored them,
and one of the bands swiftly seized the oxen reins; as soon as he
had halted the carriage in the middle of the road, a fence of white
blades came from all sides to surround the carriage, hemming it
in. First, the fellow who seemed to be chief rudely pushed aside
the curtains, then called to his companions.

"What do you say?–We have the right man now, have we
not?"

Even in his surprise the young Lord thought this puzzling, as
their attitude did not seem to be that of robbers. Having made no
movement until then, the Lord peered sideways, from behind his
fan, in his opponent's direction, and, as he did so, a hoarse voice
full of hate replied:

"Yes, he is the Lord all right!"

The Lord thought that he had heard that voice somewhere before, and he became more and more suspicious; in the moonlight, as he stared fixedly at the owner of the voice, he felt sure it was Heidaiyu who had for many years served the Lady Naka-mikado. In that moment, as one might expect, it seemed that he was so afraid that the hair on his body stood up of itself; for report of Heidaiyu's revengeful hate for the House of Horikawa had come to the ears of the young Lord long before.

At Heidaiyu's reply, the robber leader turned the tip of his sword to the young Lord's breast, and in a voice even more gruff, he menaced:

"Take your farewell of life!"

14

THEN THE young Lord, who—to the point of obstinacy—rarely lost his composure, regained his courage; complacently toying with his fan, he spoke out as though the matter had no connection with himself:

"Wait! Wait!—Since you demand my life, I shall surrender it, as I have no alternative.—But, first tell me why you want it."

At this, the bandit who seemed to be chief, steadily shifting his white blade closer to the Lord's breast, said:

"Who killed the Shô-nagon of Naka-mikado?"

"I don't know who killed him. I only know that I had nothing to do with his death. There is evidence enough of that."

"It was either you or your father.—You were surely involved, so we can be revenged on you," said the man who seemed to be chief.

From under their masks, the other bandits joined in abusively:

"Yes, we can be revenged on you!"

Stepping out from among the bandits, Heidaiyu gnashed his teeth, animal-like, as he peered into the carriage and pointed his sword at the young Lord. He said derisively:

"Resistance is useless. You had better say your prayers."

But the young Lord, with his customary composure, seemed not to see the point of the white blade.

"Then, do you all belong to the Shô-nagon's household?" he inquired, as though tossing the words at them. The bandits all seemed to hesitate before replying. Sensing the atmosphere, Heidaiyu forthwith made haste to answer:

"Yes, we do.–So, what about it?"

"Ah, nothing in particular. Supposing some of you did not come from the Shô-nagon's House?–you would be the greatest fools under heaven."

The young Lord showed his white teeth, and his shoulders shook with laughter. The cutthroats were dumbfounded. At this, even the sword point at his breast was withdrawn into the moonlight outside the carriage.

"Why I say this," continued the young Lord, "is that, having assassinated me, you will be condemned to death when the officers of the peace locate you. If you are, in truth, of the Shô-nagon's household, and you are sacrificing your lives out of loyalty, perhaps that is your desire. But, if some of you did not happen to belong to the Shô-nagon's household and were merely hoping for a little money, then he who would for that reason thrust his sword into my body would be a fool to exchange the only thing he has for the reward. Isn't that reasonable enough?"

At this the bandits looked at one another.

Only Heidaiyu raged:

"Who is a fool? That you will be killed by the sword of a fool—does not that make *you* a hundred times *more* foolish?"

"So, you, too, say that they are foolish!–Then there must be some among you who do not belong to the Shô-nagon's House. The matter becomes more and more interesting. This being the case, I have something to say to those among you who do not belong to the Shô-nagon. Your only reason for killing me can be the monetary reward. Since it is money you want, I'll give you whatsoever you ask. Is it not better to make more profit simply by helping me?"

Smiling pompously, the young Lord tapped his fan on his pleated skirt as he spoke to the bandits outside.

15

"As it happens, we would not be indisposed to such a suggestion," somewhat humbly replied the man who seemed to be chief.

A dread hush fell over the bandits. With some satisfaction, the Lord flapped his fan and said jocularly:

"Then I am grateful. What I would ask of you is not especially difficult. The old man here belonging to the House of Shô-nagon would be Heidaiyu. I understand that this man has recently declared his hate of me and has been making outrageous plans to take my life when the opportunity would arise. You have unmistakably been under Heidaiyu's persuasion."

"That's true," said each of three or four bandits, their voices muffled by their masks.

"Well–what I would ask of you is to secure the old schemer,

for I have long wanted to cut this evil root. In your strength, will you not bind him?"

The robbers were astonished at this suggestion. The chief of this masked group which surrounded the carriage, looked from one to another for a while, as if to test the atmosphere of confusion. They soon quieted down, until suddenly from among them, a hoarse voice, like the crying of a nightbird, arose:

"You are foolish. You are taken in by the speech of this Lord who still reeks of his mother's milk. You merely fumble with your drawn swords, while recklessly you even tell him that you will follow his will. Have you no obligation to me? But, no matter. I do not need your assistance. With my own sword, I can take this Lord's life in a moment."

Even as he spoke, flashing his sword, he was about to spring at the young Lord. But the chief bandit simply threw down his blade and wrested Heidaiyu aside. Whereupon, the other bandits, sheathing their swords in their scabbards, just like grasshoppers, sprang from all sides onto Heidaiyu. Being but one against so many, and that one an old man, there was no resistance. The old man was bound hastily with a rope—probably the oxen reins—and pulled onto the moonlit street. Heidaiyu, just like a fox in a trap, bared his teeth, as he panted in distress and disappointment.

The young Lord then, after observing it all, gave a mixed smile and yawn.

"Oh, well done, well done! Now I can say that my equanimity is restored. If you could escort my carriage, we will haul the old dolt to Horikawa Mansion."

The bandits did not make any objection. And, in lieu of the servants, they walked on slowly in the moonlight with the fettered old man in their midst. Though the world is wide, there would surely have been none other than the young Lord who could arrange with bandits thus to escort him. Before the strange parade had reached the Mansion, we had set out to meet the young Lord straightway on our hearing of his plight. Each of the robbers was promptly rewarded, and all stealthily dispersed.

16

THE YOUNG Lord had Heidaiyu brought to the Horikawa Mansion and tied to a post in the stables, while a servant was commanded to stand guard; and on the next day, while the garden was still enveloped in mist, he summoned Heidaiyu to the garden.

"So, Heidaiyu, your idea of revenging the Shô-nagon was unmistakably foolish; still, there is something laudable in your action. And, I would certainly say that your plan of rounding up masked men to assassinate me does not lack romantic intrigue that one would hardly have expected from you. But the locality—the environs of the Bifuku-mon was not such a good choice. For such a purpose, the Tadasu woods would surely have been better—amid the shade of old trees; on a summer moonlight night there you can hear quite near at hand the sound of a babbling stream, and the white glimmer of the *u-no-hana* adds its touch of elegance. It is perhaps unreasonable to expect you to choose such an atmosphere. But as I do commend the motive behind your action, I am of a mind to bestow forgiveness on your misdemeanor—"

The young Lord, as always, smiled brightly as he spoke.

"Since you are here, you can, incidentally, deliver a letter to your Lady.—I insist upon it!"

The expression on Heidaiyu's face on this occasion was the

strangest I have ever seen anywhere. His pained expression was a mixture of neither tears nor mirth, and his glaring eyes roved busily. His expression was laughable, but for that very reason it was all the more pitiful. The young Lord, becoming solemn, gave the gracious command to the servant who held the man's bonds:

"Well now—further detention would cause only undue bother to Heidaiyu. It would be just as well to release him now."

Even from the one night's captivity, Heidaiyu was bent stiff like a bow. Bearing a sprig of wild orange blossom attached to the young Lord's letter, he straightway crawled out through the rear gate and fled. Then, I saw my nephew quietly follow Heidaiyu through the gate, without his having asked the Lord's permission. He was following discreetly in the footsteps of the old man to make sure that Heidaiyu did not misuse the letter.

About half a *chô* separated Heidaiyu and my nephew. Perhaps conscious only of his freedom, Heidaiyu, barefooted, trudged weakly alongside the wall of one of the highways of the Capital where the smell of young persimmon leaves hung in the beclouded sky. The vegetable sellers and those others who passed along the street—they must have thought him a strange letter bearer, for some turned to look at him with suspicion, while others glared; but he seemed not to notice.

As there was no change in the old man's conduct, my nephew was on the point of turning back, but hardly had he done so when he changed his mind, and he decided to go on just a little further. As he turned into Abura-street, he saw the extraordinary priest, who was coming from the opposite direction, almost collide with Heidaiyu near the shrine of the god Sae. He needed but a glance at the female bodisâttva banner, the black robe and the weird talisman cross, to know that it was the Mary Priest.

17

THE Mary Priest suddenly drew back with a start, and for some reason stopped to stare straight at the figure of Heidaiyu. But the old man paid no heed whatsoever, and stepping aside two or three paces, he trudged on along the road. It seemed to my nephew that the Mary Priest looked with suspicion on Heidaiyu's curious appearance. The priest, standing before the Sae Shrine seemed to take a very close interest in Heidaiyu as he passed, though it seemed that the old man had not indeed noticed. Although this priest was said to be a *tengu* in human form, my nephew said that, at the time, he would not have agreed to this theory, for while the priest's attention had been fastened on Heidaiyu, there had been tears in his eyes, and his glance had been one of compassion with no trace of evil. Bathed in the shade of the green leaves of an oak which extended its branches over the roof of the shrine, he bore over his shoulder the banner of that female bodisâttva; my nephew said that this once, at least, he felt favorably disposed towards that priest who gazed fixedly at the retreating figure of Heidaiyu.

But, meanwhile, the Mary Priest showed alarm at my nephew's footsteps, and, as though awakening from a dream, he turned abruptly, and raising his hand on high, described the figure *nine*, while repeating some magic formula; then he hastily moved on. My nephew said that throughout this spell-casting he thought he had heard the priest utter a word that sounded like "Naka-mikado;" but he could never be quite sure of this. Heidaiyu, still bearing the wild orange branch, continued dejectedly on his way without once having averted his eyes. My nephew followed him right to the Nishi-no-Tôin, but, so concerned was he about the strange cavorting of the Mary Priest, that he very nearly forgot

about the young Lord's letter and said he was oppressed by a
pained feeling of uneasiness.

But it did seem that the letter was delivered without incident
into the hands of the Lady, for, oddly enough, this time there
was a prompt reply. We underlings could not be sure of what
really happened, but as the Lady had a magnanimous nature, it
seemed likely that Heidaiyu would have acquainted her of his
attempt at assassination, and of the outcome; and thus she would
be for the first time impressed with the prowess of the young
Lord. After a further two or three letters had been exchanged
between them, at length on a night of drizzling rain, the young
Lord, accompanied by my nephew, for the first time visited in
secret the Mansion of Nishi-no-Tôin which was already buried
in the shadows of the willows. Once the affair had come to that,
Heidaiyu, as might be expected, was humbled. That night, on his
coming face to face with my nephew, though he frowned, he had
no spirit for abusive words.

18

THEREAFTER, the young Lord was almost a nightly visitor at
the Mansion of Nishi-no-Tôin; and it was only when I went as
his attendant that, for the first time, I was able to reverence the
Lady's dazzling beauty. Once when the two were together, sum-
moning me to draw close they urged me to talk of the changes I
had seen in my time. I remember that the starlit water of the pond
glistened through the bamboo blinds, and a faint perfume from
the scattered remains of the wisteria pervaded the cool atmosphere. As the lovers sat quietly together over their saké with one
or two ladies-in-waiting, the beauty of the scene appeared to me

as an incarnation of a Yamato painting. I remember especially the evanescence of the Lady who, attired in a pastel undergarment over a white kimono, could not have been inferior to Princess Kaguya.

Soon, the young Lord, in a playful mood from the saké, casually turning to the Lady, remarked:

"Now, a sage once said that even in the narrow confines of this Capital, the mulberry fields would have become as the sea. It is the law of the whole world that there is unceasing change; birth and destruction rise and fall like a river; and not for a moment can the world remain still. Even in the scriptures it is preached concerning mutability that *never at one moment has there been ought that is idle!* It would seem that our love, too, cannot escape this law. Only with its beginning and its ending are we concerned!"

Though he had spoken lightly, the Lady's mood changed to one of brooding as, purposely avoiding the light from the oil lamp, she suggested:

"Ah–you say only hateful things!–then from the beginning it has been your intention to forsake me?"

Coyly she peeped at the young Lord, but the young Lord, with increasing good humor, drained his cup before replying:

"No, rather would I say, that from the beginning it has been my expectation to be discarded rather than to discard; that is a more suitable expression of my feelings."

"Tease me as you please."

The Lady smiled just the once, charmingly, but quickly again cast her eyes absently into the hues of the night outside the bamboo blinds.

"All love in this world–is it always as transient, I wonder?" she said, as though in soliloquy.

Then the young Lord, smiling as ever, showed his fine teeth.

"No one can say it is not transient. Forgetting the Buddha's laws on change, mortals can bask for a while in the wondrous pleasures of the lotus world only in moments of love. Yes, only then, we may say that we forget even the mutability of love. In my opinion, Narihira in giving himself completely to the enjoyment of love showed great wisdom. We, too, leaving the mundane agonies of this impure world, live in the eternity of Buddha (the land of bliss and serene light) by enjoying our love–a love as expressed in the *Isé Monogatari*. Somehow, don't you think there is some truth in it?"

He stole a glance at the Lady.

19

"–So the bounty could be said to be infinite."

At the length turning his gaze from the Lady who had shyly lowered her eyes, the young Lord looked in my direction, and still gay from the effects of the saké, he said:

"Somehow, I feel sure that you, too, old sir, would think as I. However, I shall not discuss love with you; but, tell me, what is your favorite saké?"

"Well, if I do indulge myself, I always grow concerned about its ill-effect on the afterlife."

In my confusion in answering I scratched my white head, but the young Lord was amused:

"Ah, it is a good answer–none better. You say, old man, that you fear its ill-effect on the afterlife, but the soul which yearns to be born anew on yonder shore of bliss, relies, as it were, on a light in the darkness; there is little difference in the soul which thus seeks to forget momentarily this world's inevitable changing. If such be so, in the end, we are both seeking the same thing–you through the Buddhist Way and I through mortal love."

"I cannot follow your reasoning. Indeed, this Lady's beauty could not even be surpassed by a celestial muse, but love is love, Buddha is Buddha, and, moreover, one's favorite saké. . . . How can all these matters be discussed in one breath?"

"But your thinking is too narrow. To my mind, Amida and women are but puppet players who help us to forget our sadness."

As the young Lord pushed this point, the Lady suddenly stole a glance at him.

"Women might dislike being referred to as puppets."

She had spoken in a small voice.

"If it be unpleasant to be a puppet, I would say that women are bodisâttva."

The young Lord was spirited in his reply, but, as if on sudden recollection, his eyes wandered towards the *otono* oil lamp.

"Years ago I was on intimate terms with Sugiwara Masahira, and often we did argue about such matters. As you would know, Masahira was different from me in that it was easy for him to have faith; one might say that he had an unstudied simplicity. I would deride the golden sutra as mere "love songs," and he would become vexed, and over and over again would rebuke me for my worldliness and heresy. Even though his voice is yet in my ears, I cannot say where Masahira would be now. . . ."

His tone as he spoke was unusually subdued, and we were all, perhaps, drawn into his mood. All of us–including the Lady and myself–held our silence while throughout the room the scent of the wisteria grew stronger. One of the ladies-in-waiting, to push a wedge into the conversation, broke in timidly:

"If I may say so, it is said that the Mary Religion has recently become fashionable in the Capital. That would be a novel expedient to help one forget the inevitability of change."

Another of the ladies-in-waiting added:

"But I would say that the priest who goes about preaching this religion, has in many respects gained a dubious reputation."

Speaking somewhat uneasily, deliberately—it would seem—she turned up the wick of the oil lamp.

20

"OH, THE Mary Religion? There, we have an unusual doctrine."

The young Lord, who had been dreaming, raised his saké cup as he turned his awakened attention to the ladies-in-waiting.

"The name *Mary* would seem to imply that it is a religion which reverences Mari-shiten."

"No, if it were Mari-shiten, it would not be so bad, but the object of adoration is said to be some unfamiliar female bodisâttva."

"There is also the theory that this Mary was the consort of King Hashi-no-ku."

I then told all about the antics of the Mary Priest when I had seen him outside the Shinsen Gardens.

"No, the figure of this female bodisâttva is not like the Consort, Mari. Indeed, it is not like the image of *any* bodisâttva—she is even embracing a naked child, and so appears very much like the female demon of the night who eats human flesh. In any case, this heretical idea is certainly something unique to Japan."

Pursuing my opinions, the Lady frowned demurely:

"Then this man who is called the *Mary Priest* really appears like some metamorphosed *tengu?*"

"That's so. He gives the impression that he came forth on wings from the midst of a burning mountain. But he would not dare to haunt the Capital in daylight in this form."

Then, the young Lord, smiling serenely as before, said:

"But such a possibility is not as incredible as you might think. In the reign of the Emperor Engi, for seven days atop a persimmon tree near Gojô, a *tengu* assumed the form of a Buddha and emitted a white radiance. Again, the female form which came every day to harass Nisho, priest of the Butsugen-ji, was in fact a *tengu.*"

"Ah, you do speak of gruesome things."

The Lady and the ladies-in-waiting all objected with some spirit; and they hid their faces in their sleeves. The young Lord's flushed face softened—

"The three thousand worlds have ever been limitless in breadth. Human wisdom is but a meager thing, and there is none who can say with assurance that *tengu* are nonexistent. For example, this *tengu*, which is going about as a priest, enamoured of my Lady, might some night stretch down a claw-like hand from the gabled peak of this Mansion!—There is no one who can say that it could never happen. But—"

The young Lord, meanwhile, with barely any change of mood, was gently stroking the collar of the Lady's undergarment to soothe her.

"It is fortunate that the Mary Priest has never even peeped at you through a cranny in the wall, so, there is no cause to take precautions against such a heretical love affair; you have nothing to fear."

Quite as though he were beguiling a child, he consoled her.

Now, the incident of which I speak happened only about a month after that. Meanwhile, little of any consequence transpired. At length, at the peak of summer–when the waters of the Kamo-gawa dazzlingly reflected the sunshine–when the traffic of cable boats had temporarily ceased along the blazing river way, my nephew–since he enjoyed angling–made his way to a spot beneath the Gojô Bridge, where crouching amid the mugwort on the river bank he could take advantage of the cool breeze which blew only in that place. Casting his line into the river, which was at a very low level, he eagerly began to fish for dace. Then, by the railing directly above his head, he heard a somehow familiar voice. Casually he looked up–saw that it was Heidaiyu, who flapped his fan as he leaned over the railing, talking earnestly to the Mary Priest.

When he caught sight of them, the strange conduct of this priest, which he had witnessed at the intersection of Abura By-street, happened to pass through my nephew's mind. He recalled that at the time he had sensed an evident intimacy between the two. He pondered over this as he concentrated on his fishing, but all the while his ears were alert to catch the conversation of the pair on the bridge. As there was almost no traffic over the bridge during this severely hot period of the day, they would have felt free from interruption. Apparently they had not observed my nephew, and their talk was loud and uninhibited.

"That it is you who is propagating the Mary Religion would be undreamed of by any other person in the Capital. Even before you introduced yourself, I knew I had seen you somewhere before, but I could not precisely remember where. It is not to be wondered at!–To compare you now as you walk scantily clad under the fiery sky–your appearance, if I may be so rude as to say so, is much like a *tengu*–to compare you now with the young man you were when you sang the *Cherry Man Song* one moonlit night in spring–then, not even the divine sorcerer would recognize you."

Plying his fan, Heidaiyu was in an obvious good humor. And the Mary Priest replied in a voice so dignified that one might have suspected him to be a lord:

"My meeting you here gives me greater satisfaction than anything. Once in front of the shrine of the god Sae, I happened to see you–you were not looking my way, but bearing a branch of wild orange to which had been affixed a letter; you trudged along deep in thought towards the Mansion."

"You saw me then? I am sorry I did not see *you*–in my old age I am surely stupid!–"

Heidaiyu would have well remembered that morning. He had spoken bitterly; but, at length, with the return of his good spirits, he went on flapping his fan.

"–Our meeting today must surely be owing to the good grace of the Kwannon Bodisâttva of Kiyomizu Temple. Never in my lifetime have I been blessed with greater happiness."

"No!–You should not invoke the Buddhist deities in my presence. Though unworthy, I have received the favor of the Heavenly Majesty's divine decree and am the priest committed to propagate the Religion of Mary throughout our land."

22

I COULD imagine how Heidaiyu knit his brow at the words of the Mary Priest, but he showed no sign of uneasiness as he used both fan and tongue.

"Yes, indeed!–I am forever making blunders in my old age. I shall take care not to invoke those deities again in your presence. However–old man that I am, I must admit I have not much inclination *to believe* nowadays. I just happened to invoke the Kwanzeon Bodisâttva; it was because I was happy at having met you again after such a long time. If I were to speak to the Lady– how delighted she would be to know that you, the companion of her youth, have fared well," he said with spirited eloquence.

There must certainly have been a change in the manner of Heidaiyu who usually found it troublesome to speak to us at all. The Mary Priest had possibly only nodded, for no reply seemed to be forthcoming; but, at length the reference to the Lady did elicit a reply:

"Well, there are certain matters I want to talk over with the Lady in private . . ." and lowering his voice he continued:

". . . Somehow, Heidaiyu, in the late evening one day, could you not arrange a meeting?"

The sound of the fan above him on the bridge had suddenly halted. My nephew was about to hazard a glance up at the railing, but as there was every likelihood of his being detected if he made some careless movement, he suppressed his desire; so he gazed at the water's flow through the mugwort along the bank, hardly daring to breathe. But Heidaiyu seemed to have lost his spirit, for he was hesitant in replying; and so long did the waiting seem to my nephew under the bridge that the sinews and bones throughout his body began to tingle.

"Well, I do live in the Capital, even if only on the river bank; naturally I have heard of Lord Horikawa's frequent visits to the Lady–"

At length, as though talking to himself, the priest continued in a normal quiet voice:

"But it is not to make love to the Lady that I desire this meeting. Though once I was consumed by worldly desires, during a sojourn in Morokoshi (China), a red-haired, blue-eyed foreign priest wooed me from such weaknesses, and now I am dedicated to furthering the work of the Heavenly Majesty. What distresses me is that this jewel-like Lady is unacquainted with the Heavenly Majesty who created heaven and earth, but rather is under the sway of the heretical teachings of fallen angels, deities, and Buddhas and makes offerings of fragrant flowers to wood and stone images of these gods. Ultimately, at life's end the Lady will, doubtlessly, burn in everlasting fire. Every time I think of that, I can clearly visualize her falling, precipitated into the dark depths of Abitaijô. Actually, last night . . ."

The priest was overwhelmed by his deep emotion, and even as he began, his words trailed off into silence.

23

"WHAT happened *last night?*"

Heidaiyu thus pressed his companion; so when he recovered his self-possession, the Mary priest again continued in a calm voice, though pausing on every word:

"Well—nothing worth speaking about. Alone in my thatched hut last night, as I slept lightly, the Lady arrayed in five robes embroidered with willows, walked near my pillow. The apparition was real and yet not real, in that her lustrous black hair was veiled in haze, and her yellow-gold hairpins diffused a mysterious light. I was overjoyed at seeing her after such a long interval and said to her, 'It is so wonderful to see you,' but the Lady, her sorrowful eyes lowered as she sat before me, did not even have the will to answer. When I observed her more closely, something seemed to be wriggling on the lower hem of her red skirt and also on her shoulders and about her breasts, and even entangled in her black hair; they seemed to scoff–"

"I cannot quite follow what you are trying to say. What might they have been?"

By this time, Heidaiyu unwittingly was being lured on by the Priest's tone, and his voice as he inquired, lacked the spirit of shortly before. The voice of the Mary Priest also had grown pensive.

"I myself do not know what they were. I could only gaze at those things as they wriggled around the Lady–strange, like countless newborn babes; and as I watched, though but dreaming, I was overcome with sadness and cried out without sparing my voice; and the Lady, seeing my weeping, could not restrain her own tears. I believe that it continued thus for a long time; but at length from somewhere, I heard a cock crowing, and I awakened from my dream."

The Mary Priest finished speaking; and this time Heidaiyu had no comment to make but began again to wield the fan that had been stilled for some time. So intently had he been listening that my nephew almost failed to notice the dace caught in his line; and while he listened to this talk of the dream, the cool damp air beneath the bridge had undefinably soaked into his body. He felt a strangeness as if he had himself seen the Lady in that wretched plight. Then, from the bridge the subdued voice of the Mary Priest began again:

"I think that those fantastic things were devils. I am sure that His Heavenly Majesty, out of pity for this Lady in danger of hell-fire, bestowed this spirit dream upon me that I might be prompted to lead her towards salvation. This is why I need your assistance to meet her."

Heidaiyu hesitated for some time, but at length he flipped his closed fan on the railing and said:

"All right, then. When some time ago under the slope at Kiyo-mizu I was wounded by the swords of bandits, my life was almost lost. By virtue of the assistance you gave me, I was able to escape. In my gratitude it ill-behooves me to deny your request. Whether or not she is converted to the Mary Religion is a matter for her own conscience, but I do know that after all this while, she will be glad of the opportunity to see you. Therefore, I shall do what I can to devise a way for you to meet."

24

ONE MORNING three or four days afterwards, I heard from my nephew the particulars of that secret confidence. Usually there was quite a gathering in the samurai quarters, but at that time we had the place to ourselves. Amidst the green leaves of the plum grove, warmed by a brilliant morning sun, the cool breeze which even then blew in gusts, foreboded that autumn was about to move in.

My nephew, having reached the end of his story, lowered his voice somewhat:

"I really don't know how the Mary Priest became acquainted with the Lady, but from the first this has seemed strange to me. At any rate, if the Priest were to meet the Lady, I feel instinc-tively it will result in unthinkable tragedy for the Lord of the Mansion. But to acquaint the Lord of these facts, his disposition being as it is, I am certain would be useless as he would take no notice. Therefore, my own opinion is that we must prevent that meeting.–Uncle, what do you think?"

"I, too, would not wish the Lady's charms to be exposed before that strange *tengu* priest. But we must not neglect our service to the Lord by constantly standing guard outside the Mansion of Nishi-no-Tôin. It is one matter to keep the priest away from her and another. . . ."

"That's the point!–Without knowing the Lady's feelings on the matter, and with old man Heidaiyu there, we cannot haphazardly prevent the Mary Priest from calling at the Nishi-no-Tôin Mansion. But, since he sleeps every night in a thatched hut on the river bank at Shijô, if we act according to my plan, we can–I am sure–prevent the Priest from ever venturing into the Capital again."

"But it's not possible to keep a watch on the hut either. I am too old to follow your devious thought. What do you intend to do with the Mary Priest?"

Dubiously I asked that question of my nephew; he looked about him as though afraid of being overheard, and, in this room alive with the shadows cast by the green plum leaves, he brought his lips close to my ear.

"You ask my plan.–What I have in mind is the only possible solution. That is–in the depths of night, to go in secret to Shijô by the river and to put an end to the priest."

At this, even I myself was dumbfounded for a while and could not continue the conversation; but, like any normal young man, my nephew pressed on in thoughtful tone:

"As you know, he is but a mendicant priest. Even if there were two or three there to help him, it should not be a difficult task to kill him."

"Still, somehow your idea is too drastic. It is true enough that the Mary Priest goes about spreading *heresy,* but beyond that, he has committed no crime that can be dubbed a *crime.* Therefore, to kill this priest is, in a way, taking the life of an innocent person."

"An excuse can be found around *any* situation. But, supposing that priest, through the power of this Heavenly Majesty of his, were to put a curse on the Lord and the Lady! To allow this to happen is no way for either of us to be worthy of our stipend."

My nephew, his face flushed, defended his plan from all quarters and was not to be dissuaded. Just then, two or three samurai, fans flapping, came in; and my nephew's talk came to an end.

25

I REMEMBER it would have been three or four days after that—a starry moonlit night. In the middle of the night my nephew and I stealthily made our way to the Shijô river bank. Even at that time I still had no intention of killing the *tengu* priest. I did not feel we were justified in killing him. But, since my nephew would not be persuaded to discard his original plan, and somehow I being too concerned to let him go there alone, there I was on an errand ill-befitting my age, wet with dew from the mugwort on the bank, and making for the hut, where lived the Mary Priest, to spy out the position.

As you would know, countless rows of shabby pariah huts line the river banks. Already many leprous beggars deep in slumber would be dreaming dreams too strange to imagine. When I and my nephew, with stealthy footsteps, quietly paused before the huts, only loud snoring issued from inside; otherwise all was quiet. In only one place a rubbish fire still smoldered, issuing a column of smoke up into the windless sky. As I looked at the smoke trailing off into the bespeckled River of Heaven, I even imagined I could hear the sound of countless specks of star dust gliding *shaku* by *shaku*, *sun* by *sun*, through the dome of the heavens over the Capital.

Meanwhile my nephew–who must have cast his eye over the hut some time previously–pointed out a reed-thatched hut bordering on the narrow waters of the Kamogawa. Standing in the mugwort of the river bank, and turning in my direction, he uttered the one phrase: "There it is." Just then, by the faint light of the rubbish fire that still spat out tongues of flame, I saw a hut smaller than any other, though no different from those nearby in that the roof was of old matting supported by bamboo poles, and a cross made from branches had been constructed there. It looked somber to us as it stood erect in the darkness.

"So that's the one?" I whispered uneasily for want of something better to say. In fact, I had still not decided whether I would kill the Mary Priest or not. Meanwhile, my nephew, showing no inclination to turn back, stared at the hut.

"It is."

At the blunt answer, an indescribable feeling overcame me– the feeling that the time had come for my sword to be stained with blood; unconsciously my whole body trembled. My nephew had quickly braced himself; carefully wetting the hilt of his sword with saliva to swell the bamboo rivet, he did not look at me as he went treading softly through the mugwort of the river bank, and like a spider watching its prey, made his way without a sound to the outside of the hut. From the rear, flattened against the matting walls in order to ascertain the situation inside, my nephew looked, somehow, unpleasantly like a large spider.

26

AT THIS STAGE in the developments I could not stand by with folded arms. While I tied up the sleeves of my hunting garb, I observed the outside layout; then, I came up behind my nephew to peer through the crevices in the matting walls.

The first thing to catch my eyes was the banner of the female bodisâttva which the Mary Priest carried about with him. Suspended on the matting of the far wall, it could be seen by the faint light of the fire which filtered through the matting entrance; the beautiful golden halo of the image vaguely glimmered like an eclipse of the moon. It would be the Mary Priest who lay before it, lost to the world from the weariness of the day. There seemed to be something like a kimono half-covering the sleeping form, but, as he had his back to the firelight, I could not tell whether it was really the *tengu* wings we had heard spoken of, or the fur of one of the fire rats which are said to be found in Tenjiku (India).

We surveyed the scene without any exchange of comment from either side. Taking up strategic positions, quietly we drew our swords from their scabbards. It was perhaps quite strange, but I had lost heart from the beginning. By then my hands had become unmanageable, and in my fumbling, a strange metallic sound rang out. With no time to be startled I saw that the Mary Priest, stretched out on the matting, who until then had slept the sleep of the dead, showed signs of quickly arousing himself.

"Who's there?" he remonstrated. Having come to this pass, I saw as well as my nephew that we then had no alternative but to assassinate the priest. As soon as the voice had spoken, without uttering a word, but slashing out with our white blades, simultaneously, we rushed into the hut from the front and back.

The clashing of our blades, the snapping of the bamboo poles, the sound of tearing as the matting was flung aside–in a moment all these dreadful sounds burst forth together and my nephew quickly–swiftly–jumped back two or three steps and exclaimed in a strained voice–"You won't escape us!" Surprised at the voice the priest had jumped up quickly; he was looking fixedly past us at the glow of the fire. What was all this about? In front of the demolished hut, that unpleasant Mary Priest, arrayed in a thin colored undergarment hanging loose from his shoulders, stooped monkey-like as he placed against his forehead the talisman cross, and stared at us and our behavior. As I saw him, I became impatient to bloody my sword as soon as possible; but for some reason or other, the darkness unaccountably deepened, and I could not seem to thrust my sword at the stooping body of that priest. It seemed as if there were some strange unseen thing whirling in the midst of that darkness and deflecting the aim of our swords. My nephew seemed to think as I. Yelling and panting all the while, we whirled the white blades above our heads in empty circles.

27

MEANWHILE, gradually raising himself, the Mary Priest waved the talisman cross from left to right, and in a stentorian voice that was like a raging storm, he bellowed:

"Yai!–blasphemously you would ignore the august authority of His Heavenly Majesty? To your beclouded eyes this Mary Priest's body would seem to be covered only with his black priestly robe–but, in truth, one and all of the various angels of Heaven, a million of the heavenly host, are my protectors. Therefore, go ahead, wield your white blades to further your exploits; what care I if you choose to compete with the might of the war-chariots–palfreys–swords–halberds–of the holy warriors following behind this priest!"

Finally he abused us in a derisive voice.

Though he threatened us in this way from the first–he did not strike fear in our hearts. When we heard him, like oxen loosed from the halter, my nephew and I struck out from both sides to cut him down. But can I say, *to cut him down?* What I should say is that the moment we waved our swords over our heads, the Mary Priest waved over his head the talisman cross; the golden gleam from the talisman flashed out like lightning into the sky before our eyes, as some fearful phantom appeared. Ah, that terrible phantom! I could never explain it, howsoever I might try. It would be like presenting a horse as a likeness of a giraffe. But, as that talisman was raised to the sky, I thought that the darkness of the river bank behind the Mary Priest was suddenly torn asunder. Then, in place of that rent darkness, limitless numbers of fiery horses and carriages and lurid dragon-like apparitions scattered sparks denser than rain, and only seeming to fall down on our heads, vividly floated up to overflow in the heavens. Meanwhile, things like flags, in hundreds–thousands–without limit, and sword-like things, sparkling, and with a frightful roaring, quite like a tempest at sea, which caused even the stones on the river bank to prance, all came boiling and seething. And in the midst, the odd figure of that priest clad only in an undergarment, bearing on high the cross talisman, sternly stood there, like some giant *tengu* leading its host of devils from the depths of hell; it was as if all heaven and hell had been transported onto that paltry river bank.

So exceedingly strange was it that we unwittingly dropped

our swords, and with our heads between our hands, we help-lessly prostrated ourselves at the priest's feet. Then, reverberating majestically in the sky above our heads, we heard once more the remonstrances of the Mary Priest:

"If you deplore your fate, you both should beseech the mercy of His Heavenly Majesty. If not, the million holy guardians of reli-gion will, at this favorable opportunity, dismember your rotting corpses!" he thundered. It is impossible to recall that extraordi-nary horror without shuddering. There at last, unable to contain ourselves longer, we raised clasped hands and closing our rever-ential eyes, we called:

"Nam-mu Ten-jô-kôtei!"

28

IN MY SHAME I shall pass over, as briefly as possible, the events which happened after that. Perhaps because we had prayed to the Heavenly Emperor, the ghastly apparition soon dissolved, but taking its place were the outcasts who, awakened by the clash of our swords, were surging around us. Here, too, as the greater part were believers in the Mary Religion, we were fully aware that since we had cast aside our swords they threatened to violate us should the occasion present itself. Wildly and brashly they abused us in unanimous voice as though we were foxes ensnared in a trap; men and women swarmed about us peering with hate-filled faces. How many of them there were I would not know; bathed in the light of the revived refuse fire, from before and behind, left and right, those leprous faces—shutting out the stars, the moon, the night—and the straining scrawny necks, seemed quite to belong to another world.

Meanwhile, as we might have expected, unperturbed, the Mary Priest, diffusing his uncanny smile as he appeased the bellowing outcasts, came forth before us and preached fervently on the essentials of the blessedness and absolute virtue of His Heavenly Majesty; but that which captured my whole attention was rather the beautiful pastel-colored undergarment draped over the priest's shoulders. The world is, of course, well-supplied with many varieties of such undergarments, but was not this the very one that had been worn by the Lady of Naka-mikado? If that were true, it might even be so that the Lady had already met this priest; and, furthermore, it was unlikely that she had already been converted to the Mary Religion. With my thoughts running in this vein, I listened only fitfully to what our opponent was saying; but, if inadvertently I were to betray my suspicions, we would in all likelihood meet with some fearful fate. From the Mary Priest's manner, it would seem that he believed that we had perpetrated our attack in the dark simply because we resented his disparagement of our deities and Buddha. Fortunately, he seemed not to have noticed that we were retainers of the young Lord of Horikawa; so, endeavoring as far as possible not to betray any special interest in his pastel undergarment, we sat down on the stones of the river bank with the set purpose of impressing the priest with our conscientious hearkening to what he had to say.

We must have assumed a somewhat commendable appearance, for, having had us listen to the sermon he preached, the Mary Priest's expression softened, and waving that crucifix talisman over us, he addressed us directly:

"In that you both are unenlightened, His Heavenly Majesty will undoubtedly pardon your misdemeanor. So, I too, will not think of condemning, or even of reproving you. Finally, that in the darkness of this night it has been yours to carry out this assault, there might come a time when you will be converted to the Mary Religion. Until that time matures, it would be best for you to withdraw from this place."

Thus, gently he spoke to us. The outcasts, though eager to seize us, and showing their ghastly antagonism, meekly opened up the way for our departure in response to the authoritative command of the priest.

Then, I and my nephew, even begrudging the time we must spend in sheathing our swords, hastily fled from that river bank at Shijô. If I were to speak of our feelings at that time, they were of indescribable joy—sadness—and again, remorse; there is nothing more I can say. Soon we were so far from the river bank that all we could see were the leprous comrades gathered like ants about the flickering glow of the fire and chanting some mysterious song. When their singing came to our ears, we both drew a long breath as, without a glance having passed between us, we went on walking.

29

FROM THEN ON, whenever we met, putting our heads together, we conferred about the involvement of the Mary Priest with the Lady of Naka-mikado, desirous as we were of alienating the two; we had various discussions, but, even so, being mindful of the fearful phantoms, no ready solution presented itself to us. In that he was younger than I, stubbornly my nephew would naturally not depart from his first plan. If the chance had arisen to follow Heidaiyu's lead, we would have mustered some highwaymen and made another attack on the hut by the river bank at Shijô. But, in the meantime, we were beset by a further manifestation of the Mary Priest's mystic powers. . . .

It was just when the autumn winds had begun to blow that the Amida-dô (Buddha Hall) in Saga, built by the Bishop of Naga-o, was completed and the time came for the dedication mass to be said. That Temple has long since been razed by fire, but, for the construction of the temple only fine timbers gathered from various parts of the country were used and only famous craftsmen were summoned, and no regard was given to the vast expenses; and besides, even though its proportions were not large, it pushed munificence to the extreme—so, we can leave to conjecture its magnificence and grandeur.

In speaking of that day on which the dedication mass was celebrated, needless to say, countless numbers of high-ranking courtiers and ladies had come there by carriage; they were drawn up along the east and west corridors lined with bamboo blinds with brocade borders; and the colorfulness of the sleeve cuffs and skirts of brush-clover pattern, Chinese bell-flower and *ominaeshi* designs, stood out in bold relief between the slits in the blinds. The whole precincts of the shrine bathed in serene sunlight were like a scene from the Lotus Treasure-land. The garden pond in the midst of the corridors was completely covered by clusters of artificial red and white lotus; and moving gracefully on this pond was a dragon boat, its brocade canopy unfurled; the ornamental oars were manipulated by boys who in *ban-é*-patterned robes sang with delicate voices, and so gracefully did they move along that tears came to the eyes of the worshippers.

Moreover, looking beyond the façade of the Temple to the railing, brightly shining with mother-of-pearl—where, veiled in the trailing smoke of precious incense, not only the Buddha, the

principal object of worship, but also the images of Seishi Kwannon and other deities stood, their unsullied gold faces bedecked
with glittering bejeweled diadems—all worshippers would have
been awed by the glory of the sanctuary. In the enclosure in
front of the Image of Buddha, on high seats in the center of the
veneration dais, sat preachers and lectors shaded by brilliantly
ornamented umbrellas, and there were the red and blue robes
and scapulars of scores of priests participating in the mass, all
blending faultlessly. The voice reading the Doctrine, the tinkling
of bells, the fragrance of Indian incense sticks, and the black
aloeswood incense rose unceasingly and receded into the clear
autumn sky.

Then, in the very midst of the mass, the vast mob which
had been waiting outside hopeful of just a glance at the interior,
suddenly, at some disturbance, began with a rush to crowd from
all directions towards the gate and like a turbulent sea, began to
push and be pushed.

30

THE CHIEF of the Guard had seen this melée and quickly ran
there; brandishing his bow on high, he made an effort to subdue
the mob that was breaking through the gate in confusion. But,
clearing a way through that wave of people, came the figure of a
strange, crude priest. The Chief had seemed about to block the
priest's path, when, all of a sudden, he cast aside his bow and
prostrated himself completely, as if he were paying homage to
the passage of the Emperor. The attention of those inside the
gate was distracted by the clamor outside, and the commotion
was very great, until suddenly all became quiet, as the whisper

"The Mary Priest!–the Mary Priest!" passed through like a breeze rustling through reeds.

His long hair, spread out over the shoulders of his black-dyed robe, was disheveled as usual, and at his breast flashed the gold talisman cross; and how cold his bare feet looked! About his head the customary banner of the female bodisâttva was boldly held aloft in the autumn sunlight by an attendant walking behind.

"I would talk with you!–As the recipient of His Heavenly Majesty's divine decree, it is appropriate that I, the Priest of Mary, should disseminate the Religion of Mary throughout our land."

After responding to the obeisance of the Chief of the Guards, the priest proceeded fearlessly into the gardens that had been strewn with sand. He had spoken out in a stern voice, and as I listened from inside the gate, a further commotion arose; but it was to be expected that the officers of the peace, though startled by the rarity of the incident, did not entirely forget their duty. Two or three who seemed to be officers of rank, holding aloft their weapons, loudly remonstrated against the tumult as they ran towards the priest. They all sprang at him from different directions as if to seize him. But the Mary Priest, staring at the officers, cried out scornfully:

"If you would strike, then strike! If you want to take me, then take me! But, the punishment of His Heavenly Majesty will descend upon you."

He laughed mockingly at them, and the talisman suspended from his breast glittered just then as it caught a ray of sunlight. As if they had been struck by lightning from the sunny sky, his opponents discarded their weapons and fell grovelling at the feet of the priest.

"Take heed, all–you have witnessed the august virtue of His Heavenly Majesty!"

The Mary Priest, grasping the talisman cross suspended from his breast, proudly raised it above his head towards the east and west corridors.

"From the outset, such display of spiritual might is not strange. His Heavenly Majesty alone has made this heaven and earth. He is the one and only God. Having no knowledge of this Almighty God, in your attempt to attain to an awareness of Truth, you have thought to hold this ostentatious mass to venerate Amida Buddha who is merely a kind of demon."

Such a reactionary speech could not be tolerated. Becoming aware of the disturbance, the monks had shortly before interrupted their recital of the sutra and with one accord had begun with agitated voices to rail and abuse the Mary Priest:

"Kill him!"

"Seize him!"

But, nobody dared leave his place to rebuke the Mary Priest.

31

AND THE Mary Priest only stared arrogantly in the direction of the monks and proclaimed:

"A Chinese holy man once said—*Do not be disheartened by your error!*—If once you would come to realize that bodisâttva are demons and thus rapidly come to be converted to the Mary Religion, you would without ado come to praise the absolute virtue of the Heavenly Majesty. But, again, if you doubt my teaching, if you find it impossible to decide whether the bodisâttva are demons, or whether His Heavenly Majesty is a false God—let us contest our power and judge which is the true Law!"—he called out in a flamboyant voice.

Yet, somehow, even the officers of the peace had lost their spirit and had fallen back before our eyes; and in the hush as they drank in that voice, of those *inside* the bamboo blinds, and those *outside*, not one among them—clergy or laity—made any move to challenge that priest's religious powers. In the end, to say nothing of the Abbot of Naga-o, even the Archbishop of the Order, and the Bishop of Nin-nanji—who were all present on that day—all were subjugated by the Mary Priest who was like an untamed god. In the enclosure, by this time, the dragon boat had ceased its music and song; it was as if the sound of the sunlight beaming down upon the artificial lotus flowers could have been heard—so silent had the atmosphere become.

The priest's confidence expanded accordingly. Raising on high the cross talisman, his scornful laugh was the laughter of a *tengu.*

"But this is all quite ludicrous! Rarely has there ever been such an assembly of holy men from southern cities and northern peaks—and yet, not one appears to rival the powers of this Mary Priest. Is it that they are beginning to pay homage to His Heavenly Majesty, and fearful of the divine light of the heavenly host, irrespective of rank or age—have all become aware of their conversion to the Mary Doctrine? So, here and now, beginning with the Abbot, should not all receive the sacrament of baptism?"—he raved in a grandiose manner.

And he was still raving when, from the west corridor, one man bearing himself with the utmost complacency, came forth—a revered monk. The gold-bordered scapular, the crystal rosary, the white eyebrows, all proclaimed his renown for infinitely virtuous conduct. He was, without doubt, Abbot of Yokawa. The Abbot was old, but carrying leisurely and ponderously his fat rotund body, he gravely advanced and came to a halt right before the eyes of the Mary Priest.

"You vile creature! As you have said just now–attending this dedication mass, there are, without mistake, in this enclosure countless holy men who follow the Way of Buddha. But, even as we disdain the vessel from which the rats have eaten, who is there who would want to contest his mystic powers with a wretch like you? You in your shame ought hastily to learn your place and leave the Buddha's Sacred Presence; your conjecture that you can vie like this with our godly Way, is extremely odd. When I come to think of it, you should be treated as a heretical priest who goes about putting into practice the Powers of Evil. Accordingly, in order to demonstrate the spiritual sword of the Three Treasures, and also to render help to those who would fall into the hell in which you are enmeshing them, I have presented myself. Even though you go about cleverly employing the sorcery of monsters, you will not be able to touch with one finger this old priest who is protected by the powers of Buddha. So, when you see the spectacle of Buddha's power, rather will you be converted to Buddha's commandments." This he declaimed authoritatively and swiftly gestured with a movement of his fingers.

32

THEN, from the hand that described that sign, suddenly, a whiff of white mist trailed stealthily into the air until it formed a canopy directly above the Bishop's head. That strange cloud-like formation–just to say it was a *mist* presents no adequate representation. If it were a *mist*, the Temple roof yonder and its environs would have been so befogged as to be invisible. It might have been that this cloud which stretched tortuously through the empty air without even dimming the brightness of the sky, possessed some mystic quality.

The people crowded into the enclosure, no matter who they were, would surely have been frightened by that cloud. Then, from nowhere, as it were, a light stirring as though a wind, sprang up—just enough to ruffle the bamboo blinds; and before that disturbance had subsided, the Abbot of Yokawa slowly moved his fleshy chin as he recited a secret incantation to alter the apparition. Immediately the vague shadowy forms of two valiant *Kinkōjin* gods wielding maces, appeared in that cloud. Even as one thought them there, they were phantoms so faint that one wondered if they really were there. But, those dancing forms seeming, as they were treading, about to swing their maces down upon the Mary Priest's crown, were invested with divine dignity. Yet, the face of the Mary Priest was haughty as usual, and, staring fixedly at the forms of those *Kinkōjin* gods, he moved not an eyebrow. On the contrary, about his tightly closed lips floated that strange shadow of a smile which betrayed an attitude of derision. It was not possible to suppress one's anger at such audaciousness. The Abbot of Yokawa, with a sudden gesture, shook his crystal rosary, and roared in a hoarse voice:

"Shitsu!"

Obedient to that voice, the *Kinkōjin* danced down through the bemisted sky, but the Mary Priest below, touching his forehead with the talisman cross, shouted something in a sharp voice. And, at that moment, a light like a rainbow was seen to rise into the sky; the forms of the *Kinkōjin* were obliterated, and the Abbot's crystal rosary was split through the center; with a metallic sound, the beads were dispersed, like hail, in all directions.

"I have seen enough of your devices.–You have learned to evoke the Powers of Evil, but not to thwart them!"

Thus, instinctively, in his triumph the priest, suppressing the tumultuous voice of the people, loftily abused the Abbot. I shall not dwell upon the extent to which, succumbing to that voice, the Abbot of Yokawa wilted. If at that time his disciples had not fought their way through to him and protected him, perhaps he would not have been able satisfactorily to make his way back through the corridor by which he had come. Meanwhile, the demeanor of the Mary Priest was becoming overbearing. He exclaimed:

"The Abbot of Yokawa is acknowledged the supreme exemplar of Buddhist virtue throughout this land. But seen through my eyes, he but dedicates himself to obscuring the glory of His Heavenly Majesty, indiscriminately, employing demons to aid him, and there is no need to say he is carnal-minded. Would it be a mistake to suppose that this Priest of Mary is the only man who understands that the bodisâttva are a kind of ogre, and the Buddhist teachings the karma for hell? If any remain who still do not seek conversion to my doctrine of Mary, I shall hear them, be they monk or layman. Howsoever many there are assembled in this place, let them here and now challenge the authority of the Heavenly Emperor."

Thus he spoke–his eyes searching in all directions.

Then, again from the eastern corridor:

"Granted ! ! !"

A voice had coolly challenged.

Composedly whisking his ceremonial Court robes as he made his way through the enclosure was the imposing presence of none other than the young Lord of Horikawa.

(Story is unfinished in original version–see introduction.)

A WOMAN'S BODY

Introductory Note:
This story, included in this volume as an example of Akutaga-
wa's levity, is one of literature's shortest tales. There is nothing
especially Japanese about it, unless it be that brevity.

The text refers to a louse ("shirami") and not to a flea
("nomi") but, as there is usually to the Western mind something
obnoxious about a human becoming a louse, the translators
have this once taken the liberty of making an alteration.

Among the Buddhists, particularly, it is something of an
amusing pastime to consider the possibility of one's assuming
the shape of various animals, for the Buddhists contend that the
soul has many transmigrations on its pilgrimage to nirvâna and
takes on many forms of life according to its measure of virtue.

"A Woman's Body" ("Nyôtai") was written in September of
Taishô 6 (1917).

ONE SUMMER NIGHT a certain Chinese named Yang, lying in bed, was awakened because of the exceedingly sultry heat. Lying on his stomach, with his head between his palms, he had been indulging in wild fancies when he noticed a flea crawling along the edge of his bed. In the dim lamplight of his room, it was seen crawling its way, with its little back glistening like silver dust, toward the shoulder of his wife sleeping by his side. He found her fast asleep, unclothed, breathing peacefully, with her head and body turned toward him.

Watching the flea's sluggish walk, Yang wondered what the world of such creatures could be. It takes the flea an hour to get to a place which is two or three human steps away from him, and its crawl is limited to the bed at that. "If I had been born a flea, how tedious my life would be. . . ."

While he was aimlessly thinking of such things, his consciousness gradually became obscure, and without knowing why, he sank deep into the abyss of a strange trance which was neither a dream nor reality. By-and-by, the instant he felt he had awakened, startled, his soul had entered the flea's body, which had all this while been walking leisurely on the bed amid a foul odor of perspiration. But this was not all that mystified him, though this thing itself was so mysterious that he stood in wonder.

In his way towered a lofty mountain, the roundish shape of which was suspended like a stalactite from its summit rising beyond the range of his sight and stretching down to the bed where he stood. The roundish foot of the mountain contiguous to the bed was in the form of a pomegranate so reddish as to suggest that fire might be stored therein. Except for this foot, the whole shapely mountain looked whitish, made up of a white mass of some fatty, tender and smooth substance. The vast surface of the mountain bathed in the light shone in a mellow amber-colored luster forming a bow-shaped curve of exquisite beauty toward the skyline, while the shady mountainside glistened like slightly blue-tinged snow under moonlight.

With his eyes wide open in admiration, Yang fixed his gaze at this mountain of fascinating beauty. But what was his amazement when he found that the mountain was one of his wife's breasts? Forgetting his love, his hatred and his sensual desire, he watched the huge breast that looked so like a mountain of ivory. In the excess of his admiration he stood as if petrified for a long time, as if stunned before this irresistible fascination, oblivious to the odor of perspiration. It was not until he became a flea that he could keenly realize the physical beauty of his wife. Nor is it limited to the beauty of a woman's body, what a man with artistic bent should stare at in wonder, as the flea did.

SUPPLEMENTARY NOTES

THE ROBBERS

"Inokuma" is situated between Nishinomiya and Horikawa in Kyôto.

"Momi-é hat"–Difficult to describe, but its shape reminds us of a blunted sea-shell.

"Obaba" is a diminutive of "Obaasan"–grandmother or "old woman."

"Rashômon"–literally translated as "Rashô Gate," lent its name to one of Akutagawa's stories which together with another of his stories, "Yabu no naka" ("Among the Bushes") provided the theme for the Japanese (Daiei Co.) film, produced by Kurosawa Akira, widely known as winner of the Grand Pix at the International Cinema Festival in Venice, and as the choice of the National Board of Review of Motion Pictures as the best foreign film of the year. The stories themselves are to be found in English in *Rashômon and Other Stories* (Liveright Publishing Corporation, New York). "Rashô Gate" was located at the southern end of Suzaku Main Street.

"Suzakumon" was situated on the southern side of the Imperial Palace and faced Suzaku Main Street. Suzaku Street is currently called "Sembon-dori."

"Azuma crow" ("Azuma-garasu") was a contemptuous term for the rough-mannered people of the eastern districts.

"Selling oil"–wasting time in small talk.

"Ken"–a measure of distance. One ken is 1.988369 yards, hence–
roughly, 2 yards.

"Tatami"–rush mats.

"Kokoroba"–plum or pine twigs which were placed on each of the
four corners of the table.

"Takatsuki"–a small stand with legs for serving food.

"Chô"–60 "Ken" or roughly 120 yards.

"Sekiyama" is currently noted for two hot springs and as a skiing
resort, about 163 miles from Tokyo.

"Hiramon" saddle–a lacquered saddle decorated with gold, silver
and gems or shells.

"Ayigasa"–a rush hat lined with silk and worn by samurai about the
streets.

"Shijôbômon"–a narrow street running east-west near Shijô.

"The Three Treasures" comprise Buddha, the scriptures, and the
priesthood. There is a story by Akutagawa called, "The Three
Treasures."

"Shichihan"–a gambling game.

"Rat's crying"–a prostitute would make this sound to attract men.

"The tripod oil lamp" ("Musubitôdai") consisted of an oil bowl
placed on three intersecting legs.

"Sôshi" are old tales written in "Kana"–phonetic syllabry.

"Sanjobômon" was a narrow street running east-west.

"Chikugo"–in Saga Prefecture.

"The Lotus" is sacred to the Buddhist and thus appears frequently
in Buddhist art and sculpture.

"Kongôrikishi" were fierce-looking "spirits" (of stone) protecting
Buddha from both sides of a temple gate.

"É-Boshi" was a soft twilled headgear with a light motif, and painted
with black lacquer.

"Ichimégasa" was a convex lacquered hat worn by women.

"Tsukushi" was the old name for Kyûshû.

"Narazaka"–a sloping road from Heijo (present-day Nara) to Kitsu in Yamaginokuni.

"The heishi" was a saké bottle.

"Zôri"–straw thronged sandals.

"The arrowroot vine binding" on the hilt of a sword ("tsuzuramaki no tachi") was also apparent on the scabbard, and was lacquered.

"Sahoyôéfu"–An officer who guarded a Palace, escorted an Imperial journey, or patrolled the Capital.

"Kamo River" ("Kamogawa") is historically famous not only for its association with Kyôto history since ancient times, but for its having been the site of the rough stage erected by Okuni, the pioneer of "Kabuki-drama."

"Kujakumyô-ô"–was an incarnate Buddha with wings like a peacock's. It rode on a peacock and was said to destroy all misfortunes. It is a figure of esoteric Buddhism.

"Sembon" was in Kamikyo-ku, Kyôto.

"Toba" is noted for its magnificent view–one of Japan's most picturesque. The "Toba Highway" was a road from Kyôto city to Toba city in Mié Prefecture.

"The arrows with turnip-shaped heads" had holes in their heads so that they would make a sound when shot.

"Higashiyama"–the hills to the east of Kyôto city.

"Koshi"–the Hokuriku district.

"The Nosenkazura" has orange-colored flowers in July and August.

"Hakama"–A skirt tied at the waist, usually worn by men over the kimono.

"The River of Heaven"–the Milky Way–a much more picturesque description than the Western one. "The River of Heaven" is the subject of one of Japan's most romantic tales, often remembered during the "Tanabata Festival."

"Otokoyama" commands a view of the rivers Yodo, Kizu, Uji and Katsura.

"Uchigi"–A woman's undergarment.

"Tonsho-bodai" is a Buddhist equivalent of "requiescat in pace."

"With whom do I sleep . . . ?"–This song appears in the "Makura no sôshi" ("The Pillow Book") of Sei Shonagon.

"Tango"–Northern sector of Kyôto city.

THE DOG, SHIRO

Baseball is popular among both adults and children in Japan. Children may often be seen playing baseball in Japanese suburban gardens and at quiet intersections in the streets.

"Taishô-ken" takes its name from the Taishô era (1912–1926).

The film and the newspaper articles referred to in the story are fictitious, but the "Nichi-Nichi," "Asahi," "Kokumin," "Jiji," "Yomiuri," were all Tokyo daily newspapers. The "Asahi" and "Yomiuri" have remained leading dailies to the present time.

"Tabata" is a (national) railway station in Kita-ku in Tokyo. From Taishô 8 (1919) Akutagawa lived at Tabata. The house in which he had lived was burned down in an air raid on July 13th, 1945.

"Kamikôchi" is in Nagano Prefecture on a plateau almost five thousand feet above sea level and is an area of hot springs, lakes, wilderness and mountain peaks.

"Odawara" in Kanagawa Prefecture is a little more than fifty miles from Tokyo. It was the seat of the Hôjô family in the fourteenth, fifteenth and sixteenth centuries, but was conquered by Toyotomi Hidèyoshi in 1590. Of the Odawara Castle, only the ruins remain.

THE HANDKERCHIEF

"Haségawa Kinzô" is modeled after Nitobé Inazô (1862–1933) a Christian, who graduated from Tokyo University of Foreign Studies and from Sapporo Agricultural University (now University of Kokkaidô) and in Meiji 17 (1884) went to the U.S.A. to continue his studies. In Meiji 20 (1887) he visited Germany. When he returned to Japan he successively became a professor at Sapporo Agricultural University, the University of Kyôto, and the Imperial University at Tokyo. Nitobé advocated world peace–imagining Japan as a pacifist nation. He married an American–Mary (Mariko) but was not favored with any children. Nitobé was associated with several unusual tales of clairvoyance of which he himself was the telepathists' subject.

"The Gifu Lantern" has slender bamboo ribs, and is covered with thin paper or silk upon which is painted some plant-life. In summer, especially during the festival for the dead (O-bon, the Feast of Lanterns, 13th–16th July), it is frequently suspended under the eaves of the house. Foreigners often have a keen interest in Gifu lanterns because the atmosphere which such decorative lanterns create is so typically "Japanese."

"Oya!" is a Japanese expression of surprise or bewilderment.

"Né" is an expression similar to the English "isn't that so?" or "don't you think?" It is a popular mannerism of Japanese speech recurring usually more often than the English equivalent, "You see!"

"Ginza" is the main business thoroughfare in Tokyo.

THE DOLLS

O-Tsuru's brother is typical of young men of the age. He was captivated by the new Western learning which had been encouraged, since the Restoration in 1868, by the Emperor Meiji and by such great educators as Fukuzawa Yukichi. Readjustment of old values is still apparent in Japan as year by year the Japanese are more and more influenced by Western thought and customs. Sometimes parents find this trend bewildering when sons and daughters insist on greater independence. In the Meiji era the reformists were commonly known as "kaika-jin" and the conservatives as "kyûkei."

The jinrikishas at the time were mostly decorated with gold-lacquer dragons, peonies, lions and other motives, painted at the rear. These were replaced after a time by red carts similar to those in use in Hong Kong at the present time. Nowadays one rarely sees a jinrikisha in Japan.

GRATITUDE

"Juraku Palace"–The Juraku-tei (House of Pleasures) was an elegant structure built by Hidèyoshi at Fushimi near Osaka. It was one of Japan's most ceremonious occasions when the Emperor honored him (Hidèyoshi) with a visit at the Juraku-tei.

"Itinerant Priest"–This priest wandered about wearing a basket hat which covered his head completely, leaving only sufficient room at its base for him to play a "shakuhachi" (bamboo flute). He would beg for alms and would frequently be offered a bowl of rice.

"Hôjôya Yasoèmon"–a fictitious character.

"The Cross"–Christianity was brought to Japan by St. Francis Xavier in 1549 and prospered in spite of persecution for a century thereafter.

"Cha-shitsu"–a formal tearoom.

"Sôshi"–old tales.

"Kyô"–the Capital (present-day Kyôto–which, if translated, means Eastern Capital).

"Ronin"–Samurai without a master. When a samurai severed allegiance from his master, he became the "hired" retainer of any who needed his services for the period of time agreed upon.

THE LADY, ROKU-NO-MIYA

"Amida Buddha" ("Amitabha Buddha")–Lord of Infinite Light. Honen (1133–1212) and Shinran (1173–1262) taught that salvation lay in absolute faith in the power of Amida Buddha–the doctrine of "tariki-hongan." It seems that Akutagawa here refers to the Jôdo sect (Jôdo-shû) of Honen rather than to the Shinshu Sect (Shinran-shû) of Shinran. The Jôdo sect requires recitation of "Namu-Amida-Butsu" ("Namo-mitabhabuddhaya"), which

formula is an act of reverence to the glory of Amida Buddha–
the prayers of the saints and the lowly being equal in Buddha's
estimation. Without this act of faith the Lady could not obtain
salvation. In any event, she lacked even the unspoken faith, it
seems, required by the Shinran sect.

"Zôri"–A development of the early "ashinaka" sandals which covered only the soles of the feet. "Zôri" have thongs which pass
through three holes in the soles and fit between the first and
second toes when worn. "Zôri" are traditionally wooden, but
nowadays may also be made of leather, rubber, or plastic. Probably "ashinaka" are meant for "zôri" in this story. It is interesting
to note that the feet of the statue of Saigô Takamori in Ueno
Park, Tokyo, are clad in "zôri."

THE KAPPA

Some traditional medicines in Japan are believed to have originated
among the Kappa.

"Buddha" (563–483 B.C.)–Prince Gautama of the Sakya clan. He was
the exponent of the eight-fold way: right views, right intention,
right speech, right action, right living, right effort, right mindful-
ness, and right meditation.

"Sen-no-Rikyû" (1520–1591) was the founder of the first rigid
school of Tea Ceremony (Cha-no-yu). Sometimes Sen-no-Rikyû
is referred to as Soéki. He offended Toyotomi Hidéyoshi, military premier of the country, by resisting Hidéyoshi's interest in
his daughter. Hidéyoshi eventually found an excuse to demand
that he commit suicide in penance for a charge of "sacrilege."

SAIGÔ TAKAMORI

"The Meiji Restoration"–Restoration of the Emperor as actual ruler
of Japan.

"Shiroyama" is a hill about a hundred feet above sea-level at
Kagoshima City. The story of Saigô's death at Shiroyama is

a controversial one. Some have even believed that he fled to Siberia.

THE GREETING

So far our research has not provided the source of the reference ". . . trararach . . . trarach," but the author is believed to be the Russian novelist Mikhail P. Artzybashev (b. 1878). In "The Story of the World's Literature" (Liveright, New York. Revised Edition: 1961), Artzybashev is described as "a queer genius . . . ," and one of his most controversial stories is "The Death of Ivan Lande" which describes "the failure of a good man in an . . . unChristian world."

Of Richepin (1849–1926), Macy writes: "A writer of genius who does not fit into any school but is most eccentrically himself . . . , a man of erratic life and thought but of great original power. His first volume of verse, 'Chanson de Gueux' (1876) . . . was so audacious that Richepin was imprisoned for violating public morals." Akutagawa, in this story, recalls one of the many anecdotes which illustrates Jean Richepin's eccentricities. Rosine Sarah Bernhardt (1845–1923) is best remembered as a French tragedienne. Of French-Dutch-Jewish descent, she entered the Conservatoire at the age of thirteen, was educated at the Grandchamp Convent in Versailles and made her debut at the Théâtre Français. In 1907 her autobiography "Ma Double Vie" was published.

One yen would have been worth about twenty-five cents at the time. In 1964 one yen is worth about 3.6 cents.

To save readers from fruitless searching, we should mention that there is apparently no existing novel which embodies the contemplated theme, to wit, "an English language teacher imbued with a revolutionary spirit, . . . etc.," as set out in the text.

WITHERED FIELDS

"Jôsô" (1662–1704)–Naitô Jôsô–One of the leading disciples of Bashô. He retired from business and became a recluse in the isolated areas of Yamashiro. His haiku style is renowned for its succinctness. He died in the first year of the Hôei era.

"Kyorai" (1651–1704)–Mukai Kyorai–With Boncho he made a representative selection of verse called "The Monkey's Rush Raincoat." His style is rather similar to that of Bashô and has no original characteristics.

"Hanaya Diary" ("Hanaya Nikki")–This deals with Bashô's travels, illness, demise and funeral from September 21 of the third year of Genroku era (1690).

"Tabi"–These are stiff bifurcated socks that fit comfortably into "zôri" (sandals) and "geta" (clogs). The usual colors are black for men and white for women.

"Samisen"–A stringed instrument with quarter tones, and somewhat resembling a banjo-mandolin. The "samisen" (or "shamisen") was imported from Canton via the Ryûkyû Islands (Luchu) about four centuries ago. Nowadays cat and dog skin is used for the sound drum, but earlier the skin of snakes was used. It has been utilized for accompanying "jôrûri" (ballad-drama) and "ko-uta" in the theatre.

ABSORBED IN LETTERS

Of Bakin's books, "Hakkenden" is the work given the most emphasis in this story. It is a historical novel based on the re-establishment of the waning Satomi family. The various eight loyal heroes represent the eight virtues–hence the beads of an eight-bead rosary: wisdom, filial piety, respect, duty, benevolence, faith, loyalty, and fraternity. The "dogs" persevere through adversity, chaos, and all manner of complications. Herein we may observe rational samurai who acted on the principles of bushidô and Confucianism throughout their exploits, rewarding good and punishing evil. And there is nothing pornographic about Bakin's work, which is edifying when one considers that his master, Kyôden, had been imprisoned for allegedly over-indulging in pornography.

Akutagawa draws to some extent from Bakin's diary; and in several chapters Bakin recreates the mood of Samba's "Ukiyo-buro" ("Fleeting Bath").

The story first appeared in the Osaka "Mainichi" newspaper, and was widely acclaimed.

THE GARDEN

"Ri" = 2.44029 miles.

"Shôchû" is a beverage distilled from rice. It has a high alcoholic content, and because it is inexpensive it is popular among the lower classes in Japan.

"Matsumoto" is about one hundred and fifty miles from Tokyo on the Shinonoi Line. This song which Akutagawa learned from his mother, his grandfather had acquired from a harlot when he had been on a visit to Tokyo. The battle was waged on the 20th of November, Genji 1 (A.D. 1864). The memorial is near Wada Park.

"Courtesan"–The courtesans of Japan were rather more respected and of a higher order than their counterparts in Western countries.

THE BADGER

"The Nihon Shoki," in "kanbun" style, spans through sixty volumes the period from the age of the gods to August of the eleventh year of the Jito era. In the fourth year of the Yôrô era (720) the work was completed by Toneri Shinno, Ono Yasumaro and others, in response to an Imperial decree.

"The Empress Suiko" was Empress of the thirty-third generation. She reigned from 592 to 623.

"Michinoku" was in northeastern Japan and is now known as the Tohoku District.

"The Suinin-ki" is the section of the "Shoki" referring to the Emperor Suinin of the eleventh generation (29 B.C.–70 A.D.).

"The Yasakani" curved gem was composed of many curved jewels linked with a cord–jadeites for personal adornment–and was shaped like the crest of a large comma.

"Yao-bikuni Myôchin" is the name of the vampire in "Satomi Hakkenden." In this case the badger assumes the form of a woman; it is really the revengeful spirit of Tamazusa. Originally a vampire called "Gyokushi" was ruined by the Satomi family; a revengeful spirit entered the badger as "Yao-bikuni Myôchin" for the purpose of cursing the Satomi family–an unusual circumstance when one considers the role of the badger is usually a comical one.

"Jinmu" was the first Emperor of Japan (660–583 b.c.).

The text refers to the Buddhist belief in transmigration (metempsychosis)–the passage of the soul at death into another living being.

The ancient Egyptians held similar beliefs as did Pythagoras and Plato. In essence, the theory is that all living things transmigrate endlessly like rotating wheels until the subjugation of desire is accomplished through right living and meditation.

"The Keiki" district was the area about Kyôto (the Capital) and Ôsaka, consisting of five provinces: Yamashiro, Yamato, Kochi, Izumi, and Settsu.

"Omi" is famous for its "eight beautiful views" of Lake Biwa.

"The Tokugawa era" extended from 1600 until the Meiji Restoration in 1868. Throughout this period, the Tokugawa family, beginning with Ieyasu, ruled Japan. Ieyasu was a descendant of Minamoto-no-Yoshiie (1041–1108). To those familiar with Japanese history both these names will already have given some inspiration.

"Sado Island," a part of Niigata Prefecture, is famous for its badgers and badger stories. "Okesa" ballads, camellias, and mild climate are all attributed to Sado Island.

HERESY

"Ryûgai-ji"–This temple is located in Takéchi-mura, Takéchi-gun, in Nara Prefecture.

"The Five Transmigrations of Life and Death"–Heaven, man, hell, beast, and plant.

"The Mary Religion"–This is evidently Christianity. Although we cannot be certain of this, it is true that at the present time unbelievers in many Christian parishes could observe the nature of Christian worship and be inclined to refer to Christianity as the "Mary Religion." Nestorian Christianity infiltrated into China from India in 650 and, it is believed, later appeared in Kyôto in the 8th century.

"Shinsen Gardens" ("Shinsen-en")–The Sacred Fountain Gardens were established when the capital was transferred to Kyôto in the reign of the Emperor Kammu (737–806). Now only a small portion remains to the south of Nijô-jô and is referred to as Ômiya Park. The Palace was razed by fire in 1177 and the Emperor removed temporarily to Fukuhara in Kobé. A temple was built on the site during the Tokugawa period. The Gardens betray a Chinese influence.

"Kwannon Bodisâttva"–The Goddess of Mercy.

"Kiyomizu Temple" ("Kiyomizuô-dera" or "Seisui-ji")–The temple is located in Higashiyama-ku, Kyôto. It was established by Sakano-ué Tamura-maro in the 17th year of Enryaku era (798). (Some historians say the 24th year, 805). The temple, on the slopes of Otowa-yama, southeast of the Yasaka pagoda, is dedicated to the Eleven-faced Kwannon.

"Abitaijô" ("or Abi-jô")–Of the eight hells of Buddhism this is the hell unto which the worst sinners are delivered.